Never Let Go

Never Let Go

E. Collins

Never Let Go and all related characters and elements are property of E. Collins.

Never Let Go is a work of fiction. Names, characters, places, and incidents either are product of the author's imagination or are used fictitiously, and any resemblance to actual persons, living or dead, businesses, companies, events, or locales is entirely coincidental.

Cover photo credit to kieutruongphoto on Pixabay

To Aaron
For the time to follow my dreams

Chapter 1

I stared down at the incoming call on my screen, at the smiling ebony face, laughing at something her brother did outside the shot. It was taken the day Misha got out of the hospital, everyone all smiles, happy she was okay and healing.

Seeing that smiling face, I'm reminded of the one I'd never see again.

My fingers twitched over the screen, ready to send the call to voicemail.

I couldn't do it.

Not today.

Not to Misha.

The owner of the studio's chirping chatter pulled me from my thoughts.

"...so if you could come back for Wednesday's class, that would be amazing!"

Ms. Cora was one of those short women with way too much energy. Though she ran around putting out fires all day and taught half the classes herself, she somehow still had the energy to bounce off the walls, high as a kite on life at the end of the day.

My own eyelids ready to drop, I looked up from my phone to meet her tawny, smiling gaze.

What were we talking about, again?

Right. Dance.

Class.

"This Wednesday?" I asked, bobbing in the waves, kicking furiously to keep my head above water. I reached for my mental calendar, searched for conflicts, before remembering. There wouldn't be any. Not anymore.

"Sure," I stretched my lips into a bright smile. Cora's eyes flitted to my phone.

"Do you need to get that?"

Why was my phone still ringing?

And what time was it?

I glanced at my phone. My eyes stuck on the three digits in the top corner.

Crap.

"N-no, but I do need to get going." I started for the door without a proper goodbye and nearly tripped over my own feet.

Darn flip-flops!

"You're sure about Wednesday?" Ms. Cora called after me.

"Yep! See you then!" I'd make myself free to teach the class on Wednesday. I'd have to.

If I had any hope of becoming a permanent instructor at Cora's Institute of Dance, I could not afford to pass up any opportunity.

I needed the money. Between bills and the renovations on the garage studio, cash went fast. The lump sum from Greg's life insurance wouldn't last forever.

Cora lifted her hand, wiggled her fingers in a dainty wave, smiled, and returned to her office.

As I crossed to my car, I answered the call, mentally reining in the exhaustion dampening my voice.

"Hi, Misha! How's it going?" I adopted my best happy tone, knowing she could use it.

"Slow... I hate it here. Everything's so structured," Misha griped. "How was class?"

I stepped down off the curb, and a wave of nausea threatened to pull me under. I slapped a hand on the hood of my car to steady myself.

One slow breath.

Easy.

My head spun as my stomach churned.

Not again.

My lips pressed to a thin line.

Misha didn't need this.

Two weeks ago, Misha checked herself back into the Winona Care and Wellness Center to help her process the loss of her brother and heal from her most recent suicide attempt.

After hearing about the crash, about Greg, Misha's parents and

I worried about how she'd react to the news, afraid she'd relapse like she had so many times before, but the last two and a half months, Misha'd been doing so good. She smiled more, spoke frequently of happy memories with Greg, particularly of when they were kids. We all thought she was working through the loss.

Then Misha's mom found her bleeding out on the kitchen floor.

"Class was good."

Class was always good. I had to get the conversation off me before she asked any more probing questions that would bring up bad memories.

"Enough about me. What have you been up to?"

"Eh, just a bunch of mandatory therapy sessions and guided meditations, stuff that's supposed to lead me through my grief and blah blah. I never should have come back."

Please be talking about the wellness center.

"Don't say that. At least you've got all that time to draw."

Misha snorted.

"You sound like Greg."

My heart squeezed painfully in my chest.

Would it ever stop doing that?

Tears pricked at my eyes as memories threatened to bust free of the vault at the back of my mind. I swiped my finger over my cheeks, forced the memories back into their cage, and climbed into my car.

I didn't have time to cry.

I had to meet Jess.

"So," I said with a deep breath meant to curb-stomp my stray emotions into submission. "I was thinking..."

"Uh oh."

God damn it, why did she have to sound so much like him?

I forced my lips to curl in an amused smile.

Greg always said my emotions shin♦ed in my voice. On bad days, he knew how I was feeling from a single greeting over the phone. Hopefully, Misha wasn't as attuned as her brother.

"How 'bout I come visit this week? You've got to be running short on art supplies by now. Maybe we can see a movie?"

Misha perked up immediately.

"Jailbreak?"

"Only with your doctor's okay, of course," I clarified. Didn't need to end up on Tracy's bad list. Greg might be gone, but she was still my mother-in-law.

"You're such a goody-goody, you know that?" Misha said with affection. "Stop worrying about little old me all the time and take a bubble bath or something."

I let out a breathy laugh.

As if.

"When the sky turns green and pigs fly."

I could hear Misha rolling her dark eyes over the phone.

Misha changed directions.

"How's the studio? Got any students yet?"

My heart dove for my toes.

Right.

My Studio.

Or more correctly, my unused garage space that I one day dreamed of opening as a dance studio.

"Listen, Misha. I've got to get going. Jess is waiting for me. Let me know when will work best for you this week. Love you!"

"Now! Come now!"

I laughed a real laugh.

"Talk to you soon."

I pulled to the curb in front of Open Hearts Family Services.

▲▲▲

Jessie closed her eyes in blissful rapture as she savored the flavors of her vanilla latte in the uncharacteristically warm late September sun.

On the other side of the table, I clung to my coffee, wishing I could find as much joy in it as Jessie.

I hadn't been able to down a cup of coffee in almost three months, ever since the crash. I don't know why I bothered ordering them anymore.

Greg used to meet me in bed in the mornings, waking me with a steaming mug filled with more cream than coffee and just a splash of white chocolate syrup. Just the way I liked it.

Those lazy mornings often lead to lazy afternoons, both of us wandering around the house in our underwear till the early afternoon. Scrambled eggs on the couch for lunch.

The day Greg left, he met me with one last cup. We talked as he dressed and gathered the last of his things. When we left for the airport, my mug sat untouched on the dresser side table, neither of us knowing it was the last.

"Jake's back." Jessie pulled me from my memory before I could slip into despondence. Her lips pursed as she took another sip of coffee.

I frowned, unsure why she'd be bringing him up.

Jessie and Jake dated in high school—before Jessie was kidnapped and her world turned upside down. Their reunion wasn't quite what Jessie had in mind when she escaped.

Their relationship was tense, at best.

But Jessie had Cole now. She was happy.

Right?

"He and Cole hanging out a lot?" I asked, unsure why we'd turned to the topic of her ex's return. Even after seven years, Jake's brief visits always upset Jessie. Guess it didn't help that her husband was Jake's best friend.

"Not too much. Cole's been busy with school starting up again. Parent-teacher conferences and all." I nodded, a familiar lump forming in my throat that always came when people spoke about their partners.

I stayed silent. What was I supposed to say? Good? *You probably don't need to be hanging out around your ex anyway?* That wouldn't work.

Jessie was determined to pretend everything was okay between her and Jake. The past was the past. And with enough willpower she could make it disappear entirely.

And for the most part, it had.

Every once in a while, though, there were little instances when the past crept back up on Jessie, usually when Jake was around. We'd all be out to dinner, and a server would drop a tray. The sharp sound of metal and glass scattered across the restaurant floor would send Jessie flying from her seat, eyes wide and searching for a man who had long since been locked away for what he did to her.

The look in her eyes after, as Cole took her hand and anchored her to his side, got me every time. Every time she'd find Jake, an accusation dancing behind her lashes.

"How long's he back?" Jake never stayed long, just long enough to throw a monkey wrench in everyone's lives and shake things up.

Jessie shrugged.

"Molley says he's here to stay."

"Mm."

And that was the weirdest part about Jessie and Jake's relationship. The third point to their strange little triangle.

Molley.

She was the girl Jake dated after Jessie, but they didn't last long. No one ever did with Jake. But despite her and Jake breaking up on less than amicable terms, Molley still talked to him. They were friends, somehow, after everything.

"Speaking of Molley," Jessie pivoted like she'd been waiting for the perfect segue. "She said she might have a job for you. Says you'll be perfect."

"Jess," I groaned, rolled my eyes. I set my coffee down on the table between us.

"I have a job."

"Yeah, two of them, I know. But this'll be easy. Something to take your mind off—"

Jessie's eyes went wide. Her pink lips pressed to a hairpin line like she could keep the end of her thought from slipping out, but Jessie was never any good at keeping her thoughts to herself.

"Off Greg, you mean."

My temper sparked and flared. I couldn't help it, even knowing Jessie meant well.

Jessie's eyes dropped in supplication. She edged back in her chair.

Guilt surged past my grief and anger like I'd just kicked a puppy or something.

"It's fine, Jess. I know you guys are just trying to help."

Even if I didn't need it.

"You should talk to her."

"Okay," I sighed. Anything to ease the tension and fear from Jessie's eyes. My hands closed tight around my disposable paper cup.

Anything to get Jessie to quit worrying.

Chapter 2

Can you come this morning?

I stared down at Misha's text.

Why? Today of all days!

One deep breath.

I rolled over and hauled myself up in the king-size bed Greg and I used to share. I typed out a quick response.

See you soon! ☺

Guess I wouldn't be working on the studio.

▲▲▲

Forty minutes later, I pulled up to Winona Care and Wellness Center, wishing I'd been awake enough to remember to stop for coffee on the way. After checking in at the front desk, I dragged myself down the hall to Misha's room.

Even without knowing her room number, I would have known which door was Misha simply from the amount of color plastered across the outside. Inside and out, vibrant drawings and paintings covered the walls. Half-finished sketches rested on the bedside table and desk, where Misha abandoned them to attend a therapy session or start on a new project.

Misha sat cross-legged on her immaculate twin-size bed.

Before coming to the center, Misha shaved her hair short. Today, it stood off her head in a neat little cap of tight, black curls. Her dark eyes, while not shining with the same joy they used to show whenever her brother stepped into the room, weren't nearly as dull and clouded as they were my last visit, when Misha refused to get out of bed for a trip down to the coffee stand in the lobby.

She offered a pleasant smile when I knocked on her open door and stepped inside.

"You came!" Misha cried like I showed up laden down with gifts or something.

It was a good day.

"I brought more pencils." I held up the box of twenty-four lively artists' tools. Misha clambered off the bed and snatched them from my hand, immediately flipping the box over to read through the colors.

"These are great! Thank you!" Without glancing my way, Misha strode to the desk and started testing the colors on a discarded scrap of paper.

"So you up for a movie? Or are you here to break me out of this joint?" Misha wiggled her eyebrows in a way that was all Greg.

Forcing a smile, I swallowed the sick that bubbled in my throat.

"Mmhmm. But isn't it a bit early for a movie?" Were theaters even open?

Misha grinned at me over her shoulder.

"Never too early for a classic."

I rolled my eyes but found myself smiling anyway.

"Misha, *Twilight* is *not* a classic."

"Mmmm, you sure? Feels like a classic." Misha pulled her laptop and a near-pristine DVD case from her desk and joined me on the bed.

"So," Misha started, sitting cross-legged against the mountain of pillows.

The opening credits played across the laptop screen. Watching the camera pan over lush green forests, I felt my heart drop into my stomach. This was precisely the conversation I'd been trying to avoid the last three months. I could feel it.

"How are you doing? Really?"

Damn psychologists. She's spending way too much time with them.

I stared at the laptop screen as it panned over a long bridge over a canyon.

Lips pressed into a tight smile. I gave a sharp nod.

"I'm good." Was that convincing? Was my voice too high? I coughed to clear my throat. "I'm doing good."

An inky brow rose on Misha's forehead.

"You know you can talk to us, right? You're still family."

Misha didn't push the issue any further, just settled into her stack of pillows, and focused on the laptop as her favorite movie played across the fifteen-inch screen.

Misha's comment threw me. I eased back beside her. My mind

ran circles as the movie played on without my notice.

What was I supposed to talk to Misha and her parents about? Greg?

That would only bring up more pain.

I lost a husband—someone I'd been with since sophomore year of high school.

Steve and Tracy lost a child, Misha, a brother—stepbrother.

Their loss was so much more significant than mine. The roots of those relationships had Greg's whole life to dig deep into every facet of their world. How could I bring up that pain for them just to get my own off my chest?

How could what I was feeling ever compare?

If they knew I still couldn't sleep in the room Greg and I shared, even after replacing the bedding and painting the walls, that seeing his smiling face in a frame on the living room wall sliced me open and left me to bleed every time I passed by, it would be a slap in the face to their grief. I couldn't do that, not to them, not after everything they'd done for me.

Taking a deep breath, I tried to shake the pain of losing Greg from my shoulders, as I'd done time and time again that summer, only for the grief to dig its vicious little claws deeper.

Would it ever stop?

▲▲▲

I left the wellness center by noon and went straight home. If I skipped lunch, I could get another coat of paint on the studio walls before I had to be at Ms. Cora's for the afternoon lesson.

Leaving my car in the driveway, I strode through the house, past the kitchen, where my fridge hummed loud taunts, promising leftovers if I just took a break. I stepped out into the backyard and stared across the stretch of grass at the dilapidated garage—more like a barn, really.

From the outside, it didn't look like much. Paint peeled from the weathered wood plank siding to reveal layers of color underneath in a chipped and faded rainbow of years of neglect. In places, the roof sagged, and in several spots the black lining stood bare, the shingles blown off in some forgotten windstorm.

It was the second garage on the property, the larger of the two. The previous owner had it built as a sort of workshop to keep his tools and loud woodworking equipment, and in a way, I was going to put it to a similar use. But instead of shaping furniture out of chunks of scrap, I'd cultivate the art of dance in the minds of the youth.

If only I could finish the remodel.

After forcing the key into the rusted lock, I shoved the door to the garage open and stepped into a small lobby area.

Unwarranted memories ricocheted painfully off my heart as I took in the walls Greg helped install last spring when I first started to pursue the idea of opening my own studio.

It had been a surprise.

Somehow, as busy as he was, Greg managed to sneak home and into the back garage without me noticing for nearly a month, where he carefully designed and crafted the most perfect little floor plan for a studio I'd only dreamed about.

It had been a gift.

Greg's last gift to me before he left for that god-awful hellhole that ripped him from my future.

We were going to work on it together when he got back. Paint the walls, replace the siding, add a tin roof so we wouldn't have to worry about any more shingles falling off. But Greg never came back.

Exhaustion tugged at my limbs.

A movie with Misha had not been a good idea.

Picking up a paint tray and roller from the paint spatter subfloor, I trudged into the largest of the classrooms.

Paint cans waited in the corner. A soft cinnamon color that would both brighten and warm the space.

But before I could even think of opening one, a wave of nausea washed over me. My breath caught in my throat as the room began to spin. I dropped to my knees, drawing in slow bits of air to calm the rising sick, but it was too late. Pulling the paint tray to me just in time, I emptied my stomach into it.

Tremors racked my body as tears forced their way from the corners of my eyes.

No. No. No.

I couldn't be sick.

Taking slow, steady breaths, I waited as the waves of nausea calmed to a slow ripple.

What the hell was going on?

I eased onto my side, pressing my cheek into the wood floor. Taking solace in the woodgrain's cool touch, I closed my eyes.

Only for a minute.

I set myself adrift.

Chapter 3

I was late.

To Ms. Cora's and to Molley's afterwards.

Sulking, I trudged up the winding walk to Molley's front porch, wondering all the while, who the heck could afford such a large house at her age.

Seriously, the place stood two stories, and I was sure it had a finished basement that spanned the length of the house. All white paint and windows.

What must it cost to heat and cool the place?

Cute little bushes mocked me from perfectly weeded beds edged with lush green grass trimmed to just the right length.

No matter how long I left the sprinkler out on my lawn, it would never be that color.

Where were all the dandelions?

It wasn't the first tie I'd been over to Molley's.

Since she moved into the house, Molley had been hosting a monthly get-together for all the old cheer girls, which was why I was there that night. Why these get-togethers had to take place in the middle of the week was beyond me.

Convinced I'd never teach another class in Cora's studio again, I took the three steps onto the porch like I'd just finished climbing Rainer, each harder than the last.

My midafternoon sob-nap did little to ease my exhaustion. If anything, I was more tired.

Hopefully, I wasn't too late to help set up.

I raised my hand to knock before remembering that Molley was probably busy in the kitchen and wouldn't hear.

I let myself in.

I stepped into an open foyer. Light from the fan overhead gleamed off the wood floors. The solid wood banister curling around the staircase brought up memories of racing down the stairs at Jessie's parents' house, chasing after her with nail polish in hand.

I cut across the entryway, down the short hall leading to the back of the house, my mind still stuck in the past before everything went south.

What would Jessie be like now if she'd never been kidnapped?

Turning the corner that would lead into the kitchen, I ran smack dab into a solid wall of human.

"Woah, sorry, didn't see ya coming."

Warm hands closed around my waist to keep me from toppling over.

Blinking, I leaned into the voice as its intoxicating, tenor cadence washed through my dulled senses.

One hand fell on a muscled arm as I regained my balance.

All too soon, the hands and the warm chest I'd been leaning on were gone as their owner stepped back.

"Molley's setting up out back."

That voice.

I looked up into deep cobalt blue eyes.

No.

It couldn't be.

He smiled at me, not quite the same cocky grin from high school, and disappeared down the stairs I hadn't noticed into the basement.

There's been no recognition in his eyes.

▲▲▲

Bemused, I turned back to the hallway and continued through the kitchen to the open back doors.

A brick patio stretched into the backyard, culminating in an intricate gazebo, housing a mini outdoor kitchen complete with grill. Lounging chairs circled an in-ground fire pit off to the left. To the right, a white patio table was set with dessert plates and wine glasses.

A petite blonde and a behemoth positioned a side table between a pair of chairs around the already burning fire pit.

The blonde set down her side of the table and turned to wave. A bright smile glowed on her face. She didn't even break a sweat moving that table.

"You made it!"

I smiled back, lacking the energy for any further response.

"Here, sit. Let me get you a drink. Red or white?"

Molley snagged a long-stemmed glass off the table, not seeming to care that it messed up the picture-perfect setup she'd crafted.

"Water?"

Molley's brows drew together. She offered up a sympathetic smile.

"Sure. Be right back."

Did I look that tired? I fought back the urge to pull out my phone to check my appearance in the camera feature.

"Here you go." Molley returned a minute later and handed over the wine glass. I took a generous sip of the clear liquid.

"So, Jake's back," I commented, nodding toward the house.

Molley took the chair across from mine.

"Oh, yeah. Got back a couple weeks ago."

Molley's husband, Will, the behemoth, came up behind her, his large hands settling on her shoulder. He kneaded the muscle there for a moment before bending to kiss her bouncing curls.

"You ladies have fun. I'll be up with Gracie if you need anything." Will turned toward the house.

Molley watched him till he disappeared from view down the hall.

When she turned back to me, her eyes held a doughy gleam of someone deep in love.

My heart constricted in my chest. Not so long ago, my own eyes reflected that same infatuated light.

"So, how are you doing? You look tired."

Molley didn't pull any punches. A quality acquired from her

psychology training? Or had she always been that way? I couldn't remember.

"Just came from a lesson." I took a gulp of water, hoping to hide behind the glass. Like Jessie the other day, and Misha that morning, Molley had that pitying tilt to her eyes that could only mean more unwanted advice was headed my way.

"You know you can talk to me, right? About what happened? Greg? Anything."

Perfect blonde brows drew together over twin seas.

Gawwd, why is everyone saying that?

Didn't they get it?

I couldn't talk to any of them, not Molley and especially not Jessie. How would any of them ever get it?

Besides, they had their own lives to worry about instead of fretting over mine. I had it under control.

Everything was under control.

"Right." Molley carried the conversation forward when I didn't respond.

"So, it's really great that you got here early, because I've been meaning to talk to you about this opportunity that's come up through my work."

Oh good. More assistance for the broken widow.

"Jessie might have mentioned something about that. But, Molley, you really don't need to be doing this. I'm covered. I'm good." My studio reno was on hold until I could build up some cash for supplies, but I had a roof over my head and food in the fridge.

I spun the wine glass between my fingers and tried to change the subject.

"How's Gracie doing? You guys getting any more sleep?"

Having decided not to have children of their own, Molley and Will had been working with an adoption agency for over a year to have a child placed with them.

Last February, they'd been put in contact with a woman looking to put her unborn baby up for adoption. Something about a one-night stand at some destination resort.

Six months later, Gracie came into Molley and Will's life.

Molley pulled a face and shook her head.

"Colic," she said. "Poor thing can't get comfortable at night. Only place she really sleeps is up against Will's shoulder, but can you blame the girl?"

A dreamy smile tugged one corner of Molley's glossed lips.

"So, about this job—"

"Molly...I appreciate it, but I really am covered.

"Yeah, yeah, Jessie told me about the bar." Molley's fingers raised to put air quotes around the word bar.

"This would be more like a favor to me. See, social services has this baby, the kid of some gangbanger the police just arrested. The mother's missing. It's a whole story. He's probably going away for a long time. We've found a family willing to take the baby, but they're in Montana."

"Hold up. Montana?"

Was she crazy?

"You've seen my car, right? It's the same dinky thing I drove around in high school. You think that thing will make it to Montana?"

"Pleeease! We really need someone to take her. You'd be perfect. You're great with kids."

Wait a second...

My eyes went wide.

No. No. No.

Back up.

"Kids, yes. Five-year-olds. Ten-year-olds. Not babies. Gracie cries when I stand in the same room as her."

"To be fair, she does that for just about everyone."

Molley waved me off.

"You'll be great. Please just say you'll think about it? You have a couple days to decide."

"Fine." I rolled my eyes. "But why the heck are you housing your ex?"

Chapter 4

Carlo's wasn't the kind of bar Molley or any of the cheer girls would willingly frequent.

From the outside, the place looked more like an abandoned barn than a bar, with its warped wood siding and tin roof.

A previous owner once painted the outside of the old building, but Carlo and all the other owners before him decided to forgo the extravagance.

Now, bits of sky-blue paint clinging the edges of worn, gray planks were all that remained of the previous owner's efforts.

If the outside didn't deter the cheer squad, one glance inside would.

Against the far wall, opposite the doors, a large stage drew all the patrons' eyes to the girls in the bright, sequined costumes. With siren's smiles and a quick flash of thigh, the girls captivated their audience, drawing many back night after night.

Weighted beats pulsed from the speakers mounted high in the corners of the large hall. Red, blue, and gold lights strobed from fixtures on the ceiling.

Tables circled the stage and spilled across the rest of the floor around the large bar top at the center of the long room.

The heels of my boots clicked on the sticky wood floors as I stepped out of the back office.

Though it was only eight, the Friday night crowd packed the space around the stage.

Several groups of patrons lined the bar top.

Raising a hand in greeting, I met the eye of the bouncer by the doors as I crossed to the bar.

Big, burly, and covered in tattoos, Eric would be an intimidating figure even in the seediest of places. At Carlo's, his main job was to look after the girls, make sure no one got too handsy or got the wrong idea.

It took all of two weeks of me behind the bar for him to realize I did not need to fall under his watchful eye.

From behind the bar, I had the best view of the entire space. I was the first to see if one of the patrons started looking for more than drinks and a show from one of the wait staff.

One glance from me and Eric would have the touchy-feeling patron out the door before he knew what hit him. Eric moved like a lion across the savanna, defending his pride. Despite his profession and overall appearance, Eric didn't relish using his fists. Usually, his sheer size was enough to scare grabby clientele into submission.

Offenders received one warning, then they were cut off. If Eric had to step in again, the patron would be leaving, by their own volition or by Eric's.

"You made it."

A cool hand closed around my elbow.

I glanced over to find a tall redhead in a feathery purple corset. Mountainous breasts spilled over the brim of her top.

I nodded and looked out over the bar.

"Busy night."

I scanned the crowd, picking out the guests most likely to cause trouble. A man leaning over the corner of the stage drew my suspicion. A short glass of amber liquid dangled precariously from his fingertips.

The woman, Ruby, blew a puff of air through her crimson-painted lips.

"Oh, Hon, you have no idea. Already had to sick Eric on a poor sap who thought he could convince Daisy to go home with him." The woman's lips curled.

Turning to the small sink to wash my hands, I found Daisy in the mirror backing the bar.

"I'll keep an eye on her." I scanned the bottles and glasses in front of the men at the bar, searching for empties.

"How have things been otherwise?"

Ruby shrugged and leaned on the bar, drawing the eye of the nearest men as her breasts rose a little higher over her top.

"Fine. But keep an eye on the guy at the end," a manicured pinky pointed toward the far end of the bar. "He's been here three nights in a row, but otherwise, none of the girls recognize him."

"Will do." Drying my hands, I pulled a black apron from beneath the bar. "Anything else?"

It wasn't strange for new patrons to come into Carlo's. The

bright Showgirls sign on the street usually drew in a few curious onlookers every night. But for them to return multiple nights in a row was odd and reason for concern.

Carlo's wasn't a strip club.

There might have been stage dancing, and the girls may have been bouncing around in heels and lingerie, but there were no lap dances, no private shows, and no touching.

Carlo prided himself in running an establishment where the dancers and female servers could feel safe.

Not all the patrons got that, and every once in a while, Carlo had to call in the police to report a possible sex trafficker.

The man Ruby indicated was definitely on my list.

One wrong move, and I'd have Eric on him and the cops there before he could spell felony.

"When you get the chance, table six is waiting for a round of shots. Bartender's choice."

Ruby winked, spun on her stiletto heel, and sauntered off into the crowd.

Taking a breath, I turned and patted Carlo on the arm as I passed behind him.

The bulky man straightened from where he'd been leaning on the bar, conversing with an elderly regular, and waved to signal I could take over.

Swiping a bottle of whiskey off the top shelf, I went to work.

▲▲▲

Time has a way of passing differently in places like Carlo's.

Stuck somewhere between a strip club and a honky-tonk saloon, the dance hall, as Carlo liked to call it, seemed to suspend the passage of time for all who entered.

Hours could pass in the blink of a song, and no one seemed to care.

I kept my eye on Daisy as she sashed among the tables in what could have passed for a saloon dress in the 1800s if it were two or three feet longer. Black fringe peeked out from beneath the tiny red skirt. The shiny fabric swished around her hips as she walked, barely covering her back end.

I flagged her down as I finished prepping another round of specialty shots.

"Doing okay?" I slid the tray of drinks across the bar in her direction.

She offered a sweet smile and took up the tray.

"Tips are good tonight."

I sent Daisy off and turned back to my customers along the bar.

Refilling a couple drinks, I glanced toward the far end of the counter, where our new repeat customer sat, both hands hugging the slim neck of his beer bottle.

Dark hair cropped close didn't make him look like your usual trafficker, but I guess you never could tell with people.

With his head hanging down between his shoulders, I couldn't make out his other features.

Not good if one of Carlo's girls went missing.

Maybe one of the cameras caught him as he came in.

I pursed my lips.

Na. I had to get a better look.

Noting the label on the stranger's bottle, I bent to retrieve another from the lower fridge, turning slightly so my barely covered ass was visible to the patrons along the bar.

With any luck, the act would get me more than a few nice tips and draw the eye of the stranger at the end enough for me to see his face.

But when I straightened, only the usuals' eyes snapped back to their drinks or the stage.

The stranger's eyes remained hidden in the dark hollows beneath his brows.

Dang.

I popped the top off the bottle.

"Another one, sugar?" I said with my most seductive smile.

Leaning on the bar in a way that made my breasts pop up, I slid the fresh beer in front of the stranger.

"Thank, but I think I'm good," he said, something in his voice oddly alluring, deep and rumbling like thunder. I let my eyes drift toward the tables by the stage, searching for empty glasses as I fought to clear my head.

No falling for customers, Hanna. Look how it ended up last time.

"Just waiting for a buddy to finish up—Hanna?"

My sleepy smile fell. Eyes snapped back to meet cobalt blue.

Shit.

I straightened.

Fought the urge to pull up my top.

"Jake? What are you—"

"I could ask you the same thing. You work here now?"

My shoulders stiffened at the judgment in his tone.

"As a matter of fact, I do. Does Molley know you're here?"

Jake's eyes narrowed to slits.

"Why would Molley care if I'm here?"

"I don't know. Why would she?" I challenged with a knowing lift to my brow.

"Moll and I are friends. Nothing more. Even if I was interested, do you really think I'd try anything with that linebacker of a husband always hanging around?"

"Then why are you staying at her house?"

A weary sigh slipped past Jake's lips.

"Where would you like me to stay, Hanna?"

I don't know. Your parents', for starters?

"Hey, can we get some service or what?"

I froze, the pompous tone taking me back almost three months. A cold wave of fear ripped down my spine, only for a second, but long enough for Jake to take notice. Something sparked in the dark depths of his eyes.

I couldn't stall forever.

Sending Jake a look to say we weren't done, I turned toward the disgruntled customer, already knowing—and dreading—the face I'd see on the other side of the bar.

Thin lips stretched into a too-wide smile that looked more like a smirk on its owner's slim aristocratic face.

Steeling myself, arms folded over my chest.

My hip propped against the bar.

In my periphery, Jake glanced from me to the too-smug man who interrupted out spat.

I glared at the lawyer.

"Thought I wasn't going to see you here again, Ethan?"

Chapter 5

They say everyone handles loss and grief differently.

Jessie closed off the world.

Misha tried to gouge it out of her skin.

My method for handling the loss of the love of my life stared back at me in the form of a regrettable one-night stand.

The man's smile widened into a mocking grin.

"Hello, gorgeous. Up for another round?"

Jake shifted at the edge of my vision.

My lip curled in disgust.

"That's never—"

Ethan held up the tumbler resting on the bar in front of him.

Amber dregs swirled around the bottom of the glass.

Right.

Ethan and his crew must have come in before my shift when Carlo handled the drinks.

I never would have let him sit down.

"For the table?" My teeth ground together as I pulled four fresh tumblers from the shelf.

"Please."

Stiff and unwilling to turn my back on the man, I filled the glasses with a middle-shelf scotch and slid them over to Ethan.

I wasn't about to send one of the girls over to his table.

Just thinking about that night and the morning after sent shivers down my spine.

There was kink, then there was whatever the sick fuck Ethan was in to.

I didn't want any of the girls ending up in that situation.

Ethan slid a couple bills across the counter. Reluctant, I snatched them up and dropped his change on the bar.

"Keep it," Ethan said with a wink. "For later."

Gross.

I left the change on the bar.

I glared at the back of Ethan's head as he made his way back to his table by the stage.

"Friend of yours?"

I turned back to Jake as he sat back on his stool. He watched me in a way that made me want to squirm.

"Why do you care?" I snagged Jake's empty and dropped it in the bin beneath the counter.

The heavy beat of the music thrummed up through the heels of my boots into my legs.

On stage, the show was heating up.

All eyes turned to follow the dancers as they seduced their captive audience.

All but Jake's.

Cobalts trained on me as I moved down the counter, wiping up spills and doing just about anything to keep from having to return to Jake's corner of the bar.

I stopped in front of a regular in his mid-sixties.

"Another, Gary?" I slipped the empty martini glass from his limp fingers.

Gary came every Friday, showing up like clockwork at 8:45, just before the cover charge. He'd sip two martinis and be out before 11:30.

Why was he still here?

"Yes, ma'am," Gary said with a hiccup.

I glanced at my watch.

11:46

A little late for his second drink.

"How're ya doing, Gary?" I asked as I pulled a local gin from the shelf.

Gary ran a hand over his scalp, smoothing back the wispy strands of gray that still stretched across the top.

He let out a bone-weary sigh.

"Been better. Marcy's niece came to stay with us. Girl's quite a handful for someone who ain't hit her teenage years yet."

"Oh?"

I let Gary rabble on about his delinquent niece as I prepped what I was sure was his third martini.

On nights like tonight, when Gary varied from his routine, Carlo or I usually drove him home.

It was shaping up to be another one of those nights.

Gary had stopped talking. He stared up at me expectantly for some kind of response.

Bartending 101. When behind the bar, you're more than just a server. You're a friend, confidant, therapist.

I cocked a hip against the edge of the counter.

"Maybe your niece needs someone to talk to," I suggested.

Movement at the end of the bar drew my attention back to Jake as he shifted down to take the empty stool next to Gary.

"I have a friend who might be able to help," I offered.

A gin-saturated puff of air burst past Gary's lips.

"You really think that'll help?" Gary sounded skeptical.

In all honesty, it didn't sound like Gary's niece was doing anything out of the ordinary. Still, if talking to someone would ease Gary's mind, then therapy was definitely an option.

I nodded, prepared to offer up Molley's contact information. She loved working with kids.

A gravelly voice stuck my tongue to the backs of my teeth.

"Helped me."

Jake sees a therapist?

"Hm. Maybe." Gary sat up straighter on his stool, his mood brightened.

"Still want this?" I help up the martini.

Gary shook his head and stood.

"Just going to watch the girls for a bit."

▲▲▲

Jake and I watched Gary weave through the crowd to an open table.

"Whats—"

A commotion near the end of the stage drew my attention.

My stomach lurched into my throat.

"Oh, hell no."

"What—"

But I was already out from behind the bar, shoving through the crowd to where I could see Gary changing course toward Daisy's platinum curls at the center of the fray.

Gary had a penchant for playing hero.

From the distressed pull of Daisy's manicured eyebrows, that's exactly what Gary had set his mind on.

We did not need Gary starting a bar brawl over a handsy customer.

I could only hope Eric was cutting across the bar somewhere behind me.

Coming up behind him, I snagged Gary's blue, plaid shirt sleeve before he could reach Daisy and pumped on the brakes. I spun him

E. Collins

"Why don't you get some air, Gary?" It wasn't a question, and he knew it.

Gary's shoulder slumped.

"But—"

"I got it."

Gary hesitated a moment. Glancing around my shoulder at Daisy one last time, he turned and started for the exit.

One crisis averted, I turned and cut a short path to Daisy.

When I reached her, I scowled.

"No touching the girls." I glared around the table, adding extra venom as I met the eye of the man who held Daisy in his lap.

Dull brown eyes stared back at me, half-masked behind drooping lids. Long, greasy hair framed a stony continence.

I reached for Daisy's hand to pull her away, but the man's hands tightened on her hips.

Daisy let out a soft whimper. Pink-painted lips turned down in a pretty frown.

"Come on, Gorgeous. They're just having a little fun."

My eyes shifted from the man accosting Daisy to settle on Ethan, lounging like a rogue prince with his scotch at the other end of the table.

My eyes narrowed to thin slits.

Ethan didn't seem to notice. His own eyes raked over my legs.

"You could benefit from a bit of fun, yourself."

I held back the shudder that fought to surge through my body.

"Not here. It's not that kind of bar."

The corner of Ethan's mouth rose in a sleepy grin.

"Wherever you like."

"That's enough." Eric's deep voice boomed from right behind me.

"Let's go, Daisy. Your set's up next." Eric turned to the men.

"The rest of you, it's time to go."

The man with the vacant stare met my gaze for a long moment before he released Daisy. I watched her race for the break room.

I'd send Ruby to check on her in a bit.

I glared down the table at Ethan.

His predatory stare stayed fixed on me as he leisurely took up his glass and downed the rest of the amber liquid inside.

His voice came out smooth, but underneath, I could hear the rattlesnake ready to strike.

"Alright, big guy." Ethan shoved to his feet.

The others around the table followed suit.

Eric's big hand closed around the arm of the man who accosted Daisy as he escorted him out of the bar, trusting the rest to follow.

With a final glare in Ethan's direction, I turned toward the bar, ready for my shift to end.

Mistake.

A hot hand closed around my wrist and spun me back around.

Ethan smirked down at me, too close, taking full advantage of the crowded space.

Whiskey wafted off him in waves.

Where was Eric?

I wasn't short by any means, but I couldn't see over the heads of the crowd of men eager to get a clear glimpse of the girls on stage.

"I'm still looking for round two," Ethan purred in my ear.

I couldn't stop the repulsed shudder from dancing across my skin.

Before I had a chance to act, an arm snaked around my waist, and suddenly, I found myself pulled against a completely different body, warm and solid at my back.

The growl that rumbled over my shoulder was deep and feral, promising hurt for any who stood in his way.

"She's not interested."

I watched Ethan's smirk fall into a sneer as his eyes raked once more over my chest and legs. When they came back to my face, they held a promise of their own.

"Next time."

With no further prompting, Ethan disappeared into the crowd like the most unwelcome of specters.

"Thanks." I stepped away from Jake and turned, arms building a wall around my body. "I had it under control."

Jake gave a stiff nod. His head tilted, and his eyes softened.

"You're shaking."

Why did he have to notice?

Jake took a step closer as I turned back toward the bar.

"I'm fine."

Jake shadowed me back to the bar.

Carlo met me there, thick arms folded over a barrel chest. His mouth set in a stiff line, but, like Jake's, his eyes were soft when they met mine.

"You're done for the night," Carlo said as I passed in front of him to step behind the counter.

"No. I'm good."

"No, you're not. Go home."

"Carlo, I—"

"You'll get your whole check for the night." Carlo glanced over my shoulder to where I could feel Jake standing, then back at me. "You know this guy?"

I nodded, and Carlo's attention shifted again.

He leveled Jake with his stare.

"Make sure she gets home safe."

"But—"

Carlo edged me from behind the bar.

"No arguing."

My mouth snapped shut.

I spun on my heel and marched toward the back room, a space reserved for the female staff to change and store their belongings.

"Where are you going?" Jake fell in beside me.

"You heard Carlo. Home. I gotta grab my bag. And you don't expect me to walk outside in this, do you?"

To Jake's credit, his eyes stayed on mine as they narrowed into suspicious slits.

My shoulders sagged.

"I really don't need an escort."

Was that pink creeping into his cheeks?

It was gone before I could be sure.

Folding his arms over his chest, Jake posted up next to the door.

"Be quick."

Before Jake could say anything else, I slipped through the door marked employees only.

▲▲▲

I didn't go back.

In the back room, I snatched my bag off a hook on the wall and slipped out the back door into the parking lot without breaking stride.

Cool air pulled my hair over my shoulders as I crossed the darkened lot.

Streetlights stood at the corners closest to the street, but only a single lamp, mounted on the roof of the bar, illuminated the near side of the parking lot.

The lot was nearing capacity.

It was quiet, the silence only broken by the occasional car passing by on Seltice Way. Most everyone was inside or lined up outside the doors on the other side of the building.

It was just me in the rows and rows of cars.

Or so I thought.

A cool wind whistled through the parking lot.

Stepping out from between two cars, the hairs on the back of my neck stood like static.

I adjusted my purse strap on my shoulder, ready to hightail it to my car near the back of the lot.

Why don't I just park by the front door like Carlo asks?

The sound of leather soles on gravel turned my head to glance behind me.

There, standing between two rows of cars, was Ethan. Alone.

Just keep walking.

But my head wouldn't turn.

The soles of my boots were glued to the gravel.

I pivoted on my heel to face the man.

Dressed in a tailored suit, Ethan didn't look like the type to frequent Carlo's.

Dust kicked up from the parking lot and clung to the bottoms of his pant legs like an adoring fan. His jacket hung over his arm.

In the diffused streetlight, Ethan's white shirt glowed.

"I'm not interested, Ethan. Leave before I call security."

Why don't I carry mace?

A smirk pulled at the edge of Ethan's thin lips.

We both knew it was an empty threat.

Ethan would get to me before I could even locate my phone in my bag, and that's assuming it was even on. Stupid battery hated to hold a charge.

Ethan stepped closer.

I stepped back, refusing and unable to take my eyes off him.

"I don't know, doll. You seemed pretty interested the last time." His smile grew nasty, relishing in the memory of our one-night stand. "Remember how you begged?"

To be let go.

I couldn't hold back the shudder that skirted over my skin.

Ethan's smile turned predatory, his teeth flashing in the moonlight like fangs.

I squared my shoulders, wishing, for the first time since starting at Carlo's, that I carried. Heck, that I owned a gun at all.

Even if I was safe in my car that very second, I knew I'd get little sleep that night. That grin burned into my mind.

Show no fear.

Not to Ethan. Not to anybody.

"Go home, Ethan." Against all my better judgment, but needing to come off unperturbed, I turned slightly and started toward my car. In my periphery, I watched Ethan to see if he'd make a move, but he was quicker than he looked in a three-piece suit.

I blinked, and an arm barred under my breasts, pulling me back into Ethan.

"Only if you're coming with me," he hissed into my hair.

I felt a hand roam up my thigh under my skirt.

43

Squeezing my thighs together, I bit my lips to hold back tears, trying to pull up what the instructor from that one self-defense class I attended after graduation said to do when grabbed from behind.

Nothing.

My mind was a blank sheet of cold dread.

"Le' da gurl go."

Eyes widened.

No.

Gary, you idiot.

Ethan's hand froze on the back of my thigh, just beneath the hem of my skirt. Fingers squeezed, bruising.

"This doesn't concern you, old man," Ethan called. "Just having some time with my girl."

A finger slipped beneath my panties.

Ethan's teeth found the fleshy space between my neck and shoulder. I wanted to gag as he bit down.

But before I could blink, the hand beneath my skirt was ripped from my skin, Ethan torn from behind me.

Confused but more than grateful, I stumbled away. Nausea tickled the edges of my stomach as Ethan's expensive cologne clung to my clothes.

As I turned to take in the scene, I tumbled into a heap of heels and skirt on the gravel.

In the space between two rows of cars, Gary gripped Ethan's wrist with more force than one would expect from a drunk old man. Gin-fogged eyes glinted with determination.

"I's said leave 'er alone."

Ethan looked ready to kill.

Barely focused eyes shifted to me.

"Ge' in yer car."

"Gary—"

Ethan dropped his fist into Gary's gut.

"No!"

Gary crumpled, falling to the ground like a discarded accordion.

"I's said leave 'er alone."

Somewhere close, gravel crunched underfoot.

My fingers fisted, closing around bits of crushed rock so tight it bit into my palms.

Tears stung my eyes.

Ethan spat in the dirt near Gary's balding head.

"Stay out of business that doesn't concern you."

Ethan turned back to me, eyes flashing with malice.

A shadow stepped in his path.

Chapter 6

A sneer slid across Ethan's face as he took in the man standing between us.

In Ethan's cold eyes, the knowledge that he'd have to retreat lashed like a viper's tail. He hated it. Hated the good Samaritan who stepped in to stop a bad situation.

Ethan might be comfortable putting down a drunk old man, but he knew better than to take on someone young and twice his size.

As quick as the sneer appeared, it dropped from Ethan's face, replaced by a placating smile that fooled many a jury. His arms fell to his sides as he forced his shoulders to relax.

"Look, man, this is all just a misunderstanding." Ethan pulled off casual better than any Grammy-winning actor.

I scrambled to my feet. Pain twinged in my ankle.

The man didn't move.

"No misunderstanding." The man's voice took on a dark timbre that promised danger if Ethan did not comply. "I suggest you go back inside."

Electricity shivered up my spine and reverberated in my limps. It settled like a time bomb ticking at my core.

A moment passed in tense silence. Ethan glared back at the man.

I watched Ethan's carefully crafted mask crack to reveal an ugly snarl.

He spit once on the ground and turned back to the bar.

"She's not worth the time anyway."

Still rooted in place, I watched him march back toward the bar.

He flashed his ID at the bounce and continued past.

The door swung closed behind Ethan with a metallic clang that I could only wish echoed finality, knowing full well I would see him again as long as I continued working at Carlo's.

When Ethan was gone, I ran to Gary, ignoring the slight ache in my ankle. I dropped beside him as Gary pushed himself up off the ground.

"Are you okay?" I brushed dust from the sleeve of his shirt.

Gary brushed me away.

"Oh, I's fine. Wha abou' you?" Gary's words came out slurred, even as he panted to catch his breath.

"I'm not the one picking drunken fights," I scolded. Once again, I moved to brush the dirt from his sleeve, only to have my fingers swatted.

"You really didn't need to do that."

"And you shouldn't be walking through dark parking lots alone."

I turned to the deep voice as its gravelly rumble slid over me.

Cobalt eyes met mine with an intensity that dared me not to look away.

My eyes dropped.

Of course, it would be Jake.

Choosing to ignore my second rescuer for the moment, I turned back to Gary.

"Let's get you home."

I looped an arm under Gary's and shoved to my feet, ignoring the sudden burst of vertigo as I pulled him up with me.

Or I would have had my ankle muscles not chosen that moment to throb uncontrollably.

Shifting, I tried to relieve the pressure building in my sprained ankle. Halfway between standing and landing back on my butt in the dirt, I wobbled.

Warm hands closed on my hips. I fought the urge to shrug them off as they steadied me. They disappeared as soon as I was stable.

"Thanks."

I glanced back up into Jake's face, my own warming.

He stared back with stoic intensity.

"Did he hurt you?"

Not this time.

Muscled bunched along Jake's jaw as he waited for my answer.

"I'm fine." I tore my eyes away, turning back to the drunk beside me.

"Let's get you home, Gary. What's Marcy going to say, you

coming home like this?"

Gary released my arm and staggered away a couple steps with a croaking sound caught somewhere between a laugh and a sob.

"Oh, Marcy'll be fine. Don't got to worry about me none."

Jake caught Gary's elbow as the older man swayed.

"Let's get you in the truck." Jake steered Gary away from where my car was parked.

"Jake—"

But he was already several steps ahead of me, leaving me no option but to limp after him.

Arms crossed, I watched Jake help Gary into the back seat of a silver Chevy.

"I can drive him home, Jake," I said as Jake closed the door softly.

He turned to face me.

Some of the ferocity had waned from his eyes, leaving them gentle, an almost midnight blue.

"It's no trouble. I do it all the time."

"Hanna, you're shaking. You're not driving anywhere."

I stiffened.

A frown formed on my lips.

"I don't need some white knight jump in to save the day, Jake. I have my own car. I can take care of myself."

"Then it's a good thing I'm no white knight. Get in the truck, Hanna."

I glared up at him, lips pursed.

Jake returned the look tenfold, promising to put me in the truck if I didn't go myself.

And I wouldn't put it past him.

"I'm not leaving my car."

He sighed, and his shoulders sagged like I was the most tiresome person in the world, the last person he wanted to deal with on a Friday night.

"I'll bring you back for your car in the morning. Just get in the truck."

I tried one last time.

"I'm fine, really. I can drive myself home."

"I know, just...humor me, darlin'. I'll sleep better knowing you got home safe."

Darlin'?

Before I could wrap my head around the endearment and come back with a snarky remark, Jake had steered me around the truck to the passenger side of his truck.

I eyed the seat, then turned ton Jake, accusing, knowing I'd been tricked into accepting a ride.

Jake gave me that small, boyish smile that made him look like he was back in high school. It was the same smile he'd offer up in commiseration after a bad play or a bungled routine.

Sweet.

"You expect me to ride in this thing?"

Jake rolled his eyes, but the smile only grew as he took my elbow to help me into the truck.

In the rearview mirror, Gary was already dozing against the window, too many drinks catching up to him.

I watched Jake slide into the driver's seat. It felt weird being in Jake's truck. How many other girls sat in the same place as me, expecting their night to end very differently than mine with the man on the other side of the cab?

It wasn't like the Jake I knew to rescue the damsel, not that I was one in any sense of the word.

With Jake, there was always a catch. You just had to find it before he caught you.

▲▲▲

The ride to Gary's farm was silent, punctuated only by Gary's bubbling snores from the back seat and my clipped directions.

We pulled up to the chain-link gate blocking the drive into Gary's house. The slowing of the truck as we pulled onto the gravel turnaround jarred Gary awake.

With garbled thanks, Gary crawled from the truck.

Jake and I watched him fumble with the gate lock, debating if we should get out to help, then watched him disappear down the darkened drive.

"Should we—"

I didn't have to finish for Jake to know what I was asking.

He shook his head, eyes still on the driveway as he turned the truck around.

"Do you usually walk him to the door?"

It was my turn to shake my head.

"He doesn't usually get like that."

I shifted in the passenger seat, angling myself to keep Jake and the windshield in my line of sight.

I studied him.

He looked the same.

Same short-cropped hair.

Same dark blue eyes a girl could get lost in.

He'd put on some muscle since high school, but I guess the army would do that to you.

Jake looked the same, but somehow he seemed wholly changed.

The Jake I'd known in high school wouldn't have stepped into the middle of a bar fight, didn't matter how pretty the girl was. He wouldn't offer a girl a ride home *just so he could sleep better at night.* If there wasn't something in it for Jake, he wouldn't take the risk.

So, what was his game?

"You do this often?" Jake asked as he turned onto the freeway onramp.

"What? Take rides from guys I haven't seen since high school?"

A brow raised over those cobalt blues as Jake glanced in my direction before returning back to the road.

Something about those eyes—I couldn't put my finger on it—was different. Something broken, deep down. Jake hid it well, as if he'd collected up all the pieces he could find and glued them back together. Deep down, he still found something vital missing.

I stared out the window into the darkness.

"Gary's a regular. He usually doesn't drink that much."

"And the asshole? What about him?"

I shook my head, unable to keep myself from laughing at the absurdity of it all.

I'm in Jake Stevens' truck.

Jake acting all protective.

I sobered quickly with another serious look from Jake.

"Ethan was a mistake. He comes by every once in a while to cause trouble, that's all."

Jake stared out the windshield. His jaw clenched as he chewed over his next words.

"He was trying to do more than cause trouble tonight," he said softly. When I looked back over, I found Jake, hard as stone, glaring out the front of the truck like Ethan stood in the headlights.

"Yeah, he was."

▲▲▲

"This is it," I said fifteen minutes later as we pulled up to a small two-story house.

Jake guided the truck into the empty driveway and cut the engine.

Neither of us moved.

Both reliving the events of the night.

"Thanks," I said, finally, my voice coming out a little louder than a whisper.

I wasn't dumb.

If Jake hadn't been there...

I didn't want to think about what might have happened.

"For tonight. For the ride."

"How's your ankle?" Jake asked, brushing aside my gratitude like it was a fly. "You were limping earlier. After..."

So he had noticed.

My cheeks warmed, and suddenly, I was thankful for the darkness of the cab. I need to get inside, away from Jake.

"Fine," I insisted as I reached for the door handle. "Thanks again."

"I swung my legs out the door, noting how my feet dangled almost a foot off the ground.

No one should drive a car that tall.

Really, what was the point?

I dropped down, hating how small the truck made me feel. I grimaced as a small jolt shot up through my calf when I landed.

Good thing I didn't have another class that week.

All weekend to rest and heal.

I slammed the door behind me and started around the front of the truck, only to hear an echoing door slam on the other side.

Jake met me on the short walk to the door and followed me up, two steps behind.

What was he doing?

It was a safe enough neighborhood.

And I was NOT some delicate little girl who needed to be escorted to safety.

It was my house, for goodness sake!

"Thanks again," I tried again to send him away as I turned on the steps, fishing my keys from my bag. "If you want to stop by tomorrow around nine? I should be ready."

Jake didn't step away from the door. Hooded eyes watched me like they could see every insecurity passing through my mind.

Shaking fingers closing around my keys, I turned to unlock the door, ready to escape the frigid night air.

Okay, and to avoid that penetrating stare.

Jake looked back over his shoulder, down the darkened street.

"You're sure you're okay here?"

I couldn't hold down the laugh that bubbled from my lips.

Who was this man before me?

It couldn't be the Jake I knew in high school.

"It's my house."

But when I turned back to face him, I found lines bracketing his mouth, a deep crease forming between his furrowed brows.

"I'm fine," I assured. "Ethan doesn't know where I live."

Jake nodded, but the worried lines never left his face.

"Pick you up at nine?"

It took longer than it should have for my brain to process what Jake meant.

Car! Right.

"Make it eight. I've got some stuff to take care of in the morning."

He nodded, still frowning.

"If that's not too early for you," I challenged. Brows ticked upward.

Jake's hands found the pockets of his jeans. He jingled his keys as he backed toward his truck.

"See you at eight."

With a small wave, he turned and drove away.

▲▲▲

I kept the lights off as I stepped inside. The door closed softly at my back.

Falling against the cool wood, I took a breath, hoping it would settle whatever churned around my core. I wouldn't name it. At best, it was stomach flu. At worst,...not even going to go there.

Nonetheless, my stomach burbled and squeezed, pressing into my throat until I had no choice but to run through the darkened house to the bathroom.

Clutching the toilet, I emptied myself. Stomach, mind, the unwarranted emotions swirling around inside.

But as I wiped my mouth on a wad of TP, the emotions remained, clinging to me like Velcro or supercharged magnets, unwilling to give up their hold.

I rinsed my mouth and swished mouthwash, nearly making me gag all over again.

Exhaustion tugged at my eyelids, weighed down my aching limbs, as I trekked back through the house. I didn't bother with the lights.

All I wanted was to curl up somewhere soft and warm and drift off for days, but when I reached my room, I froze on the threshold. Like some uninvited vampire, I found myself unable to cross, held back by memory.

Greg's specter waited for me beneath the sheets we picked out together. He called to me softly in the darkness, but I knew if I sank beneath the blankets, I wouldn't find him there.

Still, he stared back at me expectantly, wafer-thin and so intangible it hurt.

Tears pricked at my eyes. Turning back to the hall, I swiped the salty drops from my cheeks.

No more tears.

What's done is done.

Passing the linen closet, I pulled an extra blanket from the shelf and made my way to the living room, where I settled on the couch.

Greg was there as well, quieter, staring back at me from the many frames cluttering the wall above the TV.

Why?

Why can't I escape you?

But I knew why.

It was the same reason I couldn't pull those frames from the wall, couldn't change the case on his pillow, or throw away that ratty pair of grizzly bear slippers he loved so much.

Shoving against the exhaustion that begged me to stay, I levered myself off the couch and stomped to the back door.

Across the yard, a single light shined over my studio door.

Pulling the blanket tight around my shoulders, I stepped out into the chill of the October night.

A few hours of work in the studio would chase any phantom away.

Chapter 7

I fell asleep in the studio.

With a pained groan, I rolled onto my back.

I had to stop falling asleep on the floor.

My left hip ached after who knew how many hours pressed against the polished wood floor of what would become the largest classroom.

The room was pitch black, but that would happen when you built a dance studio in a barn.

I pushed up into a seated position, and the overhead lights popped on in all their natural splendor.

Motion sensors.

One of the last things Greg installed before his final trip.

A breath pushed past my lips in an audible puff.

I scrubbed at my sleep-crusted eyes.

What time was it?

I patted my pockets but couldn't find my phone.

My jacket.

Pouting my lips, I squinted against the bright light as I searched the floor for the crumpled gray garment.

Nothing.

Goodie.

Did I really take it off inside?

With another bone-deep groan, I pushed to my feet, the joints in my knees creaking in protest.

"No," I scolded my still tired limbs. "You're too young for that."

Standing, I tested the ankle I sprained the night before. Feeling only a slight stiffness in the joint, I plodded barefoot into what would be the tiny lobby.

Where were my shoes?

In the little office off the lobby, I slipped on a pair of lime green flip-flops from the collection under the card table that served as a desk.

Outside, the air was even chillier than inside the studio.

I cringed, thinking about how much it would cost to install heating and AC in the poorly insulated barn. It would have to be done if I expected to lead lessons in there someday.

Flip-flops smacked against the bottoms of my feet.

I trekked up the three steps to the minuscule back porch.

Reaching for the know, I frowned.

Did I really leave the door open all night?

Only a few inches of space between the door and the jam were visible.

Inside, the kitchen stood still and silent.

Empty.

Careful, I eased the door open and stepped inside. Back against the door, I listened to the house sounds for any sign someone else was inside.

Nothing.

Silence.

I eased away from the door.

Pale morning light filtered into the living room through the sheet curtains over the front picture window, illuminating bits of dust drifting on the still air.

A square of light stretched across the wall opposite the couch, highlighting the frames.

My eyes stalled on those at the center, bright, happy pictures in shiny silver frames. So much joy and promise.

I tore my eyes away and crossed to the hallway.

Clearing the main floor, I stopped at the base of the stairs to listen once more.

Nothing but the usual creaks of a mid-century house.

A short hall stretched at the top.

Plush white carpet engulfed my toes as I stepped off the top stair.

A large window at the far end of the hall looked out over the front yard, allowing morning sun into the narrow space.

Twin doors stood off either side of the hall, identical in every way. Four panels, white paint, a round patina-painted, brass doorknob.

The door on the right was shut. Greg's study, still full of his books, maps, and research. He'd been so excited about his trip to Kenya. It would have been his third.

Greg spent hours in that study going over books and different articles. He liked to learn everything he could about an area and its people before he stepped in, spouting off strange ideas of Western medicine.

Working mostly with indigenous tribes in remote jungles across Africa and South America, Greg wasn't one of those doctors who thought he knew the best way just because he had a few letters before and after his name. More often than not, Greg'd come back from a trip outlining a paper on some new technique he'd learned from a village healer or some bit of folk medicine he'd picked up from a community elder.

I kept the door to those memories firmly shut.

The door on the left stood open from my brief visit the night before.

Staring in at the neatly made bed, now empty of any ghosts, I leaned against the frame as more memories pulled at me.

I couldn't keep avoiding the space.

Sooner or later, I would have to reclaim the bedroom that had been ours. The studio floor was not in the least bit an adequate substitute.

Downstairs, a door slammed, sending me leaping into the air.

"Hello?" A rich voice called up the stairs. "Hanna?"

"Geezus!"

I spun away from the door and nearly toppled on the carpet.

When I looked up, Jake stood at the base of the stairs.

"You ever hear of knocking?" I stomped down to meet him, pulling the blanket tight around my shoulders.

"I did. You might want to get a doorbell."

So all the neighborhood kids could ring it at all hours of the night? I don't think so.

I swept past him.

"Coffee?" I called back as I stepped into the kitchen.

Jake followed on my heels.

I tore open the pantry door and searched the shelves for the red coffee can.

"I'm good, thanks."

Good, I thought as I picked up the can off the bottom shelf and shook it to find it nearly empty. I set it back on the middle shelf and turned, my eyes catching on the clock over the stove.

"Sorry, I'm running a little late. I'll just be a few minutes. If you've got somewhere you've got to be..."

Please have somewhere you have to be!

"Go get ready, darlin'. I'll be here."

There was that word again.

Jake leaned on the counter, arms folded over a chest that was all too sturdy and muscled to be fair.

Feeling my cheeks turn a warm shade of pink, I turned and

darted from the room.

"Thanks! I'll just be a minute."

"Take your time." Jake's voice raced me up the stairs.

▲▲▲

Pulling my damp hair into a messy ponytail, I stepped back into the living room twenty minutes later to find Jake standing in the middle of the room. He drank in the pictures scattered in frames across the wall.

I stepped up beside him.

No.

He wasn't taking in all the pictures.

Those dark blue eyes were stuck on one photo in a silver frame.

My heart squeezed.

The Hanna in that picture was so happy, so full of hope and dreams as she hung off the arm of the man she loved. Her new husband.

All in white, she let off a youthful glow, barely twenty-one, ready to take on the world.

Matching bands shined from the couple's entwined left hands, pinky promising years of love and laughter.

Neither one of them could have known it would end so soon.

I would never have those years, growing old with Greg at my side.

"I heard about what happened."

Jake's voice tore me away from the pool of grief I was so ready to drown in.

"I'm sorry."

Drawing a long breath, I swiped at a traitorous tear before letting it out.

"Me too."

My voice didn't crack.

Not this time, as it had every time before.

It may have warbled, been unrecognizable as mine, but I'd take it.

I couldn't wallow forever.

I turned and led the way out of the house.

▲▲▲

For the second time in less than eight hours, I climbed up into the passenger seat of Jake's too-tall truck.

Jake closed the door softly behind me before rounding the front of the truck and sliding into the driver's seat.

The truck roared to life with the turn of a key.

Jake glanced over and nodded to the center console.

"That's for you."

I stared down at the brown, paper to-go cup in the cupholder between the seats. A Monster Energy filled the other space next to my coffee.

I bit the inside of my lips.

"Jake, you didn't have to."

Inexplicable tears pricked in my eyes. Jake bought me a coffee.

He shrugged his big shoulders and turned back to the road.

"Figured you might want one. You and Jessie used to stop for them all the time. Vanilla Mocha, right?"

Okay, how could he remember that?

"Yeah."

What was with my voice that morning?

So soft and meek.

So unlike me.

I took the to-go cup, letting the heat soak into my palms before sipping.

Mmm.

I smiled.

Perfect.

"Thanks for the ride, by the way," I added after a few more sips of caffeine to awaken my brain.

Jake pulled out onto a busy street.

"It's nothing," Jake said with a shrug. "The least I could do." Jake turned his crooked grin on me, but I saw the shadow of a memory in his eyes. "You did keep my dumb ass out of jail."

Jail? What had he been planning on doing to Ethan?

Then I remembered.

High school. Senior year. Just after Jessie came back.

We'd all been out looking for Cole.

We found him, but in our haste, we may have forgotten to mention where we were to Jessie's parents. Naturally, they freaked.

The cops swarmed Jessie and Cole in the parking lot outside the little diner where we found Cole.

Standing in the doorway, arms wrapped tight around Jake, it took every ounce of energy I had to keep him from charging in to defend his friend.

When I closed my eyes, I still felt Jake trembling with rage against me.

In the doorway of that diner, nothing mattered to Jake but helping his friend.

"Pretty sure we're even after last night," I said, taking another sip.

"Who was that guy anyway?"

My coffee smile soured.

I stared down at the cup in my hands.

"Nobody."

Jake didn't miss the shiver that rolled through my shoulders. His hand crossed the center console to give my knee a comforting squeeze.

Damn him.

I could already feel my cheeks heating as I prepared to over-share.

"Some high-powered defense lawyer. He brings his clients out to Carlo's whenever they win a big case."

I glared out the window as Ethan's phantom hand slid up my leg.

Jake pulled his hand away from my knee. I squeezed my cup to keep from pulling it back, like the warmth of his touch could erase the memory from my mind.

Something about Jake made it easier to talk about Ethan, even Greg. Like somehow, he was a tether tying me to reality, a reminder that the past could no longer hurt me.

Ethan couldn't hurt me.

"And how's he connected to you? He seemed..."

"Familiar?" I caught Jake's eye and held it for an uncomfortable moment before he looked away.

"Yeah."

"It's stupid."

I fixed my eyes on the passing cars and buildings out the window, determined not to look back to see pity in Jake's eyes.

"I highly doubt it. If he did something to you—"

I swiped at a tear before it could escape.

"Ethan didn't do anything I didn't think I wanted at the time."

A lie, but if it got Jake to drop the subject, then I thought I could live with it.

"Sorry, I..."

Damn him.

"No." I stopped his apology.

Taking a deep breath, I forced myself to relax into the surprisingly comfortable seat.

"After Greg, I just..."

"Hey, no need to explain. I've been there. It's not a great place."

I watched Jake from the corner of my eye, knowing somehow, he understood.

"Yeah."

Jake merged onto the freeway.

"But if you ever need to talk, I'm here. 'Kay?"

Wow.

I never thought I'd see the day.

Was Jake Stevens reaching out?

I had to be dreaming.

I sent him a minuscule smile before turning back to my coffee, happy to let the rest of the drive pass in only-slightly awkward silence.

Why did Jake suddenly care what was going on in other people's lives?

Chapter 8

Carlo's parking lot was nearly empty when we pulled in.

Sunshine gleamed from a crystalline sky.

Dust plumed behind Jake's truck as he slid into the space next to my Maxima.

A sky-blue Volkswagen, two rows over, and a rusty, old van, backed into a space on the far end of the lot were the only other cars in the lot, both dark and vacant.

Cars in Carlo's lot the morning after were not unusual.

At the end of the night, it wasn't uncommon to see a line of ride-shares stretched in front of the wide double doors, waiting for their inebriated riders.

I was more than ready to put space between me and Jake. During the last half of the drive, uncomfortable questions and unwanted feelings crowded the cab of Jake's truck until it felt like we were breathing underwater, neither of us willing to look in the other's direction for long.

"Thanks again for the ride."
I sent Jake a small smile as I reached for the handle on the door,

more than eager to escape the close confines. Then, with one flip-flopped foot on the gravel, I turned back.

"And for last night."

Our eyes met then. I tried to convey everything I couldn't say out loud with that look.

Before Jake could find the stray thoughts swirling behind my eyes, I stepped from the car and let the door slam behind me.

One breath.

Brushing stray hairs from my face, I moved to the driver's side of my car and froze by the door.

"Shit."

Mouth open, I stared down at the swell of deflated rubber clinging to the front wheel of my car.

Heat rose up my neck as I noted the jagged gash torn through the tire, the site of the leak.

Nails bit into my palms as my fingers balled and my jaw clenched.

I drew in a breath meant to bring calm composure, but it only added more fuel to the fire simmering inside me.

"Fucking asshole."

"Everything okay?" Jake called through a rolled-down window.

I couldn't answer—not without screaming—nor could I tear my eyes away from the grizzly wound.

A car door slammed.

"Jeezus, fuck."

I felt Jake next to me, taking in the damage.

And though I didn't have it, and despite the anger coursing through me, Jake's exclamation had me glancing up at him with amusement.

"Guess Ethan wasn't done talking."

"Fucking asshole. You want me to call the cops?"

I shook my head before he could finish.

"No point." I popped the trunk and shoved a duffel and spare shoes aside to uncover the spare tire compartment.

"Can't prove it was him."

Jake swore again and followed me to the trunk, where he helped me lift the tire from the trunk.

"That's some mouth you've developed," I commented conversationally as I dug under the seats for the jack and ratchet.

Jake watched me with a curious look, when I came up for air.

"What?"

Jake just shook his head and held out his hand for the jack.

I leaned on the side of the car, watching Jake work.

"So, why are you back? Really."

Pocketing one of the bolts from the ruined tire, Jake's shoulders rose and fell.

"You know I can do that, right?" I waved at the tire.

Jake sent an assessing look up at me.

"I'm sure you can." He turned back to the tire. "Not today."

"At least let me—"

"Nope."

I let out a frustrated growl, earning me another amused glance from Jake.

"You're really infuriating, you know that?"

"You're not the first to say so, darlin'."

Another frustrated growl.

I stomped around the front of the car as a trill sounded from inside Jake's truck, echoing through the open driver's side door.

"Your phone's ringing," I called.

Jake leaned into the ratchet, working a stubborn bolt.

"You mind answering it? It's probably just Warren."

I climbed into the cab and snatched the smartphone from the cup holder, lifting it to my ear.

"Jake's phone, Hanna speaking. Who's this?"

"Hanna?" The woman on the other line screeched. "No, who the fuck are you, answering my husband's phone?"

Not particularly wanting to lose my hearing, I held the phone away from my ear and glanced up with a raised brow to find Jake watching me over the top of my car. The apologetic press of his lips told me he could tell from way over there exactly who was on the other line.

When the screeching quieted, I brought the phone back to my ear. A smirk curled my lips as I met Jake's gaze.

"I'm sorry, Jakey's handling something for me right now." Jake's eyes went buggy. He raced around the front of my car.

A muscled arm circled my waist, pulling me into his side as Jake reached for the phone.

Laughing, I maneuvered it out of reach.

"He's going to have to call you back after we finish."

Jake snatched the phone from my fingers before I could hang up, releasing me.

Still laughing, I bounced out of reach again.

That would teach him not to mention a vital piece of information, like a wife.

Not that I was interested.

"Gina," Jake growled into the phone, sending me a half-hearted, dirty look. I responded with an amused and satisfied smirk as he stepped around to the other side of his truck.

His voice dropped as he spoke into the phone.

"The lawyer has everything, Gina."

Lawyer?

Though I tried not to listen, my nosey nature and interest peaked.

"You should be free to go ahead with your plans...No..."

Jake's jaw bunched, and his mouth drew into a thin line as he listened.

"Gina," Jake raked a hand through his hair in exasperation. "You left me, remember? The answer's no."

He hung up before she could argue.

Tossing the phone back into the truck, he stomped back toward me.

"Uh...so..." I hedged. "You're married?"

"No more than you," Jake growled as he turned back to the tire. "Signed all the papers before leaving Texas."

"Ouch."

"Sorry, I..."

Jake's head jerked up, his eyes wide with apology.

"It's fine. Sorry I made things harder with your ex."

The look in his eyes turned mirthful.

"No harm done. Gina thought she could call up and ask for some of Ma's recipes to have the chef make for her upcoming nuptials."

"Seriously? She moves fast." I slid down the side of my car to watch Jake work. "What a bitch. You're pretty good at that." I waved toward the tire.

Another glance from Jake.

"Should be. Spent four years doing it for the army. You should be good to go now."

Jake stood and held out a hand to help me up.

Thanking Jake for the umpteenth time that morning, I took the jack and ratchet back and threw them and the ruined tire into the trunk. Choosing not to dwell on the zipping sensation still pulsing up my arm from the brief second Jake's fingers brushed mine in the handoff, I climbed into my car.

▲▲▲

There's something soothing about repetitive motion, the repeated back and forth granting the mind clemency to wander.

That afternoon, I pressed and rolled a paintbrush across the wall of the big classroom in my studio, letting the liquid motion ease my whirring mind as I deposited layer upon layer of paint on the walls, turning them a pale hollyhock blue.

Up and down.

Calming, unobtrusive, and nonthreatening.

Misha was with me when I picked out the color, days before news of Greg's accident reached us. I hadn't known then the solace I would find in the cool blue tone.

Then, I'd been worried, constantly fretting over Greg and our lack of communication in the last weeks.

Yes, he was in the jungle.

Yes, it was very remote.

But didn't they have a satellite phone or something?

What good was international coverage if I couldn't contact Greg any time to see how he was doing?

Misha pointed out the row of calming shades decorating the display in the hardware store. She encouraged me to pick one.

According to her, the blue-gray color would ease the nerves of my young students, allowing them to reach their full potential.

I blinked slowly, watching the paint pass from the brush to the drywall.

Unwarranted, cobalt blue eyes superimposed themselves over the large swath of wall I'd just finished painting. They blinked back at me. A thin sheen of levity brightened the dark surfaces, telling of some hidden joke. Unassuming and yet probing, searching for something in me.

But what?

Some unvoiced question swirled in those dark eyes.

Eyes I should *not* be exploring.

Deliberately, I dipped the brush back in the paint tray and coated over the eyes.

I had other things to worry about.

Molley's offer for one.

It was a bad idea. Really.

Who would put me in charge of a child?

When had I ever shown an aptitude for caring for another human being?

I didn't even have a pet.

Not even a goldfish.

I couldn't keep Misha from cutting when she found out about Greg. And she'd been good, healthy, happy even.

If I couldn't keep a girl who smiled and visited her therapist with little to no argument from harming herself, how was I supposed to keep a child alive, even if just for a few days?

My phone buzzed from where it rested on the floor in the middle of the room.

Newspaper crinkled under my feet as I padded over to answer.

Molley.

I slid the green circle across the screen.

Molley answered, all chirpy and happy. Full of small talk, like I couldn't see through her counselor's veneer to the reason for her call.

After ten minutes of weather and upcoming events, she finally got to the point.

"So? Will you do it?"

Molley knew she didn't need to explain. Somehow, she knew her offer had been the only thing on my mind for two days.

Was I that transparent?

I needed to work on that...

Somehow...

"I don't know, Molley..." I hedged, scuffing my bare feet across the floor of the studio.

"It would be a huge help, Hann. Just this once. You wouldn't have to commit to a new job or anything. Just this one kid. Three days, tops, and you're done."

I dropped the brush in the paint tray.

"Three days? Tops?"

"You just drive the kid to her new home, and you're done. I hear Montana's gorgeous in the fall."

Yeah, but who really wanted to make a thirteen-hour drive there and back on their own?

Doesn't matter how beautiful the scenery is.

"The pay's good," Molley tempted, and I could see the grin on her face as she dangled the bate. "Should cover those new mirrors you want for the studio."

Damn her.

"Fine."

"Really?" She sounded surprised.

"Yes. So where do I pick up this kid?" I groaned, already regretting my decision.

"Monday. I'll text you the info over the weekend."

"Great."

▲▲▲

This is a bad idea.

I stared out the windshield at the line of red taillights in front of me and worried my lip.

Not the day to forget to set an alarm.

I glanced at the clock on the dash.

9:42

Late.

I was going to be late.

Molley was going to kill me.

I took a left, then a right onto Washington.

The GPS on my phone pinged from the cupholder.

"In .3 miles, turn left into your destination."

Real helpful there, Google. Who the heck knows how far .3 miles is?

How long did it take to drive that far?

I glanced at the clock.

Ten minutes.

"In 100 feet, turn left into Rock Pointe Corporate Center."

"Thank you, Google."

My phone pinged with an incoming text.

I turned into the parking lot.

"Okay," I let out a breath I hadn't realized I'd been holding. "This is it."

After a quick glance into the back seat to collect a loose sweater and a handful of abandoned bottles—all of which got stashed in the trunk—I turned to the imposing building.

Shiny black stone and glass stretched to the sky. Three rows of windows decorated the facade. The building seemed much taller than the three stories I counted. It looked more like the headquarters of some super-secret government agency or a supervillain's lair rather than an office complex.

Who chose this place to house a child and family services office?

I stepped through the double sliding doors into the expansive lobby.

A large staircase circled the room from the left, leading up to the second floor, where a row of conference rooms was visible through the glass balcony railing.

As I crossed to the elevators, my ballet flats clicked on the marble floor tiles. As the doors slid closed, I pressed the button for the third floor.

The third level stood in stark contrast to the rest of the building. Purple carpet that looked like it hadn't been replaced since the eighties stretched down the long hallway. No windows opened into the hall to let in natural light. Only the glowing fluorescents overhead illuminated the walkway.

"There you are! I was about to call you."

I turned to find Molley approaching in that dancing, floating-on-air sort of way she had that always made her look more graceful than any of the princesses all the magazines liked to print long, scandalous articles about.

"Sorry. Ran into traffic." Not exactly a lie.

"It's okay. We're actually running a little behind, ourselves. Let's grab coffee."

▲▲▲

I let Molley lead me down to an alcove on the second floor where a small shop selling coffee and sandwiches was set up.

We ordered our drinks and found a seat near the windows.

Molley eyed me over the top of her cup.

"So." Molley crossed her legs and got comfortable in her chair. "I talked to Jake. He seems to think you might be in some kind of trouble."

Oh good. Here comes Jake, causing more trouble.

"I'm fine, Molley. Jake's just..." What? Overreacting?

Molley nodded like she understood.

"If anything is going on, though, you know you can come to me. I know people who might be able to help."

Along with working with Child and Family Services, Molley worked part-time as the city PD's in-house social worker. Unfortunately, warnings and restraining orders wouldn't solve anything with Ethan.

"I'm fine, Molley. Everything's fine."

"Good. Because I don't have the time to find another transfer. Speaking of, there's a bit you should know about the child."

Uh oh.

"Okay." I sipped at the steaming peppermint tea I ordered, hoping it would settle the nerves bubbling in my stomach.

"It's a bit of a sticky situation." Molley raked kinky curls back from her face, a move that brought a certain pair of dark blue eyes to mind.

I shook thoughts of Jake from my head and focused.

This was important.

Molley continued to explain.

"The dad's been arrested for distribution and the unlawful imprisonment of two women, along with battery and a slew of other charges. So far, we haven't been able to locate the mother. Normally, we try to keep the child with family, but in this case, it's not exactly plausible."

"Okay."

That didn't sound that bad. So, the kid came from a crappy home. Might have a bit of an attitude problem. Nothing I couldn't manage. I hoped.

"Normally, we wouldn't have a child fostered out of state, but with this guy's connections locally, we thought it best for the child's safety and that of her foster family. That's why we need you to take her to Miles City. We've found a home there willing to foster her with the possibility of adoption should we be unable to locate the mother."

I blinked back at Molley as I let the slew of information sink in.

Miles City.

When Molley told me the kid was going to Montana, I thought she meant Missoula, Bozeman, maybe. Not the other side of a state big enough to be a large European country.

The unease at my core boiled.

"Y-yea," I stammered, ungluing my tongue from the roof of my mouth. "That should be fine."

Would my car make it that far?

I bought my Maxima used just after my sixteenth birthday with babysitting money I saved. Though I remembered to change the oil and take it in for yearly tune-ups, the thing was still almost twenty years old. It struggled to get up the South Hill. How was it supposed to make it to Miles City?

Molley's slim, manicured brows drew together.

"You're sure? If this is too much—"

"I can handle it. It's fine. Besides," I forced a convincing smile onto my face. "I already ordered the mirrors.

"Good," Molley sighed. "Really, I don't know what I'd do without you. Well...I guess I could, but..." One arm slid protectively around Molley's middle, her delicate fingers splaying over her stomach in a weird way.

My eyes flashed to the tea bag tag dangling down the side of her cup.

"You're not—"

The corners of Molley's mouth tugged up in an insuppressible smile.

"Molley! That's Great! Does Will know?"

The smile on Molley's face wavered only slightly.

"Not yet. I only confirmed it this morning. I hadn't realized just how run down I'd feel all the time. At least the nausea hasn't been too bad. Sneaking off for naps has become pretty difficult, though."

Nausea?

Naps?

"You had no idea?"

Molley shrugged.

"Not really. I didn't think it was possible, but then I was almost five weeks late, so I thought, why not just be sure? Life finds a way, right?"

Five weeks.

How long had it been?

I counted back in my head, silently praying to any god I could think of that I was just missing something.

My stomach burbled. I took a sip of tea, hoping it would calm it.

No luck.

A chill swept up my arms.

Molley sat forward.

"Hanna? Are you okay? You look—"

"I'm great." I forced a smile. "That's amazing!"

"It's definitely something. Now, let's go meet this little girl and get everything squared away."

▲▲▲

Child and Family Services was housed in a cozy office space at the far end of the hall on the third floor.

I followed Molley into a little lobby with a couch and a pair of cushy-looking secondhand chairs in a haze as my mind whirred.

Was it even possible?

I mean, I'd know, right?

There'd be symptoms.

Signs.

Then again, there had been, hadn't there?

Or I wouldn't even be thinking I might be...

Molley stopped abruptly and turned to face me, a startled look on her face.

"Wait right here while I see if they're ready.

Molley disappeared down a short hall into a room, only to reappear a moment later, her glossed lips stretched into a bright cheerleader's smile.

"Alright, we're ready."

But was I?

Molley waved for me to follow her into the room.

The room was small—a ten-by-ten office with just enough room for a bean-shaped table and a handful of chairs.

Two women sat facing the door.

I blinked a moment, confused, before spotting the baby carrier on the table.

Oh.

"Hanna, this is Penny George and Dr. Rachal Eagan. They're the ones in charge of Lily's case. And this," Molley motioned to the baby carrier and the tawny infant inside. "Is Lily."

I stepped closer.

The baby blinked at me like she was as surprised by my appearance as I was by her, and just as dubious of the situation we both found ourselves in.

When Molley said I'd be transferring a child to her new foster home, I expected something like an eight-year-old—someone who could pick their own food and drink at a drive through—not a baby still on the bottle.

She was so small.

The tall woman with dark braids hanging over her shoulders stood and introduced herself as Dr. Eagan. She extended a hand over the table.

"It's a pleasure to meet you, Hanna. If you'd sit, it shouldn't take us long to go over the particulars and get everything signed and squared away."

Okay, Hanna, focus. Now is not the time to freak out.

As much as I may have wanted to.

In a sort of trance, I lowered myself into the chair across from Dr. Eagan.

The doctor launched into Lily's history, glossing over details pertaining to the father, only giving the most necessary information.

Dr. Eagan was skilled in her field.

No names were mentioned, nothing that could give away an iota of an idea of who Lily's family was.

Try as I may to focus, to take in the information the woman

presented in front of me, my mind wandered. My eyes kept drifting back to the baby in the carrier.

Blood pounded in my ears.

How was I supposed to take care of a baby?

Wide Amber eyes never left me.

The baby sat, quietly watching like what was happening around her was the most interesting thing in the world.

A folder dropped on the table in front of me.

Mind elsewhere, I flipped through the pages inside. The front flap held medical records and important documents. The other held the address for her foster home in Montana, contact information, and a brief of the foster family.

"...As you can see, it's a delicate situation. We wanted to be sure you were comfortable caring for a baby with Lily's condition."

My head snapped up to find brown eyes watching me intently from behind thick black glasses frames. I glanced over at Molley, sure I'd missed something.

"Ms. Montgomery? Is this still something you'd like to undertake?"

Amber eyes blinked up at me from behind dark, curling lashes.

So innocent.

So at peace.

How hard could taking care of such a calm baby really be?

I turned back to the women on the other side of the table, my confidence in the situation swelling.

"Yep. Shouldn't be a problem."

Chapter 9

It was going to be a problem.

The moment I stepped out of that building into the warm autumn sun, Lily started wailing.

And not the cute infant cry.

Full-on, loud shrieks that sounded like they were coming from a child double her age.

"Shh, it's okay," I cooed as I crossed the parking lot to my car, carrier slung over one arm, diaper back full of supplies in the other.

"We're going to go see your new family."

Lily cried harder.

Tears squeezed from under her clamped-shut eyelids.

My brow creased.

I set the baby carrier down next to my car and knelt in front of the infant to whisper soothing nothings to her. My words fell on deaf ears.

Nothing seemed to register to her until her tiny flailing hand closed around my finger.

Lily sniffed, sucked back tears. Little eyelids pulled back to reveal slivers of liquid amber staring back at me.

For all of two seconds, she was utterly calm. Then, her little nose wrinkled and...

"Waaa!"

I sprang up and tore open the back door to my car.

"It's going to be okay."

I glanced around to see if anyone was watching as I lifted the carrier into the car.

Did Lily even understand what I was saying?

One deep breath in through my nose, same as just before any dance routine.

I had to keep trying.

"I've got this."

God, why did I ever think this was a good idea?

Was it too late to take her back?

After ten minutes of fighting with the straps, I finally secured Lily and the car seat safely in the back of my Maxima and pulled out onto the street to the shrieking stylings of a distraught infant.

Next stop, the drugstore.

Sucking my lips between my teeth to keep from screaming, I checked my side mirror and switched lanes before taking a right-hand turn.

I thrived in quiet, in the gentle silence between the notes of a violin and piano twisting together in symphonic harmony.

I was the one to offer advice to solve problems, but there was something about Lily's discomfort I could not figure out, something crucial to resolving her worries. And it fluttered just out of reach. It was unsettling.

After fifteen blocks, I was ready to join Lily's protests.

I abandoned my plan to go to the drugstore. Answers would have to wait. I had to get Lily home.

In a last-ditch effort, I tried to calm the child in the back one last time, opting to reason with her.

"I know you're upset, sweetie, but we'll be home soon. It's all going to be okay."

Nothing.

I jabbed at a button on the dash. Soft piano spilled into the cabin space.

Stunned by the sound, Lily's shrieks cut off abruptly.

A breath I hadn't realized I was holding fled my lungs on a relieved laugh. My lips lifted.

"So, you like Uchida, huh?"

I glanced into the back seat to find Lily's long dark lashes lulling over tired eyes.

That's right. Go to sleep.

Eyes returned to the road, checked the rear mirror.

A dinged-up van sat on my rear bumper.

Ass.

I shifted lanes to get out of his way, but the van followed, staying right on my tail, its bumper just about ready to rust off.

Just to get away, I took the next left, then another right, coming out on Knox. I'd have to do a bit of backtracking to get to my house, but at least I wouldn't have to feel pressured by aggressive drivers.

I let my foot off the gas to give my racing heart time to slow back to equilibrium.

This is stupid.

You're being stupid.

Nobody was following me. Why would they?

Aside from the gentle piano drifting from the speakers, the car was silent.

I glanced back to check on Lily.

Asleep.

One corner of Lily's little mouth pulled upward. The other side fell open in slumber.

Good.

A crease formed between my brows as something the social worker said came to mind.

"Where is your mama, little one?"

Taking a right, I prepared to circle back to jump on Division and head for home when I spotted the van again, parked about half a block ahead.

Before I could reach the van, I took a right, shaking my head.

No.

It couldn't be the same van.

I wasn't in the best neighborhood. Tons of people probably

owned vans like that one.

Nothing to be concerned about.

All the same, I changed course again.

I'd take Maple north.

It might take longer, but at least it would ease my mind to leave the area.

Eager to put some distance between myself and that completely innocent, rusted-out van on the side of the road, I slid through an intersection without bothering to slow or stop for the red sign on the corner.

I just had to put a little more...

My eyes lifted to the rearview mirror.

"Fuck."

I checked the side mirrors, hoping to find a sweet little convertible following about two blocks back, knowing I wouldn't.

Crap.

Gripping the wheel, I whipped around a corner and took an immediate left after that.

Time to get out of the residential streets and out somewhere I could get some real speed.

I was just driving a little slow. Why was this jerk following me?

Talk about road rage.

If Lily hadn't been in the car, I would have just pulled over, marched back to the guy's window, and given him a big old piece of my mind. Part of me still wanted to.

But I had to keep Lily safe.

She'd just gotten to sleep anyway, no need to disturb her nap.

Maple Street was too narrow, too residential, and slow.

Redirecting toward the bigger, three-lane through-way, I cursed myself for not ordering coffee earlier. Caffeine would have gone a long way in focusing my rapidly fraying nerves.

Molley said this job would be easy.

Seeing the dark circles that managed to show through her perfect makeup, I should have known better.

Not bothering to stop at the stop sign at the next intersection, I turned out onto Monroe, cutting off a Suburban that would have laid my little Maxima flat had its driver not been paying attention.

Barely bothering to check my blind spot, I shot over a lane and hit the gas. When I looked up, the van followed two cars behind.

The hell was this guy's problem?

I switched over a lane.

The van followed, now only one car back.

Damn.

By now, there was no doubt. I was being followed.

I spared one quick glance into the back seat at my charge.

Still fast asleep, strapped into her car seat, Lily had no idea the potential danger I was putting us in.

Sorry, little one.

Gritting my teeth, I turned back to the problem at hand.

Time to lose this guy.

My flip-flopped foot fell on the gas.

A reluctant shutter undulated through the car, but it obeyed and crept up on the bumper in front of me.

How many times had Greg poked fun at my pokey car, offering to replace it with something newer, more high speed?

Why didn't I take him up on that?

The streetlight turned red.

Cars in front of my tired Maxima slowed.

Letting off a string of expletives, I took in my options as I slammed the brakes.

We couldn't just sit there and wait for the light to turn green again.

What was to keep that psycho in the van snug in their car and out of mine?

I pressed the button on the door to enable the locks.

Those aren't going to keep out anyone willing to break a window.

Gnawing the inside of my cheek, I glanced back at the van, then jerked the wheel.

Lily let out an indignant yowl as the bottom of the Maxima scraped over the edge of the curb.

Crossing my fingers that none of the businesses or houses lining the street had exterior cameras, I cut through the corner yard onto the next side street.

Back on the pavement, I refused to let my foot off the gas.

Weaving through cramped streets at speeds altogether too fast for a residential neighborhood, I tried to formulate a plan.

Okay, think Hanna. What next? The cops?

I didn't have legal guardianship of the child in the backseat. Yes, I'd come by the child on the up and up, but without any paperwork to prove so, I would spend the better part of the evening in a stinking jail cell before anyone was reached who could confirm my story.

Besides, I didn't even have a plate number for the van.

Then where?

Couldn't go home. Not until I lost the asshole.

Lily and I would be sitting ducks in that house all alone.

The flimsy deadbolt and lock on my front door wouldn't stop anyone who wanted in bad enough. They were meant for petty thieves and vandals, not scary men in vans stalking innocent women and babies.

Two rights and a left.

Checked the mirrors.

No creepy van in sight.

With a shuddering breath, I pulled to the curb in front of a surprisingly well-maintained Honda up on blocks.

Lily burbled happily in the backseat, oblivious to the danger.

Breathe, Hann. You've got this.

Think.

But my mind was blank. All actions and responses erased from my playbook.

I was back on the football field.

The homecoming game.

Half-time.

I did not know the next routine.

A tear of sweat slid from my hairline, down my forehead, and caught in my eyebrow.

Tiny quakes rippled through my body as adrenaline coursed through my veins. It was like flying. Not in a plane but through the air, tossed up high by four outstretched arms.

That rush of exhilaration as the air whooshed passed, that little catch in my breath as I started to fall, knowing there were open arms beneath to catch me.

But there was no one waiting now.

I sucked my lips between my teeth and bit down hard to hold in a sob.

Greg, if only you were here!

I pulled my hand away from the steering wheel to brush back a wayward strand of hair, noticing how my fingers shook like frail leaves in the wind.

Greg wasn't there, and he never would be again.

I was on my own.

What's my next move?

Hands back on the wheel, I let my fingers flex around the warm leather. I took in my surroundings, then chanced a peek at the side mirror.

I swore.

The rusted old van crept around the corner two blocks back.

Scrunching low in my seat, I watched the van ease closer in the mirror.

Why? Why was this freak still following me?

Breathe.

Easy.

I just had to wait for the van to pass, then I could flip a u-ey and disappear.

Heart pounding in my ears, I waited.

And waited.

Between the pounding beats of my heart in my ears, thoughts raced faster than my little Maxima had ever been able to go.

What if they recognize the car?

Or see me?

Or Lily?

What if they park and come back to investigate?

Closer.

I can't do it.

Nerves overflowing, I threw the car back into drive and swerved from my spot by the curb.

The engine cried out as my foot fell on the gas, sending the car surging forward.

A trashcan glanced off the front bumper as we sped around the next corner onto a narrow alleyway.

In the back seat, Lily started to wail.

The car hop-skipped over dips and potholes on the ill-maintained road.

Gritting my teeth, I clenched the wheel tighter. The car rattled around us.

Afraid that any second the engine might bottom out, leaving us lame ducks in plain sight of the van, I sent up a silent prayer to whoever may be listening to hold my car together just a little longer.

I did not want to find out what would happen if we stopped and the van caught up.

By sheer force of will, the Maxima kept going.

Taking the next corner a little too fast, the car flew into a skid, sending bits of dirt and gravel flying through the air behind the tires, ricocheting off the wood fence lining the left side of the road.

Wrenching the wheel, I tried to regain control, but the car blew through the six-foot fence.

This time, my cries mingled with Lily's as the tires tore a track through someone's backyard.

Fear hiccupped and burbled in my gut. My vision blurred as tears pressed at the corners of my eyes.

Please let there be no security cameras!

The car jarred on its shocks as it flew off the curb, landing one street over.

Did the van follow?

I didn't dare look.

Wasting no time, I hit the gas.

The Maxima whipped onto Division without bothering to stop for the red sign or oncoming traffic.

On all sides, cars zoomed past my beat-up little car.

Feeling like a fugitive on the run, I checked the mirrors.

No sign of the van.

Good.

Feeling slightly more at ease on the busy road, I let up on the gas and took in my surroundings.

I wasn't ready to let my guard down. Not yet.

Who was that guy?

Did he follow me from the social services office?

I shook my head at the ridiculous thought.

No.

There hadn't been a van in the parking lot when I left. That I was sure of.

I would have noticed.

...Wouldn't I?

"—Ahh!" I jumped as a car sped past, horn blaring.

Lightheaded, breath coming in short bursts, I felt the last of my composure slip as fear took complete control.

I had to get off the road before I caused an accident.

Find somewhere to lie low for a minute.

Maybe then it would be safe to go back home without some psycho on my tail.

Chapter 10

I checked my mirrors before letting my eyes slide back to the road.

Where's the van?

It had to be back there somewhere, waiting for me to slip up.

I couldn't let that happen. Not with Lily in the car.

Cl-clunk.

Beneath me, the car jerked. The check engine light flashed on the dash. Despite my foot still on the gas, the car slowed like someone pulled the old Maxima's plug.

No, no, no!

This couldn't be happening!

Eyes darted over the signs lining the busy street, searching for somewhere, anywhere to hide.

I pressed the gas pedal flat to the floor and got enough juice out of the engine to cut off a Prius in the left lane. I swerved past oncoming traffic to roll into the parking lot in front of an autobody garage.

My breath came in busts and squeezed from my lungs, leaving

me starved for oxygen, unable to catch my breath.

On its own last breath, the Maxima rolled around behind the garage before coming to a hissing halt in front of the large overhead doors.

Great.

At least I was out of sight of the road.

The engine dead, the car grew hot and stuffy in seconds, the air thick and muggy in my lungs as adrenaline drained from my system.

Barely able to pry my hand from the steering wheel, I lowered my window.

Fresh air flooded the car, clearing my thoughts and allowing me to reclaim a modicum of control.

I breathed in the cool fall air.

A door opened at the far side of the autobody shop. Out stepped a tall, dark-haired figure.

Brain still foggy, I watched the man saunter in my direction, wiping his hands on a grimy rag.

Recognition blinked at the back of my mind, and I knew I wouldn't be finding any semblance of control any time soon.

As if on cue, the waterworks started up again in the back seat, and, to my mortification, I felt my own tears prick the corners of my eyes.

"Shh, it's okay. Everything's okay." Desperation filled my voice. Was I comforting Lily or myself?

The figure drew level with the front of my car, and I lost all control of my tear ducts as I stared into dark pools over the hood.

The man slowed as he took in the dented front bumper.

Concern swam in those deep blues as the man stepped up to the open driver's side window.

"Hanna, what—"

I swept damp blonde strands out of my eyes.

"Please, you have to help us."

Jake's brow creased.

"What's going—"

"Please!" My throat constricted as I fought to decide what to tell him. How to not sound like a lunatic.

My fingers shook on the steering wheel. I squeezed it tighter to keep any more of my fear from leaking out.

Lily let out a hiccupping shriek that drew Jake's attention away from me.

The crease deepened in his forehead.

Jake's lips worked to form a question that never came.

Instead, he said, "Why don't ya'll head into the waiting area to cool off. I'll take a look at the car."

My eyes darted toward the street. Was the can still out there?

"Hanna? Is everything okay?"

"I—" Words caught in my throat as a large SUV sped past the front of the shop. I released a relieved breath as the vehicle disappeared without slowing.

When I couldn't answer, Jake reached for the door handle.

"Scoot over. Let's get the car out of the sun."

In the back seat, Lily's pitiful cries gained in volume.

My lips pressed in a thin line.

Would the car even start?

Did it matter?

Clearly, I shouldn't be driving the car right now.

With a curt nod, I peeled my fingers from the wheel.

I barely made it over the gearshift into the passenger seat when Jake slid in behind me.

His hand found the key like he'd been driving my car for years and turned it with the grace of someone comfortable behind the wheel. The engine churned but refused to turn over.

Jake's hand dropped from the key. He let the car sit a minute before trying again.

The Maxima let out a reluctant roar as it sputtered back to life.

I pressed myself to the passenger door. Jake steered my car into an open bay, and I took him in as he focused on maneuvering the car.

He'd grown since I saw him last—not physically, but in essence.

Jake had been friendly enough in high school, considering we ran in the same social circles, but back then, he'd been just like all the other boys. So self-centered, if not more self-assured than the average high school jock. There were three things that high school Jake cared about: his buddies, football, and getting with girls.

As the best friend of Jake's ex, my inclusion in any of those categories had been exclusively barred, even if I had wanted to fit into one of them.

The man sitting next to me put off an aura that was hard to explain.

There was a magnetism about Jake that I'd only ever felt around Greg.

My heart seized, clenching painfully in my chest at the thought of my late husband.

Greg.

He'd been gone three months. How could I be feeling this way about another man? Let alone *Jake!* It wasn't right.

A betrayal to the umpteenth order.

What? Suddenly, all those nights I'd spent in Greg's arms feeling loved and cherished meant nothing? All our plans, all those hours spent mourning a future that could never be, screamed vicious slurs from the back of my mind.

Traitor.

I forced the thoughts aside.

There were other things to worry about besides some wayward flutterings in my stomach, namely the baby screaming in the back seat and the guy on our tail.

The Maxima lurched to a stop inside the garage.

Through the opaque garage doors, I watched cars blur past on the street.

How far back was the van when I pulled into the parking lot?

Did the driver see me?

The van could be just one parking lot over, waiting for me to make my next move.

"Here, let's get ya'll somewhere more comfortable."

Before I could fully register what was going on, Jake was out of the car, opening my door.

Brows bunched over cobalt-blue eyes in a look I'd only ever seen on Jake's face a handful of times.

Jake wasn't one to worry... or hadn't been in high school.

Nevertheless, every time his brows bunched up like that, I was reminded of an old beagle my Uncle Hank once had when I was growing up.

Doubt sizzled on my tongue.

Actually," I started to backpedal. "I should..."

But Jake already had the car seat out, the handle slung over his arm like it belonged there. He looked like he knew exactly what he was doing with the baby in that carrier.

The muscles at my core tightened in a way I hated, as I watched Jake.

He held open a door for me that looked to lead into an empty waiting room.

I hesitated, and Jake sighed.

"Look, your car is not going anywhere any time soon. Just..." Jake paused, searching for the right words, "sit down for a second. Talk to me."

Tears surged behind my eyes. I wanted to hug Jake in that moment. Instead, I stepped into the waiting room. I selected one of several mismatched chairs furthest from the bay windows overlooking the street.

Heat pumped from vents overhead, forcing warm air over my

skin. Sitting in the embrace of heated air, I realized I was shaking, the absence of adrenaline from my earlier ordeal making my body feel like wet sand passing through a sieve. It took all my energy not to slide to the floor like an emotional heap of spaghetti.

I eyed the street wearily through the windows, waiting for the van to come into view.

On a deep breath that did little to calm my nerves, I raked sweat and tear-soaked tendrils of hair back from my face. I looked up to find Jake watching me.

Back pressed to the closed door, Jake stood like he could hold back the world till I was ready to face it again. The look in his eyes said he meant to do exactly that.

"You're back."

Stupid.

Of course, he's back. You saw him yesterday, you idiot.

Jake ignored my question and folded his arms over his chest.

"What happened to your car, Hanna?"

Lily cried angrily from her car seat, tired of being ignored.

Jake glanced down at her in her seat, resting at his feet. Cobalt eyes turned back to me.

"And whose kid is this?"

I glanced at the infant, barely five months old.

Dark wisps of downy hair curled around tan, little ears. A cute down-turned button nose and brows that would give away everything thought when she was older accented Lily's vibrant eyes. No one would ever confuse the baby as mine.

"It's...a really long story."

Fingers twisted in the ends of my braid.

In an attempt to make myself look less like my world just imploded around me, I'd twisted my long, near-blonde tresses into the simple rope that morning as I raced out the door.

It was all I'd been able to manage.

Not a speck of makeup adorned my face.

The simple tshirt and yoga pants I wore were on their second day of use, and I could only hope Jake didn't recognize them from the day before when I'd stopped by Molley's house briefly. I'd been too tired lately to bother with something as meaningless as laundry.

Strands of hair came loose from the braid and tickled my shoulders as if to scream, "Look the evidence is here! She's not okay!"

Jake's jaw tightened.

One hand scrubbed over the back of his neck as he stared out at the busy street.

"You're in trouble."

My shoulders collapsed.

"You could say that."

How was I supposed to begin to tell him what was happening when I had no idea myself?

I wasn't close to Jake, never had been, even in high school. He didn't deserve to have my mess piled on top of him.

I didn't know Jake. Not really.

Jake stared at me.

"Was it a hit and run?"

I saw the rest of the question in the silent way he watched me, suspicious.

If he thought I ran someone off the road, why was he helping me?

"No!"

"Then what's going on, Hann?"

The baby bawled at Jake's feet, letting out pathetic little gasping hiccups.

In a few quick motions, Jake had the baby out of the car seat and balanced against his shoulder. He bounced the baby gently, one hand pressed to her little back, coaxing her to sleep.

In seconds, Lily was silent.

"What are you, the baby whisperer?"

When Jake met my eye, his own danced with something fierce and feral, demanding answers even as he stood between me and the threat he still knew nothing about.

I pursed my lips.

Guess this is it.

"I'm being followed."

Chapter 11

Cobalt eyes never wavered from mine, nor did they cool.

As the seconds ticked by, a fire lit behind those eyes, churning the dark, blue pools like molten lava as Jake processed my admission.

"By who?" His lips barely moved.

"I don't know," I whispered, softer than I ever remembered my voice being. Why did it keep doing that?

"Why?"

I blinked and cocked my head.

"No idea."

A muscle ticked in Jake's jaw.

"Your car's going to take more than a little cosmetic treatment," Jake said. Concern seeped into his gaze.

"It won't be drivable for at least a week." He hesitated before continuing. "Do you need a ride somewhere?"

My shoulders stiffened.

"I can't ask that of you."

"You're not, darlin'. I'm offering."

Though his lips curved up in that crooked grin that drove girls wild in high school, the light never reached his eyes. The smile fell quickly when he saw it did little to ease the situation.

I shook my head.

"I can't."

"And I can't let you walk out of here with this baby, knowing some wackjob might be waiting for you. Just let me give you a ride home. You know Moll and Jess will never forgive me if I don't."

Breath hitched in my chest.

While I still spoke to Jessie and Molley, and I knew Jake was staying at Molley's, it was a shock to hear Jake was so close with both his exes.

I paused.

I couldn't put Jake in danger. But I couldn't put Lily at risk either. I didn't know who was following me, where they were, or what sort of threat they posed.

It was very possible this was all just a case of severe road rage.

When the guy in the van could no long see my car, he probably went on his merry, asshole way.

But what if he didn't.

I couldn't possibly accept a ride from Jake, but what were my options otherwise?

How was I supposed to sleep at night knowing the guy in the van might still be out there, waiting?

I glanced at Jake as he pulled a goofy face at Lily.

In Jake's arms, the little girl sat happy as could be, but who wouldn't?

I had to admit, it would be nice to have another adult around to shoulder some of the pressure of caring for Lily.

Jake knelt to set Lily back in her carrier.

"I'm going to bring the truck around."

"Jake, please—"

But he was already gone. The door fell shut behind him.

▲▲▲

For the third time in too few days, I climbed up into the cab of Jake's truck.

In high school, I never rode in the gigantic monstrosity, even though I was friends with Molley and Jessie when they dated Jake.

It was strange to ride in the truck now, in the same seat that used to be reserved for the girlfriend.

As it had been the day before, the cab's interior was nearly spotless.

Settling into the seat, I watched Jake in the rear-view mirror as he strapped Lily and her car seat into the back seat like he'd done so a thousand times.

Would Greg have taken to caring for Lily so easy?

Jake slid into the driver's seat.

"To the house?"

A mighty roar tore from the engine as Jake turned the key in the ignition before quieting to a low growl.

"Uh..."

Think, Hanna. Think.

I had three days before I was supposed to deliver Lily to her new foster home. Where could we go where we'd be safe if not my house?

Did I really have any other choice?

The truck pulled out onto the street. Jake merged into the flow of traffic.

"I'm sure Molley can find space for you two for the night," Jake offered.

He really needed to stop doing that.

I wasn't comfortable with gentle Jake, the Jake who cared and helped.

"No. Not Molley's."

Not with her new baby in the house. Not with her having another one on the way.

If it turned out the guy in the van was still out there looking for me, I couldn't put Molley and her family in danger.

"I'm sure she wouldn't—"

I shook my head.

"No."

"What?"

"What if we're followed?"

Jake's jaw tightened. He stayed silent.

Like me, he'd hoped it was all just a bad case of road rage.

"I can't put them in danger, Jake. Not with the baby."

Jake changed lanes, chewing over his options.

"I have some money. I can get you a hotel until we can be sure you're no longer being followed."

"No."

"Really, it would be—"

"No, Jake." Why couldn't he get it?

"Is that all you know how to say?"

Despite my fried nerves, I stuck my tongue out at Jake and folded my arms in childish protest.

"I can't take your money. Can you just drop me off at home? I'm sure it's all fine now."

I wasn't sure. I was the furthest thing from sure.

For the hundredth time since we left the garage, I checked the mirrors and the cars around us.

No van.

"Hanna." Again, Jake's voice was soft. "Is that really the best idea?"

"I don't really have any other options."

A frustrated growl tore from Jake's throat.

"Woman, there are always options."

"No."

"There it is again," Jake groaned. Callused fingers reached over and closed around my hand, resting in my lap in a surprisingly warm, almost caress. "Darlin', I'm not going to take you somewhere you could be in danger."

"And where would that be?"

If Greg's death proved anything, it was that no matter where I was, something could always find and hurt me.

Jake's lips pressed into a thin line.

Without knowing who or why someone was following me, how exactly was Jake supposed to keep me and my pint-sized charge safe?

Jake took his hand back, raked it through his hair, and scrubbed the back of his neck.

"Work with me here, Hann. Please."

The truck slowed to a stop at a red light.

Instinctively, I scrunched lower in my seat. My eyes flashed between the mirrors.

"Do you see them?"

"Hmm?" I glanced over at Jake.

"Whoever was following you." Jake didn't turn toward me as he spoke. His lips barely moved.

Anyone watching him from another car would think Jae was just singing along to the radio or something.

"No," I sighed. "I don't think they're behind us."

Jake gave a curt nod and pressed the gas as the light turned green.

"First things first. Let's return the baby to her mother."

"Yeah... about that..."

"Hanna." Jake's voice hardened with a warning I couldn't ignore.

A shiver shot down my spine.

"We can't return her."

Jake scrubbed the back of his neck.

"Man, I need a smoke," Jake murmured. Then, "Why can't we return her?"

"It's not that we can't, just not now."

"Darlin', just spit it out." Jake's words came through his teeth as he fought to keep a hold on his temper.

I took a breath and let it out. Then I told him.

When I finished, Jake blinked out the windshield.

"Foster care?"

I nodded.

"I guess. I'm a courier of sorts for kids," I said. "This is my first assignment."

Jake let out a breath and stared out the windshield, his mind whirring over the information as he navigated the huge truck through traffic.

"So where to?" There was no fight left in his voice.

"Home."

"Fine." A silent stipulation followed Jake's acquiescence. It echoed loudly through the cab. It would not be an easy task getting him to leave.

My heart squeezed with panic at the thought of another man

besides Greg in my home. The house was as much Greg's as it was mine. Was it a betrayal to let Jake inside?

With no other options, I nodded and let Jake take me home.

▲▲▲

Outside the truck, the houses went from clean, manicured lawns and cute porch furniture to dried patches scattered with dandelions as we neared my house. Rusted, old cars littered the curb along my street, several up on blocks or in varying states of disrepair.

Once more, my eyes flashed to the mirrors to find the street behind us empty.

Good.

Jake pulled to the curb a few houses down from mine.

"What..."

"Probably best to not give away what we're driving my parking in front of your house," Jake explained.

Right.

Jake's truck sat between an old Honda and an ancient red Mercedes with its hood popped.

Mine was the neighborhood where most would hesitate to leave their car unattended, but Jake stepped out with ease and pulled Lily, in her carrier, from the back. He turned to meet my eye over the hood of the truck.

Throwing the diaper bag strap over my shoulder, I motioned Jake to follow me up to my house.

In front, a sprinkler attached to a hose sat in the center of the yard, which, to my credit, was still green in the middle where the sprinkler could reach.

Jake's brow furrowed as we walked up the empty and cracked driveway. His head moved on a swivel, keeping an eye on our surroundings.

My keys rattled as I pulled them from my bag and reached with shaking fingers to unlock the door.

After three attempts, I finally got the key in the lock and let Jake and Lily inside.

"Make yourself at home," I motioned toward the couch as I took the baby carrier from Jake and set it on the coffee table.

"Let's get this little girl out of here, huh? Yeah," My voice turned high and sweet as I unhooked Lily from the car seat, making exaggerated faces for the baby's amusement.

"You're good with her," Jake noticed. "What's her name?"

"Lily."

I stood with the little girl in my arms and turned to face Jake.

Something smoldered in the depths of Jake's eyes that had me looking away as fast as I noticed it.

What was wrong with me?

I was not looking for another relationship. Not then, not ever.

Even if I was interested in guys like Jake, there was no way someone like him would be interested in me.

I banished the unwelcome thoughts that came with seeing that look to the far reaches of my mind.

Jake was there to help.

Nothing more.

I focused on Lily.

"You, little girl, smell like you could use a change." I let my eyes flit to Jake for only a second.

"We'll be right back. Make yourself at home," I called over my shoulder as I snatched up the diaper bag from where I dropped it by the door and scurried down the short hallway to the stairs.

▲▲▲

Turning toward the stairs, my eyes drifted back down the hall to where Jake stood in the dimly lit living room. Just like the other morning, he stared up at the pictures on the wall, at my life with Greg.

What did he see there in those frames?

Happiness?

Promise?

Or, like me, did he see the loss, the thousands of plans that would never come to fruition?

I jogged up the stairs before tears could dampen my lashes.

With one flitting glance at the office door across the hall, I turned into the bedroom.

To my credit, I didn't stop at the sight of the great, big, King-sized bed with the tall, intricately carved wooden pillars on each corner. Another Greg selection.

"If we're going to turn this place into our castle, we might as well have a bed fit for royalty," he said. We both knew we couldn't afford it, but Greg had a way of pulling people into his fantasy. In his mind, a pauper became a princess in the blink of an eye, and a prince wasn't made by the coin in his pocket.

What would Greg think if he could see me? If he knew all that had happened since his death?

I lowered Lily onto the cream and blue comforter as memories of many mornings past swirled in my mind.

All around, there were reminders of Greg.

The book on the nightstand that he started and would never finish, an abandoned and crumpled plaid shirt in the corner. Someday soon, it would all have to be collected up and stored away somewhere out of sight, but so far, I'd been unable to do it, unable to remove the last pieces of Greg from my life.

Tears stung the corners of my eyes. I blinked as my vision blurred and drew in a deep, settling breath before turning back to the task at hand.

Not today.

Scanning the floor for anything that would work to change Lily on, an old fleece shirt sticking out from under the bed caught my eye. Was it mine or Greg's? I couldn't remember. It had been so long since I'd done laundry. I snatched it up off the floor and positioned the shirt underneath Lily.

It would have to do.

Lily's nose wrinkled like she strongly opposed the shirt she was lying on top of. I pulled supplies from the diaper bag.

I had to work fast.

Any second, Lily would be a bawling mess once more.

You've got this.

Deep breath.

I set to work, moving at hyper-speed in hopes of outrunning Lily's seemingly impossible mood swings.

Reaching back for a wipe, I caught the edge of the nightstand with my elbow. The nightstand teetered, dangerously close to toppling. As it leveled, the book on the corner dropped to the floor.

Satisfied the table wouldn't fall on top of us, I turned back to the task at hand.

"Oh-kay! Just one more little sticky bit and... done!"

Lily was not amused by my antics.

Even as I reached for her, I could see the tears glossing over Lily's amber eyes like glaze over the acrylic paint on a mug.

I scooped her up into my arms as I stood.

"It's okay, sweet girl," I began to bounce. "Everything's okay. Don't cry."

Please don't cry!

My own tears welled up in my eyes.

I didn't know what was happening.

I wasn't a sympathetic crier. The hell was going on?

Why couldn't I make Lily stop?

"Everything okay in here?"

I whirled to find Jake peeking around the door frame.

Great. The baby whisperer, here to save the day.

I shoved down the unwarranted feelings swirling inside me. It wasn't Jake's fault that Lily preferred him over me.

"I-I don't know what's wrong," I admitted. My arms shook as I moved to hand Lily over to Jake.

Jake's eyes softened, but he didn't take Lily. Instead, he stepped around me, his arms coming under mine, guiding me until the baby rested against the front of my shoulder.

"There. Hold firm. Gentle movements."

Together, we pressed Lily to my chest and swayed in an odd sort of dance. No music, just us.

Lily quieted. A few soft snuffles pulled from her quivering chest, but nothing more.

"You've got this." Jake's breath tickled the shell of my ear, brushed over my hair.

I was hyperaware of his body pressed to my back, his arms around me like the snuggest sweater. Then, after a fleeting moment, he was gone, stepping away.

I continued to sway, afraid if I stopped, Lily would burst into tears once more.

"You're good at this." I turned to face Jake. He watched Lily with a puzzled frown.

"Na, just had lots of practice." Jake waved off my praise.

I couldn't help myself. A teasing smile curled the corners of my lips.

"Oh? Lots of little Jakes running around wherever you went when you ran away?"

A shadow passed over Jake's eyes. Jake blinked and it was gone. An almost mournful smile tugged Jake's lips before dropping away.

"Na, nothing like that. Jenn and Alexa have several, though." Jake's sisters. Molley used to complain about them in high school, in the locker rooms after cheer. Try as Molley might have, she never could get Jake's older sisters to like her while they were dating.

"Someday though, maybe."

That surprised me.

I never imagined Jake to be the family type. He was more the kind to run around from town to town, a different girl every night. But the more time I spent with Jake, the more I wondered. Maybe I never really knew Jake at all.

"So," I coughed, looking away. Jake was all too close in a room he probably had no business being in. "You want something to drink, or eat, or something?"

Lame.

Come on, Hanna. Be assertive. Sail your ship to safer waters.

But my feet stayed rooted as Jake shrugged, noncommittal, and watched Lily in my arms. I looked down to find her little lids drooping over tired eyes.

I smiled.

"You're not so bad when you're sleeping, are ya?"

In an act of defiance, Lily jerked away from my shoulder with a short cry before curling back into a tense, exhausted ball on my shoulder.

Jake let out a snort as he attempted to hold back what I'm sure would have been a full-body laugh. The sound made me want to join in his amusement, but when Lily's little muscles remained tight, I frowned instead.

The frown carried with me into the hall.

▲▲▲

"It's getting pretty late. If you want, I could..." Jake's words faded as he glanced back at me over his shoulder. Something in my face made him stop at the top of the stairs and turn to face me. In a smooth transfer, my frown spread to his face, tugging at the corners of his mouth. Silent, He took in the tears pricking in my eyes. "What?"

Damn tears.

For a second, I considered shaking my head and brushing it off. Lily was probably okay, right?

A tremor shook through her little body, her little limbs going stiff then slack. That couldn't be normal.

"She's so stiff," I forced my worried eye to meet Jake's. Something had to be wrong, but what? How could a baby be so tense when she was asleep? My heart splintered. What had happened to that little girl in her short life?

Jake stepped closer and laid a palm against Lily's back.

His frown deepened.

"Did the social worker say—"

The smoke alarm blared up the stairs like a herd of charging rhinos.

Lily's eyes flew open as she screamed her answering fury.

The hell?

My eyes met Jake's for a split second before we both turned and ran down the stairs.

It had to be a malfunction.

I hadn't been home all day, hadn't had the chance, yet, to set foot in the kitchen.

What could possibly have set off the alarm?

In the hall, hints of smoke tickled my nostrils, and by the time we reached the living room, I could see thin wisps of dark smoke drifting on the air.

Smoke? But how?

Fear spiked inside me.

Lily held tight against my shoulder. I followed Jake through the house, nearly running into his solid back as he came to a halt in the kitchen doorway.

I leaned around Jake and peered into the kitchen.

A small black mass burned on the kitchen floor, engulfed in flames beneath the smoke detector.

"What's..." I just stared. Unable to finish my thought.

While I stood frozen, Jake leaped into action, snagging the towel off the oven handle. He was at the sink in two large bounds, soaking the rag through.

I blinked, and the fire was out. The dark mass hissed and smoldered beneath the wet rag Jake threw over it from his place by the sink.

Silence floated between us on the air with the smoke and acrid stench of something dead, broken only by the soft sizzling of the dying embers.

Lily squirmed in my arms.

I shifted her to my other shoulder.

My eyes fell back to the mass on the floor.

"What is it?"

Jake looked up at me, hesitancy mixing with dead in the draw of his brows. He lifted the towel and—

"Oh god!"

My hand flew to my mouth to hold back the bile rising at the undeniable stench.

Quick, Jake lunged to take Lily in his arms as I spun and bolted for the bathroom.

Jake found me hovering over the toilet, elbows on the rim, sure more bile would bubble forth at any second.

Reaching blindly, I flushed away my mess. I tucked a loose strand of hair behind me ear as I sat back.

"Here." Jake held out a tiny bit of tissue, neatly folded.

More than a little embarrassed, I accepted the paper and dabbed at my mouth with a mumbled thanks.

"Sorry," I sighed as I leaned back against the wall. Jake slid down to sit beside me.

Happy as could be, Lily babbled softly in the crook of Jake's arm.

If only I could be so oblivious to the mounting danger around us.

Molley said it would be an easy job.

I stared up at the ceiling.

Why was all of this happening?

"Do you think... do you think it was the guy from earlier?" I asked in barely a whisper.

Jake stayed silent a long moment, his mind working behind those dark gray-blue eyes.

"I don't know. You piss anyone else off lately?"

It was meant to be a joke, but I frowned, letting my eyes drop to the linoleum floor, hoping to conceal some of the worry and doubt pirouetting inside me.

Who would do that to a cat?

"Is it..."

"Yeah," Jake affirmed. "Before the fire, from the looks of it."

How could he know that?

"Who has keys to your house?"

I glanced up to see where his mind had gone in his dark eyes.

"Just my parents," then I added as guilt swarmed inside me, "and Greg's."

Jake frowned.

"No one else? You're sure? And the door was locked?"

Silence.

I looked away.

"Please tell me it was locked."

I thought back, lips pressing into a thin line.

Was it?

"I..."

"You can't leave a place like this unlocked, Hann. Not in this neighborhood."

Lily stirred as Jake's voice rose, his sharp tone ricocheting off the walls.

My temper flared.

"You don't think I know that? It usually is... I just—I just... was running late. I must have forgotten to check it."

Jake sighed. Frustration fled his frame. Muscled shoulders drooped as Jake raked a hand across the back of his neck.

"Why don't you take Lily upstairs while I clean up in the kitchen?" I nodded, not wanting to take another look at that charred heap of fur, incapable of anything more.

"Then we'll take a look at the file that came with this one."

I looked up at Jake, confused for a moment, as he placed Lily in my arms, much to her displeasure.

"You're right. She's too tense."

Chapter 12

"Maybe we should take her to a doctor."

I watched Jake sway with Lily in the living room, cradling her secure to his chest in the only way that seemed to stop her crying.

"Let's look at the file first. They wouldn't send Lily with you if she was sick."

Some unspoken knowing in Jake's voice left no room for argument.

We settled on the couch, too close for my comfort, but Jake didn't seem to notice.

The file lay innocently on the coffee table.

Ignoring the way Jake's thigh brushing against mine sent tingles across my skin, I flipped open the front of the file.

Together, we skimmed the identification documents inside.

I turned past a blank dividing page in the file, ready to flip to the next just as quickly. Jake's hand closing over mine halted my progress.

Heat spread up my arm as my cheeks went candy apple red.

I froze.

"Wha—"

Jake's finger skimmed along the page. Halfway down the page, he stopped.

His throat bobbed as he chewed over what he'd read.

His voice came out strained and clipped, the gentle rasp that usually hid in the shadows emboldened to step into the light.

"Drugs."

I blinked.

"What?"

"Drugs," he repeated, turning all his attention to the infant in his arms. She looked so small, even for her three months.

Jake pushed to his feet and started to pace.

"She was born drug dependent. This," Jake nodded at Lily, "looks like the tail end of withdrawals. The social worker didn't say anything about this?"

Dark eyes pierced mine.

All heat drained from my body.

Had she?

Was I so tangled up in my own problems that I'd missed something so crucial?

"I...I don't...Molley—" My lips pressed tight in a line to hold in the secrets ready to spill out into the world.

"Molley put you up to this?"

"I—" But before I could answer, Lily was in my arms again. Jake strode to the door, phone to his ear.

Great. Just what I needed.

I set Lily in her car seat.

"Jake," I followed him through the kitchen.

A black stain still marred the tiles in front of the fridge. I stepped around it and followed Jake out the back.

At the edge of the cracked patio, Jake turned to face me with a deep intensity in his eyes, phone still to his ear. Evidently, Molley wasn't answering.

Please.

My brows drew together, silently trying to get through to him.

Jake didn't budge.

My jaw set.

I stepped forward and snatched the phone from his hand.

It was time for Jake to go.

"I don't need a white knight, Jake."

I ended the call before it went to voicemail and pocketed the phone.

"Thank you for being there earlier, but I think I've got it from here."

"Did you forget the burning cat someone just left in your kitchen?"

A chill raced across my skin at the memory. The fire in my kitchen hadn't been burning when we got there, so someone must have started it while we were upstairs.

I peered out across the yard toward my studio and the back fence.

Were they still out there?

Jake stepped closer.

"And thank you for taking care of that too, but I'm fine now. The doors are locked. No one else is getting inside."

Was I trying to convince him or myself?

Jake's jaw worked like he wanted to argue further.

Overhead, the sky was clear and inky, pierced through by a dusting of little white stars.

How'd it get so late?

I glanced again toward the garage-turned-studio at the back of the yard. I should have been out there finishing up the paint in the second classroom.

"Where's Lily?" Jake asked softly, though I could still feel the mule in his words.

"She's fine. She's inside. Thank you again, but I think it's time to go."

"I'm not leaving you two here alone. Not after everything that's happened."

"I'm fine, Jake. *We're* fine," I ground out. Why wouldn't he just leave?

The muscles in Jake's jaw bunched. His eyes narrowed, and mine followed. I wouldn't lose, not on this.

Wind blew through the yard, rustling the few leaves still clinging to the branches of the neighbor's maple. Another chill ran over my shoulders.

Would it be so bad if Jake stayed?

I shook the thought away.

"Let's talk inside," Jake sighed. I held the corners of my lips down, resisting a triumphant smile.

A warm hand closed around my elbow. Memories of a much different night flashed in my mind when another man grabbed my wrist, sending spikes of fear through my veins. Only heat and pleasurable tingles trailed in the wake of Jake's touch.

"Please."

Shaking off the memory, I let Jake lead me into the kitchen.

In the small room, Jake began to pace once more, glancing into the living room every time he passed the doorway to check on Lily snoozing in her car seat.

Finally, he turned to face me. Banded arms folded over his chest. The muscles in his arms bunched beneath the sleeves of his tshirt.

"You'll lock the doors."

Not a question. A command. One I wanted desperately to ignore, but I knew even if Jake hadn't said anything, the door would have been locked and sealed shut the second he passed over the threshold.

I resisted the urge to stick out my tongue in defiance.

"Obviously. I'm not stupid, Jake." Jake's eyes softened a smidge. The corner of his mouth twitched.

"And call me."

I froze.

"What?"

"If anything happens, you call me. I don't care if you think it's nothing. If anything happens, if anything's out of place, you call me."

"That's—"

"I don't care. You want me to leave. You call."

My lips pursed, and my brows bunched.

Asshole.

"Fine."

I wouldn't call.

Even if there was a reason to.

Jake's shoulders relaxed. He leaned back against the counter.

"But I won't call." Jake moved to protest. I raise a finger. "No! Because nothing's going to happen."

Jake nodded stiffly.

"I'll be back in the morning."

"Jake, you don't have to do this. You've already done too much."

I followed him through the living room to the front door. Jake turned back to stare down into my face.

I realized with surprise how little distance stood between my eyes and his.

Jake was tall but only maybe five inches taller than me. Standing toe to toe, I could see the near-black starburst around the center of his irises, how it bled into the cobalt blue of the rest of his eyes. Perfect.

Too close.

"I'll be here."

I blinked, stepped back into reality, and nodded. I forced a grateful smile to my lips.

"Thank you," I managed.

Jake reached for the door handle.

"See you in the morning."

I locked the door behind me, knowing, somehow, that Jake would stand on the other side until he heard the deadbolt turn.

For good measure, I slid a chair into place beneath the door handle before marching to the back of the house and locking that door, too.

Shaking fingers shoved tangled waves of hair back from my face. My nerves were shot. I needed to move, to do something useful.

Bottle.

I should fix Lily a bottle. She'd be hungry.

I strode into the living room and pulled everything I'd need from the diaper bag. After a quick check to ensure Lily still slept, I tiptoed back to the kitchen.

Five minutes later, warm bottle in hand, I collected Lily in her car seat and marched upstairs. As I passed through each room, I flipped off the lights, leaving the day's events downstairs in the dark.

▲▲▲

Lily remained silent all the way up the stairs. As I stepped off the last step into the hall, a moaning creak pulled from the boards beneath the carpet under my foot. Lily's face scrunched in annoyance. Tiny fists clenched as her eyes went glossy and her lips parted in the first efforts of a shriek.

I hurried the last few steps to the bedroom.

Still shaking, I lifted the stiff and fussing infant into my arms and offered a bottle.

She took it with a grudging glare.

Together we rocked as I tiptoed around the room, the only sound the gentle slurping as Lily sucked down the formula.

I stepped to the window and parted the blinds to look out at the empty driveway and street.

Shadows stretched across the yard. Loose leaves drifted listlessly over the patches of grass and dirt standing between the front of my house and the street.

The world was still, the other houses dark. Only a few lights shined in windows as night owls went about their business. Blue light flickered in the upstairs window of an elderly neighbor's house across the street.

Curious, I glanced further down the street and found Jake's Truck still sitting on the curb.

Why couldn't he just leave?

Still, a sense of calm settled around me, knowing Jake wasn't far away. I frowned at the idea.

I didn't need Jake.

I didn't need anyone.

Letting the blinds fall back into place, I turned from the window, prepared for a long, sleepless night.

▲▲▲

The night did not pass easy.

Lying in bed, nose pressed to Greg's pillow, I stared through the dark to where Lily slept in her makeshift crib, a hamper with a folded blanket for padding in the bottom.

I needed to find an alternative sleep solution. I couldn't tote that hamper all the way through Montana, not in my little car.

I didn't even want to consider the thought that I might not *get* my car back in time to make the drive to Montana.

I couldn't afford a rental.

I couldn't afford to fix the car either, but that was beside the point.

Lily needed somewhere suitable to sleep.

Besides, that hamper couldn't be all that comfortable.

I breathed in the scent of Greg's shampoo that still clung to the pillowcase.

If only you were here.

This should be his baby. Our baby.

Greg should be there with me.

In a perfect world, Greg would be snuggled close behind me as we stared down at our little baby, part Greg, part me. We'd stay up for hours counting her lashes, the seconds between her little breaths.

I smoothed a hand across my abdomen.

Did I want a baby?

Could I raise Greg's child all on my own?

Greg always wanted kids. We talked about it often, but there was always so much going on. Greg was always heading off on some trip to save people in a distant land, and I had my classes, my studio—as successful as either of those was.

Despite the ache in my heart, a soft snort escaped through my nose, and I quickly moved to stifle the sound, afraid of waking Lily.

I peeked into the hamper.

Lily's dark lashes stay still against her cheeks.

I let out a breath.

Greg would have known exactly how to care for Lily, known exactly what she needed, unlike me. I could barely distinguish if she needed a fresh diaper or a bottle.

Thank God Jake seemed to have some innate baby-calming ability. If it weren't for him, I would have gone crazy by dinner, not that I wasn't already well on my way.

Sudden tears pricked at my eyes, a thousand tiny needles.

If I couldn't last a day with Lily, how was I supposed to raise a baby of my own, or manage a studio, let alone handle the rest of my life?

All the air seemed to suck from the room. I sat up in bed. The walls were too close, squeezing me in.

Heart thundering in my chest, I pushed out of bed and tiptoed downstairs to the kitchen, sure the tumultuous beat would wake the baby if I stayed.

I breezed past all the light switches, choosing to move through the hall and living room in shadow and moonlight, letting the night blanket brush my skin in its cooling embrace.

I stopped in the open doorway to the kitchen, remembering the events earlier that evening. Even in the dark, my eyes found the spot on the floor in front of the fridge, and my heart shot into my throat.

My fingers found the switch on the wall. Light flooded the room, vanquishing the phantom shadows of a smoldering cat.

All that remained was a tiny black bit of char on the tiles.

Tea.

That's what I needed.

I moved to the pantry like a disembodied spirit, pulling a jar of shredded and dried leaves and flowers from the second shelf. I carried the tea jar to the counter, where I selected a purple narwhal infuser from the basket by the sink.

I watched my mug spin around in the microwave. The timer marked more than the passing seconds. Time was running out. Things were changing, and I wasn't sure I was ready.

But did I really have a choice?

Greg was gone.

There was no bringing him back.

And if I was pregnant, if I decided I couldn't bear to raise Greg's child on my own, could I...

No.

I reeled back from the idea like it was something scalding.

If I was pregnant, and it was Greg, I had to keep it, if only to hold a little piece of him close once again.

And if it wasn't...

I'd deal with that later.

The timer buzzed.

Mug in hand, I stepped out the back door, leaving it open in case Lily woke. I drew in a deep breath of night air.

Fragrant steam slid through the air to caress my lips as I stared into the inky darkness.

I dropped down on the back step, letting my head fall back to take in the sky.

So many stars.

For a moment, I traced patterns between the twinkling dots of light as I sipped my tea. With each passing second, the chilly night air and the outside seeped deeper into the cracks torn in my soul from the stress of the day, healing the wounds I hadn't yet readily acknowledged.

Leaves rustled in the neighbor's yard as the night breeze rattled the nearly bare branches of the maple tree hugging the fence.

My eyes fell shut to the stars.

Please let the crazy end tonight.

Cool wetness slid from the corner of my eye, slithered down my cheek to catch in the corner of my mouth.

It would be so easy to fall asleep right there on the porch steps.

So easy to succumb to the night...

A car engine roused me from my dreaming.

I sat up straight, craning my neck to see headlights cutting through the shadows between the trash bins and the fences lining the back alley.

I frowned.

None of my neighbors worked nights.

Even if they did, most parked out front on the street.

Cars rarely drove down the back alley.

Squinting against the dark, I examined the silhouette of the car.

That's what it was.

A car, not an SUV, not a truck.

Not the van from earlier.

Sleek, curved edges blended with the night.

The car must have been black or close to it. I couldn't make out an exact color.

It's probably nothing.

Fingers wrapped tight around the smooth ceramic mug, heat eased into my palms and fought to melt the ice forming at my fingertips.

I Pressed to my feet, unable to explain the unease tightening around my heart, unable to take my eyes off the car.

Through the open back door, Lily's faint cries drifted from upstairs.

I backed toward the house, slipping silently back inside.

I cut the lights as I turned the deadbolt.

Shadows devoured the kitchen.

I split the blinds, obscuring the window on the door's upper half, and stared out at the alley.

Nothing.

The car was gone.

Only darkness and night danced in the space behind the houses.

It was nothing.

Letting the blinds fall back into place, I retreated upstairs to the crying baby.

▲▲▲

From my place on the couch, I blinked into the morning sun that crept through the window, watched it slide across the living room floor.

I'd been up most of the night.

When I returned upstairs after my breather on the porch, Lily had pulled herself into a tense little ball in her car seat. As I lifted her out, her limbs shot out in protest, tense and shaking.

"Shh," I cooed as I held her to my chest. "It's okay." I rocked on the balls of my feet. When that didn't work, I danced.

Around the bed and back.

Lily's shuddering sobs subsided to hiccups.

I slowed, attempted to lower myself on to the edge of the bed, only for Lily's cries to ramp back up.

I pressed back to my feet.

No amount of rocking or gentle words would calm her.

So, exhausted, we danced.

Together, we spun and skipped through the rooms of the house, upbeat orchestral music drifting from the little speaker mounted over the TV in the living room.

Each time Lily's lashes drooped to her cheeks, I thought I could snag a few moments of sleep, but no. The second I stopped moving, she'd start up again.

Not that I minded.

In the moonlight-filled living room, music all around, the early morning house passed like water from a glass.

Smooth, easy, fluid.

Uncomplicated.

All around, the world kept on spinning, time kept ticking away, but right there, when I danced, everything stopped.

It was just me, the music, and the dance.

Lily's tiny muscles only relaxed and let her fall into a deep sleep sometime in the early hours of the morning as the sky began to lighten at the horizon.

How long she'd been asleep before I noticed, I don't know, but when I did, I slowed to a sway and sashed over to the couch.

Moving like a lazy summer breeze, I lowered myself onto the cushions.

Lily's eyes stayed closed, her relaxed little face blissfully slack.

I let out a breath, sank deeper into the cushions, into slumber.

▲▲▲

I blinked at the light streaming in through the window.

Morning.

What time was it?

I looked around the room but couldn't find a clock. Another one of Greg's eccentricities.

"The living rooms for living, not watching the clock," he'd always say when I complained about having to walk to the kitchen to check

Forgetting the hour for the moment, I glanced down at the baby in my arms, still fast asleep.

She wasn't so bad when she was quiet, the corners of her mouth turned up in a drowsy smile.

I sat back on the couch, ready to relish in the few waking moments of peace.

Overnight, tension from the previous day oozed from my muscles, leaving space for all the aches and pains of the last few days to manifest.

If I could just—

Bahhm-buhm buhm-bahhm

The doorbell rang through the house like an ancient gong.

I groaned, squeezing my eyes shut against the inevitable, knowing that when I opened them, I'd find Lily staring back at me, on the verge of tears from being so unceremoniously ripped from sleep by that offensive noise.

I took one breath, then hauled myself to my feet, the muscles in my legs and back screaming from hours spent dancing and sleeping on the couch.

Before Lily could muster the strength for another shrieking fit, I started for the door, bouncing the little girl lightly on my shoulder.

Who the heck thinks it's okay to come calling at such an ungodly hour?

What time is it anyway?

The light streaming through the living room window was strong and bright. It was well passed my usual waking hour.

Maybe not so early...

Still, who rang the bell knowing a baby was in the house?

My hand flipped the lock and turned the knob before my brain had time to regroup and process what I was doing.

When it did, it screamed for me to slam the door, to check out the window, the peephole at least, before opening the house up to a stranger.

But the door was already partially open, boots visible around the edge.

My brain screamed.

Idiot! Close it! Close it now!

Too late.

Heart in my throat, I let the door swing inward and breathed a sigh of relief when a pair of familiar cobalt eyes met mine.

"You're here early," I greeted, taking in the day's worth of dark stubble covering the lower half of Jake's face.

Jake raised a brow as I stepped back to let him inside.

"It is still early, right?" I glanced out the door, checking the clear blue sky before searching the street for any sketchy vans.

Seriously, what time was it?

In answer, Jake held out a steaming to-go cup.

My eyes brightened.

"Coffee?"

I melted right then and there.

"God, yes!"

I took the cup like a man lost in a desert falling into a cool oasis pool.

Jake slid Lily from my arms, immediately falling into a gentle sway as he peppered her with praise.

Cobalt blues never left my face as I took a long swig of coffee, my eyes rolling as sweet vanilla met my taste buds.

"You keep showing up with these, and I might never let you leave."

Anyone who knew to come bearing coffee was good in my book.

From Lily's gooey, gurgling sounds as Jake pampered her with attention, she was just as pleased with the man's arrival.

"Did little Miss let you get any sleep? You look..." Smart man knew not to finish his thought.

Stepping into the kitchen, I waved off Jake's concern.

My stomach rumbled like a Mack truck.

My face went red with embarrassment. I was too tired to even try to hide it.

"It's fine, you can say it. I'm sure I look like crap. Little Miss decided she wanted a midnight dance party." I jostled Lily's fingers affectionately as I passed on my way to the pantry in search of breakfast.

"What about you? Can't be too comfortable sleeping in your truck."

Jake ignored my pointed glance as he followed me into the kitchen.

He posted up against the counter as I emerged from the pantry with bread in hand.

Silent, he watched me pull out two slices and slather them in butter.

"What are you doing?" he asked as I raised the first slice to my mouth.

Watching him over the edge of my bread, I raised my brows.

"Breakfast. Want some?" I held out the other slice.

"I'll pass."

I shrugged and took a bite.

"Your loss."

Jake smirked.

"So ladylike..."

I ignored his jab in favor of appeasing my stomach.

Jake raised a brow at me.

"Is that all you're eating?"

I glanced down at the slice in my hand.

"What? It's toast."

Jake laughed.

Full-on, rough, raspy-edged laughed at me in that way that always pulled me in.

Lily burbled along like she was in on the joke.

Traitor.

"Here." Jake pulled the loaf of bread toward him and nudged me toward the living room.

"I've got the *toast*. You go sit."

Lips pursed. I frowned but stepped out of the way to lean on the counter.

It was still my kitchen.

Jake hiked the infant up higher on his shoulder and made a beeline for the pantry.

"What kind of fancy-ass toast are you making?" I asked as Jake reemerged, arms laden down with sugar and cinnamon.

"You'll see. Go sit."

I folded my arms over my chest and pouted.

"Can I at least take Lily?"

"If you don't mind, yeah. I'll be done in a minute."

Hesitantly, afraid to hurt or startle Lily, I eased her from Jake's shoulder. She was so small and tense.

Jake's rough fingertips brushed the back of my hand as he pulled away, sending shock waves up my arm.

My cheeks warmed.

Without a word, I turned and hightailed it into the living room. As I settled onto the couch, a trail of heat still burning across my skin where Jake and I touched.

Nope.

Not going to think on that one.

Chapter 13

Part of me knew it was a dream the second I felt masculine fingers tracing patterns across my thigh. Slow, languid strokes, like a well-saturated brush over canvas. At the same time, steady and sure while also delicate and feather light.

I'd know that touch anywhere.

So, while part of me knew I must be dreaming—knew an impassable barrier now stood between me and the man that touch belonged to—a larger part hoped I'd never wake up again.

That I could stay there forever, suspended between worlds.

At least then we could be together.

I rolled over in our feather-soft bed, the same one Greg picked for its elegance, and peered into hooded hazel eyes.

In those eyes, the future swirled in technicolor like a movie reel with all the conflict cut out.

Staring into those eyes, I watched our life fly by, the past quickly followed by the future I knew in my heart we could never have. Our first date and every subsequent date that followed filed past in the time it took Greg to blink, and suddenly, it was our wedding.

I'd been so happy.

We'd been so happy.

Standing on the precipice of the rest of our lives together, we couldn't wait to take the leap.

We danced for hours, long after the music ceased and the tables cleared away.

Greg smiled that slow, lazy smile as he brushed a wavy strand of hair back from my face.

"Remember teaching me to waltz?" he whispered, and I felt his breath on my cheeks, smelled that special brand of toothpaste he always insisted on using.

The corner of my lips pulled up at the memory. A single tear tumbled down my cheek.

I nodded, unable to speak.

"Never lost those two left feet."

And I laughed.

Because no matter how enthusiastic, or how hard he tried, Greg had always been a terrible dancer. Still, the second music came on, he pulled me from my chair out onto the floor, never one to let a moment pass.

I traced a finger over Greg's features, down his long nose, until the tip of my finger pressed to his thin lips.

"I miss you," Tears pulled at my voice, causing it to fracture in so many little lines.

Greg's hands framed my face.

"I know, babes." His thumb stroked my temple. "But it's no

longer our time."

My face scrunched as I forced back tears. I was a truly ugly crier.

"But I want to be with you." And there I was, the little girl, begging her parents not to go.

Greg shook his head sadly.

"There's still plenty of life out there for you. You just need to let it in."

"It won't be the same."

"No," Greg agreed. "But that's what makes what we have special. It's time to go."

"No."

Greg's lips pressed to my forehead. My eyes fluttered shut at the contact as I fought to memorize the feel of his touch, knowing our time was ending, that I may never feel his lips on my skin again.

I held the feeling tight, relishing in it a moment too long.

When I opened my eyes, the bed beside me was empty.

Chapter 14

I woke with a start like I'd fallen backward into a pool. In a rush my, surroundings flooded in.

Instead of my plushy, warm bed, I found my cheek pressed against a warm, solid chest.

I knew instantly it had to be Jake. My cheeks warmed.

I didn't dare open my eyes, afraid even a shift of my lashes would cue him into my wakefulness, would end the oddly weightless feeling of being cradled in another's arms.

I let myself settle, ready to pretend, for just a moment longer, that it was Greg holding me.

An aching longing shot through my chest. With everything I had, I grabbed hold of the sniffle forming at the back of my throat, knowing it would give me away.

My lip curled.

For a few more minutes, I could pretend.

I felt more than watched as we turned the corner at the end of the hall.

A second later, my foot caught on the end of the railing.

Just as quick, my illusion shattered as I flailed to regain balance. My arms shot out, waving around.

The world spun as I knocked Jake off kilter.

Together, we tumbled down the stairs, landing in a heap at the base.

Blinking, I shoved hair out of my eyes.

"You dropped me." My voice rang with accusation.

"Sorry." Jake scrubbed the back of his neck.

"You fell asleep," he said by way of explanation.

"So you thought you'd throw me down the stairs?" An unfair accusation, but I couldn't help myself.

Jake straightened, dark brows drawing together.

"You kicked me."

"So you threw me down the *stairs?!*"

I froze, the silence registering in my brain. My head whipped right and left as I searched the floor around us.

I fought to untangle myself from Jake.

"Where's Lily?"

A warm hand settled on my knee, the callused palm scrapping over the soft skin, sending skittering sparks across the surface.

"She's fine. Asleep in the living room. I thought I'd let you get a few decent hours of shut-eye since I'm here."

I stared at him, unmoving, my leg still thrown over Jake's in a way I didn't really care to examine.

I blinked.

"Oh."

"Yeah, oh. You better get going, I've got a shift at three."

"Right."

Double speed, I stood. Jake did the same.

I pressed my back to the opposite wall and took a breath, hating the air for smelling like him—like pine and dirt, a hint of smoke—hating even more that I liked it.

God, what's wrong with me?

This was Jake. Jessie's Jake. *Molley's* Jake!

I shouldn't be thinking about tingles, his skin on mine, and how he smells!

"Thank you...for that. For watching Lily, I mean."

"Don't mention it," Jake moved down the hall toward the living room, taking his intoxicating scent with him.

"Take some toast," he called over his shoulder. "You look hungry.

"Oh, no. I'm not—" My stomach butted in with a grumbling roar of protest. Traitor. Shoulders fell in defeat.

When Jake returned with a plate piled high with cinnamon-dusted toast, I accepted it without question.

Cheeks red, I turned and trudged up to my room, sure I wouldn't catch a wink of sleep.

▲▲▲

I was wrong.

Sleep came, much to my relief.

Deep and dreamless, it sucked me down into the dark oblivion of total rest and relaxation.

I rolled over in the plushy warmth of my bed. Sleep-crusted eyes blinked in the defused sunlight that snuck in through the slits in the blinds. Lashes clung together, pleading for a few more uninterrupted minutes of sleep. I tore them apart like lovers never meant to be.

Bleary-eyed, I searched Greg's bedside table for the little digital alarm clock Greg insisted on keeping.

2:15

Five hours? Really?

I threw back the covers and levered myself up on the side of the bed. Limbs heavy, I stared around the room I used to share with the love of my life. Now, all that shared the space were memories.

...and a plate of scrumptious toast.

My stomach rumbled, discontented with the distance between it and that snack. I stared at the plate on the dresser, just out of reach and frowned.

It wasn't like Jake to think about others' needs before his own. All morning, taking over toast prep, offering to watch Lily so I could sleep.

What was his game?

What did Jake want?

Maybe he's just being a good person.

I pushed aside the whispering voice in my head.

I didn't need help, and the Jake I knew wasn't the type to offer.

My stomach twisted, reminding me not so gently that I needed to find more than just a snack very soon.

Very soon, I'd need to make my way to a drugstore.

I hauled myself out of bed just long enough to snatch the plate of toast before sinking back into the blankets.

But why me?

Why was I the person he decided needed his help?

I bit the corner of a toast triangle and lost my train of thought.

Sugary warmth coated my tongue and exploded in my mouth.

Oh my god!

I took another bite, letting my eyes roll back in my head. I savored the cinnamon as it mingled with the sugar and butter on my tongue.

The hell did he do to the toast?

It was heaven.

Pure perfection.

Silky melted butter danced a three-man reel with the sugar and cinnamon, coaxed on by the crunch of the toasted bread.

My taste buds spin in euphoric bliss.

Screw what Jake wanted.

That toast was reason enough to keep him around just a bit longer.

Moving on sugar-fueled glee, I stepped from bed and ran my fingers through my hair in a futile attempt to organize my out-of-control tresses. When no amount of finger raking tamed the waves, I took up the toast plate and skipped out into the hall to go find the other occupants of the house.

I found Jake in the living room with Lily.

Sprawled on his back on the couch, Jake held Lily in the air, flying her around like a plane or a superhero or something. A great grin pulled at Lily's chubby cheeks, the first smile I'd seen on her.

Until then, I'd been sure she'd grow up to be one of the grumpy, moody girls who always sneered and rolled their eyes at me in high school whenever I walked by.

As Lily flew through the air, she looked so at peace.

No, she wouldn't be one of the mean girls. Lily was going to be a flyer.

I leaned against the wall just inside the room and took the last few bites of my toast as I took in the scene.

A wistful sigh slid past my lips before I could stop it.

Look at her now, already falling in love with the quarterback.

"You're up."

I blinked.

Jake sat up on the couch with the ease of someone whose body had yet to begin to fail him. He cradled Lily in the crook of his arm.

"Don't stop on my account," I teased as I moved to the couch.

A half-empty bottle of milk sat on the coffee table.

"Hope you didn't just feed her, or you're asking to get puked on."

Jake shrugged.

"Wouldn't be the first time," he quipped, as a lazy grin stretched across his lips.

Something in those dark, cobalt depths sparked as his eyes met mine, like flint on steel.

"We didn't wake you, did we?"

I shook my head and set my plate beside the bottle.

I straightened the coasters stacked in the middle of the table to avoid meeting Jake's eye again.

"Thanks for the toast. It was…"

"Nothing."

"Amazing!"

One brow rose up over Jake's left eye as his grin grew.

"What? You've never had cinnamon toast? Where'd you grow up? A cave?"

I couldn't help it.

Jake's smile, his laugh, was so infectious.

I smiled back.

"Something like that. Don't you have to get to work?"

Jake shrugged, noncommittal.

"Wanted to wait 'til you got up. Jenn dropped off her old Pack n' Play while you were sleeping. I wanted to get it set up before heading out."

I stared at Jake as he stood, unable to process all he'd said.

I didn't know Jenn.

Though she was Jake's youngest sister, she was still four years

157

ahead of us in school. By the time we got to high school, Jenn was long gone and moved on to the higher pastures of university life.

A college freshman couldn't be caught hanging out with her kid brother.

"That was nice of her."

Jake shifted Lily to his other arm and reached to pick up a large rectangular, tent-looking thing by the wall.

I stepped closer, catching an intoxicating whiff of pine and smoke that muddled my thoughts. Jake was too close.

"I'm sure I can figure it out. You don't want to be late."

Suddenly, all that mattered was getting Jake out of my house.

Still bent over the packed-up Pack n' Play, Jake glanced up at me, seeing the panic I knew was written all over my face. He straightened.

"You mind holding Lily?"

"Sure, but I—" He pressed the baby into my arms, and again, I was surrounded by him, even as Jake's fingers barely brushed my arm.

Jake flooded my senses.

I stepped back too fast, tripping over my feet in my haste to get away, but Jake was there.

Warm, work-worn hands caught me around my elbows and pulled me back onto my feet.

"All good?"

My breath congealed in my throat, and all I could manage was a slight nod as I stared into those dark eyes. They danced a little. I'd never been close enough to see the tiny variants in color swirling around their cores.

What, from a distance, looked like a blank sheet of night sky, was filled with wisps of light and dark that spun and twisted to some undocumented music, performing uncharted choreography that held me transfixed.

Jake's touch lingered on my elbows a moment longer as if to ensure I wouldn't topple over the second he let go.

Then he was gone.

Back across the room, collecting up the Pack n' Play and starting down the hall to the stairs before I could move past the tingling thrills racing across my arms.

Breath normalizing, I watched him go before turning my attention to Lily.

Breathing in her baby smell, I smiled down at her.

"We don't need men around taking care of us, do we? No. No we don't."

Still, I felt the emptiness at my core.

The same emptiness that drove me into Ethan's grasp after Greg's funeral.

I knew it was no good, that I should ignore it.

I shoved the feeling to the back of my mind, even as that voice in my head whispered that there was someone nearby who could fill that void.

I shook the thoughts away.

No.

Not Jake.

He was Jessie's.

...and Molley's...as weird as that was.

He would never be mine.

▲▲▲

I blinked out the window at the empty street as the roar of Jake's truck faded into nothing.

Lily squirmed in my arms. Her little nose bunched as she prepared for another fit.

I stared out at the street as a chasm yawned inside me, stretching wider with every passing second.

Alone in the house, the events and possible revelations of the past few hours piled high around me, threatening to drag me down into an endless hole.

I chewed my nail.

I had to keep Lily safe, but not knowing was driving me bonkers.

I needed answers.

Shoulders back, I sat up on the couch.

This is ridiculous.

I shoved to my feet. Lily bounced on my shoulder as I pulled up a ride-share app.

I didn't need someone to hold my hand.

The store would be more than safe enough, full of other shoppers. The ride share driver would drop me right at the doors.

Finished ordering a car, I strapped Lily into her seat and sat down to wait.

▲▲▲

It shouldn't be awkward, buying a pregnancy test.

Standing in the feminine hygiene aisle, staring at the wall of options beneath the fluorescent lights, I couldn't help but feel the eyes of every shopper who passed.

An elderly gentleman even had the nerve to quip, "Pretty soon for number two in' it?" as he toddled along.

Cheeks flaming, feeling like a preteen buying her first box of tampons, I grabbed six random tests off the rack and threw them in the cart.

Letting out the breath I'd been holding, I turned toward the front of the store and paused.

Down the aisle, staring too intently at a display of pads, a tall, slender man with greasy brown hair blocked the way to the cash registers.

At the sight of him, something slimy slithered in my memory, too deep for me to grasp or see clearly.

I couldn't say why, but somehow, I knew that man, and the idea made me crave a scalding shower.

My shoulder blades drew together, muscles bunching uncomfortably. I turned the cart the other direction and started further into the store. Surely there was something else I needed to buy. Milk. Something.

The icky feeling refused to dissipate.

A wayward thought drifted into focus.

Maybe Jake'll get off early...

I could call him, ask for a ride. It would be that easy.

With Jake close at hand...

No.

I can do this on my own.

Rolling my shoulders back to relieve some of the tension, I held my head high as I wove through the aisles, grabbing chips and microwave popcorn to make it look like I actually had a reason to be there.

My phone buzzed in the pocket of my yoga pants.

Jake.

A quaking smile pulled at my lips.

Everything going ok?

My thumbs shifted to text back before I even knew what to say.

Instinct screamed for me to let him know where I was. I ignored that natural urge and typed back.

Yep, all good here!

I paused at the end of the next aisle, looking up and down the row of shelves.

The urge to run and hide pulsed up and down my spine. Could I hide out in the women's bathroom? No. Not with Lily.

I had to get out, but the thought of going home to that empty house full of memories made my heart ache in my chest.

I turned toward the deli and froze.

There he was again, perusing the corn chips this time, only a few feet away.

Fingers white-knuckled the cart as I raced past like I hadn't noticed the creepy man.

My heart jackhammered against my ribs. My breath froze in my lungs.

He was following me.

I was being followed.

Flip-flops slapped the linoleum. As quick as possible without drawing too much attention, I cut around the outside edge of the store. Fingers fumbled across the screen of my phone, as I pulled up the ride-share app, fat-fingering the keys as I scrambled to enter my address.

A wheel spun in the center of the screen, and a second later, a list of nearby drivers appeared.

Ten minutes!

The closest driver was ten minutes away.

But that's too far! What if...

No. Everything would be okay.

Breathe. Just a few more steps and I'd be at the front of the store.

At the checkout line.

Nothing would happen in the checkout line.

Lily began to fuss as I set the last box on the counter.

The teenager behind the counter turned red as she scanned my items. Her eyes stayed fixed on her task.

Well, at least it's not just me...

"That's, uh, fifty-three eighty," the checker mumbled. Refusing to meet my eyes, the checker watched Lily with a constipated look on her face, her cheeks slowly changing from rosy to an odd shade of pasty green. Maybe I wasn't the only one who'd been reckless lately.

I scanned my card, painfully aware of how little was in my account, and took up the grocery bag.

"Have a nice day."

With a rushed thanks, I took off for the front of the store.

▲▲▲

Again, I found myself staring out the front window into the gathering darkness. Legs curled tight beneath me on the couch. My knees and ankles tingled from lack of circulation.

Upstairs, Lily slept soundly.

Though I'd insisted I could figure out how to put the pop-up crib together, Jake carried it upstairs and carefully assembled it, even pulled the tiny, fitted sheet over the portable mattress.

I just watched on, unsure what to do or how to respond to the tornado of emotions swirling around inside.

Afterwards, I followed Jake back downstairs. He stopped at the door, turned.

For a moment, when his eyes met mine, I could see the pull inside him to stay straining in those intense cobalt depths.

But again, I insisted, urging him out the door, as much for his sake as for my own sanity.

"I'll be back later." Said like a question, like he was asking permission.

Will you?

Even as I sat on the couch, waiting for that black truck to pull up, I wondered why the echoing ache of emptiness inside me felt so cavernous.

I didn't know Jake. Not really.

He wasn't a part of my life.

And after what happened with Ethan, the last thing I needed was to crawl into another man's arms.

My eyes landed on the pregnancy test resting on the edge of the coffee table, at the two pink lines on the screen.

I had other things to worry about besides boys.

Still, something like regret settled in my stomach.

Since returning from the store, my ears strained for that deep mechanical roar of a truck engine that would signal Jake's return. Part of me hoped it wouldn't come, to prove that the glimpse of the Jake I'd seen the last few days was only a mirage, vaper in the air that would fizz out and vanish as soon as things got hot.

As the sky outside darkened, I fidgeted in my seat, chewing at my thumbnail as I stared out at the street.

What if Jake didn't come back?

I chewed my lips, knowing I should start dinner. It was futile to sit and wait like a lost puppy when I had no idea when Jake's shift ended.

If he shows, he shows.

No big deal.

Needing to prove my independence to myself, I shoved off the

165

couch, not liking the amount of effort it took to pull myself from the window.

I went upstairs to check on Lily.

When I found her still asleep, I moved to the kitchen.

I had to do something productive.

Stay busy.

Dinner.

What could I make for dinner?

Mind still on the empty street out front, I wandered to the pantry. On autopilot,t I pulled noodles and sauce from the shelves and set them on the counter.

Kneeling to collect a pan from a lower cabinet, I froze, ears perked.

Was that crying?

I stood, focusing in on the silence of the house.

Nothing.

Lips pressed in a thin line, I waited.

Maybe she went back to sleep?

A few more seconds passed.

Still, nothing but silence drifted down the stairs.

Fingers curled around the edge of the drawer.

Lily probably went back to sleep.

...but what if she didn't?

What if something was wrong?

I shut the drawer and crossed into the living room.

The street outside still sat empty, the streetlights just flickering on.

Shadows swirled around the edge of the illuminated circle surrounding the nearest streetlamp.

Unable to shake the nagging feeling, I turned away from the window and jogged upstairs.

It doesn't matter if Jake doesn't come back.

▲▲▲

Lily was awake.

She grinned up at me from her bed as I came into view, then she noticed the empty space over my shoulder.

A little bit of light fell from her eyes.

I know, sweetie. You're not the only girl he's disappointed, trust me on that.

Lifting Lily into my arms, I took a deep breath of baby and let it swirl in my sinuses as I settled her against my shoulder.

I turned back to the hall, my eyes catching on a picture of Greg and me before senior prom.

The photo shook loose a flood of memories in my head.

I'd been with Greg since freshman year. From day one, it was me and him. I never really took part in the whole high school dating scene, but I'd seen it play out around me. I watched the other girls fawn over Jake and the football boys, who seemed to spend more time following a ball than the curriculum of any one of their classes.

Greg and I passed down the halls as love blossomed and

bloomed around us, only to wilt under the undiscerning eye of oblivious teenage boys.

Sometimes, at night, I wondered what it was like, how it felt to have one's young heart pierced so shallowly but to feel the wound so deeply.

Then I remembered the mess Jessie became after finding out about Molley and Jake, how, even with Cole there with her every second, her mind wandered to what she'd lost. To the could have been she built up in her mind.

Would it be like that for me?

If I chose to move on, to find someone new, would I find myself comparing every suitor to the love I lost?

Would anyone measure up?

Lily threw her fist up like she couldn't stand the light streaming from the center of the ceiling. Her lip scrunched, and her amber eyes glazed.

A pint-sized whimper split from Lily's lips.

My head whipped toward the hall and the stairs.

Beneath Lily's soft cry, I could have sworn I heard...

Hiking Lily higher on my shoulder, I tilted my head to listen.

I called out into the house.

"Hello?"

Nothing.

Only the echo of silence filled the house.

Then, the hall, the room around me, went totally dark.

Chapter 15

My scream echoed off the walls.

In a rush of discombobulated thoughts, instinct took over, and I slammed the bedroom door shut. My fingers fumbled for the lock.

Oh god. Oh-God-oh-God-oh-God!

Someone was in the house.

Someone was in *my* house!

Where's Jake?

Lily whimpered in my arms. I glanced down at her in the darkness. Lily's little gleaming eyes filled with frightened tears. Her lip shook.

I sucked in a breath.

"It's going to be okay. I've got you."

Only...how was I supposed to get us out of that room?

The only switches for the hall lights were at the top and bottom of the stairs, so there would be no going back through the bedroom door.

My eyes began to adjust to the lack of light in the room. I took in my surroundings.

Wait a second.

If someone flipped the hall switch, why did the bedroom light go out?

I breathed a heavy sigh of relief and smiled down at Lily.

"It's okay."

Everything was going to be okay.

It was just a power outage.

It wasn't exactly common to experience power outages in the area, but from time to time, a tree limb or something would fall over a line, and the street would go dark for a few hours.

At least that time, it happened at night. Lose power during the day when everyone is going about their business, and everyone loses their mind.

Eyes fully adjusted to the lack of light, I turned the lock and opened the door.

There was nothing to be afraid of.

It was just a power outage.

In the living room, I collected my phone to check the power company's website for an update on when we'd have power back.

I bounced lightly as my thumb scrolled over the screen, trying to dissuade Lily's down-turned mood.

The website crawled, bogged down by too many users.

I glanced up from my phone and paused, frowned.

Mist and shadows danced in the street around a yellow pool of light at the base of a streetlamp.

Weird.

My eyes wandered to the house across the street.

A tv flickered in an upstairs window.

But...

A board creaked at the back of the house.

Blood froze in my veins. The last bit of air in my lungs caught in my throat. Fingers tightened on Lily.

No.

Please, God, no.

I didn't turn around. Didn't look.

Somehow, I knew what I'd see.

Movies taught me enough about intruders to know I'd find a tall, dark figure looming just inside the kitchen, cloaked in a false shade of his own creation. If I stopped to look, I'd be wasting precious time.

Precious time that I could use to cross the ten feet to the door.

Five steps. That was it.

Would I have enough time?

Could I get out before he caught me, or would I be better off if I stayed and fought?

I sucked my lips between my teeth on a breath. Hands pressed Lily against my chest, but she didn't seem to mind the extra tight hug.

On three.

One.

Two.

I bolted for the door, too afraid to wait a second longer. Afraid my resolve would falter, that I'd stay frozen in place, waiting for whatever the intruder had in store.

My shoulder slammed into the door with a deafening thud.

Lily screeched.

Fingers found the deadbolt, then the lock on the handle, and I was outside, sprinting across the yard.

Gravel and bits of cold grass poked and tickled the soles of my bare feet as I sprinted for the street. My feet would be black with dirt, but I didn't care.

We had to get away.

"Help!" I cried into the night, hoping someone, anyone, would hear me and come running outside.

My head whipped to the houses on either side of the street as I ran, afraid to slow in case the psycho who decided to break into my house took chase.

Moisture licked at my cheeks.

Tears.

Lily's or mine?

I didn't stop to check, didn't even wipe them away.,

Fear blurred my vision. I ran on, not knowing what would happen if I stopped, unwilling to risk finding out.

Cutting through the yard on the corner, I shot out into the next street.

Feet slapped the pavement in a disjointed staccato rhythm that would have been thrilling to spin and stomp along to if I weren't running for my life.

Breath came in rasps. My chest ached.

Another block at full sprint, then I slowed, took in my surroundings.

The houses on the street were nicer, the yards better kept.

Spokane was like that.

One second, you were in a shit neighborhood, worried about getting mugged for your cheap drugstore sunglasses. Two blocks over, you'd find yourself in a cheery little park full of moms and nannies with little kids running all over the place.

What I would have given for one of those happy little, populated parks right about then.

Up and down the street, all the houses were dark. No signs of life. I ran up to the closest houses anyway.

I needed to call the police.

I patted my pockets. Nothing. No Phone.

Exhaustion clung to my muscles like molasses, a slow ache that usually came after a good, hard day of dance, leaving me ready to collapse on the couch for hours. There was no time for that now.

I hammered on the door.

"Hello!"

No answer.

I banged harder.

"Hello! Please, help!"

Nothing.

A frustrated growl tore from my throat as I peeled off the porch like a mad woman.

Lily, held tight to my side, stayed miraculously silent, terrified of the coo-coo-nut-lady I'd become or content to come along for the ride, I'd never know.

I skirted down the street, hugging the curb, and crossed an intersection.

My eyes darted all around, over my shoulder.

Wind pulled at the branches of the trees and bushes lining the yards, ruffling the leaves covering the grass.

In the dark, the shifting leaves sounded like muffled footsteps.

I picked up my pace.

By the time I reached the next cross street, I was sprinting, trying to outrun my pursuer, be that the wind or the man from earlier.

The air shifted. Lily hiccupped the beginning of a sob.

I pulled her tighter into my side, offering what little warmth I could. I glanced down the street and skidded to a stop, eyes widening.

No.

Nonono, i-it couldn't—it couldn't be.

Twin headlights stared down the street from several blocks away.

Holding my breath, I watched the car creep closer, knowing if I stayed still, I'd go unseen.

But that wouldn't last long.

Soon, the car would be close enough it wouldn't matter what I did. I'd be spotted.

It wasn't a t-rex driving that car.

All it would take was a little pressure on the gas, and those headlights would be on me.

No more hiding.

Hitching Lily higher on my hip, I shot across the nearest yard.

Dew off the grass spattered my feet as the wet blades slapped against my toes.

I had to get Lily away.

It was very possible that car wasn't driven by the same man who broke into my house, but I couldn't take that chance. Not with Lily.

I swerved around the side of the house.

The backyard was dark, shrouded beneath the branches of tall pines, older than most of the buildings in the area.

Bits of shredded bark stabbed at my feet.

A chain-link fence stretched across the back length of the yard. I was on top of it before I caught the moonlight glinting off the metal.

Hair lashed at my cheeks as my eyes slashed back over my shoulder.

The car hadn't come into view around the side of the house, but somehow, I knew it was still out there, crawling up the street. Searching.

I couldn't stop, couldn't go back.

Winging a leg over the fence, I vaulted over, taking off as soon as I touched down on the other side.

Streetlights flooded the next street over. Running down the center of the pavement where the light couldn't reach, my toe caught on the asphalt. One arm flew out to regain my balance, even as I curled around the little bundle in my arms. Stumbling several steps, I glanced down to find Lily passed out cold, peacefully rocked to sleep by the jostling of our escape.

Good.

One of us deserved to get some sleep.

My legs ached.

The muscles in my thighs and calves pulsed with exhaustion, begging me to stop.

To just slow down.

Only for a little while.

One block, tops.

I kept going.

Try as I may, though, ten blocks later, I couldn't keep going.

I stumbled through another intersection, not bothering to avoid the streetlight on the corner. Wheezing, I fell against the pole to catch my breath.

Air entered my lungs on halting gasps. No matter how many times I sucked in more air, I couldn't get enough. It felt like a dam had been erected between my lungs and brain. The air just couldn't get through.

A car turned the corner at the far end of the street, headlights blinding in the darkness. But these lights weren't creeping. The headlights blazed down the road like a bat out of hell, straight for me.

"Why?" It came out on a choked sob.

With no other options, I took off back the way I came, shot around the nearest corner, praying to whoever was listening that the car wouldn't follow.

Seconds behind me, the car careened around the bend.

My heart leaped into my throat as the roaring engine grew closer and flew on past, hulking and loud.

Not a car.

A truck.

The hell?

I slowed, staring after the glowing red taillights.

Maybe it wasn't...

But one block up, those red lights disappeared as the truck spun in the intersection.

It was coming back!

Fast.

I stumbled back, frantically trying to get out of the way.

There was no time.

I turned to protect Lily from the oncoming impact.

Blinding light from the high beams forced my eyes shut as I prepared for the crush of bones against metal fender.

Brakes squealed. I tumbled back.

Asphalt fast approaching, my mind sputtered back to life with just enough time to shift and land on my backside. Arms wrapped tight around Lily. I braced for impact.

An indignant cry mixed with my own startled shriek as I landed butt first on the road and rolled in on myself, around Lily.

Eyes squeezed shut. I quickly assessed for damage.

Head, shaken but not rattled.

No real damage to my back. Thank you, cheer and dance, for teaching me how to fall.

Butt was a little sore, but whose wouldn't be and...

A car door slammed.

He's coming!

Unable to hear over the blood pounding in my ears, I pulled myself up. The man stepped in front of the truck, his form silhouetted by the headlights at his back.

I skittered back in a clumsy, one-armed crab walk.

One thought ran through my mind.

Protect lily.

"P-please. I-I don't... I n-ne..." Through the gasps and my hammering heart, the words could get out.

"Hann?"

The whiskey tenor voice cut through the fog of terror in my mind. The little rasp at the edges brushed over my skin like the softest of caresses. Every muscle in my body breathed a sigh of relief.

"Jake," I sobbed, my voice crackling as the last of the adrenaline fled my body.

And he was there, kneeling in front of me.

You came.

Warm, calloused hands cupped my face, brushed tangled strands of hair back off my damp cheeks.

"Hey, it's me. Hann, what's going on? Hanna, why are you out here in the cold?"

Jake shrugged out of his jacket and threw it around my shoulders.

"In the house," I stammered as Lily began to fuss. I held her tighter to my chest, refusing to let go. I bounced her softly.

"He was in the house."

"Who?"

Hair flew in my face as I shook my head.

Again, Jake caught the wayward strands and brushed them behind my ear.

Rough pads rasped over my cheek, sending shivers racing down my limbs that had nothing to do with the frigid temperatures.

Mistaking my shivers for chill, Jake scooped Lily and me up into his arms and carried us to the truck.

Chapter 16

The cab of Jake's truck was toasty. Heat pumped from the vents in the dash, sending warmth fanning over my face as I shrugged deeper into Jake's Jacket.

In halting movements, I scooted across to the passenger side. Jake followed me in.

His hand found mine trembling on the center console.

"Hann, what happened?"

I took a shaky breath and told him everything.

Almost everything.

About checking on Lily.

The lights and the intruder.

Running.

I left out the part about the store and how I spent the afternoon at the front window, the part where I couldn't stop wondering when he'd be back—*if* he'd be back. That afternoon, every cell in my body screamed for me to beg him to stay, to skip work for me.

But that wasn't me, and I couldn't let Jake see that moment of weakness.

"And then, there you were," I finished, eyes stinging with fatigue and too much bottled-up emotion.

The truck still sat on the curb.

Jake's fists constricted around the steering wheel. His mouth worked, trying to find words.

The silence that slipped in around my last words to mingle with our breath was shattered by Jake's phone chirping in the cup holder.

"That's Molley," Jake reached for the phone.

I raised a quizzical brow in his direction as the moment shattered around us.

Jake let out a sigh.

"I called her when I got to your house and found the door open. I..." Jake looked away, staring out into the night. He raked his hand back through his hair. His fingers shook as he scrubbed the back of his neck.

"We've been looking for you."

I didn't have a chance to respond.

Jake lifted the phone to his ear.

"I found them." He sounded like someone had a noose around his neck. The words scraped through his throat with a reverberating rasp.

Jake paused. From the passenger seat, Molley's muffled voice filtered through the line.

Jake nodded.

"Do that. We'll be there soon."

Molley's Mercedes sat in the driveway in front of my house.

I stared up at the dark facade. Was the intruder still around? Was he still inside?

The front door stood ajar. Through the crack, I caught the glint of moonlight off the picture frames in the living room.

A light lit up the interior of the Mercedes as Molley stepped from the car. She was halfway across the yard when Jake stepped out of the truck to meet her.

Molley stormed past Jake, tore open the passenger side door of his truck, and pulled me down into a fierce hug.

Molley pulled away, holding me at arm's length as she searched for any injury.

"I'm so sorry." Seeing nothing beyond bumps and bruises, she turned her attention to the baby in my arms.

"The police are on their way. Once we get everything sorted, we'll head back to my house for the night."

I stepped from Molley's embrace.

"You don't have to do that. I-I'm sure we'll be fine."

"Like hell."

Our heads shot to Jake standing in the middle of the lawn. Every muscle in his body bulged with tension, ready to leap into action at a moment's notice. Something dark and bulky stuck out of his jeans' waistband, kissing his back.

Was that a gun?

Where the hell did that come from?

Since when did the high school quarterback carry a gun?

Dark cobalt eyes bore into me, refusing to look away. Muscles in Jake's jaw ticked.

"Excuse me?"

"You're not staying here alone."

My brow bunched.

"It's my house."

"I don't give a damn if it's Fort Knox. I'm not leaving you here alone.

My eyes narrowed.

"Well, it's a good thing it's not up to you. Besides, I won't be alone. I'll have Lily."

I shifted the infant to my other shoulder.

"Actually, Hann..."

Molley fidgeted.

Her long, manicured fingers twisted.

"Lily's coming with me. For her safety. You should come too."

"But Montana."

"You don't even have a car. What if—"

"I-I can rent a car. I-I'll—"

"He's right, Hanna. I appreciate you being willing to do this, but things have gotten out of hand, and you shouldn't be on your own tonight." Molley cut the winds from my sails before turning a quizzical eye on Jake. Messy blond curls bounced as Molley cocked her head to one side like she'd just solved some obscure riddle.

Dark eyes met Molley's with a silent warning. The corner of Molley's mouth curved upward.

I hated the silent way Jake and Molley seemed to communicate.

Molley turned to me with that same knowing smile.

"If you want to stay here, fine. But Jake's staying with you."

Jake's shoulders relaxed, but I glared at Molley.

"No."

It was ridiculous.

I didn't need a babysitter.

I'd done perfectly fine the last three months on my own.

Had it really been that long since Greg passed?

Traitorous tears burned the backs of my eyes.

I forced them back.

Tears would only hinder my argument.

I was fully capable of taking care of myself.

Prepared to argue as much, I blinked my eyes clear as a pair of police cruisers slid to a stop behind Jake's truck.

▲▲▲

A burly officer with a rusty, close-trimmed beard stepped from the driver's seat of the first cruiser, followed close behind by a tall, clean-shaven officer.

The burly officer nodded in greeting as he approached. Beneath his beard, his mouth twitched as he glanced at Molley.

"Someone called about a break-in," Officer Blair said after introducing himself and his partner.

A pair of cops from the second cruiser came to flank Officer Blair.

Again, I recapped the events of the night.

As his partner took notes in a on a little pad, Blair listened intently. Through his warm, olive eyes, I watched him sort through the details, formulate his next moves. The dark red-blond hair of his mustache bunched over his lips as they pursed.

Blair gave a nod as I finished.

"Mind if we take a quick look around? Then you can come in and make sure nothing's missing."

Standing there on the darkened lawn, Blair's words seemed so casual, so easy, like there might not be some crazed psycho waiting for me in the bushes. It was oddly refreshing.

I wanted nothing more than to run inside and lock out the world, but of course, that hadn't kept out the world the last time, had it?

A shiver sashed over my skin.

I pulled Jake's coat tighter around me, tucking Lily inside the woolly lining.

The burly officer's eyes softened as they landed on the infant.

"Why don't you all wait in your car? Should only take us a few minutes," the officer said before nodding to my leg.

"You should get that tended to. Want an ambulance?"

My brows knit in confusion. I glanced down to find an ugly red smear of blood down my left calf.

"How—" My vision blurred. The world tilted on its axis.

"Fuck."

My stomach flipped, and my throat burned.

Stumbling forward, I fell against a solid chest as the little I'd eaten that day spilled onto the dirt.

Someone pulled Lily from my quivering grasp.

For the second time that night, I found myself cradled against a wall of warm muscle.

Exhausted and still queasy, my head rolled against Jake's shoulder. I pressed my face into the crook of his neck to hide my embarrassment creeping into my cheeks.

I clung tighter to him as the world swayed with his loping stride.

Jake's earthy, spicy scent filled my lungs, somehow grounding me as it sent my heart racing.

When Jake deposited me into the passenger seat of his truck, I immediately felt his absence, even as he stood a step away.

I glanced up with a sheepish smile.

Over Jake's shoulder, Molley looked a bit queasy herself, her cheeks tinged a soft green as she rocked Lily.

"Thanks." A self-deprecating laugh none of us expected burst from my lips. And once I started, I couldn't stop.

Tears I'd been holding back all night tumbled off the tips of my lashes to rush over my cheeks like so much water over Niagara.

"Guess I'm not too big a fan of blood."

Jake watched me with an uncharacteristic sternness. Concern bracketed his mouth as he squeezed my knees.

My cheeks heated at the pleasurable trails left on my bare skin by Jake's work-worn finger pads.

Molley appeared around Jake's shoulder, cocked her head. By the grace of God, she kept her mouth shut, though I saw the corners of her lips twitch upward.

"How about that ambulance?" the officer called from where he stood in the yard.

Jake growled over his shoulder.

"I got it."

The officer's eyes hardened. He squared his shoulders.

"Right." He cleared his throat. "We'll only be a few minutes."

I shot Jake an admonishing look as the officer turned toward the house.

Over Jake's shoulder, I watched two cops disappear around the side of the house as Blair and his partner jogged up the front steps.

"He was only trying to help."

Jake gave an unconvinced grunt as he turned his attention to the scrape on my leg.

"Climb in the back, Moll, no point in freezing."

"I should call Will."

"I said, I've got this," Jake growled.

"Not everything is about you," Molley purred with a sharp smile that could pierce armor. She moved around him to climb in the back.

"He'll be worried if he doesn't hear from me soon. I don't want him waking up Grace for no reason."

Jake gave no sign he heard Molley. He turned my leg to get a better look at the cut. I kept my eyes fixed on Jake's face, watched as dark eyes took in the jagged, torn edges of the abrasion before pulling away.

Without a word, he strode to the back of the truck and returned with a First Aid kit.

Jake made quick work of cleaning and bandaging my leg.

I blinked in wonder as he secured the end of the bandage strip.

"Where'd you learn to do that?"

Jake shrugged.

"Army. Everyone learns field dressing."

I opened my mouth to question him further but stopped as Officer Blair stepped back onto the front step.

"All clear," the officer called. Jake smoothed a hand over the bandage on my calf before settling on my bare thigh. Heat radiated from his palm like a furnace as he applied the gentlest pressure, asking for my attention.

I bit down on my lips, staring at Jake's long, tanned fingers against the pale of my thigh, wondering, not for the first time, what the touch, the looks, and the sudden insistence on staying close all meant.

I could worry about that later.

Unwilling to make the situation any more awkward, I sat up in my seat.

A witty comment primed on my tongue, I tilted my head back to meet Jake's gaze, only to have the words wilt against my teeth as I fell into the wealth of emotion swirling in those cobalt depths.

"You ready?" Jake's voice floated to me as if I were in a dream.

His grip on my legs was firm and surprisingly reassuring, promising to never let me fall.

Too late.

If only I could believe that touch.

The look in his eyes.

"Yeah," I breathed.

I hopped down out of the truck, landing all too close to Jake.

My chest brushed his as I drew a startled breath. Twinging pain shot up my injured calf as I landed on the curb. In seconds, warm hands settled on my hips to steady me.

Heat seeped up my neck into my cheeks.

"Thanks," I mumbled before stepping away, ever aware of Molley's eyes on my back.

On the other side of the truck, the cab door slammed as Molley climbed out to meet us. Lily slept soundlessly against her shoulder.

Molley looked up at the house.

"You guys take a look around. Tell Shawn if anything's missing. I'll take Lily back to the house and get her fed and back to bed. Come over when you finish up here."

Molley's eyes flitted up and down my form before meeting my eye.

"I'll have a room ready for you."

Too exhausted to argue, I set her a weary smile.

"Thank you."

"Okay, now go. Don't keep Blair waiting." Molley waved to the burly cop as he looked up from his partner's notes.

"Thanks, Shawn. I own you one," she called with little regard for the late hour or my sleeping neighbors.

Blair raised a hand in acknowledgment.

"Just bring one of those fancy coffees next time you come by."

Molley grinned and strode back over to her car.

▲▲▲

Inside, the house was dark.

Habit drew my fingers to the switch on the wall, but no lights came on.

Jake pressed his phone into my hand, the flashlight app open on the screen.

"Here."

I gave him a shaky smile in return, my frayed nerves sparking like a live wire as I stepped into the living room.

I had to get the test. Before Jake saw. Before he knew.

I shined the beam around the room.

Everything looked the same, untouched and in place.

The pillows on the couch, the pictures on the wall, even the coasters.

I frowned, the light shining on the clean coffee table.

"What is it?" Jake stepped to my side, close enough for his breath to tickle across the shell of my ear.

Crap.

Think Hanna.

"My phone. I must have dropped it when I ran, but it's not here."

It was true. Somewhere in my escape, I'd dropped the phone. I thought I'd find it here, on the couch or the floor.

"Let's check upstairs."

▲▲▲

Something was wrong.

I knew it the second I stepped onto the stairs.

Each step up lodged unnerving unease down my throat.

Only Jake's hand on my back kept me moving.

A prisoner on her way to execution.

Something vital would die when we reach the top.

Each step took more effort to keep from turning back, running out to Jake's truck like the coward I was.

I couldn't do this.

Every fiber in my being screamed to turn back.

To close my eyes against the carnage that would tear through my life.

I kept going.

And as my foot touched down on the final step, all air fled my lungs. I stared at the open door.

A strangled squeak eked past my lips.

Jake was at my side, his hand warm around my shoulder as he tried to turn me to face him.

I stared at the open door.

"What is it?"

Dark eyes searched mine with frenetic urgency, like if he found all the shattering pieces, he could hold me together with sheer will.

"Greg's office."

Darkness pressed around me.

Jake stood close.

I watched the frown spread across his lips.

He said nothing, waiting for me to make the next move.

I took a measured step closer, unsure, afraid of what I'd find.

Surely, the cops had been up there, searching for any intruder.

No matter how many times I told myself the room would be empty, I couldn't help but feel eyes on the back of my head.

Probably Jake.

But a small part of me hoped and feared it was Greg.

I hadn't been in Greg's office since he left.

That morning, Greg shut the door and it had stayed that way ever since, holding in the things he'd been most passionate about.

His research. Plans.

I told myself there was no reason to go in there.

I didn't need the space.

All those books and papers weren't hurting anybody being in there.

And if a little bit of Greg got to stay alive in the house because they were there, was that such a bad thing?

In truth, I wasn't sure I could bring myself to open the door.

Didn't know if I could stand to see all the medical texts and anthropology studies lining the shelves, waiting for Greg to return and plan his next trip.

I didn't need to lift Jake's phone to see the ransacked.

Even when Greg was home, his office was never clean, but now all the books and printouts were strewn across the floor, books lying open, pages ripped. The top of the expansive desk, usually covered in disheveled stacks of research and maps, reflected moonlight off the nearly clear surface.

The swivel chair Greg spent hours searching for online, searching for the chair with the best lumbar support, lay toppled on its side, a jagged gash sliced in the leather. Stuffing spilled from the cushion like guts all over the floor.

Books lay discarded on top of a layer of paper, flayed open, pages torn.

Tears pressed at my eyes.

All that work, Greg's dreams, discarded like trash.

Heart beating the insides of my ribs, I stepped around the desk to find the drawers ajar, their contents riffled and abandoned.

A fat, salty drop escaped my lashes and tracked down my cheek to tumble off my chin. A wave followed in the first drop's wake. Unstoppable and unbending rage and sorrow mingled in my tears as they cascaded off my lashes.

I bit my lips to hold back a sob. Failed.

Greg's office was a sanctuary. A place where Greg could research and prep for his travels. Why that room? Of all the rooms in the house, why would someone tear that room apart?

"Hanna?" Jake's hand brushed my arm as he came up behind me. He only said my name, but Jake asked a million questions in that one word.

What's going on?

Are you okay?

"Why?" I choked, panning the flashlight over a scrambled stack of maps and research papers.

"I don't know." Jake's answer came soft, almost a whisper. Any louder, and I may have shattered like fragile china on the floor.

What is wrong with me?

I don't crumble. I don't cry.

"He was a *freaking* doctor," I cried, not caring if the officers downstairs heard. "What could he possibly have had that would make someone do this? What did he know?"

"I don't know." Again with that placating tone.

Jake's hand closed around my elbow, ready to pull me away from the tattered remains of Greg's office.

With a feral growl, I tore away. I knelt to collect the maps off the floor, straightening them into a neat pile on the corner of the desk.

Greg wouldn't want his research left out for people to step all over. He might not have been the neat and tidy type, but Greg had a system all his own. At a moment's notice, he could pull a book or research paper from a pile and provide you with a source or fact.

Now that system, all that research, had been destroyed by some asshole intruder looking for God knows what.

I reached for another stack of papers.

Jake's hand closed on my wrist, and with a gentle tug, he turned me to face him. I glared up into cobalt blues.

"Hanna, should we really be messing with this? The cops might need—"

"I can't leave it like this. It's—It's..." I bit my lips as a wave of emotion tore through me, threatening to pull me out to see, drag me down deep into a spiraling pool of despair I'd have no hope of pulling myself out of.

I drew in a slow breath and forced the wayward feelings aside.

"Greg wouldn't want it left like this."

Jake held my wrist, tethering me to the earth.

We stood there in the dark.

He was right.

I knew it, deep down.

Whether I liked it or not, Greg's office was a crime scene.

"We'll take care of it tomorrow. Okay? In the daylight."

I nodded.

It would take hours to clean up Greg's office, even longer in the dark.

Gingerly, Jake slid the papers from my hands and set them back on the floor with a level of reverence one would expect to be shown to a newborn or someone's elderly grandmother.

Jake was right. The police would dust for prints or something. Greg was the only person who ever came into that office. Surely whoever trashed the place left behind prints, or DNA, or something.

Jake led me out into the hall.

▲▲▲

"Anything missing?" Officer Blair asked, turning to face us as we returned to the living room. The other officers were gone. Only Blair and his partner remained.

I shook my head.

"Not that I can tell, but Greg—my husband's office, they tore it apart. I-it's trashed."

"It looked like they were searching for something," Jake filled in from behind me.

"Any idea what they might have been searching for?" But Blair's olive gaze never returned to me. It stayed fixed on Jake. My brow creased as I answered.

"No. H-he was a doctor. Worked with the Red Cross and Doctors Without Borders."

The cop's bushy brows rose as he glanced from me to Jake.

"Apologies, but you don't exactly strike me as the medical type." My eyes went wide. I nearly choked. A warm hand I hadn't realized I was holding pulsed around my fingers, in silent assurance.

"I'm not..."

Gathering the last of my strength, I straightened, releasing Jake's hand.

"My husband is dead, Officer Blair. Just over three months now."

"Oh." Blair scrubbed a hand over the back of his neck and tugged at his beard.

"Apologies, and my condolences, ma'am. Do you have any idea what your husband was working on before he died? Any new treatment methods or research someone might be interested in stealing?"

I shook my head.

"I know it's dark—looks like the power has been cut. You'll want to call the power company in the morning to have them reconnect the wiring—but could you tell if anything was missing from your husband's office?"

My throat bobbed, and my shoulders sagged in defeat. I shook my head.

Officer Blair pulled a card from his pocket and held it out.

"If you notice anything, please call."

There was no dusting for prints, no DNA testing, no molds made of shoe prints left on the carpet.

Maybe I watched too many crime dramas.

Blair and his partners left without another word, and Jake and I were alone in the dark.

As the door closed behind the officers, the full weight of the evening settled around me.

My eyes trailed around the room, searching for where the last of my energy fled.

Trounced from the events of the night and the dead-end Jake and I found ourselves marred in, I let Jake lock up and lead me back to his truck with little argument.

Chapter 17

"Molley, you really don't need to go to all this trouble," I protested for what felt like the hundredth time since arriving at her house. As she had the last ninety-nine times, Molley ignored me and dropped two fresh pillows on the queen-size bed in her upstairs guest room.

"Seriously," I continued, following her into the adjoining bathroom, where she pulled several towels of varying sizes from a small linen closet. "I'm fine with the couch. This...it's too much."

Molley turned and deposited the towel next to the sink.

"Bullshit."

I blinked.

Was this the peppy girl I knew in high school?

Molley was usually so put together, so strait-laced.

Not to say she didn't swear every now and again, but it was so rare that when a four-letter word did slip out, it threw me for a loop.

It wasn't what I expected to come out of the bubblegum lip gloss painted mouth of a bouncing blonde mini fashionista.

When my brain finally rebooted from its momentary short-circuit, Molley had moved on from the bathroom. I had to jog to catch up with her in the hall as she turned toward the stairs.

"I don't mind sleeping on the couch. I don't want to be a burden."

Molley halted on the stairs. She spun on her kitten heels to face me.

"Hanna, listen to me. You are not a burden. The grumpy lump that drove you here? That remains to be seen, but you? Never."

"I heard that!" came from the kitchen.

A smug smirk slid across Molley's face as she led me back down into the kitchen, where Jake and her husband, Will, stood in an odd sort of face-off. Jake posted up next to the fridge. Will leaned casually against the sink. Both men's muscled arms were folded tightly over their chests. Despite putting up with each other for more than six years, neither of the men in the room was too fond of the other.

"Besides," Molley thumbed in Jake's direction. "If you knew how frequently that one ended up on the couch at three am, you wouldn't be so eager to claim it for a sleeping space."

Molley's blue eyes sparkled with mischief, but it was Jake's curious gaze that pinned me in place.

"It's not that often," he protested.

"Oh, it really is," Molley interjected. "Won't go see someone about it either."

"What happened to doctor-patient confidentiality?"

"That," Molley said as Will pulled her snug against his chest, "would require you pay me."

Jake sent Molley a half-hearted glower that earned him a smirk in return.

I claimed a stool at the island to watch the two banter back and forth, utterly perplexed by their relationship.

Somehow, since high school, Jake and Molley went from hating each other's guts to thicker than thieves. If their coloring weren't so different, a stranger might see them and assume they were siblings.

And what was up with Jake sleeping on the couch? I thought he had a room in the basement.

Unsuccessfully suppressing a yawn, I rested my head in my palm.

With a gentle kiss to Molley's hair, Will slipped from the room to check on the babies. And just as quickly, the conversation shifted.

"So," Molley eyed me like a wolf eyed a skittish rabbit. "In light of everything going on, I called the foster family that agreed to take Lily. They've agreed to take her on early. Thought it might be a good idea to get our little girl out of town sooner rather than later."

Molley's sea-blue eyes never shifted from mine.

Even at midnight, she looked flawless, her eye makeup unsmudged and perfect after hours of wearing.

I couldn't even manage to apply liner and shadow without smearing it all over the place.

Silence stretched.

Molley wanted an answer.

I straightened on my stool.

"That's great, but I don't have a car, remember?"

Jake had to have told her the tale of how he ended up chained to me.

"I—" Molley stopped and pursed her lips. I could have sworn her eyes flitted in Jake's direction.

As if on cue...

"I'll drive you."

I turned accusing eyes on Jake.

They'd planned this.

Somehow.

"Even if it was available, your Maxima wouldn't make the drive. Not this time of year."

I frowned.

It was early October.

What did the time of year have to do with anything? There wouldn't be snow or anything in the mountains yet, would there? The ski resorts in the area wouldn't open for another two months.

My Maxima would be fine.

"I can't ask you to do that. What about your work?" I implored, sure I'd found the perfect excuse.

The thought of being stuck in a car with Jake for ten-plus hours sent an annoying shot of tingles racing over my skin. With my recent record of bad decisions, I couldn't trust myself for that long, alone with him in close quarters.

A muscled shoulder rose and fell like it was nothing.

How could he be so at ease? So nonchalant?

This wasn't a trip to the grocery store!

"Warren will cover for me. He'll understand, especially since it's you."

My eyes darkened.

"And what's that supposed to mean?' I folded my arms to lean forward on the island counter.

Again with the shoulder shrug.

"You're an old friend, Hann. Warren will understand."

Oh.

A traitorous piece of my heart shattered away from the whole.

Friends.

That was what I was to him.

I stared into dark cobalt, watching as the darker, near-black centers churned, obscuring the emotion behind them, leaving only a heated stare pinning me down.

That look didn't say we were friends.

Molley glanced between us, that smirk back on her painted lips, and pushed off the counter.

"Well, I'll leave you two to figure everything out. Night!"

The little blonde traitor disappeared down the hall.

I whirled away, tearing my eyes from Jake, looking anywhere but at those molten blue eyes.

"I should check on Lily."

"I don't mind driving you, Hann. You're not a burden. I'd feel better if you let me."

I froze in the doorway, glanced back over my shoulder, only to get caught once more in the web of Jake's stare, so sincere and packed with muddled emotion. He stood by the island, watching me.

"Why?"

That infuriating shoulder rose and fell.

"I don't know." A troubled frown tugged at his lips. "Just think about it, okay? Sleep well."

Jake's shoulder brushed mine as he passed.

"You too."

▲▲▲

I blinked up at the ceiling.

Why was it always the nights you needed rest the most that sleep became the most elusive?

Hours ticked away on the little bedside alarm clock as I tossed in the sheets, ears primed for the slightest creak of someone on the stairs, for Lily's muffled cry from one room over, anything that may signify danger and the need for flight.

Danger couldn't be far behind.

The last two days were born of nightmares. I knew the events of the past forty-eight hours would be waiting for me the moment I shut my eyes.

The sandman waited in the shadowy corners with a sinister grin, promising a full recap.

But I needed sleep, no matter what awaited me.

After days of running, the bits of bone and tissue holding me together ached with fatigue.

And who knew what lack of sleep would do to the little life growing inside of me.

As it did every time I thought of that seed, just beginning to sprout at my core, a tendril of fear shot through with excitement twisted in my gut.

What if it was Greg's?

What if it wasn't?

I squeezed my eyes shut on the thought, counted back from ten, focused on my breath.

Deep breaths.

In.

And out.

In...

A frustrated growl tore from my lips, and I flung back the covers.

I would not find sleep. Not there in that bed.

Might as well check on Lily.

The clock on the nightstand proved it to be too early to be up, but I couldn't sit still any longer.

My toes sunk deep into the plushy carpet as I padded down the hall to the room Lily shared with Molly and Will's daughter.

Maybe I'd curl up on the floor in there to sleep. God knows it would be soft enough.

The door to the nursery was cracked, allowing enough room for one to lean in to check on the sleeping babies without making the door squeak on its hinges.

Though, in Molley's house, I doubted anything squeaked.

Muted moonlight filtered through gauzy curtains over the two large, east-facing windows, casting the room in a soft blue light.

In the corner, the sound machine whirred, sending soothing ocean sounds to lull those around into slumber.

It must work. Both Lily and Gracie snoozed without a peep.

I stepped back out into the hall.

Now what?

Though my brain could use a good nap to help stitch all the frayed edges back together, my body was wired, craving movement, activity.

A challenge.

I tramped down the stairs, making as little noise as possible.

Molley and Will had done so much for me already. The last thing I wanted to do was wake them.

Crossing the foyer toward the back of the house, I let my fingers skirt along the surface of the maple side table, running along the wall. My stockinged feet skated over the polished wood floors.

If only I could have these floors in my studio.

Unable to resist, I executed a series of turns and spun around the corner into the hall. I slowed.

A light was on in the kitchen.

Geez, I knew Molley and Will had to be loaded to live in this house, but I didn't think they were leave-the-lights-on loaded.

I toed toward the corner and peered around.

Empty.

And the light wasn't coming from the kitchen.

I froze.

Molley and Jake sat close on the steps down to the lower porch in the backyard, their backs to the sliding glass door.

A thin stream of smoke pirouetted over their heads in sloping circles as it freestyle twisted into nothing.

What were they doing out there?

Molley's hand grazed Jake's back on its way to his shoulder. Her head fell against him in a way that spoke of an intimate knowledge of one another that spanned years.

I was halfway across the kitchen before realizing I'd moved.

I couldn't look away.

As easy as she fell against him, Molley pressed away.

With a pat on Jake's shoulder, she stood and said something I couldn't hear through the glass.

A thick plume of smoke rose over Jake's head in response.

Hesitating only a moment, like all she wanted was to return to Jake's side, Molley turned toward the house.

I watched her step falter as she spotted me.

Caught.

Sky-blue eyes widened. To Molley's credit, she only slowed for a second before stepping inside. A kind smile tilted her lips.

No sign of guilt shined in Molley's eyes.

"Can't sleep?" she asked as she moved to the coffee pot on the counter and pressed a series of buttons. A soft burble pulled from the device. Seconds later, a stream of dark, silky caramel-scented coffee dribbled into the pot.

I shook my head, unable to keep my eyes from straying back toward the porch where Jake sat alone.

Molley's eyes were too sharp for so early. She effortlessly fell into counselor mode.

"Everything okay? The girls wake you?"

"No...I don't know." Like a magnet, my eyes stuck on Jake's dark form.

Molley took a seat at the island. Her eyes never left me. She watched me like I was a puzzle she could solve if only she found the right pieces.

But I wasn't a puzzle, and the broken parts were long lost, shattered to dust the moment I heard the news of the crash.

"Do you think about him a lot?"

I bit my lips.

Why was she doing this?

I shifted around the island, putting space between us and Jake out of my line of sight.

A small guilty part of me tried to drag my eyes back in his direction.

My hip fell against the counter. Sighing, I raked a long, tangled mass of hair back from my face.

"More than I should," I admitted.

Every goddamn day.

Greg was the music in the world. Though his passions differed from mine and dragged him away from me, Greg had a way of pulling me from an all-consuming quagmire with the lightest of touches.

Molley's pink lips tugged down. Thin brows drew together.

Molley's hand found mine from across the island, settling over my fingers and squeezing them.

"You were together, what? Ten years? That's a long time, Hanna. It's okay for you to think about him. To miss him. I know how much Greg meant to you. We all do."

The world. Greg was my whole damn world.

"You don't have to hide how you miss him."

Molley let out a short bark of laughter as she took her hand back, brushing a bunch of tight curls behind her ear.

"Fuck, if anything happened to Will, I'd..." All signs of amusement melted from her face. A deep, very real fear settled in around her eyes.

"How do you do it? When it comes back?" It wasn't a secret that Will had been fighting cancer since he was a child. He'd been in remission the last four years, but just knowing it could come back at any second would leave me a tangled ball of anxiety. The thought that one day the person I loved could go in for a routine doctor's visit and find out he had months to live would be more than I could bear.

"Hope it doesn't," Molley said softly, a small, almost miserable smile on her lips. "All I can do is be here. Live every day. I can't spend every day thinking it might be the last. Our last kiss, touch. I'd go insane. So, I don't."

Molley studied me a moment.

"You can do the same, you know. Live, I mean. Greg would want you to. But it's okay to miss him."

The sliding door squeaked as it opened.

Tobacco and fresh air waft in ahead of Jake.

"You're up early." Jake's voice was rough and tight, as if he hadn't spoken in days.

"So are you," I met his dark gaze and was caught in their depths before I could look away.

Molley cleared her throat.

"So, you two come up with a plan?"

Plan?

"I can be ready by ten this morning, if that works for you, Hann," Jake said, like he was asking where I wanted to go for breakfast.

I shifted around the island's edge, away from Jake, searching for room to breathe, but found my new place just as devoid of oxygen.

"I can't leave today."

Dark eyes speared me.

"Why?"

A shiver shot through my body.

"I-My mirrors. For the studio. They're supposed to come today," I stammered.

"What time? I'm free most of the day. I can be there when they arrive."

Then why don't you take Lily to Montana?

A wave of guilt rose over my head. My shoulders sagged. Lily was my charge. I would be the one to take her to her new home, to keep her safe till she got there.

"I can't ask you to do that."

"You're not. I'm offering." Molley popped off her stool and grabbed a mug from the cabinet by the sink. As the last drop fell, she pulled the pot from the warmer.

"It's okay to accept help, Hanna."

Heat flooded my cheeks. I glanced over at Jake to find him watching me intently.

Molley set the coffee in front of me.

"I think I heard Gracie. Better grab her before she wakes Lily."

Awkward silence settled in Molley's wake as she disappeared down the hall.

Determined not to be the first to speak, I lifted the mug and took the tiniest of sips, deliberately avoiding Jake's gaze.

Jake stepped around the island to claim Molley's stool, placing himself directly in my line of sight over the rim of my mug.

He was about to step into a conversation I did *not* want to have with him, so I beat him to the punch.

"I didn't know you smoke."

Jake met my challenging stare, his mouth a thin line.

"I don't," he nearly growled as he raked both hands over his face and back through his mussed hair.

"Looked a lot like you were," I nodded toward the porch.

"I quit."

I raised a brow.

"I'm quitting," he relented.

With a nod, I let it go and took a sip of my coffee. I took the mug to the couch in the living room.

We all had our vices.

Jake followed me, dropping onto the opposite couch in front of the large windows looking out on the backyard.

Silence settled around us like a blanket.

"So."

No one should make leather cushions so comfortable.

How was I ever going to enjoy my second-hand fabric couch again?

"What now? Now that you're done with the army thing."

Did I say that? Did I really just ask that?

I wanted to flee, run back up the stairs, and hide in the guest room, but it was too late. The words were out.

I stared at Jake, taking in his relaxed posture as he lounged on the couch, one arm stretched over the back. Something in his face kept me from running back to my room like I knew I should. Held me in place.

For a moment, Jake said nothing, his brows drawn together, dark gaze pensive. I looked away but still felt his eyes on me like he was searching for something.

Darkness clung to his chiseled features, sinking into the grooves and angles of his face. The shadows and dim lighting cast Jake in sepia, the image of a man not quite whole.

I hated it.

In Jake's eyes, I saw the hopeful star he'd once been, the brooding soul he'd become—lost and wandering. Mixed in amongst it all, I caught glimpses of the fierce protector he'd been to me for the last few days.

It was dizzying.

Then light caught in his eyes, brightening the silvery gray swirls in the depths of the midnight pools, and the turmoil inside was carefully masked once more.

Jake's shoulders rose and fell with a sigh.

"Ya know," Jake drawled, "people keep asking that."

Jake stared out the window into the forlorn black.

Molley switched off the back porch light when she went back to bed.

Silence echoed in the space between us. I was convinced that was all the answer I was going to get. Conversation over. Door closed.

"I don't know," Jake admitted with a self-deprecating laugh. A difficult admission for a man who once thought he had the world at his feet. The unknowing weighed on his shoulders, an immovable stone crushing the man beneath.

My heart ached for him.

"I guess I'll just...keep working at Warren's 'til I figure everything out."

Head falling into my hand, I searched Jake's features, taking in the insecurity, uncertainty, and self-loathing that came through in his moment of vulnerability.

There was too much pain in his face. My fingers itched to reach across the distance and wipe it all away.

Where'd the carefree superstar go?

"Everything seems like a lot all at once."

Jake's head fell back with a sigh. Strong, blunted fingers scrubbed over his face.

"Yeah."

There was something else he wasn't saying beneath it all. Something that pulled at him and held him back. Deep down, I knew that hidden something was what brought the purpling hue to the space around his eyes and kept him up at night.

How long had this sat on his shoulders, festered in his mind?

"So," when Jake spoke next, the shadows vanished from his voice. "Ten work?"

And like that, the mood around us shifted.

Jake sat up on the couch, eyes fixed on me for the first time since we stepped into the room.

"I can push it back a little if that helps, but I've got to make a quick stop at the shop to—"

"Why are you doing this?" I cut him off, unable to stand the stark contrast between this kind, generous Jake and the boy I went to school alongside. What was he trying to prove?

Jake tilted his head and frowned.

"You don't need to," I continued, "I can rent a car." *Maybe...* "Or take the bus, or anything else. Why are you going so..."

"So what, Hanna?" Jake leaned toward me, elbows pressing into his knees, his own challenge embedded in his stare.

If I accepted, I knew I'd be making a mistake, but it was too late now.

"It's not like you. Not like the you I remember."

Jake tore his eyes away from me, shoved off the couch.

"People change."

Without another glance in my direction, Jake stormed from the room.

"I'll be out front at ten," Jake threw over his rigid shoulder before disappearing.

Great.

Nice going, Hann.

Chapter 18

I stared out at the street from my perch on Molley's front steps, feeling so out of place.

I couldn't remember the last time I'd waited on the porch steps for someone to pick me up, but there I was, fidgeting and nervous, unsure Jake would even show after all I'd said earlier that morning.

Lily sat quietly in her car seat beside me, occupied as she tried to snag the little button-sized flowers off the planter by the door. She had no idea the turmoil swirling inside me.

A minute ticked by.

The street remained empty.

I'm an idiot.

After everything Jake had done for me, I went and screwed it all up.

My toes flexed in my flats. I was eager to escape to my studio, lock the door, crank the music, and lose myself in movement—anything to erase the past few days.

Let Jake and Molley handle getting Lily to her new family.

Forget the intruder.

Definitely forget about Jake.

Almost on cue, the deep rumble of a truck sounded in the distance moments before a familiar Chevy pulled around the corner. The silver paint reflected the bright sun like some shining steed as it rumbled to the curb.

Lips pressed tight as I fought the urge to smile.

Jake wasn't a white knight in high school, but he definitely had been for me the last few days, or as close to it as I'd ever witnessed.

And what did I do?

Shoved it all back in his face because I was afraid of a feeling.

I refused to call it feelings.

Molley was right.

Greg would want me to live my life.

Unbidden, ice-blue eyes and an arrogant smirk flashed in my mind.

Tears pressed at my eyes as the memory of one night, one mistake with the wrong man filled my mind. Guilt swarmed.

It was too soon.

Greg's memory was too fresh.

God knows I'd already screwed up too many times to count in the last few months.

What would Greg's family think if they knew?

What would Misha think if she found out about Ethan?

Bile rose in my throat.

I couldn't do it. I couldn't—

A car door slammed.

"Everything okay?" Jake stood before me on the path, hands in his pockets, eyes soft.

I froze. Words wouldn't come.

Sensing my unease, Jake scooped up Lily's carrier and my small duffle with an athlete's grace.

My tongue pulled itself from the roof of my mouth.

"Why wouldn't it be?"

Jake looked unconvinced, but he turned back toward the truck anyway.

▲▲▲

The ride was torture.

Awkwardness slunk into the cab behind Jake and me and coiled around us like a deadly viper. The event of the night before threatened to suffocate us all if not dealt with soon. To top it all off, Lily decided she suddenly did not like car rides.

In the back seat, the baby shrieked at the top of her lungs.

No amount of cooing or comfort seemed to calm her.

I was ready to start ripping my hair out.

Desperate, I turned to Jake and found him unperturbed by the volume of Lily's orchestrations. His hand fell loosely over the top of the steering wheel as he stared out at the road.

I unbuckled and climbed into the back with Lily.

Big amber eyes blinked at me in surprise as I dropped onto the seat.

Oh. There you are.

"Hey, sweet girl," I cooed as I extracted a bottle of water and formula from the diaper bag on the floorboard.

Maybe she's hungry.

Hoping a little snack would ease the little tyke into a peaceful sleep, I screwed on the bottle cap and shook till the water turned milky.

"There you go."

I offered up the bottle like a sacred sacrifice to the gods. Breath breezed past my lips as Lily took the bottle without fuss.

I caught Jake's bright smile in the mirror.

"You really are good with her," he complimented.

Oh, so that's the game we're gonna play.

Last night never happened.

"Did…" the smile faltered on Jake's perfect lips.

"Hmm?" I cocked my head as I observed the flow of emotion filtering across Jake's face. What was going on in that brain of his?

"Nothing, it's…"

"No, go ahead," I pressed, meeting his eye in the mirror before he turned back to the road.

"Did you and Greg ever talk about kids? You don't have to answer that."

"Jake," I nearly choked as I swallowed back a wave of grief and confused emotion that surfaced like a sea monster from the deep.

"It's fine. And no, not really."

A crease formed in Jake's forehead.

I frowned, finding I didn't like that worried canyon in his skin.

I should have left it at that, let the conversation fizzle and die like my dreams of growing old with Greg, but something compelled me to go on.

"We were always busy, ya know?" I rolled my ankle where it hung off the front of the center console.

"Greg spent so much time out of country. When he was home, he was always preparing for the next trip."

"Sounds lonely."

Blinking, I tilted my head to meet Jake's eye in the mirror, surprised to see recognition and understanding shining back from their depths.

I shrugged and looked away. Focusing back on Lily, I tilted the bottle higher so she could get the last drops.

"Sometimes," I admitted.

Loneliness never crossed my mind when Greg was home. Even when we went days barely seeing each other in passing, Greg had a way of letting me know he was there, that he was thinking of me, that chased away even the possibility of despondency brought about by time apart.

"What about you and *Gina*?"

Despite the lilting taunt in my voice, I really wanted to know. *Really* wanted to know that Jake hadn't ever considered having kids with that woman. Something about the idea made my skin crawl.

Jake deserved someone kind who cared about him. Someone—

I don't know, but definitely not someone like Gina.

It wasn't like I ever really thought about having kids myself. I got my kid fix through teaching dance, with the added bonus of being able to step away at the end of the hour when the children were exhausted and cranky.

For some reason, it mattered if Jake wanted kids, especially if he wanted them with his obnoxious ex-wife.

It still sounded strange in my head, Jake having an ex-wife. Jake having a wife at all was a foreign concept to me, though I felt the same way about being a widow.

To me, Jake was still that cocky boy from high school.

"Gina wasn't the having-kids kind."

The heck did that mean?

But Jake didn't elaborate, and I didn't ask.

▲▲▲

We stopped in Missoula mid-afternoon for food and gas.

Sending a smile back over my shoulder to the cashier at the combination Mcdonalds-Kwikstop, I stepped out of the glacial AC into the parking lot.

The sky was clear blue overhead, stretching cloudless to the snowcapped mountains in the distance. I stopped for a moment to bask in the sun.

It was beautiful.

Even in town, I got the sense of the wild that still clung to much of Montana. Bright pines and fir trees were everywhere.

Any direction I looked, craggy mountains stretched on the

horizon, reaching with outstretched arms for the swath of blue sky overhead.

I glanced down at the cracking asphalt beneath my feet at the wild that fought to reclaim the pavement. Moss and grass shot up through the cracks they'd managed to wedge themselves into.

Montana was the kind of place a girl could get lost.

Bag of greasy burgers and fries in one hand, sugary treats and jerky in the other, I absorbed my surroundings like a sponge, relishing in the virility we missed out on, even three hours west in Spokane.

Sucking down a lung full of chilly air, I scanned the busy lot.

A couple blocks off the interstate, the gas station got plenty of traffic, both local and travelers passing through. Cars and trucks filled most of the pump stations.

On the far side of the lot, Jake removed the gas nozzle from the truck's tank. The sun caught in his dark hair as he turned, shooting it full of ruby and amber-gold streaks. Jake's dark eyes scanned the lot, squinting against the sun as he assessed each of the other vehicles in the vicinity.

God, that man's nice to look at.

Muscles in his arms and upper body fought against the confines of his tshirt. Worn jeans hung low on his lips, concealing what I realized to be the pistol I noticed the night before.

Memories from high school said Jake packing should have been more than concerning, but oddly enough, as his dark gaze zeroed on me, I felt a warm security wrap around me, knowing he had the gun.

I smiled back at Jake as I raised the bag of greasy burgers in greeting.

Jake met me at the truck door, pulling it open. I ducked under his arm to dump the sweets onto the front seat.

"Ready to go?" Jake asked, peeking over my shoulder to check out the haul.

Easing the paper bag from my hand, Jake snuck a couple fries.

"Just about. I need to check on Lily."

"Already done. All clear," Jake said around a mouthful of fries.

I stopped, One foot on the step up into the back seat.

"Oh.

Jake changes diapers?

I fought the urge to climb in and check his handy work as my heart gave a strange little skip. A hoard of butterflies took off in my stomach.

With how easily Jake handled Lily's tantrums, he was probably a pro at diaper changes.

Better than me, anyway.

▲▲▲

"The heck did you do to the fries?" I stared down at the two half-empty cartons of french fries as I pulled them from the bag and settled them in the cupholders.

Jake gave a sheepish shrug but didn't take his eyes off the road as he pulled from the parking lot.

I dug into my cheeseburger.

"God, yes!"

A smirk stretched Jake's lips as I swallowed greasy goodness

222

and went in for another bite.

My eyes narrowed on Jake as he went in for another fry.

"What?"

"Nothing. You don't strike me as the fast-food type," Jake eyed my soft pink yoga pants.

My eyes drifted to the window as I licked ketchup from the side of my pinky.

"In most cases, I'm not. But you gotta love road food.

I counted the cars behind us in the side mirror.

The road wasn't crowded, but with the freeway stretching to three lanes through the city, everyone seemed to pack together, each trying to get ahead.

"I like that." My head lifted in surprise to catch Jake still watching me. He sent me a wink as he popped another fry into his mouth and turned back to the road.

Heat rising in my cheeks, I let a small smile slip as I returned to my burger.

The sky and landscapes around us were spectacular, unobstructed by tall buildings, airplanes, or the constant buzz of news helicopters. Just trees and mountains and wide open spaces.

"I ran into Keith Liniquart."

A crease shot between my brows.

Should I know who that is?

I turned back to Jake with a question in my eyes.

The name touched a fuzzy memory deep in my mind from a simpler time.

"The assistant coach?"

Jake nodded.

"He's the head coach now." Jake's voice was light, casual, but the apple in his throat bobbed.

"How's he doing?"

A shrug.

"He wants me to come by and check out a practice, give some pointers."

My brows flew up my forehead.

Why was he telling me this?

Dark eyes peeked over to gauge my reaction.

Something fragile ringed those eyes.

Why did my opinion matter so much to him?

No matter.

This game was safe.

I could play this game.

I plastered an enthusiastic smile on my face.

"That's awesome! You're going to do it, right?"

Jake's mouth pulled to the side, noncommittal.

"What?" I leaned forward, invading his space a bit to rest my arms on the center console. "You'd be a great coach."

"I don't know." A big hand scrubbed the back of Jake's neck.

I watched the lines in the muscle there grow more defined and nearly swallowed my tongue.

"It's kind of pathetic, isn't it? The washed-up QB crawling back to the one place he'd been somebody?"

My back shot straight. A troubled frown tugged at my lips.

"Is that really what you think?"

Jake's jaw tightened.

I resisted the urge to push for an answer. It wasn't my job to fix Jake's mental and emotional hang-ups. Jake's problems were Jake's problems.

"I think you should call him."

So much for staying out of it.

"Maybe."

It felt like a brush-off.

My lips pursed.

I bit the tip of my tongue to hold back my retort as I turned toward the window.

If you don't want advice, don't ask.

I glared at the cars as they passed.

Jake was not my problem. Why was I letting him get to me?

A flash of rust in the mirror caught my eye. My mouth went dry as the Sahara. Any humor in my face slipped away like a greasy patty over a skillet.

No.

It can't be.

Setting my burger aside, I leaned forward for a better look, glancing back over my shoulder.

It had to be my imagination.

How did that guy find us?

"What is it?"

Jake caught on to my mood shift in seconds. It should have bothered me how quickly he was able to read me.

Cobalt blues darted to the mirrors.

"I think we're being followed."

"Fuck. Alright." An authoritative calm slid over Jake as he switched lanes. His shoulders relaxed, his keen eyes immediately finding the van in the rearview mirror before turning back to the road ahead. A booted foot pressed the gas, and we eased ahead of a semi.

"What do we do?" I turned in my seat to peer out the back.

"I've got this."

Wow.

The speedometer crept up on triple digits as we shot around a curve.

Without my say-so, my hand shot across the invisible line I'd drawn between Jake and me and latched on to his thigh. Jake's hand dropped from the wheel to close around mine.

As we passed behind a large outcropping, the truck slipped into the right-hand lane. The semi between us and the van, we were obscured just long enough for Jake to jerk the wheel at the last second and send the truck veering off at the next off-ramp, too quick for anyone in pursuit to follow.

Jake barely slowed at the stop sign at the bottom of the ramp as he turned onto a local road then immediately onto a state highway as we passed under the interstate.

Warm, calloused fingers squeezed mine in an unrelenting grip like Jake needed the connection to me as much as I needed one to him in that moment.

A mile down the road, Jake lifted his foot from the gas, allowing the truck to slow back to a reasonable speed.

I peered out the back window, finding nothing but empty road in our wake.

"Clear," I sighed, dropping back into my seat only long enough to unhook my seatbelt.

In a handful of quick movements, I fell into the back seat to check on Lily.

I sagged into the bench seat.

Asleep.

At least someone wasn't traumatized by our high-speed chase.

In the front seat, Jake fished his phone out of his jeans pocket and tossed it back to me.

"Do we have service?" Jake asked as I fumbled to catch the device.

I ran my finger across the screen.

"Yep."

"Good. Pull up Maps. Find us an alternate route."

My brow creased.

"Why?"

Couldn't we just circle back in an hour?

Jake raised a brow at me in the mirror.

"Settle in, Darlin'. We're taking the scenic route."

Chapter 19

Night has a way of creeping in in the Northwest as the year nears its close, leaving you with little time to prepare. One second, the sky is bright and blue. Blink, and it's shot through with orange and purple. The next second, it's darker than Satan's asshole.

I stared out the windshield at the single-lane road as we moved through sagebrush fields.

Montana was a completely different place after dark.

Gone were the beautiful vistas and the bright sky stretching from horizon to horizon. All around us was black, save for the swath in our headlights as we sliced through the night.

Overhead, a symphony of stars dazzled in the inky black.

I suppressed a yawn as I checked the time on the dash.

Almost four hours passed since our last stop for gas.

An uncomfortable pressure grew low in my belly.

I had to pee.

"Maybe we should stop for the night," I suggested.

Jake looked worse than I felt. The skin around his eyes was

drawn and tight, purple in the deep hallows underneath. I had a feeling he'd gotten less sleep than me in the last few days.

A pang of guilt shot through me.

Jake wouldn't be in this mess if it weren't for me.

"I can drive."

Dark eyes flitted to the phone balanced on his thigh, the Maps app still open, though we'd last service and GPS almost an hour ago.

"There should be a decent-sized town in about an hour," Jake said, ignoring my offer. "We should be able to find a hotel there." In a second's glance, he took me in before turning back to the road.

"You should sleep. There should be a sweatshirt in the back."

"I'm okay," I insisted, suppressing another yawn.

Eyes still on the road, Jake reached into the back seat and pulled a sweatshirt from the floorboards.

"Here."

"You still have this?" I turned the sweatshirt to run my fingers over a gold and blue high school football logo. A reminiscent smile ghosted across my lips.

When Jake and the rest of the football players weren't in jerseys or their letterman jackets, every one of them could usually be found in the navy blue sweatshirts all the school athletes owned.

"Found it when I got back, among other things," Jake said, pulling a face that said he'd rather not discuss what else he found in his truck after leaving it sitting for years.

So, it's not just me who finds the truck to be a bit of a time capsule. Interesting.

I bundled the sweatshirt and wedged it between my head and the window. Fingertips pressed to the icy glass. I focused on the chill that seeped into my hand before letting it drop to my lap.

Might as well get a few minutes sleep.

At least in the truck, with Jake right there, I didn't have to worry about being disturbed by any unwanted intruders.

Lashes fell against my cheeks.

Ah.

"Hey, before you pass out, you mind opening the jerky?"

"Sure."

Lugging myself off the window, I snatched the jerky off the floorboards and tore the top of the packaging.

A tanging cloud wafted up from the bag.

"Oh, God!" I threw the package of jerky at Jake as bile rose up into my throat.

My finger found the button for the window.

Frigid air whipped against my cheeks. My nose cleared, filling instead with the crisp scent of grass, sagebrush, and coming snow, but it was too late. The damage was done.

"Pull over!" I choked as my throat clogged.

The truck hadn't come to a full stop when I threw the door open and stumbled into the ditch along the side of the road.

I spewed the contents of my stomach into the weeds.

Coughing, I dropped to my knees and vomited again and again.

A car door slammed.

I spit into the dirt.

Gah, bleh! I hate puking.

The acrid taste of bile clung to the walls of my mouth.

Tips of my hair dangled dangerously close to the mess I left in the dirt.

A warm hand settled on my back. The wavy curtains on either side of my face pulled back as Jake drew my hair back over my shoulders.

"You okay?" he asked softly. "What was that?"

I dropped back on my butt and leaned into Jake, registering for the first time just how cold it was out.

Shivers shot down my bare arms.

"Here." Jake pulled the athletics sweatshirt over my head. I slid my arms into the too-long sleeves like a toddler learning to dress herself.

"Thanks." I drew in a deep breath of night air.

"Hanna?

"Hmm?" My eyes fell closed as I held on to the heat wafting off Jake's body.

"Are you okay?" Jake's calloused hand cupped my shoulder.

"...Yeah."

"Is it food poisoning?" Jake asked, his arm tightening around my shoulders.

"Nope."

What's with the twenty questions?

Can't we just get back in the car?

"Here, drink this." Jake pressed a water bottle into my hands before settling into the dirt behind me.

I took a big gulp, swished, and spit to clear my mouth. Who cared if I ruined any lady-like image of me Jake might have in his head.

Sipping the cool, clean liquid, I pressed further into Jake's side, needing his warmth to settle the quakes still racing through my body.

"You're not telling me something."

I pulled in a shaky breath through warbling lips and laughed.

"Hann?"

Tears pricked the corners of my eyes.

"I think...I'm pregnant."

Jake's arm around me tensed.

A long moment passed.

"Is it...?" Ethan's or Greg's.

"I don't know."

"Think you're ready to get back in the truck?"

What?

"Depends."

I turned to fix Jake with a leveling stare.

"Are you done with the jerky?"

Jake pressed to his feet, bringing me with him, his arm still around me. He steered me toward the open passenger-side door.

"Pretty sure I'm done with all food for a while." A hint of amusement lit Jake's eyes in the moonlight.

My cheeks heated, mortified.

"Sorry." I climbed into the passenger seat, intentionally avoiding looking at Jake.

Jake rested an arm against the car over my head, leaning into my space.

"Don't be." He brushed a strand of hair back off my face.

"Just get some sleep. I'll find us somewhere to stay for the night."

Unbidden tears sprang up in the corners of my eyes. I forced a small smile as I fought to hold back the waterworks.

"Thank you."

Jake's mouth rose in a lopsided smile in answer.

"Anytime."

▲▲▲

An hour and a half further down the road, Jake pulled the truck into the rut-filled parking lot of a little motel in a town barely large enough to have its own gas station.

Jake pulled the keys from the ignition.

"Lock the doors. If anyone besides me comes near, blast the horn."

Seriously?

"Do you think—"

"No. Just humor me."

Jake disappeared to check in to the motel.

Alone in the truck with Lily, the darkness pressed in on all sides. Every shadow and shift of light made me jump. As the minutes ticked by, my mind invented noises to send me searching for invisible assailants, but I pursed my lips when Jake appeared in the exterior light of the motel and the muscles in my shoulders eased.

The rooms—yes, rooms plural—were much what I expected from a roadside motel in the middle of nowhere: cramped, outdated, under-stocked, but clean. And after nearly twelve hours on the road, clean was all I cared about.

Stepping into one of the two rooms, I set Lily, still in her carrier, on the floor, dropped the single small bag Jake let me carry from the car on the chair against the wall, and collapsed on the floral print bed, unsure if I'd be able to get up even if I had to.

The bed wasn't exactly comfortable, but it felt so good to stretch out.

When I opened my eyes, Jake stood in the doorway, his shoulders filling the space, arms folded like he could hold off the night's chill through sheer will if he wanted to.

After the day we'd had, I had no doubt he could if he put his mind to it.

My cheeks warmed as I sat up.

"It's not exactly the Hilton," Jake eased the door closed and pulled Lily from her car seat.

I shrugged and wrinkled my nose.

"Those places are always so snooty anyway. I can watch her," I objected as Jake adjusted Lily against his shoulder and lifted the diaper bag. "You should sleep. You've been driving all day."

Jake was shaking his head before I could finish. He stepped toward the door.

"I'll be fine. Get some rest. Back on the road by eight."

I huffed and folded my arms over my chest but stayed silent, putting up no further protest.

Jake stopped in the doorway and turned to laugh at the irritated draw of my mouth and brows. A smooth, caramelized sound pulled from deep in his chest. The corners of my lips lifted.

"Sweet dreams, darlin'." I shook my head at the endearment.

"You too, cowboy."

▲▲▲

By noon the next day, we rolled into Miles City, a little city that screamed of cowboys and years of history. Bars and little boutiques lined the main street, housed in two-story brick buildings that looked like they had fallen out of a Clint Eastwood movie.

Sitting in the gas station parking lot, a cloud settled around me as I watched Jake fill the tank, knowing that when the car started next, he would be driving the short distance to Lily's new home.

Already, the address was plugged into Jake's phone in the cup holder.

Lily slept in the back seat, at peace.

In the front, I searched the lot around us.

All day, I felt eyes on my back, waiting for me to let down my guard.

I kept expecting to look up and find that rusted-out van approaching or the man from the other night outside my car window.

After more than twenty-four hours on the road, my nerves were shot. I couldn't wait to take a nice long nap after we dropped Lily off, but the thought of not having her put me just as on edge as the men on our tail.

One look at Jake's tense, rock-solid shoulders, the purple shadows under his eyes, I knew he was just as exhausted. Despite all that, Jake's dark eyes stayed laser-sharp as he scanned the parking lot, pausing after every pass to peek into the truck at Lily.

On one such pause, I caught Jake's eye and offered up a slight smile that he quickly returned.

"Ready?" He asked, climbing back behind the wheel.

"I—" My answer caught behind my teeth. Before I could blink, tears pressed at my eyes.

A half-hysterical laugh burst from my lips as the tears slipped free.

"No." I swiped at my tears as Jake's hand crossed over the center console.

"I'm okay, I promise," I waved off his concern, pressing a smile onto my lips.

Jake's hand fell onto my knee.

"It's okay to miss her."

"I know. I don't know why I'm crying," I admitted. Jake's thumb drew circles on the crook of my knee, sending tantalizing thrills shooting over my skin with every touch.

Unbidden, more tears filled the corners of my eyes.

If Jake didn't stop that nice guy thing, I wouldn't be able to step away when I needed to.

The truck pulled off the highway just outside town onto a long, dusty driveway. We passed under a twisting archway. Corder Ranch stretched across the top in what appeared to be hundreds of welded horseshoes.

Wood fences circled the flowing yellow fields, dividing up the property. Cattle and horses dotted the distant hills.

Up on a rise, a log cabin-style home stood tall. A thin smattering of bedraggled firs shielded the structure from the wind, the only trees in sight.

It was perfect.

Plenty of room for a girl to run and explore, far from the noise and dangers of the city.

Jake pulled up near the porch next to an old pickup with Dave's Feed Store printed in faded blue lettering on the side.

Silence settled around us as we stared up at the large house.

What next?

How exactly did you go about delivering a baby to its new home? Was there some special kind of protocol? Should we check out the place before bringing Lily inside? Make sure it's safe? Or do we just hand her off?

Luckily, our next move was made for us.

The front door flew open, and a middle-aged, plump woman with curly brown hair scooted out onto the wrap-around porch in her house slippers. A big, expectant smile lit her jovial face.

A tall, weather-worn man followed close behind the woman, securing a trucker's cap over his thinning, gray hair as soon as he passed under the threshold onto the porch.

With no other option, I eased open my door and stepped from the truck, sending Jake one last nerve-filled glance.

"Hanna?" the woman greeted me from the edge of the porch, her plump arms going around one of the beams at the top of the porch steps.

She had the look of a woman who'd survived many battles and was used to taking care of herself, a warrior in her own right, though as she took in Jake and me and our bedraggled appearances, worry swam in her eyes. Her bright smile dimmed.

For some reason, I wanted to put that light back in her face. She looked like someone who deserved that brightness in her life.

"That's me. You must be Dawn and Mark Corder."

A cordial smile curled my lips.

The last hour of our drive, I studied Lily's file extensively, trying to learn as much as I could to ease the unexpected concern that bubbled up inside me upon waking that morning.

The woman's smile broadened once more. In a rush, she released the beam and descended the stairs.

"That we are. How was your drive? You both look exhausted."

My eyes drifted to Jake. How much did we want to tell them? How much did they know?

Jake took over the conversation.

"More scenic than expected, but not bad."

"Well, that's Montana for you," Mark said from his place on the porch.

The corner of Jake's mouth quirked upward.

"I think we have someone in the truck who'd love to meet you both."

Dawn let out a little squeal of excitement.

Jake really could be charming when he wanted to be.

"Oh yes! We've been waiting for her. Mark has everything ready for her."

A smile cracked across my lips as I watched the joy blossom through crumbling doubt on both Dawn's and Mark's faces. The doubt that settled around my heart in the last few miles of the drive evaporated into the thin Montana air.

I turned to pull Lily from the truck and found Jake already there, Lily burbling in his arms. With ease and so much care, Jake passed Lily to me for one last hug.

After a long nap in the car, Lily was all smiles as we turned to her new family.

Lily's gummy grin widened as she caught sight of Dawn.

"Oh, she's darling!" Dawn cooed as she eagerly took Lily into her arms. A plump fingertip ran down Lily's nose and over her rosy cheeks.

Another chunk of my earlier anxiety chipped off and tumbled away.

Lily would be okay with Dawn and Mark.

Happy even.

With so much land to explore, who wouldn't be?

Chapter 20

"I'm going to miss her," I said as we rolled down the dirt drive away from Dawn and Mark's home later that afternoon. Dawn insisted we stay for lunch, and after one last tear-filled goodbye, Jake and I were on our way.

In the rearview mirror, I watched the log house on the hill grow smaller.

Mark waved farewell from the porch; his slim frame leaned up against one of the porch beams.

Jake gave a rueful smile.

"I thought you might."

We stopped where the dirt road met the highway to let a shiny black sedan speed past.

In the rearview, Mark straightened as his eyes followed the car down the road, his slim shoulders rigid beneath his flannel shirt. The corners of my mouth fell.

When I turned back to the road, the car was gone. Only empty asphalt flowed over the next rise.

"She'll be okay," Jake assured as he turned toward town, "They're good people."

"I know."

Molley wouldn't let Lily go to a family that would mistreat her. After watching Dawn with Lily as we devoured heaping bowls full of stew, I was fully confident in her ability to care for Lily. Dawn was a natural mother.

"How come they don't have kids of their own?" I wondered.

Wheat fields flew by in shades of sunny gold and brown beyond the truck's windows.

Jake's hand dropped over mine on the center console.

"For some people, it's just not in the cards." He squeezed my fingers. When I looked up, Jake grinned at me, but melancholy and regret circled in his eyes. I wanted desperately to know what put it there but held my tongue.

It wasn't my place.

He probably just missed Lily.

Jake didn't let go of my hand.

"So, I was thinking." I cocked my head in his direction, my feet folding up beneath me. Even with the heat on, my toes were always cold if left immobile too long.

"I have an old army buddy who's living just outside of Bighorn. He said we could stay the night if we're in the area. It doesn't get us much closer to home, but..."

I smiled and squeezed Jake's hand as he started to ramble.

"It sounds perfect."

I didn't know how much longer I could sit still in the truck anyway.

My muscles ached from disuse, begging to move and stretch.

A genuine smile met my approval, the first one I'd seen on him that actually reached his eyes.

Something almost like butterflies stirred inside me, but I refused to dwell too long on the feeling.

Probably just gas.

Or morning sickness.

When we got back, Jake and I would each go our separate ways, but even as I denied the butterflies at my core, I caught myself wishing to seek out more of those sunshine smiles.

▲▲▲

Jake's army buddy lived in a converted apartment over a utility barn on a working horse ranch fifteen miles outside of town. A large second-story deck overlooked a field full of mares and their foals.

Brent Joyner was the last thing I expected when Jake said we would be staying with an old army buddy.

Brent was neither old nor did he look like he'd ever been a part of any rigidly structured organization, let alone the army.

Long-haired and hollow-cheeked, Brent looked like he might actually be thinner than the fence lines around the outside of the ranch he spent so many days repairing.

The man laughed easily and couldn't keep from badgering and ribbing Jake every chance he got, despite the fact Jake could easily put the man on the ground.

On the second-story deck, Jake and I sat in handcrafted

Adirondack chairs around a blazing fire.

Brent's lady friend—his description for her upon introductions—Tallulah had her chair scooted as close to Brent's as she could manage, a curtain of straight, raven hair glided over her shoulder to brush against the back of their hands where they were intertwined between the arms of their chairs. Dressed in jeans and an oversized, plaid shirt that looked way too big to be borrowed from Brent, Tallulah looked every bit like she belonged in the wilds of Montana.

While I had my stockinged feet bundled tight under a lap throw, snagged from the back of the leather couch just inside the sliding doors, Tallulah's painted toes stood out bare against the dark stained wood of the deck, unbothered by the night's chill.

Stars twinkled overhead in a sky so clear I couldn't help but stare up into it.

From the moment we arrived, Jake and Brent were lost in conversation, reminiscing over their time in the army and their many adventures.

I listened intently, soaking up every detail.

It was interesting hearing Brent talk about Jake.

It seemed Jake's time with the army acted as the genesis for this new Jake sitting beside me. In Brent's stories, Jake wasn't the arrogant footballer I remembered from high school, but a confident young man, desperately trying to improve and find a place.

"I swear, Hanna, you should have seen him," Brent laughed. "This bull was pissed when we pulled up, but Stevens just had to prove he could kick it with the locals."

"Oh no," I smiled across the fire, pulling the blanket tighter

E. Collins

"Okay," Brent admitted, raising his hands. "There may or may not have been a woman involved."

"With Jake? You don't say!" My eyes widened with humor as I glance at the brooding man beside me.

"Yeah, yeah, can we leave out all the lovesick puppy crap?" Jake griped as he relaxed back into his chair, one hand around the neck of his beer bottle as it dangled over the arm of his chair.

Jake stared up at the stars, just as mesmerized by them as I was, but I could still see the slight upturn of his lips.

"Aw, but Jakey, that's the best part."

On the other side of the fire, Brent guffawed, slapping his leg.

"I like this one, Stevens. Not sure how you convinced her to stick around, but I like her."

"Of course you do," Jake said as he stood, sending a quick wink in my direction as he finished the last of his beer.

"Anyone need anything?" Jake called as he crossed to the door. A chorus of "no's" and "I'm good's" echoed behind him.

"Well," Tallulah chimed in her husky voice as Jake slid the door open, making him pause. "Maybe another blanket for Hanna? She looks like you dipped her in the creak. I swear, do you let the girl eat?"

Jake tensed as all eyes turned to me.

"I'm fine, seriously. But thank you." I glanced at Tallulah, more than a little unsettled by her observation.

Was I eating enough?

Jake stared at me from the doorway.

Okay. Staring was the wrong word.

Dark, cobalt eyes skirted up my frame and over my face before landing on my eyes. I stared back, unabashed by the appreciative gleam in the depths of Jake's eyes, not caring that we were very much not alone.

"I've got that sweatshirt inside if you want it," Jake's voice turned sultry, the rasping at the edges like little burrs catching in a wool sweater.

Damn him!

Heat crept up my neck.

"I'm good," I ground out. Knowing eyes watched from across the fire, amusement dancing with the firelight in their depth.

I ignored Brent and Tallulah as they whispered to each other.

There's nothing to see here, people.

"You two seem close," Brent commented as Jake disappeared into the apartment. Fingers twining through Tallulah's, Brent relaxed back into his chair.

"Do we?" I feigned ignorance.

Brent gave a nod as he lifted his beer to his lips.

"Closer than I've ever seen Stevens with a woman. And I knew Gina. You've heard about her, right?"

My shoulders tensed at the mention of Jake's ex. I gave a stiff nod.

"Real piece of work, that one. If I knew it weren't still such a sore spot for 'im, I'd tell you all about her. So, how'd ya'll meet?"

E. Collins

I blinked at both the flood of information and the sudden shift in conversation. My mind twisted, trying to make sense of it all.

Jake was still messed up over Gina?

Was that what he and Molley were talking about the other night on the porch?

The hell did that she-devil put Jake through?

I let out an awkward cough, realizing I'd been silent a beat too long.

"High school, actually."

Jake stepped back onto the porch.

"Ah, so you knew All-State Jake." An unattractive snort burst past my lips.

"Is that really what you called him?"

"That and Brady." Ouch.

Knowing how the nickname must have stung the fallen football star, I glanced up at Jake, catching the tail end of a grimace as it vanished behind an easy smile.

"Hey, never would have made it to state without the prettiest cheerleaders on the sidelines," Jake joked, sending a playful wink my way that did more to my insides than I cared to admit.

Jake pressed the sweatshirt I said I didn't need into my hands as he claimed his seat next to me.

And my face went cherry red.

Thanks, Jake. Thanks a lot.

With the light streaming out through the sliding glass door, there was no hiding my new coloring.

I slid my arms into the oversized sleeves but refused to pull it all the way on, afraid to add more kindling to the fire.

"Cute," Tallulah laughed, "the cheerleader and the football star. So, how long have you been together? Any secret hookups beneath the bleachers you care to divulge."

Jake tensed beside me. I winced a second too late, remembering why Jake looked so uncomfortable.

He dated a cheerleader in high school, but it hadn't been me.

"Actually..."

"No!" Tallulah's dark eyes went wide as she realized the true status of Jake and my relationship. "Girl, you can't be serious."

She turned on Jake.

"What's wrong with you?"

Jake looked like a deer might in the headlights of his truck, frozen, unsure how to react to get himself to safety.

"Easy, Lulu," Brent massaged Tallulah's palm. "Not all of us are so quick on the draw."

The heck did that mean?

Tallulah stole Brent's beer and took a swig before sending an apologetic smile in our direction.

"Sorry. Too many romance novels!" Tallulah laughed and rolled her eyes.

Conversation ease back into safer waters. In seconds, I zoned out, losing track of the topic.

My head fell back to count the stars, tracing patterns between them until my eyes drifted closed.

"Hanna?" My eyes batted open lazily. I peered up at Jake.

"Let's get you inside." Jake pulled me to my feet. Brent and Tallulah had already moved into the living room.

The coals in the fire pit flickered dimly, more ash than fire.

"Goodnights" were quick and in passing as beer bottles and paper plates were tossed in the trash.

"Guest room is at the end of the hall," Brent said. "If you want, we can make up the couch for Jake."

"No," I insisted. "It's fine. Wouldn't be the first time we've had to share a room," I added with a peek in Jake's direction, knowing he'd remember the countless away games where the cheerleaders and the football team had to sleep in the opposing team's gym due to lack of funding or the unavailability of affordable hotel accommodations.

While the girls and the boys were supposed to sleep on opposite ends of the gymnasium, many bent the rules to find a space near their significant others.

Greg didn't do organized sports—didn't have time with everything going on at home with Misha and his classes—so I never participated in the rule-bending, but I knew Jake and Molley often snuck off together once the lights went out.

With one last goodnight, Jake followed me down the hall.

▲▲▲

I stared up at the ceiling, blinking into the darkness, acutely aware of the heat radiating off Jake's body, only inches away in the full-sized bed.

So, I thought with dismal amusement, *this is becoming a trend.*

Falling asleep did not seem to be a problem for Jake. He drifted off as soon as his head hit the pillow.

Lucky bastard.

Steady breathing permeated from the other side of the bed like a vindictive taunt.

I rolled onto my side and fixed my eyes on the wall.

What were those tricks people used to force themselves to fall asleep?

Somehow, I doubted counting sheep would help.

Sheep and deep breathing couldn't push aside the fact that someone was following me. Or the ache in my chest after giving Lily up, knowing another little one would be coming soon.

What would it be like, raising a baby on my own? Diaper changes and late-night feedings, no one there to help shoulder it all, to lean on when things got tough.

Lily was better off with Dawn and Mark. A part of me wondered if maybe the little life sprouting inside me would be better off with a family like that, far away from me and whatever creep decided to make me his new target of creep-tastic affection.

With so much going on, how could I possibly just shut off my brain for eight hours?

It wasn't going to happen.

I zeroed in on the night sounds around me.

Wind whipped against the side of the building, causing the room and boards to screech their objections into the twilight.

Somewhere, water dripped slowly from a leaky faucet.

In the distance, I imagined wolves calling to each other, because that's what happened in Montana, right? The wild lived to be wild.

There, in the dark, I would have given anything to escape all that was going on back home, leave everything, family, friends, my studio, my past, and start over somewhere new.

But even as the thought filtered through my mind, I knew it would never happen. I couldn't leave Misha, not now that Greg was gone. Running away from my past would be as easy as outrunning the sun. It just couldn't be done.

No.

I'd have to learn to live with it all, starting with my little stalker problem.

First thing, when we got back to Spokane, I'd call the police officer from the other night to see if they'd found anything.

I held my breath as Jake flopped over in his sleep, pulling the blankets and sheets with him. I was left with little more than a corner of the blankets to squeeze under.

My fingers closed around the edge of the blanket, ready to tug back my fair share, when Jake let out a soft, strangled sound that almost, almost, sounded like a word.

Breath slid slowly over my lips. Frozen, I listened, convinced that whatever caused the uncharacteristically Jake sound passed without incident.

A large hand shot out from under the covers and clamped around my wrist.

"Jake."

I rolled over and propped myself up so I was half seated as a second strangled cry broke from Jake's lips. His hand tightened around my wrist.

His eyes were closed, still sleeping.

"Jake." I closed my free hand over Jake's tense grip, wrapped around my arm, and tried to wake him gently. The last thing I needed was for him to wake up thrashing and accidentally get myself smacked.

I edged closer. My knees brushed the skin over his ribs.

"Jake, wake up."

His head flopped to the other side. Messy brown hair fell over his forehead that creased with anxiety caused by whatever tormented Jake in his sleep. He showed no sign of waking.

I couldn't just sit there and let him ride out the nightmare, even if his thrashing about wasn't a threat to my safety.

The soft, guttural cries slipping past his lips tore at my heart.

I had to wake him.

There was no other option.

And that meant getting closer.

I'm gonna get myself hit.

Resignation fell from my lips on a sigh.

I pressed my free hand to the center of Jake's chest.

"Hey, Jake, wake up." My hand rubbed circles into Jake's sternum as I tried—unsuccessfully—to ignore the toned muscle spreading out in every direction. A dusting of freckles peeked through sparse, light brown hairs that curled around my fingers.

Jake's fingers flexed on my wrist.

Please don't break my arm!

Leaning closer, fingertips skirted over the crease in Jake's brow, down his temple.

A microscopic smile tilted his lips before his brow puckered once more.

Jake shot up, eyes wide with horror, as his brain fought to process his surroundings.

I ripped my hand away.

Wide eyes found mine.

"I didn't do it," Jake rasped, his voice choked with sleep and unexpressed emotion buried deep, "I couldn't do it!"

"I know. It's okay." Jake's fingers tightened on my wrist.

"No. I wouldn't do it! I shouldn't—I—"

He wasn't fully awake, still partially trapped in the nightmare.

Tears glossed over cobalt pools.

Whatever was causing this was more than just some dream.

I reached for him, pulled him into my arms. Jake collapsed against me. His hand dropped from my wrist.

"Shh. It's okay. Whatever it is, it's over now." Hands splayed across the backs of Jake's shoulders. I traced the groves in the muscle, fingers dancing over skin damp with sweat.

Jake's head fell to my shoulder. Big arms circled around me. With little effort, Jake flipped the tables, dragging me into his lap, one knee on either side of his muscled thighs.

"It's over," I breathed again as my fingers skipped up the back of Jake's neck to tangle in the short dark hair at his nape.

Needing the security of the touch as much as Jake, I pressed myself closer and held him to me as he took a shaky breath.

He lifted his head.

"It's not over."

Jake's voice came like sandpaper, rough and tormented.

"It'll never be over. Not for her."

"Jake." I sat back and stared into his face, searching for some clue as to what he was talking about as fear lanced through me.

What had he been through?

I brushed back a lock of hair off his forehead, my fingers settling against his jaw.

"What's going on?"

Jake tore his gaze from mine.

My hand fell from his face, landing in my lap, as Jake stared somewhere into the past beyond my shoulder.

Memory contorted his face as the crumbling mask he wore so well fell away to reveal the anguish left to fester for years underneath.

He drew in a deep breath that left on a sob as his head fell between his shoulders.

"Jessie. I should have been there."

Oh.

"Jake, what happened to Jessie...It's not your fault." Fingers feather-light on his skin, I lifted his head so I could see into his eyes.

The self-loathing I saw in the depths of Jake's eyes twisted my soul.

Why was he doing this to himself?

How could he still think, after so many years, that he was the cause of everything that happened to Jessie the summer before our senior year?

"Can't you see? If I'd been there, like I said I'd be, instead of off…"

He didn't finish his thought.

We both knew where he'd been that night.

We'd both been there, at the pizza parlor, with the rest of the cheer squad and most of the football team. It was tradition, the night before a game.

"It shouldn't have been me."

Now, what did that mean?

"Jessie doesn't blame you, Jake. She never did." Lids drooped over cobalt.

Moving on impulse, my fingertips stroked his cheek from temple to jaw, and he leaned into my touch.

"No one blames you."

Jake's eyes flashed to mine, spearing me with their intensity. Only inches away, I could count the number of times those memories plagued Jake in the crisscrossing of angry scars in his eyes. He kept them well hidden during the day, but here, in the dark, they gleamed bright as stars in a clear night sky.

Jake spoke in barely a whisper of breath.

"You should."

My heart splintered in my chest.

I couldn't breathe, watching Jake hurt like that.

Unable to watch the pain play across his face any longer, I leaned in.

My lips pressed to Jake's, taking his mouth aggressively and wholeheartedly.

If asked why I kissed Jake in that moment, I wouldn't have an answer. There were so many better, safer, more responsible paths I could have chosen. I should have crawled off him, for starters. Put distance between us so we could talk through the tangled mess of memories knotted in Jake's head.

How had Molley not tackled this in all these years? *She* was the therapist, not me.

Instead of pushing me away, strong hands tightened around me, dragged me flush to Jake's bare chest as he devoured me with the same fervor I did him.

I dove in with reckless abandon. All outside forces fell silent—my mind fell silent—until all there was Jake and me together.

Tongues and lips joined in an exploratory freestyle dance. My fingers slid further into Jake's hair, afraid to pull away, knowing if I did, we'd both come crumbling apart at the seams.

Jake's hands firm on my hips, he rolled, taking me with him until my back pressed to the mattress, and he was on top of me, chest to chest.

Forearms pressed into the mattress on either side of me, caging me in. Jake allowed only the slightest press of his weight on top of me as his lips tore from mine to kiss across my jaw.

"Is this okay?"

My head fell back, offering further access that Jake greedily accepted.

"Mmhmm." More than okay.

Jake's lips traveled down my neck to the hollow of my throat.

"We should stop," murmured against my skin.

"No." I shook my head, lost in his touch, in his calloused hands on my body, unlike anything I'd ever felt before.

Jake eased back to hover above me. He met my eye.

With the gentlest of touches, Jake brushed a wave of tangled sandy brown hair from my face. His eyes roared with a hunger that raged inside him.

Jake pressed one last kiss to my lips, chaste and sweet in comparison to the battle we waged on each other only seconds before.

"What about Greg?"

My head fell back on the pillow.

He was right.

What about Greg?

It had been three months. Three *God-damn* months!

I told myself, after Ethan, I wouldn't do that again, wouldn't seek comfort in someone else's bed, burying my grief in their sheets, hoping to lose it forever. And there I was, doing it all over again, with Jake no less!

What would Jessie and Molley say when they found out? I'd have to tell Jessie, and Jake, no doubt, would tell Molley at one of their next heart-to-hearts.

God, I probably just ruined two of my closest friendships for a micro-makeout with their ex!

"Hey," Jake ran a fingertip over my temple. "Where'd you just go?"

His eyes softened, like a midnight winter sky, as he searched my face. Jake's thumb caught a tear as it slipped languidly down my cheek.

"I didn't mean…"

"I know."

This new Jake wouldn't hurt me, or anyone. Not intentionally. But I couldn't be sure I wouldn't hurt him, and that was a problem.

Jake didn't deserve to be used as some rebound, an emotional sedative.

"I'm sorry, I shouldn't have…"

"Don't."

I blinked.

"What?"

"Don't ever say you're sorry for kissing me."

Another tear slipped past my lashes.

Like the last, Jake caught the tear and sucked the salty drop from his fingertip as he rolled off me to sit up.

"But…"

E. Collins

"Uh uh."

"But—"

"Nope."

"I'm not like that, you know." And I was rambling. Once I got going, I couldn't stop. "I—I don't go around jumping every guy in sight, I don't..."

Jake's hand found mine in the sheets and squeezed my fingers like one would cradle a baby bird.

"Hanna, I know."

"But Ethan, and now this and—" The muscles in Jake's jaw bunched.

"I saw the way you looked at that guy at the bar. It's nothing like you're looking at me now. It's not the same, darlin'."

"No," I sighed. "It's not."

My fingers tightened around his, needing the warmth of his touch to anchor myself to this reality. The reality where it was okay to have kissed Jake, no matter what Molley or Jessie thought.

It was okay.

"Thank you."

Jake let out a short, dark bark.

"I should be thanking you."

My brows tilted.

Jake backtracked.

"That came out wrong. What I meant was—"

I pressed my fingers to his lips.

"I know what you meant," I said with a small, teary-eyed smile. Jake's lips puckered to kiss the tips of my fingers, and I laughed as I pulled them away.

"We should get some sleep."

"You're right."

But Jake didn't move to roll over and go back to sleep. Instead, he continued to stare into my eyes.

I waited.

The seconds ticked away into the night.

"Hanna," Jake paused to collect his thoughts.

"I know you're not over Greg. I don't expect you to be. I just want you to know I'm here. I've never been into the whole one girl, two guys thing, but if there were anyone I had to share you with, it would be Greg."

I blinked in the darkness. A moment passed in stunned silence. Then another so we didn't end up right where we started.

Did he just...

I leaned over and pressed a soft kiss to the corner of Jake's mouth.

"I'll keep that in mind."

Chapter 21

I woke before the sun, before Jake, wrapped in a warm cocoon of blankets and muscled arms. Jake's calloused hand splayed languidly over my hip. Heat radiated off Jake. Even if I hadn't somehow ended up snug against his chest, I would have felt him from the far edge of the bed.

Keeping perfectly still, I memorized the rhythm of his breath, counted the seconds between each exhale, waiting for the one that would signal the end of this fantasy I woke up in.

I wanted to stay there forever, reveling in Jake and his warmth and the smooth plains of muscle that covered his body. But that wasn't how life worked.

As the first rays snuck through the blinds, it hit me.

This wasn't real.

It couldn't be.

The kisses and heated touches the night before were a dream.

The soft words whispered in the dark, the promises, meant nothing.

This.

Us.

Meant nothing.

It had to.

I wasn't over Greg. Jake clearly had plenty to work through on his own, and I was a far cry from his usual type.

I wasn't strong and resilient like Jessie or bold and beautiful like Molley. His ex-wife seemed like a bitch, but I'm sure she fit neatly into the fold of women Jake dated in the past, another stunning bombshell that I had no hope of competing with in my grief-stricken, damaged state.

Silent, I eased out of bed, thankful to find my shorts and tshirt still in place. At least I didn't make a total fool of myself.

The air outside the protection of the insulated blankets was icy.

I grabbed the first piece of warm clothing off the floor.

Slipping my arms through the sleeves, I let Jake's sweatshirt fall against my thighs and slid like a ghost from the room.

But in the hall, I paused. My shoulders fell back against the door like I'd reached the end of some invisible tie. Breath fled my lungs as shaky fingers raked back through my hair, sending a thousand tingling reminders of the night before racing over my skin.

It meant nothing.

He didn't mean it.

Any of it.

He couldn't.

My heart squeezed feebly in my chest as if to whisper, "But what if he did?"

I shoved off the door.

I need coffee.

The apartment was silent, the dawn barely creeping in through the wide windows as I stepped into the open kitchen.

I spun in a slow circle, eyes sliding over the counters, searching for a coffee maker, Keurig, heck I would have settle for one of those little instant pouches.

Brent was ex-army. There had to be coffee somewhere. Tallulah had to drink coffee, right?

But after three passes through the little kitchen, I found nothing to suggest the existence of my morning beverage of choice. I let out an angry snarl and spun toward the closed pantry doors.

Screw politeness.

I needed caffeine.

A smoky laugh wafted over my shoulder and froze me in place.

I turned.

"Looking for coffee?" Tallulah gave a knowing smile from where she perched on the back of the couch. Her dark eyes were already lined in smooth coal.

"You won't find any."

My palms slapped on the counter.

"Seriously?"

A dark brow rose on Tallulah's forehead.

"How the heck did these guys get through the army without

coffee?"

Tallulah was entirely unfazed by my outburst.

"It's addictive, you know?"

You don't say.

Tallulah's arms crossed over her chest in a move that screamed superiority and powerplay.

Those dark eyes slid over my face like she could read every detail of my past written clearly on my skin.

"You two will be good together." She gave a satisfied smile like she'd just made a declaration on a furniture set rather than a nonexistent relationship.

Unbidden tears pressed at my eyes.

"Oh no. I..." My eyes pulled to the hall and the door still closed at the end.

"I'm not good for him. I don't know that I can be."

"Does he know that?"

"It doesn't matter what he knows."

"Huh." Tallulah hopped off the couch and sauntered toward a closed door, off the living room. "You and I must have heard some radically different stories about Jake then."

With a cryptic smirk, she disappeared behind the door.

Alone in a totally caffeine-free kitchen, I stared at the door.

The hell?

She was wrong.

What did she know anyway?

I had Greg.

He was my love, the one I was supposed to grow old with.

'Til death do we part wasn't supposed to come so soon.

Greg, why'd you have to go?

And like that, I crumbled. My nose scrunched in a futile attempt to hold off the onslaught of emotion threatening to burst forth. My body went limp. I slid down the cabinet faces until I was a pile of tangled hair and tears on the tile.

How was I supposed to go on without Greg?

It would be so easy to be with someone like Jake, but it wouldn't be fair.

Sure, Jake said he didn't mind if I never let Greg go, but even if he meant it, how long would it last.

A week?

A month?

Even if we beat the odds and figured something out, who's to say, in three years or five, Jake wouldn't look at me in the mirror and see my love for Greg shining back from my eyes and decide enough was enough. He'd leave, and I'd be twice shattered, knowing I could have prevented the pain.

No.

I couldn't let it happen.

Fingers quaking, I scrubbed my face dry.

I couldn't be found crying on the kitchen floor.

Not by Jake or Brent, and most definitely not by Tallulah.

"Let me guess, no coffee?"

My head tilted back to find dark cobalt eyes and a lazy smile watching be from over the island. Some amusing secret twinkled in the depths of Jake's eyes as he leaned over the counter.

He was so at ease, so present in the moment, so full and ready to love.

He deserved someone who could give him as much in return.

No.

Jake and I could never happen.

Chapter 22

Mornings after are always awkward. Tiptoeing around each other.

Who showers first?

Can't shower together because that would mean the night before meant more than it did.

What if someone suggested breakfast?

Accepting any form of food after a one-night stand was a mistake. A joint shower *and* food afterward made it real when it shouldn't ever be more than a one-night stand. And that's what the night before between Jake and me was... or the PG13 equivalent.

Just a one-night stand.

And the number one rule of one-night stands?

Always have your own way out.

If he has to drive you home in the morning, it's going to get weird.

Silence filled the cab of Jake's truck like sand tumbling into an hourglass, slow and steady. Soon, the oppressive lack of sound would fill all the space around us, squeezing out the last of the air, making it impossible for either of us to go on breathing easily.

I wanted to say something, erase the strange quiet building up around us.

Jake did, too.

I caught flickers of dark eyes glancing in my direction. His lips parted like he had the beginnings of our next conversation, then he'd turn back to the road, and the silence continued to build. Because it wasn't just silence circling around like sharks but an awkward knowing that something happened last night that at least one of us refused to acknowledge.

But how could I?

You don't acknowledge one-night stands.

You go home.

If, by some chance of ill-gotten fate, he has to drive you home, you say your goodbyes with some vague statement about meeting up later.

I'll call you.

Then lose his number immediately.

There can be no temptations.

Except it's an eight-hour drive home, a long time for the silence and the awkwardness to build, a long time for unwanted questions to bubble up into unwanted conversations.

I stared out the window, counting the trees as we followed a road around a lake.

Alternating strips of light and show cast by the tall firs striped the highway, empty save for our truck.

It was beautiful.

The kind of place people wrote ballets and symphonies about.

My legs itched to move, to carry me away from the tension building in the cab in leaping twirls.

God, what I wouldn't give to take off dancing through those trees.

I stretched my legs straight in front of me. My calves ached.

It was going to be a long drive.

Jake drew in a breath.

My heart dropped.

Here it comes.

"Could we—shit!"

The back corner of the truck dropped with a deafening pop.

Jake slammed on the brakes and swerved into a pull-off next to a trailhead sign.

The truck rolled with a disjointed thump-th-thunk as we came to a stop in a shaded strip of roadway.

"What just..." But Jake was already out of the truck.

"Fuck!"

I tracked Jake out of the corner of my eye as I slid from the cab, already knowing what I'd find when I rounded the truck to stand beside him.

Jake raked a hand through his hair and scrubbed the back of his neck as we stared down at the deflated tire. There wasn't an ounce of air left inside.

Wrapped in the flabby rubber, the metal wheel rested on the asphalt.

H-How?

Tires don't just go flat out of nowhere.

I stared down the road the way we came.

"Did we drive over something?"

Jake knelt next to the tire without a word.

Deciding it best if I remain silent, instead of bombarding Jake with questions he clearly did not have the answers to, I watched him pull the and tug at the loose rubber.

Jake stood after a moment and strode to the back of the truck.

"Do me a favor," Jake called as he dug through a metal box in the truck bed, "pull the jack from under the passenger seat."

Right.

The jack.

We needed to change the tire.

With a jerking and wide-eyed nod, I jogged back to my side of the truck and threw open the door.

Unsure what I'd find, I jammed my hand under the seat and felt around until my fingers bumped up against cool metal.

A new tire lay on the road next to the truck when I came back around.

Unease tickled across the back of my neck as I stood like a useless child, watching Jake jack up the back corner of the truck.

"This isn't right."

Tires don't just go flat.

Under the truck, Jake gave a noncommittal grunt.

"Not really how I saw the morning going," he agreed.

Heat rose in my cheeks. The question came across loud and clear in Jake's voice. I had to get away before he asked outright rather than offering me an easy out.

I paced back down the road, eyes on the ground, searching for anything, a sharp rock, a pothole, a pile of nails that fell off the back of a truck.

A hundred yards up the road, I turned back to the truck.

Nothing.

The road was in perfect condition and clear, nothing lying about that could have punctured the tire.

Heavy with failure, I started back, taking the unobserved moment to take in Jake's sleek, muscular profile.

He wasn't bad to look at, quite the contrary.

All hard lines, his shoulders held just the right amount of muscle to make me wonder what it would feel like squeezing them as he...

Oh no. We are not going there, Hanna.

Just crazy pregnancy hormones.

That was a thing, right?

No use indulging in thoughts that could never be.

It wouldn't be fair, not to Jake.

Jake deserved to be someone's everything. I couldn't even guarantee that he could be a something to me.

I needed to take a step back, distance myself.

It was the only option.

Jake sat back on his heels, swiped the back of his hand across his forehead to catch the sweat gathering there despite the cool Montana temperatures.

I bit my lips, forcing back the memory of his work-roughened hands catching my tears the night before.

Jake turned and I lost my breath at the depth in his eyes, visible even from a distance.

Don't go there, Hann.

It wouldn't work.

"Nothing," I stopped by the truck.

The flat tire lay in a heap on the asphalt, the spare already in place.

Jake palmed the jack and tossed it back in the cab.

"That was quick. You're good at this."

Jake shrugged, staring at the road at my feet a moment too long. He stepped around me without a word and threw the ruined tire into the truck bed.

Crap.

Jake didn't turn back to face me.

I watched his back, counted as his shoulders rose and fell with his breath, hating the memory of his skin on mine in the dark that sent thrills trilling to my core even in the bright of day.

I chanced a step closer, fingers itching to reach for him.

Muscled shoulders tensed, and I froze.

What did I...

"Hanna." Jake's voice was halting and rough around my name.

Oh no.

This was it.

The conversation that would blow up the rest of our trip.

Guess I wouldn't be attending any more events at Molley's.

After what I was sure was coming, it would be all too awkward to be around Jake for any prolonged amount of time. For the both of us, I'd have to cut those events from my calendar.

Might as well dive in feet first.

I stepped closer, reached for Jake's hand.

"Jake, I can't—"

"Quiet."

Oh no. He did not just—

"I don't know what y—"

"Listen."

I froze, hearing the urgency in his voice.

A low rumble rolled over the top of the nature sounds around us.

"What, it's just some other car?"

Jake speared me with his dark blue eyes.

"And how many of those have we passed since we left Joyner's?"

I swallowed back the fear that spiked at the implication of Jake's

273

question.

"Get off the road." Jake turned to face the coming sound.

"Jake, It's probably just—"

Jake's hand closed around my wrist. Before I could process what was happening, he darted across the street, pulling me with him up the short embankment into the thick trees and underbrush.

Pine needles and branches caught in my hair, scratched as my arms.

Stumbling over a fallen tree the Forest Service hadn't yet come to clear away, I fell into Jake's back.

"What's going on?" I whisper-hissed, moving beside him.

"I don't know."

Twenty feet from the road, Jake pulled me down behind a tree in a thick cluster of pine bushes.

"The hell are we doing then?"

"Shh."

My lips pressed tight. I gave a sniff as I folded my arms over my chest.

Fine. Jake wanted to play it cold. I could play it cold.

We listened in silence as the roar of the engine grew louder.

Jake squinted through the bushes, jaw tight.

Impatient, hating the quiet, I kicked at a fallen pinecone, earning a sideways glance from Jake before he turned back to the road, ignoring my attitude.

I almost missed it, it was so slight, but Jake's hand shifted toward the gun holstered at his hip.

I tensed, hesitated, then turned to see what he was watching.

There can't be any real threat...

The thought flattened as I tracked Jake's line of sight.

Behind Jake's truck, a rusted van rolled to a stop.

No way.

"That's—"

"I know." Jake's hand snaked out to close on my arm, pulling me behind him.

Jake drew his pistol.

I leaned out around Jake and the tree.

A man with scraggly hair in a hoody dropped out of the van. He glanced up and down the road, his head moving on a lolling swivel before settling on Jake's truck.

A second man appeared from around the van, dressed in designer jeans and jacket. A ski mask obscured his face.

I held my breath. Hands tightened in the fabric of Jake's shirt.

"That's him, from the bar."

"Shh!" If possible, the muscles in Jake's shoulders grew more rigid as he stared through the bushes.

A tense minute passed.

"Find anything?" Ski Mask called to the man in the hoody, who was half buried in the cab of Jake's truck. The voice tickled something at the back of my mind.

"They're not here, boss," the man in the hoody answered.

"You don't say. Just search the damn truck!"

Ski Mask turned to the forest on the other side of the road.

"They have to be out here somewhere."

A terrified squeak slipped past my tightly sealed lips.

Jake's hand tightened around my wrist, squeezing a warning. He didn't take his eyes off the men by the truck, nor did he release me.

They were going to find us.

I couldn't say how I knew it; I just did.

And what then?

Unable to move, I stared at the man in the ski mask, sure that any second, his head would whip in our direction, and it would all be over. We'd be found and have nothing left to do but run or fight to get away.

Both of those guys were bigger than me, and the guy in the ski mask looked mean.

There was a manic glint in his eyes that said he fought dirty.

Who knew what kind of weapons they had hidden up their sleeves.

If it came down to it, I couldn't let Jake fight them. Not alone.

I shook Jake's hand from my arm and leaned further around the tree for a better look.

The man in the hoody circled around the truck, looking in all the windows.

"It's not here," he called.

"Well, no shit, shitbrain. They're not going to leave it in the car. Check the glove box."

Hoody pulled open the passenger side door and started to rifle around.

Even from a distance, I could hear the mess he was making.

I cringed at what the inside of Jake's truck would look like when they were done.

"What are they looking for?" I whispered as softly as I could manage.

Jake's eyes cut to me like I'd decided to shout or something, before returning to the men digging through his truck.

"I don't know," Jake popped up into a crouch. "Stay down."

With one hand, he nudged me behind the tree as he slipped around the other side of the trunk.

I stuck to Jake's side, peering through the bushes.

"Find anything?" Ski Mask paced beside the truck.

Hoody held some papers out the door of the truck. Ski Mask took one look at them and tossed them back inside.

"The hell am I supposed to do with that?"

"Well...I don—I don't know. I thought—"

"Do I pay you to think?"

"I—I don't..."

Ski Mask grabbed Hoody by the shoulder and tore him from the cab of the truck with enough force to send Hoody stumbling into the street.

"Search the woods. They've got to be here somewhere."

"Y-yes, boss."

Tripping over his own feet, Hoody ran around Ski Mask and stopped, staring up and down the road and the long line of forest like he didn't know where to go next.

A weighted sigh packed with unsurprised disappointment hissed past Ski Mask's lips as he rubbed at a spot over his eye.

"Start by the lake. They're probably stretching their legs."

With a shaky nod, Hoody decided on a direction and took off, full tilt, into the forest on the other side of the road.

Ski Mask waited a beat, peered up and down the road, then scanned the trees on either side of the road with a shrewd, narrowed gaze that sent chills up my spine.

As those cruel eyes passed over our hiding spot, I held my breath, afraid even a single shifting pine needle would give us away.

But there was no hitch in Ski Mask's movement. He kept turning until his attention landed back on the spot where Hoody disappeared into the trees.

Another sigh rattled past the man's lips, and with slow, almost reluctant strides, he took off into the forest on the side of the road closest to the truck.

I didn't dare move.

Sitting like a stone at Jake's side, I waited, watching for either man to return.

It had to be a trap.

They were just waiting on the other side of the thick foliage for us to show ourselves.

A minute passed.

Then another.

Jake let his knee drop to the earth.

My breath came in slow, audible puffs like I'd just finished a particularly challenging dance number.

Jake's gaze shifted to me.

Unblinking, I met his stare as he searched my face, his own a fine mask of focus.

"Are you okay?" Jake asked, his voice a low, earthy rumble.

Afraid to be heard, I bit my lips and nodded.

Jake made one last pass over my face, searching for any sign I was about to crumble beneath the pressure of our situation.

I wouldn't let that happen.

Not right now.

The stress would have to wait.

Satisfied, Jake gave a brief nod, like he could read my thoughts, and turned back to the road.

I don't know how long we waited.

It felt like hours, but really could only have been a handful of minutes.

Without warning, Jake pressed to his feet, his hand finding mine and pulling me up with him.

When he released me, his keys were in my palm.

I stared down at the shining metal as it glinted in the dim forest light.

"What..."

"When I say so, run to the truck."

My jaw tightened.

Jake's eyes were on the road again. He refused to look at me.

"And where will you be?"

"Don't worry about that. Just...if anything happens, you go. Okay? You get away."

"No."

Cobalt eyes pinned me, sharp and dangerous as daggers.

"Hanna," he said my name through his teeth. "This isn't a game. If anything happens, you drive."

"Not. Without. You."

"Hanna, those people are dangerous. I can't let you—"

"You can't let me what, Jake?" My hands found my hips. "Last I checked, I was not your responsibility."

"Just get in the truck and lock the doors. For the baby." His eyes flashed to my still flat stomach, but it was enough to set guilt swarming inside me.

It wasn't just about me anymore.

"I'm not leaving without you."

"Fine," Jake ground out, looking ready to throw me over his shoulder and lock me in some cave.

Together, we eased from the bushes and picked our way back to the road, keeping our eyes peeled, waiting for the moment the men would step from the trees.

My heart lodged in my throat. My pulse hammered against my skin, so hard I was sure Jake could hear it from several feet ahead.

Jake paused at the tree line, keen eyes scanning the forest on the other side of the road. I stopped at his side but couldn't stand the anxiety that came with immobility, knowing I was being hunted.

I stepped from the cover of the trees, ready to be out of there, safe in the truck and back on the road, but I only made it a couple steps.

Strong fingers closed on my wrist, tugging me back around. I glared up into dark eyes, and I knew, then, he felt the frenetic energy coming off me in waves.

"Hanna."

My lips parted.

Was he crazy? The men could be back any minute. We had to get out of there!

"Lock the doors."

I nodded once, foolishly waiting for what would come next. For the sweet words that always followed the unexpected pullback.

Jake's eyes smoldered with the intensity romance novels were written about.

"If anything happens. Drive."

Not gonna happen, buddy.

But, frowning, I nodded, knowing he wouldn't let me go if I didn't.

Jake's fingers peeled away from my wrist. I felt the loss of every one.

The burning intensity in his eyes shifted to determined steel as he broke away.

No lingering glances or declaratory words of devotion.

No earth-shattering kiss.

It is not the moment for wasted time.

Besides, I wanted distance.

The night before was a fluke, nothing more. A moment of weakness.

I'd had a lot of those lately.

But no matter how I told myself this was what I wanted—*needed*—every cell in my body screamed for me to stick with Jake.

Don't separate.

I pulled my eyes away from his back and jogged the short distance to the truck.

Sliding behind the wheel, I was at once startled by the sense of power that came with sitting behind the controls of such a big machine. Though, by then, I'd spent plenty of time in Jake's truck, it never struck me till then, how much higher off the ground I sat in the truck than my little Maxima.

I ran my hand over the smooth leather of the steering wheel before glancing into the passenger seat.

"Seriously?"

In his search of the truck, Hoody pulled almost everything from the console. Papers and receipts lay crumpled and strewn over the seat and floorboards, hanging from the open compartment.

Leaning over the gearshift, I scooped up all the papers and

shoved them back into the glove compartment before turning to the knick-knacks scattered about the cab.

Stretched out, reaching for the far back of the passenger foot space for a small cluster of change, I didn't look up as the passenger door opened.

"That was quick," I commented as I plucked the coins from the floorboards. "You sure you don't want to dri—?"

A hand clamped around my wrist, squeezing hard.

I froze, staring at the pale fingers, at the cracked nails as they cut into my skin.

"Out of the car."

With a painful tug on my arm, I fell across the cab.

Gasping, I jerked back, clawing at the man's hand to get free.

It was no use.

With one sharp yank on my arm, I was dragged across the cab, tumbling out into the dirt.

"Get up," a growl and another tug on my wrist.

I made a show of getting to my feet, letting out a soft sniff.

As my hair fell over my shoulder, obscuring my face, I searched my surroundings.

The trees were too thick to make for a feasible escape, even if I could get up the steep incline of the gulch on the side of the road.

If I ran down the road, the man would be on me in seconds.

Jake.

I had to get to Jake.

But…where'd he go?

Feigning imbalance, I tripped toward the man, his face still obscured by the thick ski mask.

Close enough, I stomped down on his foot and drove my elbow up into his stomach.

Grunting in pain, the man's hold on my wrist loosened.

I took my chance and darted to the back of the truck.

But Ski Mask recovered much too quick.

Fingers snagged in my loose hair. Pain seared my scalp as he ripped me back.

My lips parted in a scream as I fell.

Pulling me up by my hair, the man threw me against the side of the truck.

"Where is it?" He growled.

Stale breath settled on my face like a dense city fog. I gagged as a wave of nausea overcame me.

"I-I don't know."

Hand still wrapped in my hair, the man slammed me against the cab, sending my mind spinning. I blinked away the dark spots from the edges of my vision.

"You're lying!" He pressed close, pushing me into the cool metal of the truck. "You don't want to see what I do to liars."

The man's teeth grazed over the shell of my ear.

Tears stung my eyes as they spilled over my lashes.

Struggling against the man's grip, I let out a strangled sob.

Where was Jake?

I wasn't the kind of girl stuff like this happened to.

The hell did this guy even want?

I shifted, trying to free my arm from where it was trapped between my body and the truck.

Ski Mask shoved me harder into the truck.

Fear spiked in my gut.

Please. Not like this.

"Please," I sobbed. "The baby."

Pain blossomed across my forehead.

"I don't know what you're looking for."

My head throbbed where the man slammed me against the car. Already, I felt the tissues swelling.

There'd be a goose egg on my head in the morning.

...If I was lucky.

The man loosed a feral sound as he pulled back on my hair. My neck strained as he forced me to look back at him. I stared into cold, lifeless eyes, chin against the cool metal of the truck.

"The baby," the man growled. "Where is it?"

Fuck.

Lily.

What did he want with Lily?

Even as fear spiked at my core and the pain in my head grew blinding, I knew I couldn't tell him.

"What baby?"

My temple made solid contact with the truck with the man's next blow, knocking the air and sense out of me.

Was the world spinning?

The blow echoed in my ears, just the sound of my skull cracking against the truck over and over again.

Hope I'm not leaving a dent in Jake's truck.

The pounding only stopped with a metallic click close behind me.

Oh God, what was that?

A knife?

A gun?

The fist in my hair tensed.

I readied for the next blow, sure this was the end.

"Step. Back. Slowly."

Chapter 23

I almost didn't recognize the voice, deep and gravelly, thick with violence. It didn't just threaten carnage. It promised it to whomever chose not to follow his every command.

Like a butterfly unfurling from a cocoon, the fingers tangled in my hair loosened, pulled away.

The head against my back vanished as Ski Mask stepped back. Montana chill rushed in to fill the void.

Trembling hands rose against the side of the truck, unsure of my precarious balance after multiple blows to the head, afraid I'd fall if I took one step away from the support.

I blinked to clear the blurry edges of my sight. The black spots refused to dissipate.

"Get in the truck, Hanna, and lock your door."

Unable to process the situation, or do much else other than follow simple commands, I gave a tremulous nod and shuffled to the front passenger door.

I scrambled awkwardly inside and let the door slam behind me.

Fingers numb, I jabbed at the lock button until the soft click resonated throughout the cab.

Only then did I look back out the window.

On measured steps, Jake walked the man around the front of the truck to a small stump on the other side of the road. The gun Jake usually kept secured in his waistband leveled on the back of Ski Mask's head.

He'd pull the trigger.

I had no doubt.

If given the chance and a reason, he'd do it.

Murderous vengeance shined in his eyes, a prehistoric instinct to protect what was his. It was both alluring and frightening all at once.

A tiny voice in my head questioned if maybe it would be safer to jump out and run while both Jake and Ski Mask were distracted.

But Hoody was still out there.

I stayed in the truck, another, more basal part of me knowing it was where I belonged.

At Jake's not so gentle urging, Ski Mask knelt on the ground, wrapped his arms around the fallen tree.

With quick, deft movements, Jake secured the man's hands, never lowering the gun.

Jake stepped back and said something to the man I couldn't hear through the glass.

Jake backed toward the truck, only lowering the gun after he opened the door.

He slid behind the wheel, scooping the keys off the seat where I'd dropped them in my struggle.

I pressed into the door on my side as the truck roared to life.

We were half a mile down the road before my brain began to function enough to speak. Even then, my words came out small.

"Thank you."

Jake's eyes cut across the cab. He said nothing.

The muscles in Jake's jaw worked, his arms and shoulders tense as his fingers clenched the steering wheel. His Adam's apple bobbed in his throat.

We rode around a curve, past several cross streets that looked to only lead deeper into the forest, before Jake turned down a narrow dirt path.

A wood sign stuck out of the brush, half obscured by branches and too faded to make out what it once said, pained in neat black brush strokes.

Trees reached for each other over our heads like long-lost lovers reunited if only for the narrow gap of the road between them.

Bushes and pine branches scraped along the sides of the truck as we wound deeper into the forest.

Another quarter mile and the road opened into a wide clearing.

Thick pines and fir trees gave way to long grasses, yellow potentillas, and purple coneflowers with their bronze-red centers.

A round dirt parking lot took up space along one end of the clearing.

Jake spun the truck around to face the road we came in on before bringing us to a halt in a cloud of dust at the center of the lot.

Jake didn't move, didn't speak.

His hands gripped the wheel like he imagined them wrapped tight around the neck of the man in the ski mask.

...or mine.

"Jake?"

With a sign, Jake dropped his head between his shoulders.

"Are you okay?"

"I'm fine. What happened back there..."

"I told you to lock the doors."

My spine straightened. A frown flattened my mouth into a thin line.

"It was only a second."

"And that guy seized it."

"Are you trying to say this is my fault? Where were you?"

"If you'd locked the doors..."

I couldn't help it.

A sharp burst of angry laughter blasted past my lips.

"Seriously?" Jake lifted his head to eye me over the top of his arm. Everything in his expression was hard. His cobalt eyes turned to stone. The muscles in his jaw ticked.

"You're unbelievable."

I couldn't do it.

Not a second long.

I threw off my seatbelt and pushed open the door.

E. Collins

"What are you—Hanna!"

I slammed the door on Jake and strode across the lot, kicking up dust in my wake.

"Hanna."

I resisted the urge to turn back, to face Jake. I needed a few more seconds alone to keep myself from saying something I shouldn't.

Jake's boots crunched on the gravel, drawing closer.

I sucked in a breath, hating how wobbly I felt on my own feet.

Pulling hair away from my face, I raked my fingers over my scalp, feeling the tender places where my head met the metal of Jake's truck.

I'd scream if I wasn't so afraid I'd draw Ski Mask right to us.

How far did we drive before Jake pulled over?

I had no idea.

"Hanna, can we just talk?"

I whirled.

"Why? So you can tell me what I did wrong, again?"

"If you'd locked the doors—"

"And I would have! Enough with the god-damn doors! I just didn't get that far."

Tears pressed free of my eyes.

I swiped at the drops, angry at myself for crying in front of Jake.

"Hanna...I—" Jake stepped closer, reached for me.

"No!" I shuffled back, tripped on the heel of my shoe as it caught in the dirt.

Jake lunged, arms outstretched, but I shied away.

Unceremoniously, I dropped into the dirt. Dust plumed around me. Protective, my arms circled my middle, thoughts turning to the little life inside me.

I glared up at Jake.

He moved to lift me back to my feet. I shuffled back like a crab. Wisely, he didn't follow.

"Hanna, I..."

"I don't need your help," I said, struggling to get my feet under me. "I got it."

"I know."

"Do you?" I fixed Jake with a severe stare. "Because from where I stand, it seems you've been trying to jump all over my life with this white knight shit. I don't need saving, Jake. Thank you for...back there," I waved vaguely toward the woods. "But I can take care of myself."

Something shifted in Jake's eyes. Mid-morning sun glinted off their dark churning surface.

Was that amusement?

The corner of Jake's mouth tried to curl. He held it down. His hand rose to scrub across the back of his neck.

"I know. I just...forget it." Jake turned back to the truck.

What?

I moved to follow, but once more, the world tilted, and I stumbled. The edges of my vision blurred and darkened.

"Jake!"

E. Collins

The fear in my voice as it warbled over his name brought him back to me. In seconds, Jake was there.

One arm around my waist, Jake brushed hair from my face, met my eyes.

"Hanna, what's happened? Talk to me."

"I-I don't know. I—" A hand settled on my abdomen. I wrenched from his grip and lost my breakfast in the dust.

Jake held my shoulders as I spit and wiped my mouth. He watched as I straightened, lifted my gaze to meet his.

Fear equal to my own shined back at me from cobalt pools.

"The baby."

Jake's arm was around me, guiding me back to the truck.

"I'm taking you to the hospital."

▲▲▲

Jake's mind was made up about the hospital.

Even as worry surged inside me, I argued the whole way back to the truck.

Jake helped me up into the seat and circled around the truck without a word. Turning the truck toward the closest major city.

I tried to tell him that any clinic in any of the little towns on the way home would be able to reassure him I was fine, but Jake insisted on taking me to the hospital.

If I disliked protective Jake, worried Jake was worse.

Every few seconds, cobalt eyes darted toward me from across the cab. A little crease dug between Jake's brows.

I rested my aching head against the cool glass of the window and tried to ignore Jake's concern, but any time I let my eyes shut for longer than it took to blink Jake was calling my name, gently shaking my arm to wake me.

Soaking in Jake's worry, my own grew, feeding off his concern like a ravenous beast.

Forehead pressed to the window, I wondered, where would Jake be if he showed this sort of concern and care in his previous relationships?

He'd been right, the other night, even if I couldn't admit it to him. If Jake had shown even an iota of the care he showed me, in the last few days, to Jessie back in high school, she never would have been kidnapped, her life as she knew it destroyed.

But at the same time, if Jake had been the man he seemed to be now back in high school, would Jessie and Colt ever have ended up together?

Would Jake and Molley ever have dated? If so, would they have broken up? And where would that leave Will?

I shook the what-ifs from my mind as the truck rolled into city limits.

Jake found the hospital and parked in the large lot near the front.

He met me at my door as I shoved it open.

I met Jake's gaze, letting my legs dangle off the side of the truck. With me still in the passenger seat, we were almost at level with each other.

"Are we really doing this?" I asked wearily, blinking back at Jake.

Long, calloused fingers skirted over the bruise that spread from my hairline all the way down my temple to the edge of my eyebrow. The purple skin was tender to the touch, but God, I wanted to feel his fingers trace along my cheek, down my neck, and over my collarbone. Lower.

He brushed back a wave of light brown hair.

"You have a concussion, Hanna."

My eyes flashed open.

When did I close them?

Jake wasn't forcing me to do anything—the slight warble in his voice said he knew it as much as I—but I couldn't stand seeing the worry bleeding in his eyes every time he glanced my way, which happened all too often.

I let out a sign and met Jake's gaze.

"You know they're going to think you did this?" I motioned toward the bruising across my face.

Pain and hurt flashed together in cobalt eyes before He buried the emotions.

When Jake spoke, his voice was hard with conviction.

"I don't care what they think, as long as you're okay."

I was afraid of that.

With another sigh, I slid out of the truck and took Jake's offered hand.

"Then let's do this."

Chapter 24

I didn't like hospital rooms or doctor's offices in general. Not that I'd ever really had a reason to be in one outside the yearly physical for cheer.

There's something about knowing you are surrounded by the sick and dying that always leaves me feeling uneasy. I got the same feeling at funerals.

I stared at the posters and charts on the walls of the little ten-by-ten exam room we'd been shown to upon check-in at the emergency room. Thankfully, at two in the afternoon on a Sunday the ER wasn't terribly busy.

The few minutes we sat in the cramped, ultra-modern waiting room almost sent me over the edge with nerves.

Was the baby okay?

What if something was wrong?

I sat in the uncomfortable black chair next to Jake, wringing my hands. I looked around at the few other people, waiting with us, with suspicion.

What were they in for?

Were they contagious?

Should I be worried?

An older man sat against the opposite wall near the door, his skin pale and papery. He wasn't particularly thin or fat, but somehow, his face sagged around his features like the things he'd been through made holding everything in place too monumental a task. His body hunched in his chair, and uncut gray hair stuck out from under a trucker's hat that looked like it had seen better days many, many years ago.

A sense of frailty clung to that man that I couldn't pull my eyes away from. His eyes, never wavering from the double doors leading to the examination area, were clear and keen.

A young couple, maybe college-age, took up two seats near the back wall, both looking in relatively good health if not for their slurred speech and the fact that one of them clutched his arm to his chest like it was his last prized possession.

Jake's arm slid around my shoulders. His free hand dropped over mine with a gentle squeeze that only let up when I pulled my gaze away from the other patrons to meet his stare with a question in my own wide, rattled eyes.

"You'll be fine," Jake murmured only for me. I nodded and turned back to my suspicious inspection of the waiting room.

In the exam room, I wasn't much better, but Jake sat patiently in the extra chair, pulled close to the exam table where I sat, wringing my hands. He watched me for any signs of flight, ready to step in with a calm word.

"Just a few minutes."

"Just a routine check to make sure everything's okay."

"This is normal."

"What's taking so long?" They already took my weight and had me pee in a cup upon finding out I was pregnant.

The crepe paper covering the table I sat on crinkled beneath me as I shifted uneasily. We'd been in that tiny room longer than the waiting room.

Jake glanced at his phone.

"Just give them a minute. Water?" Jake held out a bottle he brought in from the truck. I shook my head and turned back to the posters on the wall.

A second later, I leaped into the air at a soft knock on the door. The door cracked open, and a smiley nurse in pink scrubs stuck her head in.

"Hanna Montgomery?"

"That's me," I squeaked, my voice tight as a windup toy. I tried to force my lips upward but knew from the way Jake hid his own smile behind his hand that I failed.

"I'm Bethany. I'm just going to get your vitals before the doctor comes in. Is that okay?" The smile never left Bethany's face; it even shined in her dark, nearly black eyes.

I nodded my consent.

Bethany shut the door behind her and stepped to the sink to wash her hands.

"So, what brings you in today?" Bethany asked cheerfully, like I'd stepped into some boutique rather than a hospital covered in bruises.

"I uh..." I glanced to Jake for help, something Bethany's sharp eyes did not fail to miss as she scrubbed her nails against her palms under the running water.

"She was attacked," Jake answered for me, barely succeeding in keeping his anger from dragging his voice into the animalistic growl he'd unleashed earlier.

Guess we're going with the truth.

I watched the smile crumble and fall from Bethany's face as she finally took in the extent of the discoloration to my own.

Drying her hands swiftly, Bethany took up the tablet she set on the counter and began to click away at the screen. Her eyes moved accusingly from the bruises peppering my face to Jake and back.

"Did you report the attack?"

Why hadn't we called the police?

"No, I...it happened so fast. We were..." I bit my lip.

I must be more concussed than I thought.

My brain refused to come up with a story.

I couldn't tell her the whole truth.

The nurse had the look of someone who fully intended to call the police the moment she left the room. Judging by the way her eyes kept pitching daggers in Jake's direction, she would not be reporting a random attack.

Great, just what we need.

"We were camping out by Fort Peck," Jake explained. The regret and self-loathing that leaked into his voice made my heart ache. "She went back to the truck for something after dark, and he grabbed her." Jake's eyes shifted from the wall to meet mine, and I hated the anguish I saw there. "If you hadn't screamed—"

"You saved me." A hint of a smile lifted my lips.

Bethany's eyes softened ever so slightly. She tapped away on her tablet.

Maybe we can convince her Jake didn't do this.

Simmering heat seeped into Jake's gaze, saying he'd do it again in a heartbeat.

The nurse cleared her throat, breaking me free of Jake's spell.

Lashes dropped.

Heat rising into my cheeks, I looked away.

What was going on? I wasn't supposed to be feeling like this, not for Jake.

I decided earlier. It wouldn't work.

Greg.

Greg was enough.

My eyes flashed back to Jake and away as Bethany strapped the blood pressure cuff around my arm.

I kept my attention on the nurse, watching to see the little frown she quickly covered up before typing a note on the tablet.

As hard as I tried to keep them away, my eyes always strayed back to Jake, finding him watching me every time.

What was happening here? Between us.

Jake couldn't possibly have feelings for me. Sure, he'd sounded convincing last night, and the longer it stayed there, the harder it became to deny the heat in Jake's eyes. That, at least, was very real, but what if it wasn't what I wanted?

What if I let him in to feel that heat, the passion that pulsed in every one of his muscles, and in the morning, he was gone?

Because they were always gone in the morning.

I'd be left broken, because I wasn't what Jake wanted. Not really. I couldn't be.

I wasn't the curvy blonde or the bold athlete, just the willowy widow, tall, too skinny, pathetic.

"Alright, Hanna," Bethany chimed, her chipper tone and smile returning like it was some switch she could flip. "That's all I need. I'm just going to ask that you step out with me for a second. We just need a quick urine sample. Just come back into the room when you're done. The doctor will be in shortly.

A hood fell over Jake's eyes as they narrowed.

They were separating us. Bethany didn't buy our story.

"I already gave a sample."

"Please, just come with me." That too-bright smile never left her face.

Jake squeezed my hand.

"It'll be fine," he murmured before releasing me.

I stood stiffly to follow the nurse from the room.

I'd fix this.

▲▲▲

Bethany led me down the hall, past a marked bathroom, and around a corner before turning to face me.

The facade dropped, leaving behind a woman dead-set on saving another.

Here it was.

A deep breath flared her nostrils.

"Hanna," Bethany whispered. "If you're in trouble—if he hurt you—you can tell me. We will get you out of this situation."

I didn't like the savior light shining in her eyes, so desperate to help, so quick to accuse in a situation she knew nothing about. Arms folded over my chest.

"Jake didn't do this to me," I said slow and clear, meeting her dark eyes. She could not call the cops.

"I was attacked. Jake would never hurt me."

"Mmhmm." Bethany did not look convinced. "If you change your mind, just let me know, and we will get you away today. He won't hurt you again."

"Jake didn't do this."

"Right." Bethany nodded back toward the bathroom. "There's instructions on the poster opposite the toilet for leaving your sample." Bethany turned and walked away, off to butt her nosy nose into someone else's business.

Great.

I'd just have to convince the doctor.

I strode past the bathroom door back to the exam room.

▲▲▲

Jake was alone in the room when I returned.

Easing the door closed behind me, I met Jake's eyes as he stood and crossed the short distance between us. I folded into his chest, leaning in, reveling in the warmth and security that wafted off his body.

Strong hands drew soothing circles over my back.

"She doesn't believe us."

"I don't blame her."

I stepped back to look up into Jake's face.

"That bad, huh?" I tried for levity and failed miserably. That animalistic look flashed in Jake's eyes for the briefest of seconds before sinking back into the depths, replaced by the agony I so hated to see in him.

A hand rose to brush over my cheek.

I hated that the soft caress made me wince as Jake's rough finger pads skirted over the edge of a bruise. The touch vanished in a blink.

I bit back a frustrated scream, wanting Jake's touch like it was my next breath, hating myself for it.

I should be stronger than this.

But I wasn't.

"I should have come sooner."

Yeah...that would have been nice.

A crease formed in my forehead.

"What were you doing?"

Jake scrubbed a hand over the back of his neck, his eyes flitting away.

"I uh...slashed their tires."

I blinked.

Smart move.

"All of them?"

"All but one."

My lips pursed as I fought back a smile.

"Good."

Another knock sounded at the door.

My heart dropped, dreading having to go another round with the nosy nurse.

I'm sure she'd helped many women out of bad situations, but she was completely misreading mine.

The head that popped around the door was not the dark-eyed nurse but an older blonde woman in braids.

"Hanna Montgomery?" She didn't wait for my response as she strode into the room and sat on the only other available chair, a stool near the counter. Her eyes didn't lift from the tablet in her hands for a long minute.

"So," she said when she finished perusing my chart. "It seems you've been through a bit of an ordeal."

To the woman's credit, when she glanced toward Jake, her eyes did not send sharpened spears like the nurse's had. Her attention quickly returned to me.

The woman introduced herself as Dr. Karen Hartford.

"So, let's get down to brass tacks. Are you comfortable with me discussing your condition with all present?" The doctor's hazel eyes met mine directly and didn't waiver. I gave a definitive nod.

"Well then, it looks like you have a mild concussion, but that isn't what we're interested in here, is it?"

Jake leaned closer as the doctor leveled us with a stare over the top of her glasses.

"I assume you're aware you're pregnant?"

Another nod.

Jake's hand closed around mine.

Dr. Hartford glanced between us, then swiped her slim finger across her tablet.

"Well, I want to do an ultrasound to check out how baby's doing in there. Have you established care with an OB in Spokane?"

"No, I...It's pretty recent."

"Alright. We'll be sure to get you some good pictures then and establish a date."

My forehead creased.

"I'm sorry. Date for what?"

Dr. Hartford smiled kindly.

"Why, your due date."

Chapter 25

Pregnant.

I blinked as the doctor stood.

Though I'd known for days, somehow, the idea of actually seeing the baby made it all real.

"A nurse will come for you when the technician's ready for you."

I was pregnant. But that would mean...

Dr. Hartford stood with a nod to Jake and me and left the room to schedule the ultrasound.

Pregnant.

The door closed with a soft click.

Jake was up in seconds, big hands pulling me into his arms. Lost in my thoughts, I leaned into his chest, needing his warmth like it could fix everything.

I felt his chin rest atop my hair.

"Hanna. Darlin', talk to me. What's going on in that head?"

I shook my head and bit my lip as I stared at the closed blinds over the window.

No. This couldn't be happening.

Memories of that night flashed in my head.

I couldn't say it started out innocent, because nothing to do with that man was innocent. I knew it then, and I knew it the first time I saw him at the bar in his out-of-place suit.

There was something about Ethan that screamed danger and set off all the warning bells in my head, but of course, that night, I hadn't been looking for someone safe.

Just oblivion.

Someone to wipe the memory of Greg from my mind, even if just for an hour.

What was supposed to be an easy one-night stand turned into the stuff nightmares were made of the moment we got into that room of his, deep in his mini-McMansion.

And now this?

I thought he'd used a condom, but really, after the drinks and those cuffs were tightened around my wrists, there was little I remembered clearly through the thick fog of fear that wrapped itself around that night.

And now I was supposed to have his baby? A constant reminder, even if I didn't keep it. I'd know somewhere out there was a child with our shared DNA.

"Hanna, look at me."

When I refused, Jake's finger curled under my chin until I met his gaze. His hand smoothed over my hair.

"It's going to be okay. We'll get through this. You can get

through this."

I felt my face crumpling before my lips even parted to speak.

"I don't know that I can."

Jake found my hand, squeezed it.

"That's okay. We'll figure it out." A frown tugged at his lips as a new thought passed through his eyes.

"Could it be anyone else's?" Jake's mind went to the same place as mine.

I shook my head.

"No. I-I don't..."

"Hey now," Jake pulled me back into his chest as the first tears plummeted off my lashes. "It's okay. You can get through this, whatever path you choose."

I was still pressed into Jake's chest when the nurse came for us.

Jake eased back and met my eye.

"Ready?" like I had much of a choice in the matter.

"Yeah." I nodded, knowing if I said no, Jake would have sent the nurse away, told her to come back later after I had a few more minutes to collect myself.

Sniffing back the last of my tears, I swiped under my eyes and took Jake's offered hand.

▲▲▲

The room where they conducted the ultrasound was dark. A low hospital bed sat beside a desk loaded with computer screens. On the wall opposite the head of the bed, a tv was mounted.

The nurse directed me to lie down on the bed. I stared at the tv as I laid back on the crepe paper. Jake claimed the chair by the bed. Warm fingers threaded through mine, offering up a reassuring squeeze.

I'm here.

"Alright, let's take a look at cutie pie, shall we."

I folded my shirt up. Staring down at my stomach, at the flat plains, it was hard to believe a little life was in there.

The technician squirted a sizable dollop of gel into her palm.

"This may be a little cold," she warned apologetically.

It wasn't, though the slimy texture beneath the wand felt odd against my abdomen.

The technician pressed the end of the want into my stomach and waved it back and forth before settling on a location and pressing further. I squeezed Jake's fingers. It wasn't painful, just strange.

"There's cutie pie!"

What?

How could she...

Movement on the screen caught my attention. My head flew up to find the grainy outline of what was clearly a baby, all large head and long limbs scrunched up into a tight little bundle.

My hand tightened around Jake's as a new feeling spread through my chest. Fresh tears slid down my cheeks.

"We're just going to take some quick measurements, then we'll see about getting you some pictures, okay?" The technician didn't wait for a response, not that I could have given one.

I stared, enraptured, at the screen.

A baby.

My baby.

A cursor darted around the screen, clicking points and drawing lines.

"I'd say you're about sixteen weeks along."

My head snapped to the technician.

"Sixteen? You're sure?"

"Pretty darned."

The laugh that burst past my lips was loud and shrill, verging on hysterical. Tears fell in force down my cheeks, and the grainy image of the baby on the tv screen blurred as the wand bounced on my belly.

Sixteen weeks.

Not Ethan's.

That means...

"Alright. I think we've got all we need. Looks to me like you've got a healthy little cutie pie in there." The technician pulled a small hand towel from a shelf and wiped the gel from my skin. She handed over a long strip of film paper.

Sitting up, I adjusted my shirt and stared down at the images with a smile.

My baby.

Our baby.

▲▲▲

I was floating on air.

Sixteen weeks.

Not Ethan's.

The baby was *not* Ethan's!

Jake practically dragged me back to the examination room, where the doctor waited for us once more.

The doctor rattled off care instructions for my concussion and the baby, but everything passed over my head.

Though I tried to listen, to pay close attention, my eyes kept drifting to those grainy images in my hand. Everything else faded to nothing.

Thank God for Jake, who seemed to be paying close attention to all the doctor's advice.

I'd have to borrow his notes later once the high wore off.

It was almost three in the afternoon when we walked out of the hospital. Well...Jake walked. I couldn't seem to move at anything less exuberant than a skip.

I swung our joined hands between us as we crossed the lot to Jake's truck.

Amusement tilted the corners of Jake's mouth and crinkled around his eyes as he watched me.

Jake opened my door.

"Thank you," I said. The smile that supplanted itself on my lips widened as a slow, crooked grin spread across Jake's face.

I climbed into the truck but let my legs hang out the door, not ready to turn away from Jake.

"I'm missing something." Jake's hands massaged my knees.

"Uh huh," I agreed, unable to wipe away my smile. My eyes twinkled with mischief as I held onto my little secret a moment longer.

"You going to fill me in, darlin'?"

I took one last moment, pretending to contemplate, loving the impatience that flashed in Jake's cobalt eyes.

"Not Ethan's."

"B-but you said..." Jake stopped, his mind working. Counting. "No! Really?"

My relief bubbled forth to join with Jake's in the form of uncontrollable laughter as I nodded.

A wide grin stretched Jake's mouth.

Before I could push back or even realize what was happening, he scooped me up out of the truck and spun me around in the parking lot.

My laughter grew as Jake's own deeper tones mixed with mine.

As Jake set me back on the earth, I felt the pieces of my world slide closer together in a way that was all at once terrifying and thrilling.

At least for the moment, I wouldn't worry about the future, or what it might bring, or the people who were following me.

For the moment, I was happy, glad to have someone to share in the joy alongside me.

Before the high could fade and common sense sank back in, I pressed my lips to Jake's, riding the lightning thrills racing over my skin into my core.

Chapter 26

The sky was dark as we rolled back into town, the clock on the dash showing near midnight.

I stared up into the inky blue that matched Jake's eyes, my head rested against the cool glass.

For the first time in days, I relaxed, my hand snug in Jake's on the center console. Jake's thumb drew slow circles over my skin.

We drove all afternoon with no sign of the van.

When we stopped for a bite to eat, Jake suggested finding a hotel, but I needed to be home, in my own bed, someplace familiar.

A part of me knew some part of that need was to be somewhere Greg had been, had loved. Even as a contented smile lifted my lips, I recognized the unfairness of my desire, but when I brought it up, Jake didn't put up a fight, only nodded in acceptance.

We turned onto my block.

It's too late to wake Molley and her family.

At least, that's what I told myself.

Parked in my driveway, Jake was out of the truck in seconds, pulling our bags from the back seat before I even managed to tumble out of the passenger door.

I didn't miss how Jake glanced up and down the street before following me up the front steps or how his head moved on a swivel until we were inside, the lock secured on the door behind us.

A shiver raced over my arms as I turned to Jake, standing in the center of my living room.

"Do you think they'll come back?"

"Probably," Jake answered. I nodded, Jake's honesty oddly comforting in the darkness.

"You want this upstairs?" Jake turned toward the stairs before I could answer, taking my bag with him.

"I can take it." But I was already chasing Jake down the hall.

The man could be so infuriating.

Jake set my bag inside my room and turned to find me at the top of the stairs.

I let my shoulder fall against the wall, my lips barely lifting at the corners.

"You're unbelievable, you know that?" My voice was soft as I watched the light flecks in Jake's eyes leap and dance.

"Might have heard it once or twice," Jake admitted as he stepped closer.

My lashes fluttered against my cheeks as he caught a loose tendril and placed it behind my ear with the utmost care.

"Never in this context thought."

I opened my eyes and nearly lost myself in the galaxies staring

A teasing smile tugged one side of Jake's mouth, lined with the slightest hint of self-deprecation.

My heart squeezed.

"Those other girls didn't see what they were missing."

Jake's hand brushed my shoulder in a gesture altogether too intimate. My mind skittered about, lighting on all the possible meanings behind his caress.

"Hanna," Jake's voice held a warning, an easy out.

And like that, the spell holding me shattered.

I stepped away, feeling the loss of Jake's touch immediately.

"No. You're right."

I wrapped my arms around myself to hold on to the tiniest bit of the moment before it escaped into the night.

"I'm sorry, I..."

Jake watched me. What looked like hope caught in the moonlight in his eyes.

I turned away, searching for something, anything, to look at that wouldn't end with me doing something we'd both regret.

The open door of Greg's office stood like a dark sentry just down the hall. A tangible reminder of where my feelings should lie.

The kiss. All the hand holding and gentle brushes of skin.

None of it should have happened.

"I shouldn't have—"

"Hanna, don't."

Jake was before me, stepping into my space. His hands slid around my waist like they belonged there, caging me in.

"I'm here, remember?" Jake's breath was a murmur against my hair, brushing softly over the cell of my ear like a cool breeze.

I pressed a hand to his chest, feeling the heat of his heart hammering beneath the thin cotton of his shirt.

"What if I'm not? What if I can't be?" Pain seared my heart at the truth that followed me all afternoon like a silent wraith.

A sigh slid from Jake's lips. In it, I heard all the exhaustion resting on his shoulders, the hours of driving, keeping me safe. His forehead fell against mine.

Reluctant, I met his eye.

"Then I'll be here."

Jake was too close.

His warm hands on my hips were too inviting.

Tears filled my eyes.

I shook my head furiously.

"Jake, that's not... I can't make you..."

"You're not, darlin'."

A calloused hand pressed to my cheek.

Tears slid off my lashes.

I broke free, eyes darting to the open office door around Jake's shoulder.

Fingers caressed my cheek.

"You miss him terribly, don't you?"

His hand fell away.

Unable to do anything else, I nodded, sucking back a sob.

"Greg was a good guy. He loved you. He'd want you to be happy."

I was shaking my head before Jake could finish.

"It's too soon."

It would always be too soon.

Greg was supposed to be my forever.

"No one's rushing you. I just want to make sure you're safe, that you're okay. Greg would want that, too."

"No," I croaked, hating the froggy scratch in my voice.

Before I could draw another breath, everything was running: my eyes, nose, my mouth.

"Not you. Not this, whatever it is." I took Jake's hand and pressed it to my heart, knowing he'd feel it pounding fast and heavy as a kickdrum behind the rise and fall of my breath.

"It's too soon for me to feel this. For you."

Jake's lips parted. His thumb stroked the exposed skin at my collarbone.

"See? It's not you. It's all me." I bit my lips, hating myself for the next words about to come out of my mouth. "I thought I loved Greg, that I still love him, but if I'm feeling like this, like the other night, for you, what does it mean about my time with him?"

A frown tugged Jake's mouth. Compassion lit in his eyes.

Jake swiped the tears from my cheeks.

"Darlin', nothing you feel for me or anyone else will ever lessen what you feel for Greg. He was supposed to be your forever. Anyone could see that. I'm only asking you to let me fill in while he's gone. If that's as friends, so be it. Greg wouldn't want you to cry. Not over feelings like this."

Jake's thumb made one more pass under my eyes to catch the last of the tears. It took everything in me to stay still.

"But," heat rose up in my cheeks, filled my eyes with fire as I met Jake's gaze, "I don't want to be friends."

"Good."

And Jake's lips were on mine.

Chapter 27

I was water over stone, muscles and bone free-flowing and heavy in a cocoon of warmth as the morning sun eased across the room.

I nuzzled closer to the source of that warmth beside me. A smile curled my lips as an arm drew me in tight.

I wasn't ready to open my eyes, to let this dream end, drift into nothing.

After the last few days, I reveled in the luxury of peace and comfort, breathed in the masculine, earthy scent I'd come to recognize as all Jake.

A callused fingertip brushed the hair from my cheek.

He barely touched me, but the pleasant scrape of skin on skin set memories of the wee hours of the morning we spent together spinning through my mind.

Tangled up in sheets and each other, those same fingers brushed over other parts of me, parts I hadn't realized craved attention until Jake came to them.

Those same fingers danced over my shoulder and drew twisting designs down my ribs.

Jake's morning voice rumbled over the sheets, craggy as the monolithic volcanoes scattered through the Cascades, and oh so tantalizing as it soaked into my skin.

"Good morning, darlin'."

I pressed into his side, fingers playing over the plains of Jake's chest.

"Is it morning already." I lifted a lid to peer up at Jake through my lashes, a satiated smile lazing over my lips.

Crystalline sunlight streaked through the window on my side of the bed, bathing Jake's hard features in a cottony light.

Jake kissed my lips, and my smile broadened.

So...

Not a dream.

"Can we just stay here all day?" I batted my lashes as I listened to the beat of Jake's heart beneath my cheek. It was quickly becoming my favorite place as I listened to the steady thrum of his life-force.

My fingers wandered lower, past ridges of abdominals. I thrilled when the beat in Jake's chest accelerated with my progress.

Jake caught my hand with the most unthreatening of growls.

I let him roll me onto my back. Jake shifted over me, balancing his weight on his forearms on either side of my head.

"I think that is the best idea I've heard in weeks."

Kisses peppered around my mouth and down my jaw.

An impatient moan pulled passed my lips as Jake slowed at the hollow of my throat, licking and sucking there until my fingers tightened in the muscles of his shoulders.

He dove lower, licking and nipping his way down my chest until I couldn't take another second of this slow torture.

I lifted my hips in search of one thing and one thing only, and...

A phone rang.

My eyes flew open like I'd been torn from a dream. Jake held himself frozen over me, dark cobalt eyes on mine.

A question passed between us.

Do we answer?

Seconds ticked away.

The phone continued to ring.

Once, twice, three times before switching over to the answering service.

The room fell back into blissful silence.

Jake's shoulders relaxed beneath my hands. He pressed a kiss to my jaw and resumed his slow, torturously sweet descent.

I breathed his name into his shoulder, fingers twisting in his hair.

Jake answered my touch by dragging his tongue, slow and languid, over my nipple. Teeth grazed over the sensitive skin.

The phone on the bedside table trilled into the silence.

Jake's forehead fell against my chest as he released me with a gentle kiss, promising more to come later.

"Answer," I urged, against my better judgment.

Every cell in my body wanted to beg Jake to ignore the siren's call, to return to me.

But it could be his work.

Whoever it was must really need to get a hold of him if they called twice.

With a sign and one last slow kiss on my lips, Jake rolled off me. He answered the phone on the final ring.

"What?" Jake raked a hand back through his hair, leaving it standing up in random bits all over. My own fingers itched to dive into those dark, soft depths once more.

"What?!"

I knew immediately the person on the other line was not someone Jake wanted to talk to.

Jake pushed up in bed, his spine ramrod straight. His jaw stiffened beneath several days of stubble. Fingers, that only moments ago roamed my body with the delicate touch one would afford a baby bird, fisted in the sheets.

I sat up, watching anger and panic mingle in Jake's eyes.

A quiet rage crackled in Jake's voice.

"No. Why are you even—you know what, never mind. I don't want to know. Do us both a favor and get back on whatever plane brought you here and..." Jake's teeth clenched around the rest of his words as he fought to remain civil.

On the other end of the line, a woman's voice screeched through the phone. Jake went dead still, the muscles in his neck and jaw bunching.

Then.

"Wait, what?" I saw the moment Jake's skin went from golden

tan to ghost white. His eyes widened as the earlier panic returned, wide and darting like a cornered animal searching for escape.

More screeching through the phone.

I found Jake's hand in the sheets and squeezed it tight in mine. Jake's fingers closed around one of my hands and held on like he feared he'd drown.

"Go home, Gina. If you go anywhere near..." Jake lowered the phone, the call screen flashing the final call length.

Squeezing his fingers, I drew Jake back to me, out of the clutches of his ex-wife on the phone.

Jake dropped his phone on the bed like touching the device left him feeling slimy.

I pulled my knees to my chest, hugging them close beneath the sheets. A chill raced up my arms.

We wouldn't be falling back into each other's arms. Not that morning.

"What did she want?" I asked, watching Jake over the tops of my knees, afraid the fragile bliss we'd found would shatter with one wrong move.

Something had changed, but I couldn't see what.

Jake scrubbed the back of his neck.

"Nothing. It's stupid. You want coffee?"

Eyes narrowed at the obvious attempt at distraction.

"That would be great, but I don't have decaf. Are you okay?"

"Fine." But he was drifting.

Already, Jake was miles away.

A moment passed, the silence shoving us further apart, even as I clung to his fingers.

Jake rolled out of bed.

"I'll be right back," Jake shoved into his jeans.

I sat up, watching him dress.

"Where are you going?"

"Just a quick trip to the store."

Buttoning his pants, Jake leaned in, his lips finding mine.

"You," he pulled back only to place a peck on my lips. "Stay right there."

▲▲▲

I didn't stay in bed.

I couldn't.

When the front door slammed, I was already at the window, peering through the blinds.

Something was wrong.

I watched Jake cross the grass to his truck, phone pressed to his ear.

Was Gina on the other line?

Part of me wanted to stay, to watch until Jake was out of sight around the corner, hoping to glean some minuscule microexpression or shift in his posture that would indicate what the hell was going on.

But I wasn't one of those girls.

Or was I?

Panic set in.

I'd only ever been with Greg. How was I supposed to know what kind of girl I was when it came to jealousy and dating? We were basically an old married couple since sophomore year of high school.

I didn't hover.

But I didn't think I was the kind of girl to throw herself blindly at men either.

Despite what some might think when they find out, I knew what I was getting with Jake.

I forced my shoulders to relax.

Everything was okay.

Sheet still wrapped around me, trailing on the floor, I wandered into the hall.

Greg's office stood open.

I stared into the mess of papers and scattered books.

Why would someone break in just to rummage through a bunch of medical texts?

I stopped in the doorway, surveying the room, books, maps, and research everywhere. A toppled cup of pens lay scattered over the desk.

I stepped further into the room, stooped to pick up a heavy black bookend shaped like the head and shoulders of a man. Some famous scholar, probably.

There was so much work to be done.

I slid the bookend onto the shelf with its mate.

Fingers trailed over my still flat stomach.

What are we going to do?

Aside from the room at the front of the house, Greg's office was the only other bedroom. Could I really dismantle the last piece of him I had left?

A tear slid down my cheek as I picture the room in shades of blue and green, pink and purple. A crib would fit perfect between the windows overlooking the backyard, leaving plenty of room in the corner for a rocker.

It shouldn't be so easy to erase someone so meaningful.

Guilt dragged me to the floor next to the desk.

How?

How could I feel like I do with Jake and still miss Greg so much?

With Jake, I felt so safe, at ease, seen in a way I'd never felt before, even with Greg. With Jake, I could relax and not worry about every little thing like I had with Greg. Greg loved me deeply with his whole heart, but he'd been too consumed with his humanitarian missions to think about the dishes piling up in the sink or dinner.

With Jake, I was the mission.

Some small part of me loved that. I'd never been the center, always an orbiting planet around someone else's sun. It felt good to be the star.

Another tear slipped off my lashes as I collected the papers scattered around me and shuffled them into a semi-neat pile. I reached for a thick anatomy text wedged under the corner of the desk and weighed it in my hands.

Greg loved his books, each of them kept in pristine condition.

They deserved to be used, to offer up their information to

whoever may need it.

I peered around the room.

Such a wealth of information.

I folded back the cover of the anatomy text, flipped through the thin pages.

All black and white, text with a smattering of diagrams.

Leave it to a book on the human body to be dull as bones.

I flipped back through the pages and frowned when a flash of color caught my eye between the pages.

Back pressed to the side of the desk, I turned back the pages, listening to the soft whish of the paper as it passed over the ends of my fingers. I scanned each page, searching for that pop of color as I passed over diagrams of organs and the circulatory system.

A macabre sketch of a human skull paused my page-turning. In slow, precise motions, I traced the hollows around the eyes with the tip of my finger. There was a strange beauty in it.

Something dropped into my lap.

Small.

More square than rectangular.

I stared down at the piece of paper no larger than a recipe card.

Greg must have hidden it between the pages to mark his place.

A date scrawled in sloppy script in one corner.

I stared, knowing there was something significant about that particular collection of numbers, unable to put my finger on it.

6/18/2016

What did it mean?

Nothing else was written on the card.

No smudges on the crisp backing.

I lifted the card delicately, weighing the paper. It turned, revealing a polaroid.

At first, I didn't know what I was looking at.

I drank in the colors and features of the image for a long moment before it finally clicked.

On a gasp, I flung the photo and scuttled back against the wall.

No. Nonono.

Why did Greg have that?

Resolve settled.

No.

I had to be mistaken, misread the collections of lines and color.

I crept closer, somehow afraid the lifeless girl in the photo would somehow come alive and jump out of the paper at me, drag me back with her to endure a similar fate.

Bile rose in my throat.

Nope.

There she was, one leg bent at an impossible angle, party skirt hiked up above her waist, exposed on the floor.

Dark spots covered the girl's arms, which were raised up over her head and tied by a thin green and blue cord.

The girl's straight blonde hair fell over her face in a shield, obscuring her identity.

I flung the photo once more and turned away.

Fingers pressed into my lips as I dug for a reasonable explanation for such a photo to be in Greg's possession.

In his *office.*

It didn't make sense.

It had to be some kind of snuff porn.

It had to be fake.

But if it was real...

No!

Greg wasn't into that sort of thing.

Or was he?

I shook the thought away and began to pace over the scattered papers still covering the floor.

The picture looked real, but even Polaroids could be faked.

An actress.

She had to be.

Or model.

The bruises on her arms weren't real, just carefully applied costume makeup.

I'd seen it all the time on tv. You could make anything look real with the right lighting.

That's what this was.

A carefully staged fake.

But why was it here?

What if there were more?

I tore an undisturbed textbook from the shelf and leafed through the pages.

Nothing.

Suddenly, not caring for the well-being of the book's pages or spine, I dropped it and moved on to the next and the next.

Three shelves stood bare before I changed tactics and crossed to the desk.

I cringed as I lowered myself into the chair.

All the gross and depraved things and thoughts that may have taken place in that chair flooded my mind.

The long top drawer of the desk stood open, its contents thrown about in disarray.

I picked through the pens and papers, searching for more pictures, more evidence that the man I thought I loved was a monster.

I found nothing.

Absolutely nothing.

Sitting back, defeated, I snatched the stack of papers off the desk.

Maybe there was something in them, some clue as to the depth of his depravity.

But they were nothing more than a sociological study on the use of native herbs by some African tribe.

▲▲▲

"I'm back." Jake's voice echoed through the house, followed by the front door slamming behind him. "Hanna?"

But I couldn't answer, unable to gain enough control of my emotions to speak. Wrenching sobs pulled sniveling whimpers past my lips.

Jake found me on the office floor, papers and books strewn around me from my search.

Something wild swam in Jake's eyes as he stepped into the doorway and released a breath. A smile curved his lips.

"There you are." He froze, taking in the blubbering mess I'd fallen into in his absence.

"Hanna." One had reached for me as he discarded a paper to-go cup on the bookcase.

I stayed on the floor, unsure if my legs would support me if I stood. I pulled them to my chest. Tears streamed down my cheeks like a small child waking from a nightmare.

I was awake alright, but there was no escaping the nightmare.

Jake approached with caution as if I was a wounded animal ready to strike if provoked. But he had nothing to fear from me. There was no fight left.

I was drained, as lifeless as the girl in the photo.

I crumbled into Jake, drawing on his warmth and strength as his strong arms closed around me. Long, capable fingers massaged soothing circles across my back.

"You were thinking about him again," Jake spoke into my hair, not accusing. "Greg."

My head fell to Jake's shoulder. Unable to form words, my lips and nose scrunched to hold in a gasping shriek of pain for the life that had been torn away from me, for the man I'd loved. I nodded, rubbing my cheek over the cottony soft fabric of Jake's shirt.

"Tell me." Jake had no idea what he was asking. No idea the dumpster fire he'd walked back into.

Minutes passed in silence as I wrangled control of my emotions.

"It was all a lie." My voice came out strangled and broken.

"Ah, Hanna, no." Jake turned me in his arms. Callused fingers brushed hair from my eyes. As he tilted my chin up.

Silent, Jake searched my eyes for some clue as to what dampened my mood. I stared back, finding solace in the dense, dark swirls of his eyes. Tears slowed.

Had anyone ever looked at the girl in the photo the way Jake looked at me?

A hint of fear mixed with concern and care molded together in a look of complete devotion.

Did someone hold her like she was the most precious thing on earth, like any moment spent away from her was a moment too long?

Jake ducked to meet my eye.

"Greg loved you." Jake's hands closed around mine. In his, my hands felt cold and stiff. "Only you. Anyone could see that, even in high school."

I stilled, pain searing my heart.

How could Greg have loved me with pictures of other girls in his office?

How could I feel so deeply for someone like that?

I pulled my eyes away from Jake's.

"Why couldn't it have been you?" I asked.

A worried crease formed in Jake's forehead. Frowning, he squeezed my fingers, trying to draw me back to him.

"Back then, in high school. Why couldn't it have been you?"

"You wouldn't have wanted me then, Hanna. I'm not sure you should now."

I shivered, the cool air in the room drying the wet track on my cheeks.

"Greg couldn't have loved me." Air shuddered into my lungs.

No more tears.

I had no more left to spill.

My voice was flat, hollow.

"Not really."

I reached for the photo, face down on the carpet, and thrust it at Jake.

"Look."

Caution returned to Jake's eyes, unsure what to do with this new Hanna that crawled free from the rubble of my miserable and wrecked life.

Jake drew the photo from my fingers like a card from the grip of a shady street magician. His eyes stayed on me as he turned it, searching for some indication of what he'd find on the other side.

When Jake's eyes finally dropped to the photo, he froze, trapped in the details.

The muscles in Jake's jaw tightened and bunched. His frown deepened.

"Where did you find this?" He asked.

"Over there." I waved toward the bookshelf. "In one of Greg's books. There's a date on the back."

Jake flipped the photo to read the date.

"So, you see. Greg couldn't have loved me. Not really."

Chapter 28

"That can't be right."

Jake flipped the photo back over, taking in the details.

"There has to be another explanation."

My laugh came out harsh and humorless.

"Like what?"

Jake stared back at me.

His mouth opened and shut, but nothing came out. His jaw worked before he raked a hand across the back of his neck.

I shoved to my feet, tired of wallowing in my own self-pity when anger felt so much better.

I strode from the room, needing to find something, anything, to take the hurt away.

Air.

I needed air.

I had to get outside.

Taking the stairs two at a time, I started for the back of the house, remembering halfway there the extra cargo I carried.

In the living room, I stalled, eyes catching on the collage of memories scattered across the wall in shining frames. All happy, smiling memories.

Me with friends and family.

All the important milestones.

Prom.

Graduation.

Move-in day.

My wedding.

Each one colored by the man I thought I'd spend the rest of my life with.

All lies.

My hand moved to my middle of its own accord.

And now I had another reminder of the fraud that had been my life. Would I be able to hold my baby—our baby—without thinking of Greg and that photo I found in his office?

I tore myself from my memories.

A streak of sunlight cut across the room. I stared out the front window at the frozen ground, at the white frost clinging to the last surviving weeds in my yard.

A walk would be nice. To feel like I was actually going somewhere, rather than treading water, running in circles, trying to avoid the next disaster. The thought of the road beneath my bare feet, the wind pulling my hair, chilling my cheeks brought a smile to my lips.

But with those men on my tail, a walk was beyond impractical, even if Jake would have allowed me out the front door.

The smile crumbled.

I wouldn't be going anywhere on my own any time soon.

After the weekend, there was little doubt that I was being pursued.

Why?

My brow creased as new rage surged inside me.

I was trapped in my house, caged, unable to live and fly as I pleased.

My metaphysical wings ached to stretch wide, their beautiful muscles dying to feel the pulse of blood pumping through their veins as they shot me forward into the sky.

There was no forward.

Not now.

Not with those men out there and not after what I found in Greg's office.

How could there be a next move when the entire history, my entire history, had been ripped from behind me, rewritten by some cruel twist of fate.

With no other option, I stormed through the kitchen to the back door, forgoing a blanket or a coat, needing to feel the icy bite of the breeze on my skin.

I strode into the frosty outdoors.

On the back stoop, arms instantly wrapped around my chest.

It was colder than expected. After the warmth of the house, the outside air felt like knives slicing shallow cuts across my bare arms and legs, but at least I was feeling something.

The burning, bubbling rage tempered inside me.

At the back of the yard, a wood bench rested amongst the bare brambles of a rose bush and the fence. I crossed the lawn on quick feet, the frozen grass tickling my toes.

Hands fell in my lap as I dropped on the bench.

Now what?

There was so much to be done.

Class to arrange with Cora. The mirrors in the studio needed to be hung.

Sometime soon, I'd have to call Carlo and request extra shifts to make up for the weekend I missed at the bar.

Carlo's wasn't the most conventional of jobs; bartending at a saloon-style dance hall never made it on my list of potential careers in high school, but most nights, it felt safe, and Carlo paid well. I really did enjoy working with the girls.

Maybe they could use a new routine.

Choreographing the sensual twists and turns, dips and shimmies that would pull the bills from drunk observers' pockets was a welcome distraction from the mess of my life.

Eventually, I'd have to go back upstairs to Greg's office and clean out all the books and papers.

Hands settled over my belly button.

Soon, someone new would be moving into that room. If I had anything to say about it, there would be no hint of the man who occupied it first left when I was finished.

E. Collins

The back door squealed as it opened. Jake stepped out onto the step, a fleece blanket folded over his arm.

Dark shades of blue and lime green peeked through folds, the edge of the sports team logo just visible.

It was Greg's, pulled from the pile on the back of the couch.

Jake hesitated, seeing me there, staring back at him with a stiff back and tense jaw and as fierce a look as I could muster. I didn't need to be coddled, and I most definitely did not want *that* blanket.

I turned away, eyes flat and dismissive. I stared instead at the building that would soon be my dance studio.

It needed paint, I decided, remembering the day, the previous summer, when Greg and I coated the outside of the building in that calming pale gray color to match the house.

Now, something bright and exciting seemed more appropriate. Something garish to stand out and draw the eye that screamed, "Look at me!"

It was the kind of dance I preferred, the wild and modern movements paired with heavy drumbeats of popular music.

A warm and soft layer dropped over my shoulders. A cloying, soapy scent wafted off the minky fabric, making me want to gag. It still smelled like him. After so many weeks, Greg's scent clung to the blanket like herpes.

I shrugged out of the warm blanket as Jake sat beside me on the bench.

"Hanna, I know this is hard. It's one picture. Aren't your memories of Greg stronger than that? Who knows, it could be—"

I ground my teeth to crush the anger inside me before it surged forth. I did not succeed.

"How? How do I know it's just one picture? Huh? And even if it is, shouldn't that be enough?" I shoved off the bench and paced out into the lawn.

My next words crumbled off my lips as I spun to face Jake, some part of me still looking for him to give me some plausible explanation to save my memories of Greg.

"You saw it. Did it look fake to you?" My eyes bore into Jake's.

"You don't know why it was there." So calm, consoling. Why couldn't he just fight me?

"And you do?"

"No, but if we just go upstairs—"

"No." Shutters fell over my eyes as I shook away his placating words. "No, Jake. I'm done. I need to forward."

"But—" Jake stood to follow me across the yard, but I pinned him in place with a glance.

He couldn't come any closer, not if I was going to maintain the fragile hold I had on my emotions.

"He was my husband, Jake. I'm pretty darn sure I knew him better than you," I spat the words as I pointed to the second-story window overlooking the yard. "The only thing I'm going to find in that room is more pain and heartbreak, and quite honestly, I'd rather not. If you can't accept that, I think it's time for you to go."

"Hanna." Jake stepped closer, dark eyes brimming with worry, lit by the fire that now burned in both our souls. We set something free last night, something neither of us could bottle back up.

I just wanted to fall back into bed and curl up in his arms, but there would be no more wallowing. No more bad decisions made on grief.

"Go, Jake." My voice was hard. "There's nothing you can show me that will change my mind."

Jake's eyes cooled. Hurt pulled at their corners. He bit down on his response, holding it back. His jaw ticked, and his throat bobbed.

Without a word, Jake turned and walked away.

▲▲▲

When I went back inside, his stuff was gone, cleared from the space along the wall in the upstairs bedroom.

I prowled through the house, fueled by the heat of our argument. It made me itch.

I needed a shower, to wash away the negativity of the morning.

The hot water in the shower felt like heaven on my skin. I stood under the water, letting it sluice over me until it ran cold.

Dressed, I wandered back downstairs.

A note sat on the coffee table in the living room, Jake's phone with it.

If you need it, written in Jake's slanted blocky hand, followed by four numbers. *1017.*

I frowned at the numbers, wondering at their meaning. A birthday maybe?

I palmed the phone.

It felt weird having it, intimate and yet intrusive in a way I wasn't entirely comfortable with.

I made a quick call to Carlo, setting up some weekday shifts before moving into the kitchen. Switching on the radio in the corner, the room filled with soft rock as I dug trash bags from under the sink. Jake's phone lay abandoned on the counter.

I couldn't hide from the office forever. The sooner I got it cleaned out, the sooner I could forget about the whole thing, the photo, Jake, those goons on my tail.

A song faded as the DJ's voice filtered in.

I only half listened as I pulled a bag free and turned toward the living room.

"Ethan St. James of Gordon, St. James and Associates, lawyer of one Brandon Tippins, one of the two convicts to escape Airway Heights Correctional earlier this month, made a statement the morning to local county police."

I gasped as Ethan's smug voice invaded my home.

"I was not aware of any escape Mr. Tippins may or may not have planned. Had I any knowledge, the police would be the first to know."

The DJ returned after the short sound bite. "St. James asserts that his client was confident in the legal system and his council's abilities and eagerly awaited his upcoming appeal. An appeal St. James claims they likely would have won with Tippins' impeccable transformation behind bars."

An involuntary snort pulled from my nose.

Of course Ethan would defend violent criminals. After seeing the group he was with at Carlo's the other night, I was not at all surprised.

I turned down the radio, but loneliness seeped in to fill the silence, wrapping around me like some feral predator. An overwhelming need to escape welled inside me.

I snatched up Jake's phone and found Jessie's number in the contacts.

My thumb pressed call before the strange feelings could throw me into an emotional tailspin.

I needed a distraction, fast, and maybe, just maybe, to vent.

Jessie picked up on the first ring.

"Hello?" Her voice was tight. Had she been crying? "Jake, this really isn't a good time, I've got—"

"God, it's good to hear your voice."

"Hanna? What are you doing with…" I could hear Jessie moving around on the other end of the line, paper and books shuffling. "Jake was that intolerable, huh? Molley mentioned he drove you to drop off the foster. If you want, Molley and I can—"

"No, no, Jake's been a lifesaver, actually." In more ways than one. "I was wondering, can we grab coffee? I could really use some girl time."

Silence.

The static lasted so long I was half convinced Jessie hung up.

In the background, Jessie's doorbell chimed.

"I'm pretty busy with something, Hanna. Can we rain-check the coffee?" Was it just me, or was her voice more strained?

Who the heck was at her door so early?

Why wasn't she at work?

"Would this afternoon work better?" *I just need out of this house!*

"I'm going to be pretty busy all day. I'll get back to you, 'kay?"

"Sure." My chipper tone sounded thin as Teflon, too sugary sweet.

Another weighted pause.

"Hanna... Is everything okay?"

I couldn't do this to Jessie, not after all she'd been through, the day she was clearly already having. She didn't need to hear about my sham of a marriage and failed almost relationship with Jake.

"Yeah," I sighed across the line. "Everything's just fine."

▲▲▲

I didn't make it upstairs.

It started in the hall, a tingling hesitance at the back of my mind, some small part of me still clinging to the hope that Jake was right. That it was all just one huge misunderstanding, the photo somehow connected to one of Greg's cases, in no way some strange fetish.

Garbage back clenched in my fist, I forced past the feelings and dragged myself up the stairs.

Tears started by the third step.

Halfway up, I came to a gridlocked stop, cheeks drenched, unable to force my foot up to the next stair.

Letting out a huff, I dropped down on the step. I took a breath, then another, and swiped away the moisture on my cheeks.

Hands settled against my stomach, clinging to the last real thing in the world.

Slowly, the muscles in my back and shoulders eased.

I sniffed.

I've got this.

I can do this.

I couldn't.

It wasn't the time to clean Greg's space.

Soon.

But not now.

I left the garbage bag on the stair.

The girls at Carlos had been asking for new material for weeks. Losing myself to music and movement sounded like bliss on a cake. Plus, I could check out the new mirrors.

I detoured to the pantry on my way through the kitchen and reached up into the bowl on the fourth shelf for the studio key.

Already, I felt lighter.

I pressed to my tiptoes. Fingertips met only the smooth bottom of the little wooden bowl.

Frowning, I dropped back onto my heels, hands going to my hips.

Where'd I leave those keys?

I made a pass through the living room, checking between the cushions on the couch, under the edges of all the furniture.

My frown deepened.

I tried to conjure an image of when I had them last but came up blank.

I'd been a little scatterbrained since Greg's passing, tired and exhausted, but how could I not remember the last time I had the studio keys?

It's okay.

Deep breath.

One last place to check.

I took the stairs at a jog, hopping over the trash bag and bypassing Greg's office, the door still gaping like a slack-jawed maw, and turned into the bedroom.

Dresser top, clear

Floor clear.

Sheets and blankets lay in a rumbled mess at the foot of the bed.

The corner of my lips quirked up involuntarily as I remembered Jake's paradoxical touch exploring every inch of my skin. His lips chasing every feather-light touch, simultaneously rough and gentle. Water and stone.

Jake's hands were nothing like Greg's.

Greg's hands were smooth—a surgeon's hands, his dad used to say, never mind that Greg focused his study on natural field medicine and internal med.

Greg's hands were always sure. He didn't make a move without thinking it through thoroughly.

Jake's hands were warm and strong, a workman's hands, but also hesitant, something I never expected from the high school quarterback who always seemed to know exactly what to do.

All night, Jake's eyes stayed on me, gleaming in the dark as he watched for any subtle queue that he'd gone too far, that I was uncomfortable in any way.

My fingers twitched with the need to hear his voice, to call him back, apologize for earlier as long as I could be back in those arms, but Jake's phone was downstairs, and despite my sudden inexplicable need to be constantly coddled in muscular embrace, I was not ready to talk to Jake.

Instead, I knelt to pick up the book lying face down and open on its pages under the edge of the bed. It must have been knocked off the bedside table in the night.

I stood.

A thin slip of paper slid from the pages, falling to the floor.

Cold dread froze my veins. My heart plummeted.

No.

I stared down at the white rectangle on the carpet.

No.

It couldn't be.

Not another one.

Not here, in our room.

I set the book aside, unable to look away from the unassuming piece of paper.

Every cell in my body screamed for me to run like a mad woman down the stairs and out the door, to never look back.

But I had to know.

It could just be a bookmark.

A postcard.

Postcards aren't blank on the back.

I could wait for Jake, let him check when he returned.

I didn't have to know.

No.

I had to do it.

I didn't need Jake.

I took a microscopic step closer.

Come on, Hanna. You can do this.

But I couldn't.

I shook my head and took several steps back, distancing myself.

I stared down at what I knew was another Polaroid, wishing I could blink it away like a speck of dirt in my eye.

This photo.

The one in Greg's office.

The break-in.

The jerks following me for no good reason.

But no matter how hard I blinked, it was all still there.

The unassuming rectangle still sat on the carpet.

It all felt dirty, like a thick coat of sewer grim slathered it all. If I touched it, even to flip it over and see, that grim would spread.

My eyes blurred as I stared at the paper before returning to focus on a series of numbers in one corner.

If I thought my blood froze earlier, it was nothing to the frost that flushed through my veins in that moment. Color leached from my face.

I knew those numbers, that date. I knew beyond a shadow of a doubt who would be in the photo on the other side.

Bile bubbled in my throat.

My vision blurred.

Tears bubbled up on my lashes, spilled over.

How?

How was that here?

Why did Greg have it?

Of all the dates, why did this one have to have that one?

My eyes flashed to the cover of the book resting on the side table, searching desperately for answers.

I frowned at the title, unable to remember if it was mine or Greg's.

It had to be Greg's. I knew *I* didn't put the photo in between the pages.

I tasted bile as it slid onto the back of my tongue.

Turning before it was too late, I ran from the room and down the stairs.

As I lost what little remained in my stomach into the toilet, the date on the back of the Polaroid seared itself across the backs of my eyelids.

05/17/2013

The day Jessie disappeared.

Chapter 29

A phone ringing drew me from a fear-stricken fog as it echoed off the walls of the house.

Wiping my mouth on a wad of toilet paper, I flushed away my mess and hauled myself from the bathroom.

On autopilot, I followed the ringing to the kitchen and picked up Jake's phone.

A photo of Molley pulling some silly, ornery face with her tongue hanging out peered up at me from the call screen.

I was going to catch hell from Molley for answering Jake's phone, but I needed someone, anyone, to be there, to pull me away from the hellish things surrounding me in that house. I slid the green call button across the screen and lifted the phone to my ear.

"Hey," my voice sounded dead. "Jake's not here right now, but..." I faded off as my voice warbled.

Molley didn't bother with a greeting.

"I'm not looking for Jake. Jessie called."

"Oh." I leaned on the counter.

"Everything okay? You sound..."

A sob tore from my throat. Fat, salty tears slid between my lashes.

"Hanna, what's going on? Where's Jake?"

"I don't know," I sobbed, as the loneliness and what I'd done finally sank in. "I sent him away."

Silence, then—

"I'll be over in a minute. Sit tight."

Molley didn't wait for an answer or an explanation.

The line went dead.

I dropped Jake's phone back on the counter and tried to curb my tears, but nothing helped.

It's the house, I decided, looking around the homie kitchen. It was tearing me apart with all the memories held within its walls.

I took a determined step toward the backyard.

I may have lost the key to the studio, but what were the chances I remembered to lock the door the last time I was inside?

Even if the studio was locked, I'd rather freeze outside than waste away another minute beneath the suffocating weight of that house.

Forcing one foot in front of the other, I crossed the yard to the converted garage.

The building itself was more akin to a barn, really, with its size, but I'd never been able to envision animals living on the property.

When Greg and I bought the place, the realtor said the previous owner kept his cars inside, but I always saw a dance studio when I stepped inside.

The wood exterior had been freshly painted in the spring, and the tin roof gleamed in the stream of sunlight peeking through the clouds.

I closed my hand around the doorknob. A wave of horrified relief washed over me as it turned in my hand.

Did I leave it unlocked?

The mirrors.

No. I couldn't have. Molley would have said something.

Maybe she forgot to lock up after the delivery men left?

I stepped inside, letting the door fall closed behind.

With no windows, the door to the office closed, the tiny entryway was pitch dark.

In the black, I felt the closeness of the walls around me, the stillness in the air.

I sighed.

Alone.

No memories would find me there.

I felt along the wall for the light, but when I flipped the switch, the room remained dark.

Fantastic.

Praying it was just a blown bulb, I started across the short entryway, more hallway than anything else.

Hanna said the mirrors were in the back classroom, so that was where I'd start.

Having spent more hours in my studio than in the actual house, I could navigate the place with my eyes closed. Finding the back room would be no problem in the dark.

I took two steps and leapt back with a squeal.

"Oow!"

Pain shot through my big toe, radiating out into the ball of my foot.

On one leg, I hopped back and flung open the door. Sunlight streamed across the floor.

Thick drops of crimson beaded at the end of my big toe and dripped onto the floor, where they splattered like watercolor roses. Just below the nail, a thin shard of glass stuck from my skin, pink with blood coalescing around it.

Gah.

I fought to focus and keep down my breakfast.

Blood.

Breathe.

Pulling air deep into my lungs, I leaned on the door to yank the glass from my foot.

Near the center of the room, hundreds of little shards, just like the one I pulled from my foot lay scattered across the tile.

The bulb that once lit the room must have shattered somehow.

When the power was cut, maybe?

Dismissing the how and why, I hobbled around the mess to my office to collect the little hand-broom I kept in the drawer. In seconds, I had the mess squared away.

Abandoning the cleaning supplies against the wall in the entryway, I hop-skipped on my injured foot into the back classroom.

The rooms were going to look so good once I got the mirrors hung.

Both classrooms were painted a pale lilac color, with beautiful gleaming oak floors. Extra high ceilings allowed for magnificent crystal chandeliers in the center of each studio. Natural lights would fill the rooms with the glow of the sun.

But when I flipped the switch just inside the back classroom, no light.

My shoulders fell.

"Seriously?"

The electric company restored power to the house but not to my studio?

With a huff, I spun and stomped back to my office for a flashlight.

After the week I'd had, I needed something positive in my life.

I wanted to see my mirrors.

Equipped with the Maglite from the bottom drawer of my desk and an extra set of batteries—because it had been that kind of week—I returned to the studio.

I flipped on the flashlight as I cleared the doorway and froze.

A—

What?

My lip trembled. Tears blurred the room.

I gripped the door frame, knowing my legs would give out any second.

Blinking to clear my vision, I took in the carnage.

Graffiti and what I sincerely hoped was dirt smeared the walls.

Trash and what looked to be torn forms from my office littered the floor.

Flashlight light bounced off tiny bits of reflective silver shattered and strewn about the room.

Tears overflowed my lashes.

In the center of it all, cut down, lying on its side, the fractured remains of the chandelier.

Bits of crystal mixed with wrappers, paper, and glass.

Hand gripping the door frame, my legs finally gave out. I slid to the floor as a sob wracked through my frame.

How?

All that work. Gone.

All that time spent picking colors and the perfect lamp manufacturer, painting the walls. Wasted.

I'd be lucky if the floor wasn't dented and gouged.

It looked like someone threw a party in my studio.

Tears tumbling off my cheeks, I crawled into the room, brushing aside bits of trash and broken mirror until I reached what remained of my chandelier. I picked up an egg-sized, faceted crystal bead that—thankfully—was still mostly intact. One finger stroked the blunted side of the bead as I cradled it to my chest.

Who would *do* this?

If I'd been home, if I'd been here, would this have happened? If I hadn't lost the key, if the doors had been locked, would the teenagers, or whoever decided to trash my studio, have been deterred enough to find somewhere else to take part in their hoodlum shenanigans?

I peered down at my shattered reflection in the bits of mirror scattered across the floor.

Could I have stopped this?

"Hanna? You in here?"

Molley's voice echoed through the defaced husk of my studio.

With a sniff, I blinked my vision clear and swiped at my cheeks before Molley could find me.

"In here." I gulped a breath and swiped again at my cheeks.

Molley's voice bubbled ahead of her, all cheer an airiness.

"Checking out the new..." Her chipper comment died on a horrified gasp.

Molley froze at the door, eyes wide as she took in the destruction.

Slow, she stepped to me, her heels cracking bits of mirror beneath her feet.

"Hanna, I'm so sorry."

I reined in my emotions, pulling them back inside with a sniff.

"Was it locked? When you came to meet the guys with the mirrors?"

Molley blinked at me for a moment.

A crease formed between her perfect brows.

E. Collins

"Hanna, your friend, Angie, called and said you asked her to let them in."

My brow scrunched.

"I don't know an Angie."

Where are my keys?

Molley squeezed my hand, trying to pull me back, but I kept drifting away, back to the graffiti, the trash, the shattered bits of my dream all over the floor.

"Come on," she coaxed. "Let's go back to the house while I hunt down Jake and Will to get them to stop by Ziggy's or somewhere for supplies."

Another squeeze to my fingers, calling me back.

"We'll fix this, Hanna."

In a fog, I followed Molley back into the sunshine, but when she started toward the house, I came up short.

My toe stung where I cut it, but I dug my heels into the grass.

"I can't," I stepped away from the house with a shake of my head. "I'm sorry, I—"

"Well, you can't stay out here. You'll freeze. Come on, just a few minutes."

When did Molley grow up and become a mom? Her fingers stayed loose around mine, her eyes soft as she turned back to face me.

Another head shake.

Molley frowned, tiny brackets forming around her mouth. The old Molley never would have let those worry lines show.

"What's going on, Hanna?"

I folded in on myself, arms going tight around my ribs.

"Upstairs. In the bedroom."

Molley's frown deepened as worry seeped into her gaze.

"Did—"

Oh god.

"No! It's..."

Sending me one last worried glance, Molley turned and stepped into the house.

She was only gone a few minutes before returning, eyes wide with fear.

"Hanna, come with me."

▲▲▲

Standing in the front yard, I blinked away tears. For the second time in less than a week, I was letting strangers search my home. A steady stream of police officers flowed in and out, all around me and the house, like some messed up whirlpool.

I recognized a couple of the officers from the other night.

Officer Blair was there, along with his partner, but many of the faces were new.

I scrubbed a hand under my eyes to clear away the moisture collecting in the hollows. Behind me Molley was on the phone again, calling around as she tried to locate Jake.

An unexpected wave of longing swelled around my chest and flitted about my lungs as I caught myself wishing Jake was there with me.

Why'd I have to send him away?

I paced on the grass, trying not to fidget too much.

Where was Jake?

What was taking so long?

I paused as a rough-looking, blond detective stepped out of an older model brown sedan parked in front of my neighbor's house. Dark sunglasses obscured his eyes like some tv cop as he scanned the scene from the curb, then he strode into the house.

"Detective Carter," Molley explained. My suspicious stare softened with recognition.

"He worked Jessie's case."

"He works in sex crimes now, but he never let go of her case. Considering what you found, I figured he'd want to be informed."

Right.

Spring of our junior year of high school, my best friend—Jake's girlfriend at the time—was kidnapped out of the school parking lot and held captive for over six months before Jessie managed to escape. Jessie was so messed up from drugs and trauma she couldn't tell the cops a thing about the man who kidnapped her or where she'd been held right away.

Detective Carter and his partner spent countless hours tracking down Jessie's kidnapper, even going so far as to arrest Cole one night.

The detective had been younger then, his blond, swept-back hair free of the silver that peppered it now.

The years had not been kind.

To any of us.

So much had changed since high school.

An engine roared.

I looked up, and my heart did a cha-cha. Jake's truck careening around the corner at the end of the block. Like a mechanical silver steed, the truck sped toward my house before screeching to a halt at the curb inches from Detective Carter's bumper.

Jake might say he was no white night, but as he stepped down from the driver's seat, I couldn't see him as anything else.

Air fled my lips in a rush. In an instant, I turned into one of those swooning girls on tv who claimed to be a strong, independent woman but really just wanted to fall asleep in a loving man's arms.

Forgetting Molley beside me, and how I sent him away earlier that morning, I ran for Jake, needing to be in his arms for some reason I didn't care to look at too closely.

The thoughts followed on my heels.

What if Jake rejects me?

Pushes me away for how I acted that morning.

What if—

But seeing me come, Jake's arms opened wide. He pulled me into his chest in a bone-crushing hug. Lips fell to my hair.

Warm hands splayed over my back like a shield as he pulled me closer to breathe in the lavender scent of my shampoo.

I held on just as tight, clinging to Jake's shirt as I buried my face in the curve of his neck.

It was like every cell in my body craved more of him. I breathed Jake's spicy scent.

He'd been smoking again.

"You came," I whispered into his skin.

Bits of my hair caught in the day's worth of stubble across Jake's jaw.

Unbidden, a lazed memory of that stubble against my most delicate skin in the early hours of the morning surged forth, flooding my senses in technicolor.

I stepped back, feeling the heat rise in my cheeks.

"Of course," Jake's fingers skirted along the underside of my arm to my hand. His eyes shined as he squeezed my fingers and didn't let go.

Jake nodded toward the police roaming around the outside of the house.

"What's going on?" Cobalt eyes shifted over my shoulder to where Molley stood.

"You want the bad or the worse first?" Molley countered when my voice caught in my throat.

Tears bubbled up on my lashes. My shoulder ached with pent-up stress.

Sensing my growing anxiety, Jake's hand slipped back up my arm to pull me into his side.

Jake stood with such ease, ignoring the curious glance Molley sent between us.

"Just tell me what's going on, Moll." Despite his relaxed stance, Jake's voice was strained, the gentle rasp at its edges amplified like he'd been snacking on nails on the drive over.

"Hanna found another photo."

There's a certain kind of anxiety that takes hold when your space is invaded, amplified when there's nothing you can do but stand back and watch.

Standing on the front lawn, a suffocating weight settled in my chest, slithered down to pool at my core.

Cops moved like little worker ants in and out of my house, picking through my things—Greg's things—searching for clues, snapping pictures like peeping Toms breaking into my life, chipping away at bits of my already fragile composure.

Thank God, for Jake and Molley.

Both stayed by my side through it all, Jake with his arms wrapped firm around me like an iron wall as Molley took charge of the situation.

As soon as the cops cleared out, Will showed up with a car laden with cleaning supplies. Everyone set to work on the studio, sweeping up the shards of my sweat and tears, scrubbing away the dirt, grime, and nasty words plastered across the walls and floors until every surface gleamed with new hope.

By then, I was well and totally drained.

Standing at the center of the room, muscles aching, crying out for sleep, I took a turn around the space, taking in our progress, marveling at all we'd accomplished in a few short hours.

I never would have been able to do it on my own, not so quickly or so thoroughly. Molley or Jake would have come by to find me passed out in a pile of glass and rubble, too drained to carry on.

Tears pricked my eyes.

How could I ever repay them for all they'd done? Not just today but over the last week—heck, since Greg died. Despite my efforts to stand tall and composed in my grief, Molley had been there for me, waiting patient for me to open up, to lean on her offered shoulder.

Jake's hand slid over my waist as he came up behind me.

The rasp of his five o'clock shadow tickled my shoulder as he pressed his lips to the curve of my neck.

Lingering only a moment, I stepped away.

As much as I loved the tingling butterflies that shot across my skin and down my spine at the touch, Molley was right across the room, and though it looked like she was preoccupied scouring the last bit of spray paint from the wall, I knew she was watching through that bouncing curtain of curls.

I bent to pick up a trash bag.

Jake's hand found my shoulder as I straightened and turned for the door.

"I've got it. Rest." Concern shimmered in the dark blue depths of Jake's eyes as he slid the bag from my fingers.

New tears slid onto my lashes. They'd been doing that a lot lately. Though I wanted to protest, I let Jake take the bag.

My arms twinged from too much sweeping and scrubbing. My hair was knotted, and I'm sure I stunk.

It felt like I'd been run over by an emotionally abusive Mac truck.

Molley and Jake had done so much for me that day. They jumped into cleaning the studio when I could barely stand looking at the mess that had once been my sanctuary.

And bless them for it, because looking at the studio, fresh and renewed, ease seeped back into my mind.

It was nice, I decided, having someone to lean on, to let someone else take the reins for a change, at least for a little while. I wasn't ready to give up complete control, and I didn't want to take advantage.

I snatched up another trash bag off the floor.

▲▲▲

The backyard was empty when I stepped from the studio. The gate to the alley stood open.

Pausing in the waning sunlight, I drew in a breath of brisk evening air.

But in my hand, the bag grew heavy. My fingers shook, wrapped tight around the straining plastic.

I stepped around the gate into the alley and froze.

There, knelt by the trashcans, Jake crouched, head bowed, hands fisted in his hair.

My brain sputtered, trying to come up with a reason for this sudden shift.

He'd been fine a minute ago, open and affectionate in a way I never expected to experience from him, let alone in front of one of his exes.

What could have caused such a quick change?

I paused.

Could he have found...?

"Jake."

I eased the trash bag to the ground and stepped closer.

Words formed on my lips as Jake's cobalt eyes found me over his shoulder but died on my tongue as I took in the briefest glimpse of the squalling storm at the core of his eyes. Only for a moment, then his carefully crafted mask fell into place.

Jake stood.

Turned.

That signature quarterback's smirk curled his lips.

"What's—"

"Nothing. Let me get that."

If I hadn't just seen him on the verge of breaking down in the alley, I would have believed Jake's swagger and bravado.

Jake stepped around me to collect my abandoned trash bag. He clutched his phone in one hand.

My eyes narrowed.

Slamming the lid on the trashcan, Jake started back into the yard on long, relaxed strides.

Nope.

Not this time.

I wasn't going to let him bottle up whatever that was in the alley. I was tired of the men in my life keeping things from me.

"Jake."

He came to a halt at the gate like he'd reached the end of some invisible lead but didn't turn.

"About earlier, I'm sorry. I wasn't..." What? I wasn't what?

Sorry, I got mad? That I can't believe my dead husband could have those photos in his possession and still be a good person?

"I'm sorry for sending you away."

A weighted sigh fell from Jake's lips.

"It's your house, Hann. You had every right."

"Still, I shouldn't have sent you away. All this—with Greg. I'm having a hard time processing it all. I shouldn't have lashed out when you tried to help. I didn't mean to make you—"

Jake turned.

The bravado and swagger were gone.

In their place, a hollow void, marked only by the scars of what almost looked like regret.

"You should have sent me away the second I offered you a ride home from the garage."

Oh no. We weren't doing this.

Not now.

Part of me wanted to point out that I'd tried, but it wouldn't have helped.

I shook my head. Steel coalesced in my eyes as I stepped closer.

This wasn't the Jake I'd come to know the last few days.

This man before me was broken, shattered by too many disappointments and some invisible final blow that came so swiftly that I missed it entirely.

Muscles in Jake's jaw feathered as he bit down on his next words.

"You're not safe with me, Hanna."

My jaw set. This wasn't happening.

Not now.

I crossed the short distance between us and wrapped my arms around his waist, half expecting Jake to step away.

When he didn't, I pressed in close until I felt the beat of his heart hammering against my cheek.

"I don't want to be anywhere else," I murmured into his chest.

"Hann..."

I shook my head to silence him, squeezed a little harder.

Jake sighed.

One hand fell to the small of my back, pressing me closer like he, too, had felt my absence the last couple of hours.

Jake's voice cracked when he spoke again.

"Shit like this is going to keep happening, Hann."

I edged back to look up into his face with a question Jake didn't need me to articulate.

"Gina called, my ex. She wouldn't admit to anything outright, but...she did this, Hanna, I know it, and I'm so, so sorry. But if I know Gina, she's not finished."

"I really made an impression on her, huh?" My words came out casual, but I was anything but. Jake sent me a deadpan look and shook his head.

He kept talking, apologizing, but I'd stopped listening.

My fingers knotted in Jake's shirt as red seeped into the world.

Gina—not some faceless thugs—destroyed my studio. Broke into my home to do so because she couldn't let go of a guy *she* left.

When all this stalker shit was finished, that bitch was going to pay.

Chapter 30

It was late when we got back to Molley's house. Delivery pizza was consumed in a zombie haze before everyone dragged themselves off to their beds.

But as the minutes passed in that dark upstairs guest room, sleep would not find me. Limbs heavy from hours on the move, I stared up at the ceiling, listening to the seconds tick away on the obnoxiously large wall clock opposite the bed.

I'd need to stop by the police station sometime soon to provide a statement, explain how I found the photos.

When I tried to explain to Detective Carter earlier, the craggy detective just looked at me over the top of his sunglasses with a haggard stare and told me to come in at my earliest convenience for a formal statement.

Jake protested, of course, in a deep growl that cut through the air like churning gravel, but Carter was insistent.

A tingling sensation danced on tiptoes over my shoulders and down my arms. This protective Jake was something entirely new to me in so many ways.

Greg had been so many things—supportive, fun, kind—but he'd never been one to step into the line of fire, to turn himself into an impenetrable wall, refusing to back down.

And the Jake I'd known before had been hotheaded, sure, refusing to back down from a fight, but those fights were always for him. As bad as it sounds, the Jake I'd known in high school never would have stood up for others, not without something to gain.

I blinked up at the ceiling.

Could I trust this new Jake?

My mouth fell open in the silence as I realized the truth of it.

I didn't need to decide if Jake could be trusted.

Something deep in my core already tethered itself to him in a way that would be all too painful to separate.

I drew in a breath, trying to relax enough to claim a few hours of sleep before the sun came up.

I squeezed my eyes shut. They snapped back open the second the muscles eased.

Fine.

Before I could change my mind, I swung my legs over the side of the bed.

So many questions swam in my mind, with so few answers to pair them with.

I needed a remedy soon, or I'd drive myself crazy.

My heart craved to accept these pieces of Greg he'd kept hidden from me, this Greg that would keep those photos hidden away in his office, but I couldn't. As hard as I tried, there was no explanation for the Greg I'd known choosing to keep those photos for himself. There

E. Collins

had to be another reason they were in the house.

In my head, I knew I probably never really knew my husband. It was the most likely answer—Occam's Razor and all that—but a piece of my heart shut the door to that idea and refused to see reason.

I should be sleeping.

I pushed to my feet instead.

▲▲▲

The hall was dark when I stepped from the guest room.

On tiptoes, I skirted down the hall, passed the nursery when Gracie slept soundly.

Soon, I'd have one of those in my own house.

It was surreal. Unsure how to process the idea of a baby, not knowing how to feel about the fact that I may not really know the father of my baby, I pushed the thoughts aside, choosing to live in the here and now.

I stalked through the main floor of the house, thinking myself aimless until I found myself at the base of the basement stairs.

What were the chances Jake was up?

I bit the inside of my cheek.

Slim.

Much of the space beneath Molley and Will's house consisted of a single open room. A large TV and couch were set up in one corner. A foosball table claimed much of the remaining space.

Two doors branched off the open room, one closed, the other leading to a combination bathroom laundry room.

Emboldened by the darkness, I crossed the room in long strides.

371

My hand settled against the closed door.

Steady breathing slid around the wood, the only indication the room was anything other than a storage closet.

My heart hammered in my chest like heavy tribal drums.

Before I could think better of it, I turned the knob and slipped inside and was swallowed into pitch black.

Breathing, steady and rhythmic, called to me through the darkness.

This is crazy.

What was I thinking? Sneaking into Jake's room? Really?

This could go so very bad.

But I didn't turn back.

I took a cautious step forward, then another.

Before I knew for sure what I'd do when I got there, my knees bumped the edge of the bed.

The even breathing I'd been following like a beacon faltered before starting up once more, slower.

I closed my teeth over my lips, holding in the nervous squeak threatening to break free.

One hand touched down on the mattress.

I reached for the blanket, ready to slip beneath.

The breathing stopped.

Before I could think to drop the blanket and skitter back to safety, a hand closed around my wrist and tugged me onto the bed.

A keening squeal escaped my lips as I was pulled flush to a very solid, very naked chest.

I sighed at the contact.

Jake.

My body relaxed into him, sure that, by then, Jake realized it was me.

The grip on my wrist tightened, almost bone-crushingly so.

"Jake," I whispered, breathless. My free hand settled on his shoulder and gave a little shake.

"Jake, let go. It's me, it's—"

Jake blinked in the darkness, hard. When his eyes opened again, they were clear.

Jake dropped my wrist like a hot brick.

"Jeezus, Hanna, I'm—"

"Shh." I ran a hand over a stubbly cheek.

"Don't worry about it. I'm fine. I shouldn't have come down here like this." I was rambling, scooting back toward the edge of the bed, ready to flee.

Jake brushed my shoulder.

"Stay."

I froze, blinking in the darkness as Jake propped himself up on his elbow and leaned over me to turn on the lamp on the side table.

A whoosh of air blew past Jake's lips as he dropped back to the mattress, his eyes wild and ragged with worry when they turned on me.

Feather-light, Jake's hand slid beneath mine and eased it closer to examine my wrist.

A faint purple bruise circled my arm where he'd grabbed me. Just above the wrist joint, three smaller round bruises darkened my skin.

"Fuck, Hanna, I didn't mean—I didn't know—"

"It's fine. I shouldn't have startled you." Jake let out a dark rumbling sound at my defense.

"It's not fine." His thumb grazed over the purpling skin on my wrist.

"I hurt you," his voice was soft, broken.

I scooted closer.

"Not on purpose."

"No," Jake admitted. His eyes remained dark, troubled.

"Then I think we can let it go." I took Jake's hand in mine and squeezed. Why was he being so hard on himself?

I needed to change the subject, draw him away from the damage he'd caused in the dark.

"I couldn't sleep," I admitted. "I keep thinking about those photos, the studio. Maybe you were right about Greg."

Jake watched me a moment, taking in my eyes, the set of my lips, then brushed a lock of hair behind my ear.

"Greg only had eyes for you, you know? Even in high school." My lip wobbled. How did Jake always know what I needed to hear?

"I'm beginning to see why."

Heat rose in my cheeks, and I knew that if it hadn't been so dark, they'd be red hot.

374

E. Collins

Jake's admission sent lightning down my spine and feather-light flutters to my core. It would be so easy to let Jake pull me into his arms, to lose myself in his kisses.

"I need to know how those photos got in my house."

"We'll find out," Jake pulled me closer to his chest and laid back on the pillows. "And about the studio..."

"There's no way to prove Gina broke in, Jake." Even if it would be nice to see Jake's noxious ex dragged away in cuffs.

A noncommittal grunt pulled from Jake's chest.

Callused fingers traced rivers up and down my spine.

My eyelashes dusted over my cheeks.

Jake's heart thrummed in my ear, sure and strong, lulling me toward dreamland.

"I have a shift at Carlo's tomorrow," I murmured into Jake's chest, not entirely sure why I was so unwilling to let the conversation die. We could both use the sleep.

Jake's hands slipped beneath the thin fabric of my tank top to splay across my back. I followed the tantalizing warmth as it radiated out from his touch.

"Hanna..." Jake hedged. I tilted my head to find his eyes in the dark. "Is that really safe?"

"It's my job, Jake. I need the money."

Jake's lips parted, ready to offer me the world if I just stayed away from the bar. They shut without a sound when I speared him with a fierce unyielding glare. I saw the moment the fight fell from his shoulders.

"I might be able to have your car running by then, but I can't

375

guarantee it'll be reliable."

"Mmm." A smile quirked my lips. My eyes fell closed. When they opened again, I slid my hand up Jake's torso to rest over his heart, enjoying the little hitch my touch caused in his breath.

"I wasn't really asking about my car." My lashes pulled back like a butterfly's wings in flight to find Jake watching me, his eyes bright.

"Could you give me a ride?" I asked before adding in a rush, "if it's not too much trouble."

"Yeah. Of course."

My eyes narrowed.

"But I don't want you sitting around glaring at everyone who comes up to the bar asking for a drink."

"I wouldn't..." I fixed him with a look.

"Fine." Jake didn't sound pleased with the idea. "But you'll call if anything happens? Anything at all."

"Mmm," I let my fingers drum against his chest. "I would love to, but I don't have a phone."

"Yeah... about that..." Jake leaned over me again. The scrape of wood filled the room as he opened a drawer in the side table.

My lips curled.

"I don't really see the point in a condom," I drawled as Jake dug around in the drawer. "All considering."

Jake sat back with a grin on his gorgeous face.

"Aren't you presumptuous." Jake pressed something cool and rectangular into my hand. Way too big to be a condom.

I sat up and opened my eyes before letting out another squeak as I dropped the object on the bed.

"Jake, what's that?"

Jake tilted his head and looked at me from under his brows, lips pressing thin in a mocking expression.

"Pretty sure it's a phone. Your new one."

"Y-you can't do this. It's too much."

Jake's fingers slid around mine.

"You can't be without a phone, darlin'. What if something happens? What if you need help?"

"I don't know. Not sure what good a phone's going to do, though." They weren't exactly durable, and so far, I didn't have the best track record with phones.

"Just hold on to it for now. Please? For me."

Vulnerability slipped back into Jake's eyes, sending silvery gray specks swirling in the cobalt spheres.

I frowned, knowing already I'd be taking the phone.

"I don't need help like this," I insisted.

"I know." Jake pulled me back down to his chest and turned off the lamp. "Please, for me, take it. I'll feel better knowing you aren't completely stranded somewhere."

"Okay," I said like it hadn't been decided with Jake's first puppy dog look.

My head dropped onto Jake's chest as his arms wrapped tight around me in the best kind of embrace. I fell asleep counting the steady beats of his heart beneath my hand.

Chapter 31

"You're sure you want to do this today?"

Jake's truck sat in front of my house. Morning sun peeked through the layer of fog that hadn't yet burned away.

"Yeah." Even I thought I sounded unsure.

I stared up at the modest two-story I shared with Greg's memory. So unassuming from the outside, benevolent even. At street level, it was impossible to see the secrets hiding within.

Jake's hand lifted mine from the center console. With a gentle squeeze, he kissed my fingertips. His eyebrows wiggled in an attempt to draw a smile from me.

I tried, but the twist of my lips came off more like the ugly child of a frown and a grimace.

"If this is too much…" I held up a hand.

"I have to do this, Jake. Even if it weren't time, I have to know what was going on." I didn't have to say, "with Greg." We both knew who and what I was talking about, could feel Greg sitting there with us in the truck.

Jake didn't fight me. His fingers brushed a waving lock behind my ear with a resigned nod. I closed my eyes as his fingers trailed down my neck.

"I don't want you doing this alone." This time, I smiled as I opened my eyes.

"I'll be fine," I assured. "I'll lock all the doors."

"Noted and appreciated, but not what I meant." Jake threaded his fingers through mine. "Are you sure you're okay going back in there? You were pretty upset yesterday."

I wanted to trace the creases that formed in Jake's forehead and let him carry me off somewhere if only it would vanquish his worry for me.

Instead, I sat on a deep breath as I processed Jake's concern.

He wasn't wrong.

The house was a great paradox.

I'd filled the rooms within those walls with so many happy memories of life, Greg, and the future we planned. My dance studio blossomed in the living room.

But now those happy memories were tainted with the secrets that sprouted up over the last few days.

It's awful how quick years of joy and love can be wiped away.

One piece of paper shouldn't evoke so much change.

"I'll be okay," I promised as I glanced up at the house.

"I'll be fine."

Jake lifted my fingers once more to his lips, stubble tickling the sensitive skin.

"Call me if anything happens."

My lips fell flat.

I didn't want to depend on Jake. I handled my own shit, even when Greg was around. Heck, I was a one-woman watchdog for the girls at Carlo's.

My fingers went limp in Jake's hand as I tried to pull away. Jake's fingers closed around mine. His eyes sharpened.

"Anything, Hanna."

I forced my frustration out through my nose.

"You don't need to do this." I met Jake's hard stare with one of my own. "I can take care of myself."

"I know."

I blinked.

What?

Jake let loose an amused snort.

"Don't look so surprised."

"No, I...It's not that." My brows pulled close as I looked up at Jake, a mixture of realization and surprise in my eyes. "High school you wouldn't have said that."

The laugh that filled the cab was loud and explosive.

"God, I hope I'm not still who I was in high school." Beneath the laughter was a dark undercurrent of insecurity. Jake worked hard to become someone other than that self-centered boy I'd known in high school, and the idea that anyone could still see him as such troubled him.

"You're not," I said, leaning over to peck his lips.

"Good. But seriously, darlin', those guys we ran into in Montana? They're bad news. Real bad. If anything were to happen to you..."

"I'll call. Promise."

"Okay." We shared one last scorching kiss that made me question every plan I'd made that morning.

Was it just me, or was it hot in the truck? The air felt too close, squeezing around me.

"Let me know if you find anything."

I shoved open the door, grateful for the sudden rush of cool fall air that blasted my face.

My flip-flop sank into the half-frozen lawn. It would need to be cut again before the snow.

Behind me, the whoosh of a window descending.

"Let me know when you're ready to be picked up."

I fought the urge to roll my eyes as I turned and smiled back at Jake.

"Jessie's picking me up for coffee later."

Jake's lips pouched in a pout that almost yanked me back across the lawn to kiss it from his face.

"Don't give me that look," I laughed and truly enjoyed the sound as I turned back to the house. "You've got plenty of your own shit to take care of today."

I turned and waved from the porch, just in time to see what looked like indecision flash across Jake's face. He looked ready to follow me into the house, fire burning in his dark eyes.

Muscles in my legs tightened.

If I didn't put a solid door between Jake and me, I would get very little searching and cleaning done.

Sending one last wave, I unlocked the door and stepped inside.

▲▲▲

Dropping the last stack of loose papers into the trash bag, I let out a long breath.

I was so done with cleaning.

All the books were back on the shelves, the pens back in the mug Greg kept on the edge of his desk. The floor was clear of all debris.

The room looked exactly as it had when Greg inhabited it.

Okay, cleaner.

It took me hours, and I hadn't found anything else interesting amongst the piles of research. No more photos. Not even a loose scrap of paper with an unknown phone number scrawled across it.

I stepped around the desk and dropped into the cushy leather gaming chair with a sign.

I'd never seen inside Greg's desk.

A strange thought. I would have thought at some point in the last five years, I would have gone looking for a pencil, pen, something that would have led me to its drawers. But nothing had.

I slid open the first drawer to find...

Notebooks.

All colors and sizes, all half-full of Greg's neat print.

Random bits of information.

Charts and maps from his various trips.

Each dropped into the trash.

I skipped over the next drawer entirely after opening it to find nothing but dried-up pens and an empty stapler.

The lower drawer was the largest, its metal handle gleaming in the morning light like a beacon. My fingers tucked beneath the handle and gave a gentle tug.

Nothing.

I pulled again.

The drawer wouldn't budge.

I sat back in the gaming chair, eying the little copper keyhole on the front of the drawer.

Locked.

Why?

What was Greg hiding?

A sickening feeling settled in my gut.

More pictures?

Maybe the ones I found were just misplaced and forgotten.

What if the rest of his collection rested somewhere he thought was safe?

Whatever was in that drawer, it must have been something he was trying to keep from me.

I was the only other person with access to the house.

Knowing it was futile before I tried, I yanked once more on the drawer before standing.

I had to find something to get that drawer open.

▲▲▲

A hairpin, butter knife, and screwdriver later, I dropped to my knees in front of the drawer with a little worn hatchet in hand.

Giddy energy bubbled inside me as I eased the leather case off the ax head.

I mean, I didn't intend to keep the desk. Why'd it have to stay in one piece? Could it even be taken out of the room whole?

A wide grin spread over my lips.

This is going to be fun.

Drawing the hatchet back over my shoulder, I drove the blade into the side of the desk. The dark stained wood splintered with a deafening crack.

Yes.

It was ridiculously satisfying.

I swung again and again. Slivers of wood confetti filled the air.

Swiping hair out of my face, I surveyed the damage.

One side of the bottom drawer lay in tatters on the carpet, the side of the desk destroyed.

Finally!

The hatchet fell from my fingers with a thud on the carpet.

I brushed the last bits of the drawer away.

A single manila folder peeked through the gaping hole.

I jumped as my phone chirped with an incoming text.

"Gahhh."

My fingers itched to tear into the file's contents.

But with everything going on...

I paused to check the text.

Jessie.

Out front.

Right. Coffee.

A whoosh of breath slid past my lips.

Great.

The girl had the worst timing.

Be out in a sec

Pausing to snatch the file from the drawer, I shoved it into my purse on the way down the stairs. I'd have to look through the file later.

Chapter 32

I strode into Carlo's that evening, wishing I'd taken the time to try on my usual work uniform before rushing out to meet Jessie.

Running on the high of breaking into the drawer and finding the file, I had to turn back on the stairs, on my out the door, for a spare change of work clothes.

In my rush, I grabbed the first bits of clothing I came across without considering that my body may have changed in the last week. I'd been in yoga pants and stretchy shorts since my last shift.

My black, thigh-high boots pinched at my toes and squeezed my calves as I crossed to the bar to store my purse.

The moment I pulled—and I mean *pulled*—on the sleek hip-hugging booty shorts at Molley's, I had an overwhelming urge to take them off. I stared at my ass hanging out of the shorts for a full minute in the bathroom mirror before stepping out.

Really, the shorts weren't that short, no shorter than anything I would have worn for cheer in high school, but in the last week or so, something changed in my hips. It wasn't perceptible. When I looked at myself straight on, I looked the same. But in my bar clothes, I felt like a whale.

Jake's eyes found me the moment I stepped around the corner into the living room, his eyes going wide and buggy from his place on the couch.

He recovered quickly, realizing I planned to leave the house like that.

Brows dropped over his eyes as a frown tugged the corners of his mouth.

"Ready?" he asked, his voice gravel and shattered glass.

Wishing, then, that I had another outfit choice on hand, I pasted on my most confident smirk and nodded.

Hey, if Jake reacted like that, at least the tips would be good. Lord knew I needed them.

By the time we reached the freeway, I was ready to beg Jake for his shirt.

The little red corset I'd chosen for a top was fine when I was standing, but the second I bent for anything, it became my own personal torture chamber. The fishbone ribs dug painfully into my sides and breasts, even though I'd fastened the clasps down the back on the loosest setting.

I tumbled out of the truck when we finally stopped outside Carlo's, grateful for the ease of pressure on my lungs.

Out of the corner of my eye, I caught motion in the mirror, Jake moving to get out of the truck as well.

I whirled.

"Oh, no. I don't need a babysitter here, Jake. You'll scare off all my tips."

Jake frowned stubbornly.

"Carlo's crowd can keep their tips to themselves." I gave Jake a stern look that said to get to the point. Jake knew me well enough to know I could take care of myself.

"What if..."

"No," I cut him off. "Carlo has bouncers on staff for a reason. I don't need my own personal bodyguard."

Jake's jaw bunched, but in his eyes, I saw that he heard me, that he'd listen.

"Fine." I grinned and leaned across the cab to kiss the tension from his jaw.

"Thank you."

Jake's expression didn't brighten.

"Let me know when you're ready to go. I'll be here."

Unbidden, tears pressed at my eyes.

I sniffed back the welling emotions.

Why did he have to be so amazing?

"Thanks."

I blinked away the moisture.

No point ruining my eyeliner.

I stepped away from the truck.

▲▲▲

From the back of the lot, Jake stared down the rusted metal doors in front of Carlo's. He shifted, unease in the driver's seat of his truck.

He'd promised Hanna he wouldn't hover, so he wasn't. Jake said nothing about leaving the premises. That was just something he couldn't do.

Even if there wasn't someone following Hanna, she'd already had one too many interactions with a particular scumbag lawyer at the bar for Jake's comfort.

Yeah. He'd done his research. Jake knew Ethan was some fancy-pants defense attorney and probably knew the law too well for Jake to intimidate the man into leaving Hanna alone.

If Hanna didn't want Jake inside, he'd stay in the parking lot just in case the pest—because Jake refused to see the smarmy lawyer as anything else—decided to show his face again.

▲▲▲

Carlo's got busy fast. It always did. One second, the place would be next to dead; the next, a horde of concertgoers from next door would come streaming through the doors, all loud and rowdy.

Tonight was no different. I wasn't ready for it.

Tonight, the crowd that filtered in clutched their shiny new Stetsons as they took a dubious look around the open space, taking in the multiple bars and the long stage across the one wall adorned with gleaming silver poles.

Daisy mentioned the country bar down the street had some big-wig singer performing. Our crowd seemed to be those who were too slow to snatch up tickets.

I sucked down my own discomfort and pasted on a cordial—verging on flirtatious—smile as I leaned on the bar to take their orders.

Get a few drinks in them, direct them toward the tables by the stage, and most newcomers would be there all night, their concert long forgotten.

That was the advantage of being so close to a major music hall in a small town. The tickets were bound to run out long before the people's interest. Carlo's reaped the benefits every time.

Popping tops and sliding beers across the bar to a group of guys and their skeeved-looking girlfriends, I glanced around the hall to check on the girls.

It was still early, but the tables were quickly filling up.

So far, there hadn't been any trouble, but I wasn't about to relax my watch.

Nights like tonight, when half the patrons came in moderately disgruntled, having expected to spend their evening elsewhere, people tended to get pushy, if not downright belligerent.

I'd bet money that Eric and the other bouncers would get some work that night.

▲▲▲

There were too many people.

Hands clenched around the steering wheel, Jake squinted through the dim parking lot at the faces squeezing toward the front doors of the bar.

What was going on?

Who went to a place like Carlo's in the middle of the week?

Night came too early that time of year, offering a natural shroud for anyone looking to commit actions of devious means.

I don't like it.

Jake's hands shook with unease. He scrubbed the back of his neck, hoping to relieve the itch in his fingertips to reach for the pack of Camels buried in the center console.

One won't hurt. Just a few drags to take the edge off.

Jake shook the thoughts away.

No.

He was quitting. And he couldn't spare a second to go find something to mask the stench of the tobacco smoke that would cling to his clothes and his breath.

Focus.

Jake reached into the cup holder for his phone, the screen casting the cab in a blue light.

Nothing from Hanna.

He swiped his thumb across the screen to clear the notifications collecting at the top.

Thumbs tapped the screen to open a new text.

She probably didn't have time to answer, wouldn't want him checking up on her either way.

How's it going?

No.

Jake deleted the text, dropping the phone back into the cup holder.

He would not be that guy.

Turning back to the parking lot and the crowd collected at the bar entrance, Jake settled in. Hopefully, there would be no need for him to be there.

Jake wasn't that optimistic.

▲▲▲

"Six tequila shots."

"Coming up, hon," I sent a flirtatious smile over my shoulder to the pretend cowboy on the other side of the bar, gritting my teeth against the stabbing pain in my ribs.

If I could get enough air into my restricted lungs, I would have screamed my discomfort.

Might as well use my attire to my advantage.

The place was packed. It had been go-go-go for the last hour and wasn't showing signs of slowing.

Pressing up onto my tiptoes, I shifted my hips seductively as I reached for a bottle on a higher shelf.

A twenty-dollar tip slid into my hand when I turned back around with six lime-adorned shot glasses full of golden liquor.

"Enjoy!" I slid the tip into the jar beneath the bar.

Offering up refills to those lounging on the bar stools, I searched over the heads of the crowd, checking on my girls.

Ruby Sauntered through the crowd with a tray of test tube shots held high over her head.

Daisy and Chandra were in the back, preparing for their turn on stage.

Kiera, the newest to the crew, seemed to be holding her own at the tables with Renee.

For the most part, the patrons were content to sit, drink, and watch the dancing.

One booth in the corner, though, was getting a bit rowdy. Nothing I couldn't handle.

After one last pass down the bar, ensuring everyone was covered and happy, I slipped into the crowd to regulate the rambunctious table.

"How ya'll doing?" I asked, cocking my hip as I came to a stop at the edge of the booth.

The young man on the end looked to be barely twenty-one and was easily distracted by the proximity of my barely covered breasts.

I offered up a platter of wings, to which I was greeted with much enthusiasm.

Satisfied that the group was distracted from whatever squabble they'd been in the middle of, I sashayed my way back through the crowd.

On nights like tonight, I hated being away from the bar. Everyone was too close, bumping into each other, spilling drinks. I brushed off multiple wandering hands, eager to take advantage of the overpacked bar. Most were just horny drunks hoping to get lucky, easy to deter, afraid of any real confrontation.

I caught Daisy's eye across the hall and offered an encouraging smile.

A hand tightened around my shoulder.

The smile fell from my face as I was pulled around.

I stumbled, struggling to stay up in my heels as an arm barred across my chest, forcing my back flush to a too-hot body.

My heart spiked. Adrenaline poured into my system as fight or flight took over.

I'd been too distracted, trying to keep my balance, to twist out of the hold before I was trapped.

"I could use a bit of service." An oily voice slid into my ear, breath hot on my neck. A hand grazed down my body, tightened on my thigh, as the man ground into my ass.

No.

I'd know that voice anywhere.

Not sparing a second, I rammed my elbow back into soft tissue.

The grip around me loosened, and I spun away, turning to face my attacker.

A small clear space formed around us, onlookers getting out of the way of flying limbs, not wanting to get involved in whatever squabble was about to go down.

I glared at Ethan.

"If you ever touch me again, I swear to God, I'll—"

Ethan closed the gap between us in two quick strides.

"You'll what? Press charges? Do you really think those'll stick after the police find out about the night we met?"

Color drained from my face. A cruel smile curled one side of Ethan's thin lips.

"I'm sure the cops would love to see the photos," Ethan continued.

My eyes widened.

What?

My memory of the night we met was clouded by too much alcohol, grief, and fear. He had pictures?

"You didn't think I'd let you leave without something to remember you by, did you?" Ethan's voice was too smooth, too calm.

Altogether deadly.

"Stay away from me."

The corner of his mouth rose further up his face.

A disgusted sound caught in my throat as I turned and waltzed away.

Space. As much as possible. That's what I needed.

▲▲▲

The text came in a little after ten.

Three little words that sent Jake's heart rocketing in his chest, adrenaline surging through his veins.

Come get me

Brows creased. Jake frowned down at the screen. His thumbs flew across the keypad.

Outside. Want me to come in?

Muscles in Jake's jaw feathered with tension as a minute passed with no answer from Hanna.

Sparking cobalt eyes lifted from Jake's phone to scan the parking lot. Trucks and large SUVs circled the full lot, searching for open parking spots. The crowd outside the rusting metal doors to the bar had doubled in the last hour.

Girls in short shorts and bedazzled cowboy boots clung to beefy men in flannel, waiting to get inside.

It was going to be murder getting through that mess.

Jake's phone buzzed in his hand.

b out n a sec

Jake fell back into the seat to wait, his phone dropping into the cup holder. Hands clenched around the steering wheel and released, only to tighten around the leather a second later.

Eyes trained on the doors, Jake waited, knee bouncing, for Hanna in her ridiculous red top to step out into the night.

Seconds ticked away, turning to minutes.

Jake's eyes flitted toward the back of the building.

Would Hanna leave out the back like last time?

But there was no wavy-haired beauty crossing the lot in his direction.

Unease clenched in Jake's chest.

He couldn't just sit there.

Not for another second.

Snatching up his phone, Jake bound from the truck.

His phone was to his ear before he passed the front bumper on his way toward the growing crowd outside Carlo's.

One ring, then straight to voicemail.

The heck?

Hanna just texted him. Why would she turn off her phone?

Maybe it died?

No. Hanna's phone had been fully charged when they left Molley's. Jake had checked.

There was no reason for her phone to be off, except—

"Fuck."

Jake picked up his pace.

Pebbles and gravel skittered away from the fronts of Jake's boots as if fearing his wrath.

Anyone who stood between him and Hanna in that moment should have been concerned for their life upon seeing the lethal glint in Jake's dark eyes.

As if sensing the fatal energy coursing off him, people shifted out of Jake's way as he stalked up to the door.

The bouncer from the other night eyed Jake with dubious recognition as he approached.

"I'm here to pick up Hanna," Jake all but growled.

The bouncer nodded once as he scanned the ID of a woman with short, curly black hair.

"Hanna hasn't come out," he answered as he took the ID from the next person in line.

"Mind if I..." Jake gestured toward the door.

The bouncer waved Jake through.

Inside, Jake made a quick sweep of the bar.

A little blonde and a busty woman with auburn hair dominated the stage at the other end of the hall. The patrons stared, captivated in the women's direction, crowding the tables surrounding the elevated platform.

Music pulsed through the air.

Even without the music pumping from the speakers mounted in the rafters high above, Jake wasn't sure he would have been able to hear himself think over the general cacophony of voices echoing off the walls.

What kind of max capacity did a place like this have?

Jake wove his way to the bar.

A short, burly man stood behind the counter, taking orders.

Where was Hanna?

Jake's eyes swept over the tables around the bar and stage.

Nothing.

Jake motioned to the bartender, who stepped over, a glass and rag in hand.

"What can I do ya for?"

"I'm here for Hanna," Jake shouted over the raucous. "You seen her?"

A crease formed between the bartender's bushy brows as he thought a moment too long before shaking his head. Holding up a finger, the burly man bent to check something under the counter.

"Purse is still here. Might be in back."

Sparing a stiff nod in thanks, Jake turned to scan the rest of the bar as he waited.

He sent another text.

At the bar. Where are you?

A minute passed.

No new text.

Unable to sit still and do nothing, Jake paced around the edge of the room like a tiger in a cage, searching for prey.

A woman in a short Victorian-styled outfit—it was too short to consider a dress—stopped Jake on his second pass by the bar.

"You're Hanna's friend."

It wasn't a question.

Jake's pulse, already ringing in his ears, picked up several decibels, challenging the music.

"Have you seen her?"

The woman jerked her chin toward the back toward the changing rooms.

"Left out the back a few minutes ago. Looked pretty spooked."

Fuck.

Jake's heart lodged in his throat as his stomach shriveled in his gut.

"Was she with anyone?" Jake's words leapt off his lips in a panicked fervor.

The woman pulled her curls over her shoulder and shook her head.

"Can't say. You might still catch her in the parking lot."

Hanna must not have told anyone about her car.

"Thanks." Jake shoved toward the exit.

Busting out into the cool night air, fear ruled Jake's movements, propelling him through the crowd to the back of the building. The bouncer at the door hollered after him, but Jake didn't hear.

He searched the parking lot for any sign of the wavy-haired woman in the red top.

"Hanna!" He called, shoving a man in a too-tight tshirt out of his way. Jake called again as he stumbled onto open gravel.

Dust plumed around Jake.

No answer came to his call.

No sign of Hanna,

Jake punched her number in his phone.

Nothing.

Straight to voicemail.

Hanna's sweet, chirpy voice told him to leave a message, and she'd get back to him as soon as she could.

Breathing hard, Jake ran up and down the rows of car, scanning each one.

She has to be here.

A long-buried fear slithered up from the depths of Jake's mind, threatening to paralyze him where he stood.

Jake stopped, forcing a breath into his lungs outside the door leading into the back of the bar.

Puffs of steam billowed in the air.

Hands shaking, a mix of withdrawal and adrenaline coursed through Jake's system, forcing him forward.

He had to find her.

Hanna has to be her.

Somewhere in the lot, an engine backfired, loud as a shotgun blast before rumbling to life.

Jake's head snapped toward the sound.

He knew that engine.

Cobalt eyes darted over the lot. Heart rate doubling in his chest, Jake broke into a run.

No.

It had to be a mistake.

He'd been watching.

They couldn't be there.

Even as the thoughts passed through Jake's mind, he knew what must have happened.

They must have beat them to the bar, been lying in wait somewhere on the other side of the building.

A cloud of dust plumed three rows over. Tires squealed.

Before Jake took his first step in that direction, a rusted-out van busted into the open and swerved out onto the main road.

Jake didn't waste a second.

Tracking the van's movement, Jake sprinted for his truck, keys in hand.

The silver pickup peeled out of the lot seconds later, roaring with every ounce of rage Jake felt as it barreled down the road after the van.

Up ahead, Jake's headlights met empty pavement.

Foot heavy on the gas, Jake kept driving, undeterred.

He knew which way the van went, and if it was the last thing he did, he'd catch it.

Driving mad, Jake didn't see the county cruiser on the side of the road until he'd well passed it.

Blue lights flashed in his mirror. A glance down at the speedometer showed the dial nearing ninety.

Shit.

The cruiser's siren whirred.

Debating the consequences if he kept going, Jake glanced in the rearview. Hands strangled the steering wheel. The muscles in Jake's jaw twitched.

He couldn't find Hanna if he was behind bars for evading the cops.

Fist slamming the steering wheel, Jake let his foot off the gas.

Chapter 33

Something wasn't right.

I knew it before I opened my eyes.

A strange chalkiness clung to my tongue, sticking it to the roof of my mouth and cheeks.

I licked my lips, hoping to alleviate the uncomfortable, dry feeling.

No luck.

My throat ached like I'd been screaming for hours. Cotton filled my head, slowing my thoughts as they passed through my mind like walking through mud.

I furrowed my brow, concentrating, trying—to little avail—to remember what came after my altercation with Ethan. I'd been upset; I knew that much.

I went straight back to the bar and texted Jake to come get me, but then what?

And why was I sleeping on the floor?

My arm felt numb, bent up under my head.

A shiver skittered over my skin.

The floor was like ice.

Did I fall asleep in the studio again?

How'd I get home?

I shifted, arm scraping over stone.

I peeled back my eyelids, lashes crusted with salt, reluctant to part from each other.

Blinding light speared my irises.

Lashes dropped as I tried to clear my vision, pulled back.

Eyes adjusting to the intense glow emanating from overhead.

Through bleary eyes, I took in my surroundings.

The room was small, with concrete walls and floor. A root cellar? A single bulb dangled from its cord in the middle of the room.

I looked to the heavy wooden door but found no light switch around its edges.

The fuck?

A single window sat high on the opposite wall, small and narrow over a precarious stack of logs.

Oh God, where am I?

Pain throbbed at the back of my skull. Pressing my fingers to my hair, they came away sticky and red, wreaking of iron.

Blood.

I wiped my hand on my shorts and pushed onto my knees.

A wave of nausea surged, drawing bile into my throat.

Bending over my knees once more, I emptied my stomach on the floor.

Gross.

Strands of hair dangled into my mess.

I swiped them back and peered around the room once more.

There had to be a way out.

Eyes settled on the window. A sinking feeling dropped into my stomach as memories of late nights at Jessie's after graduation filtered to the forefront. Nights when Jessie divulged details of her abduction she hadn't even shared with Cole.

Oh God.

This is—

Breath came short bursts. My vision blurred with tears.

This wasn't good.

I shrieked as a thump sounded overhead. I stared up at the ceiling. My heart hammered in my chest. Blood billowed through my veins at double pace. My chest heaved, searching for air I just couldn't seem to find.

It's okay, Hann.

You've got this.

Think.

But my mind was well past rational thought. There was nothing clear or level-headed about how my brain was functioning.

Sound overhead meant people. People who could help me. People who might know what's going on.

Pressing higher up on my knees, I drew in a deep breath and shouted as loud as I could.

"Hello?"

I waited. Listened.

A scuffle, then the thump of rapid footsteps.

Then silence.

Without warning, the room went dark.

A startled cry tore from my lips. I scuttled backward in a frightened crabwalk. My back slammed into the wall. Sobs wracked my chest, stealing what little air I'd found. My cries echoed off the walls around me, disorienting me further in the inky black.

I blinked as I tried to even out my breathing. As minutes passed and nothing happened, my vision returned little by little as I grew accustomed to the dark.

Pushing past the ache in my head, I focused on a point high up in what had to be the corner nearest the door.

My heart bottomed out.

I'd been wrong.

I wasn't alone in the room.

In the top corner, nearest the door, a little red light blinked.

▲▲▲

Jake glared at the police officer through the open window of his truck as the cop finished writing up the ticket.

He'd tried desperately to convince the cop to let him go, that he had to find his friend. The officer wouldn't budge.

For a long moment, when the officer returned to his car to run Jake's registration and license through his system, Jake seriously considered taking off. If he was quick, Jake may be able to escape. Chances were, even with the head start, the officer would still catch up to Jake before he reached Hanna.

The officer handed Jake a slip of paper through the window with his ticket information and instructions on how to pay the fine.

Jake blinked at the infraction.

Ten over? Seriously?

Either the cop's radar gun needed to be calibrated, or his eyes needed checked.

Either way, it was Jake's lucky day.

"You slow down and drive safe, you hear me?"

The officer met Jake's gaze through the window as he handed back Jake's ID and registration.

Not wanting to push his luck any further, Jake nodded, stiff.

Jake's jaw ticked. Blood rushed in his ears.

He mumbled a "thank you, officer" and threw the documents into the passenger seat where Hanna should have been sitting in that skimpy get-up she called an outfit. Jake knew she'd been uncomfortable the moment she stepped into Molley's living room. The way Hanna's nose bunched, roses seeping into her cheeks as he took her in, were the only things that kept him from commenting on the look then and there.

She'd been stunning.

Hanna was always stunning.

And now she was God knows where, with some creep, in a

creepy, rusted-out van, and Jake had no idea how to find her.

His fist slammed the steering wheel.

Jake meant to stop after the first blow, but as his fist collided with the leather, something in him snapped. A numbing heat shot through his hand that was oddly cathartic.

Over and over, Jake punched the wheel until a warrior's cry, laden with frustrated loss and pain, ripped past his lips and filled the cab.

Breathing in bursts, Jake stared out the windshield into the night.

The van was gone, with it, Hanna. There was little chance of him catching up now.

It happened again. Another one gone, because of him.

Somehow, Jake had to find Hanna.

He reached for the key.

A white, nondescript card caught his eye in the coin holder below the radio, a six-pointed star in an evergreen circle in the upper corner.

Frowning, Jake reached for the card and read through Officer Shawn Blair's contact information.

Hanna must have left it in his truck after her house was broken into.

Jake's jaw tensed just thinking about how shaken up and frightened Hanna had been that night, knowing whatever she was feeling now had to be ten times worse.

All Jake wanted to do was pull Hanna into his arms and hold her until all the bad disappeared from her world. He'd hoped that by driving Hanna to the baby's new foster home in Montana, he'd be doing just that.

He hadn't expected how his feelings for Hanna would shift.

In high school, Jake never saw Hanna as someone he might be interested in romantically.

Sure, she was beautiful, anyone could see that, but she was Jessie's friend, Molley's teammate, and she'd always been with Greg. One look at Greg and Hanna together, and anyone would see they had eyes only for each other.

But now...

Jake wasn't sure what he and Hanna were to each other, wasn't sure that he deserved to be happy with someone as generous, and caring, and funny as Hanna, but he intended to find out.

First, he had to find her.

Jake picked up his phone and dialed the number on the card.

▲▲▲

Jake barely slept that night.

Returning to Carlo's, the truck was barely parked before Jake was out and storming toward the crowd still mingling outside the double doors, past the bouncer, to the burly man at the bar.

Palms slammed onto the bar.

"Who'd Hanna leave with?"

The man behind the bar eyed Jake warily.

"I don't discuss employee's personal lives," before turning back to the other patrons.

Jake pressed further over the bar.

"I was supposed to pick her up. She never came out, and now she'd not answering her phone."

The man shrugged a beefy shoulder as he filled an older gentleman's glass, completely unbothered by Jake's raging show of masculinity.

"Must have found another ride."

Jake was ready to jump over the bar and show the burly man what he thought of his suggestion.

The edges of his vision tinged with red. Fighting for control, Jake's hands clenched around the edge of the bar.

Fuming, Jake tore his eyes from the bartender to scan the room, hoping Hanna would come bouncing through the crowd in that tiny red top and all his worrying would be for nothing.

But Hanna wasn't there. Jake felt her absence settle into his chest. He knew in his gut, that she was in that van.

Taking one final pass over the room, Jake froze, focus settling on a familiar, smug man in a suit, the last person Jake wanted to see at Carlo's.

Fury burned in Jake's throat as he shoved off the bar.

In seconds, rage carried him across the room, and Jake had the man by the front of his shirt, slamming him back into the wall before anyone could blink.

There was no more red in Jake's sight, just a blank, white-hot sheet.

"Where is she!"

The man was several inches shorter than Jake and quite a bit leaner. In his rage, Jake could have put him in the ground with minimal effort, but the man just smirked up at Jake.

"So, she ran out on you too, huh?"

"Where is she?" Jake slammed the man into the wall with enough force to topple a linebacker.

Before Ethan could answer, Jake was hauled off him by the bouncers.

"What's going on here?" a tattooed bounced demanded. He didn't take his hulking hand off Jake's shoulder.

Ethan straightened his suit jacket.

"Nothing at all," he said smoothly, like he hadn't just been lifted off his feet.

"Just a misunderstanding." Ethan's lips curved in a placating smile meant to sway a jury. It didn't little to fool the bouncer or Jake.

Glancing between the two men, the bouncer's gaze settled on Ethan.

"Thought I told you last week not to come back here."

Hands raised in the air. Ethan's smile turned oily.

"My mistake. I'll be going."

Jake made to follow Ethan to the door, but the bouncer's grip tightened on his shoulder.

Ready to tear the muscle-bound man a new one, Jake spun on him. He paused as he met a curious stare.

"You're Hanna's friend."

Jake's face tightened, and he swallowed back a snarled retort, answering only with a single nod.

He shrugged out of the bouncer's grip.

"She's missing. I think she might be in danger.

The bouncer nodded.

"She went out the back about half an hour ago." Jake followed the bouncer back to the bar and watched as the big man slipped behind the counter.

The bowling ball of a bartender eyed them from the other end of the counter.

"Purse is still here."

A small light brown bag plopped onto the counter in front of Jake.

Jake's frown deepened as he stared down at the purse.

He didn't know much about Hanna, didn't pretend to be an expert when it came to women, but Jake was pretty confident Hanna would never leave her purse behind.

The bartender stepped up next to the tattooed bouncer, creases deepening into canyons cutting across his forehead.

"What's going on, Eric?"

"Hanna's missing."

The bartender's chin jerked toward Jake.

"The boyfriend?"

Jake tensed as he met the man's shrewd stare.

"Something like that. I have reason to believe she's in danger."

"From you?" the bartender, Carlo, Jake realized, leveled his stare on him.

"I'd never hurt Hanna." Several uncomfortably tense seconds ticked away. Carlo gave a curt nod, convinced by the conviction in Jake's words.

"There's not much else we can do here," Carlo explained with a note of apology, "if we hear anything, we'll let you and the police know."

Jake nodded his thanks.

"Mind if I take this?" Jake nodded to the purse.

"I'm sure Hanna'll be wanting it when you find her."

▲▲▲

In the parking lot, the freezing air barely registered to Jake as he crossed to his truck.

Dust plumed around his boots with each charging step.

Where were the cops?

Where was Blair?

Breath coming in heavy bursts, Jake threw open the driver's side door.

Who knew where Hanna was, what she was going through. If the men who'd been following them in Montana had her—

Jake shook his head.

Focus.

He had to focus if he was going to find Hanna. To do that, he needed to get a grip and calm down.

Breathe.

"Hanna's strong. She can take care of herself," Jake reminded himself.

But what about the baby?

No matter Greg's connection to that photo she'd found, Hanna would never forgive herself if something were to happen to her child.

Drawing a slow breath, Jake tossed Hanna's purse into the passenger seat and pulled out his phone.

It was too late to call, but what other choice did he have. If he weren't out of ideas with nowhere else to turn, Jake wouldn't have bothered.

Molley is going to kill me.

The phone rang in Jake's ear.

Icy tendrils slithered up Jake's spine to twist around his neck like a noose. Breath came in gasping breaths as he fought for control over the rising panic.

Hanna, where are you?

If he'd caused another girl to—

No.

He couldn't think like that.

He'd find her.

He wasn't that stupid kid in high school anymore.

Unable to sit still, Jake dumped the contents of Hanna's purse on the passenger seat.

Lotion, spare socks, a wallet, Chapstick all spilled out on top of a manila folder.

The phone at his ear clicked, abruptly cutting off the ringing.

"Hello?" Will.

"Can I talk to Moll?" Jake's words came out rushed, more vulnerable than he'd planned, but he was having a hard enough time keeping himself in one place waiting for Blair without worrying about some made up rivalry with Molley's husband.

Jake listened as the man on the other end of the line threw off blankets and sat up in bed.

"Do you have any idea what time it is?" Will groaned.

"It's Hanna."

Silence.

A weighted sigh came over the line.

"Hold on a sec."

Balancing the phone against his shoulder, Jake unclasped the latch on Hanna's wallet and flipped through while he waited.

A fond smile lifted the corner of his mouth as he found the money slot jam-packed with coffee-house punch cards.

Shuffling over the line.

"What's going on, Jake?" Molley answered, sounding like she'd both been awake for hours and just been pulled from something important.

The noose around Jake's neck tightened.

"Hanna's missing."

"She what? You're sure?"

"Yes, I'm sure," Jake growled.

"Are you sure she's not, like, in the bathroom or something?"

"She's gone. Someone grabbed her. I saw the van."

Silence.

"Have you called the police?"

Attempting to swallow back the lump in his throat, Jake nodded.

"Yeah," he forced out. He explained about the text, Ethan, the van, then finding Blair's number in the truck.

"What did he say?" Molley asked when he finished.

"He's not here."

Molley was quiet for so long Jake was sure she'd hung up.

"Give me one minute. I'll fix this."

Jake suspected this was one of the few situations Molley could not fix with her many connections, but he stayed silent, knowing not to interfere when Molley was on a mission.

He flipped open the front flap of the folder on his passenger seat. Printouts and photos filled the folder.

"I'll call you back." Molley came back.

"Moll," Jake forced out before she could end the call. His heart hammered in his throat, wedging itself in tighter with every second. He swallowed, but it wouldn't budge.

Molley stilled on the line.

"Hanna's pregnant."

"Shit."

Yeah. That about covered it.

"Jake, I'm..." The pity in Molley's voice grated Jake's ears. He wished he could wipe it all away like a smear of grease.

The pity, the pain threatening to rip his still beating heart from his chest, the whole damn situation.

Hanna should be somewhere far away, safe in his arms, not alone and afraid God knows where.

Jake's eyes burned.

Needing something, anything, to make him feel like he was making progress, Jake flipped through the pages in the folder he'd found in Hanna's purse, hoping to find some clue to help lead him to her kidnappers.

Hanna must have found the folder in Greg's office somewhere.

Was this what Hanna's house was broken into for?

It had to be.

"Jake, just sit tight. I'll handle this."

The call ended.

Jake skimmed through the pages of notes.

Natalie Dormer

Disappeared April 237, 2009

Found dead August 6, 2010, Spokane River Indian Canyon

Last seen...

Jake froze, staring down at a single name underlined in red.

This was it.

This had to be it.

Heart a jackhammer in his chest, lungs aching for more air, Jake shoved out of his truck and searched the parking lot.

Where is he? Where'd he go?

The crowd outside the bar doors had cleared, most moved inside.

Only a few people lingered around the gravel lot. Tendrils of smoke wafted over most of their heads as they let off steam or caught a breath of tobacco-flavored air.

None were the smarmy blond lawyer Jake was looking for.

A ferocious growl tore from Jake's lips, more animal than man, as he spun toward the street.

Where was he?

He couldn't have gotten far.

A police cruiser pulled into the lot, flipping on its lights to clear bystanders from its path.

Finally.

Jake ran back to his truck to snatch the page of notes from the folder.

The cruiser barely stopped in front of the silver truck when Jake slammed the paper to the driver's side window, his burning blue eyes meeting the officer's moss green glare through the glass.

"Ethan St. James took Hanna."

Chapter 34

The lights never came back on.

Frozen on the floor, I listened in the darkness for any movement overhead, beyond the door.

My teeth chattered.

Beyond that silence.

I stared up at the blinking red light.

At least with the lights off, I didn't have to worry about being watched.

I bit my lips, holding in what bit of control I still possessed.

Drawing a breath through my nose, I held it until my lungs screamed before letting air rush past my teeth in an audible whoosh.

Okay.

What next?

I scanned the space around me, hoping some source of light would jump out at me, sneaking in around the edge of the door or window. But in the dark, I couldn't even pinpoint where the door and window were.

Another breath to settle my mind.

There had to be a way out.

There was always a way out.

I rolled onto my hands and knees and crawled forward until I met the wall, fingertips bumping the rough concrete.

And the door is this way...

I felt along the wall only to come to a corner.

Great.

Or this way?

One hand on the wall, I pushed to my feet, turning back the way I came, only to stump as my toe caught in a divot in the floor.

"Ow!"

I clutched my throbbing foot.

Was it bleeding?

Where were my shoes?

Not that I was upset to be out of those boots. My arches still ached from the steep heel.

When I got out of there, I'd need to make for the nearest outlet mall to find more sensible shoes.

How'd I even get into that little...basement?

Please don't be a buried shipping container!

Kneeling in the dark, I tried once more to fit together the shattered fragments of my memory leading up to...what?

I must have been kidnapped.

By who?

Jake sure as hell wouldn't leave me in this freezer of a room.

Flashes of a van.

Men in the front seats.

The longer I concentrated, the blurrier the edges of my memory.

Fatigue and frustration slid like a blanket over my mind.

For the moment, I left the past behind to focus on escape.

It didn't matter how I got in that room.

Not really.

What mattered was how I was going to get out.

▲▲▲

Jake glared out the windshield at the large glass doors leading into the building that housed the law offices of Gordon St. James and Associates.

It wasn't hard to find.

Housed in a newer, brick-faced building on Riverside, the edifice looked like it had been transplanted from some university campus.

Large plate glass windows flashed in the sun, stretching three stories over the front doors. White stone capped the building in a scalloped crown, declaring its superiority over the other buildings living around it.

The clock on the dash read five past eight.

Already, the street was crowded.

Cars and SUVs crammed into the metered parking around

Jake's truck along the curb.

Busy people rushed along the sidewalk, moving past the shuffling homeless with their lives laden on their backs.

Focused on the doors, Jake paid little mind to the morning traffic.

Ethan would be there soon.

Jake scrubbed a hand over his face.

He hadn't slept the night before, spending the hours driving up and down the streets around Carlo's until Molley finally called and forced him to come back to the house. There, he dropped on the couch, search engine already open on his phone, as he searched for any bit of information on Ethan that might lead him to Hanna.

Unfortunately, the law office and a few news articles cataloging Ethan's career were all Jake could find on the elusive lawyer.

No past criminal history.

No home address.

Jake only skimmed over the article headlines.

Ethan had been busy in his short career.

Article after article documented the numerous high-profile cases the man took on over his short career.

Ethan's climb up the career ladder had been swift, just under ten years.

But none of the cases in those articles would help Jake bring Hanna home.

Hanna's petrified screams echoed in Jake's mind. No matter how he tried to quiet them, they were there, mingling with images that should have been long forgotten. Images that were forever burned in Jake's mind, his own personal atonement for his shortcomings.

He couldn't let Hanna become another one of those memories.

Jake dressed as soon as he heard Molley and Will moving around upstairs, threw on his boots, and was out the door before either of them could come downstairs.

On the seat beside him, the file folder from Hanna's purse rested with its secrets.

Jake didn't know what he would do when Ethan got there. His rational brain had quit working hours before, but even Jake knew there was no way the man would talk to him, not after Jake put him in the dirt the other night for touching Hanna.

He had to try.

Jake glanced at the folder.

There had to be something in there to make Ethan talk.

Knuckles wrapped against the driver's side window, startling Jake from his thoughts.

A familiar bearded cop stared in at Jake from the other side.

Jake scowled and rolled down the window.

Blair didn't bother with pleasantries.

"Do I want to know what you're doing outside Ethan St. James' office?" A steaming paper cup passed through the window. The roasted scent of coffee grounds wafted into the car.

Jake set the go cup between the seats, a sick feeling settling in his gut. Hanna would have had that cup out of his hands in seconds. Half of it would have been gone before he could blink. The woman had a serious caffeine addiction.

"Same as you, I suspect." Jake strained to keep a scowl from his face.

Bushy brows lowered over narrowed shamrock eyes.

Despite the officer's tendency to get in Jake's way, Jake had a feeling in any other circumstance that Shawn Blair was the kind of man he could grab a beer with.

"The police have this handled. Don't make me write you up for interfering in the investigation, I don't care how much the girl means to you."

Jake glared back at the officer. It would be so easy to let the pent-up rage spiraling in his gut do the talking, but Jake was no good to Hanna behind bars, and that's exactly where his mouth would get him if let loose.

"Don't you have your beat to get back to? Some hoodlum kids to harass?" Jake snarked anyway as he turned his attention back to the building's glass doors.

"I can't let you go in there."

"What are you doing here anyway? Ethan's not going to keep evidence in his office."

Blair nodded as he stared up the sidewalk. His mustache bunched over his lip.

"You're right."

Jake couldn't take it any longer.

"So do something!" There's got to be something hidden away in his house. Hanna could be locked up in some underground vault."

If possible, Blair's brows fell lower over his eyes as he nodded to a man passing on the sidewalk before speaking in a low voice.

"It's not that easy. We can't just barge in, guns blazing. This isn't some Criminal Minds shit. Police need evidence. A warrant."

One corner of Blair's mustache rose as he eyed Jake. He slapped a stack of napkins into Jake's hand.

"We'll get there. We just need some proof."

A pointed look passed between the two men before green eyes flitted to the napkins and back to Jake's face.

"Find some evidence. Then we'll talk."

Smacking the hood of the truck, Blair swaggered toward the double glass doors like some wisdom-spewing cowboy.

Jake shook his head, watching the cop disappear into the building. The man made no sense.

Tossing the napkins onto the passenger seat, Jake reached to roll up the window, ready to be out of there, when a dark smudge on the napkins made him pause.

A crease formed in Jake's brow as he folded back the top napkin. His lips parted.

Oh.

On the second napkin, an address had been scrawled in hasty block letters.

Jake's lips curled.

If Blair wanted evidence, Jake would find him evidence.

▲▲▲

I pulled my knees up to my chest, squeezing tighter into the alcove behind the door.

With no light and no clock to judge the passage of time, I had no way of knowing the hour or how many had passed as I sat there in the dark.

I stared across the room at the only hint that more than a few minutes passed. On the far wall, a faint glow seeped around the edges of the plywood secured over the window.

Morning.

Though my captors tried to keep it out, the sun had found me.

And if the sun could get in, I could get out.

Chapter 35

Jake stared at the tall wrought-iron fence standing fifteen feet off the road. Spear-like points stood across the top of the fence like a row of black teeth.

The address on the napkin led Jake North of town, out past the Indian Painted Rocks, up a bluff covered in thick pines. A narrow single-lane road twined up the hillside, lined for miles by that tall black fencing. Every half mile or so, a turn of lead to a gate and keypad, the only indications of a break in property lines.

He hadn't seen a single house.

Jake drove until he reached the gate corresponding to the address given to him by the cop. Then, he drove another quarter mile before stashing his truck in a secluded space off the road.

Dressed in a dark sweatshirt and worn jeans, Jake hoped the wide hood would obscure his identity from any passersby or cameras.

He stepped to the fence, listening for any sign of security.

A place with fences and gates, like the one Jake was sizing up, was bound to have guard dogs, armed security, cameras at the very least.

Jake's hands shook as they closed around the bars.

Here goes nothing.

Taking one deep breath to calm his nerves, Jake hauled himself up and over the fence. His boots crunched pine needles on the other side as he landed in a crouch.

On bated breath, Jake waited for alarms to sound, for someone to come running.

When the only sounds to reach him were the wind in the pines high overhead, Jake straightened.

▲▲▲

Footsteps roused me from a fitful half-sleep. My shoulders ached from the cold and my cramped position against the wall.

Were those voices?

Louder, I listened as heavy feet thudded down a flight of stairs, echoing through the walls.

Scrambling to my feet, I pressed flat to the icy concrete wall.

I'd only get one shot at this.

I had to be ready.

Voices, clear and loud, through the thick door.

I held my breath, afraid to make a sound.

"All I'm sayin' is, I don't like it. It's the first place they'll come lookin' for me."

The high, nasal whine scratched something in my mind.

"Don't see why we can't jus' take her to yer place. Plenty of

space there."

Compared to the first voice, the one that came next was teeth and wrath, seething rage and indigence.

"Because, thanks to some chivalrous do-gooder, I've got the cops breathing down my ass. You couldn't have picked a worse time to break out, could you? Between the cops and the media, it's a fucking miracle I was able to slip away this afternoon. Where is she?"

A key rattled in the lock.

My world narrowed to a pinprick as the lock turned.

The click echoed through my skull.

The door swung in.

A spear of light cut across the floor.

"God damn it, Tip. Where's the fucking light?"

Fumbling beyond the door.

The single bulb blinked back to life, casting the room in sharp white rays that pierced my eyes.

"FUCK!"

My eyes burned from too long in the dark, but I squinted through the pain.

I couldn't afford to mess this up.

Someone stomped into the room.

"You let her escape. That's two, two that you've lost. Do you have any idea what will happen if we don't find her?"

Around the edge of the door, a neat blond head of hair and a tailored suit came into sight.

No way.

The breath I'd been holding fled past my lips.

I'd known he was slimy, but I never thought he was this dirty.

Primed to strike, I waited.

It didn't matter who he was.

Just a few more steps into the room.

That's it.

One more.

Run!

Springing forward, I shot from my corner. I was around the door before the slap of my feet on the concrete could reach Ethan.

Hair everywhere, flying in my face, sticking to the tracks of tears and fear streaming down my cheeks, I slid, half-blind, into a dim hallway.

Straight into the arms of my second captor.

▲▲▲

Gulping back a scream, I stared up into dull brown eyes. Sickening recognition sank in as I took in the hallows around those eyes and the man's gaunt features.

Scraggly dark hair stood off his head in tufts, hanging down over his forehead like the floppy scruff of a dog. Beer and stale cigarettes wafted from his mouth.

Fear drove into my spine like railroad spikes, halting time in its tracks.

I knew this man.

Ten years had passed, but still I saw the snarl on the man's face as the police dragged him away from Jessie in front of that house party, captured in the many photos that filtered through the high school halls in the weeks that followed Brandon Tippins' arrest.

Something was wrong.

Very, very wrong.

This man should be in jail, not running free.

I'd been at his sentencing. The prosecutor had been convinced the man would never see the light of day again as a free man for what he'd done to Jessie and many girls before her.

A blink and the seconds began to tick away once more.

I drove my head forward and struck out against the man. Limbs flew in all directions as I fought for freedom.

A keening squeal peeled from the man as my knee found something soft. The fingers around my arms loosened.

I tore myself free and turned to the far end of the hall where a second door stood open, natural light shining in.

Freedom.

Tripping and stumbling, I shoved off the man and scrambled to get nowhere before a hand snaked around my neck.

Feet flew out from under me as I was pulled back.

Ready to fight, bite, whatever it took to get free, I gulped in air as the hand tightened over my windpipe. In a second, I was gasping air through a sliver of a straw.

Cruel laughter bound over my shoulder as Ethan pressed

himself into my back.

Oh god! Was that...

Something hard rolled across my ass.

Sick fuck.

When I get loose, I'll—

Like the snake he was, Ethan's grip constricted around my throat until spots flickered across the edges of my sight.

This was it.

I wouldn't see Jessie, or Molley, or Jake again.

Gahh!

Jake.

He'd be looking for me.

Not just because of whatever was growing between us, but because of the guilt my disappearing like I did would cause in him, so similar to Jessie's kidnapping.

Ethan's fingers pulsed, letting my lungs fill with air before my airway closed again.

Only then did I see my error.

A pressure bomb settled in my chest, pressing at my lungs, ready to explode.

Vicious laughter slid from Ethan's lips like poison.

"Now, Hanna. Is that really how we play nice?"

Chapter 36

A hundred yards from the fence, trees blocked Jake's view of the street.

Before him, lush green grass stretched over shallow hills and valleys to a magnificent three-story mansion.

Neither the house nor the vibrant lawn was visible from the road.

God, who could ever use so much space.

The mansion's sandstone exterior caught the sun like a copper disk.

Huge plate glass windows gleamed in the midday glow of the fiery orb in the sky.

Between the coloring and the sheer craftsmanship that had to have gone into the construction, the expansive house was blinding to look upon.

The place had no business being a single guy's house.

Jake didn't care how good a lawyer Ethan was. How could some guy no more than ten years his senior afford such an obscenely ostentatious home?

Up close, the gigantic structure was even more over the top.

Beneath every window, intricate carvings cut into the stone, framing the glass in swirling scallops and spirals.

The stonework alone had to cost more than Jake made in a year at the garage.

A long driveway looped in front of the house, circling around a large flowerbed full of evergreen shrubs. At its center, a burbling found sat in a deceptive calm as water burbled over the sides.

It was easy to see how one might be distracted enough by their surroundings to miss the viper guiding them into his lair.

Jake took in the house as he circled around the back, keeping to the trees and out of sight.

No cars in the driveway.

No one lounging by the crystal blue pool.

Both balconies stretching the back length of the house were empty.

Halting near the corner of the lower deck where the trees met the grass, Jake scanned the backyard.

The lower porch was tiered, stretching out over the yard and around the pool.

From his place in the trees, Jake made out a low row of egress windows beneath the tallest tier of the deck. The perfect place to break in undetected.

One last glance around to make sure no one else was about. The windows on the back of the house were dark, shielding anyone who may be standing on the other side, but for Hanna, Jake had to risk it.

He shot across the short stretch of grass in a handful of long strides into the darkness and relative shelter beneath the deck.

Staring down into the hole around the closest egress window, Jake frowned.

Sealed.

Through the glass, Jake had a clear view into a large room outfitted with dark leather couches and utilitarian black end tables.

Some kind of living room?

It looked more like a waiting room for some twisted sex dungeon.

Even the floors were an easy-to-clean black marble.

Is that a drain in the corner?

Jake didn't even want to consider what that was for.

He didn't have time for this.

He had to get in, find Hanna, and get out.

But how?

A place like that was bound to have a security system.

If Jake broke the class, an alarm would sound before the first shard fractured on the tile floor.

There had to be a way in.

Some way to...

Jake froze, standing over the third window.

A sliver of open space stood between the bottom of the window and the sill.

Perfect.

Overhead, the patio door slammed.

Jake stilled, breath held in his throat as short, quick steps clicked over the deck.

Shit.

The heeled steps stopped.

Not daring to move or breathe, Jake stared up through the boards, waiting.

A shadow stood against the railing.

Silence stretched so long, Jake glanced down at the open window, considering going for it.

But it was too risky.

Familiar metallic clicks snapped overhead. A temping sulfuric scent wafter over the railing and down to Jake a second later. The sweet tobacco scent filled his nose.

A long audible drag. A scratchy woman's voice spoke through the exhale.

"Hey Marcie...Yeah, just taking a break.

"You wouldn't believe the mess he left this time."

Jake cocked his head.

Cleaning lady.

Jake glanced back at the window.

Cracked only a couple inches, the open window was precisely the break Jake was looking for.

Judging by the sound of the woman's phone call, Jake had at

least ten minutes alone in the house before the cleaning lady returned from her smoke break.

He'd have to make every minute count.

No longer concerned with being overhead by the clearly overworked and underpaid maid, Jake crept to the window and eased into the shallow pit around the outside.

Easing the window up, Jake dropped into the room.

Bits of gravel and dirt flaked off Jake's boots onto the gleaming floor.

A nauseating wave of bleach washed into Jake's senses.

Oh.

Jake blinked hard, his vision blurring from the noxious fumes. He tried to uncross his eyes.

So that's why the window's open.

Jake stepped around the couch.

What apathetic bastard decorated this place?

The walls were a bare, hospital-white tile stretching up the bottom five or six feet.

The fuck?

Jake stared at a small, elevated platform against the far wall encircled by couches.

A single iron ring was affixed to the center of the platform.

Afraid to touch anything, Jake stepped around the platform to a black door leading to a dark, narrow hall.

Jake's eyes adjusted quickly to the lack of light, still stinging from the bleach vapors in the air.

Three doors lined one side of the hall.

Like a shadow in the night, Jake slid soundlessly down the hall to the first door. Shaking fingers closed around the knob.

The cool metal turned in Jake's hand, but the door held firm.

He tried the next door with the same result.

Jake released the knob and turned to move on to the next.

As the rubber sole of his boot met marble beneath his first step, Jake paused.

He didn't know why, couldn't remember anything distinct, but Jake could have sworn he heard movement behind the second door. Faint, blink-and-miss-it quick.

Jake pressed his ear to the wood panels, held his breath to listen.

Yes!

Definitely movement.

Someone—or something—was in there.

Jake pounded the door, his heart threatening to burst from his chest.

"Hanna!" he called as loud as he dared. "Hanna, can you hear me?"

A soft whimper.

Then, nothing.

Silence.

Dark, still, silence.

A growl tore from Jake's chest. He tried the knob again.

Nothing.

He pressed closer to the door.

"If you're in there—if you can hear me—I'm coming back. I'll get you out."

Silence.

Jake couldn't afford to waste any more time.

He had to find something, anything, that could get the cops a warrant to search the house.

Expecting to find the final door locked as well, Jake turned the knob and nearly stumbled into the room on the other side as the door swung inward.

Jake blinked, sure he was imagining the small, dirty room. Barely long enough for him to lie across the floor, the room had space for a small, stained mattress and a tin bucket in the corner.

The longer he stood there in the doorway, the more the sights and smells seeped into his senses. Despair and panic clung to the room.

Something bad happened there.

Bile rose in Jake's throat as he pulled out his phone and snapped a couple pictures.

Returning to the hall, Jake pulled the door shut on the tiny prison cell before his stomach found a use for the tin bucket.

Breathing in sharp, shallow bursts, trying to rid himself of the slimy feeling the room left on his skin, Jake stepped from the door.

The hall continued around a corner, ending with one final door at the base of a stairwell.

Jake stilled as a chill raced over his arms. Dread at what he'd find behind this new door tightened like a noose around Jake's neck. He forced himself forward, grasped the handle with a sweaty palm, expecting another cell, maybe a sadistic torture chamber, all leather, steel, and chains.

The handle turned.

Plush carpet and an ornate oak desk met Jake on the other side of the door. A large bookcase covered the wall behind the desk.

Clean natural light filtered in through a high window running along the top of one wall, casting the room in shades of green as it passed through the bushes growing on the other side of the glass. It was oddly calming, a stark contrast to the nightmare down the hall.

It looked like Greg's office in a way, though it lacked the bright airy feel.

It only took Jake a moment to clear his head enough to step back into his search.

Hanna wasn't there, but maybe Jake could find something that could point him toward where she'd been taken.

Jake couldn't put his finger on why exactly, but the whole room—more so than the hall, cells, or even the weird showroom—had a foreboding sense of death about it. Maybe not physical death—God knows the place was too clean for that—but an emotional, spiritual death that left its mark on a place far longer than any corporeal event ever could. There had to be something incriminating hiding close at hand.

Jake approached the desk.

Every neuron in his brain screamed to bolt, turn and run the other way before any more horrors could be added to the toybox of nightmares living in Jake's brain. He almost listened.

But he had enough regrets to keep him awake for the rest of his life without adding anything more.

If Hanna was gone forever, Jake didn't know how he'd carry on.

He had to find her.

Jake lifted a file off the corner of the tidy desk, flipped through to find it full of invoices.

The rest of the files piled on the corner appeared to be client files, notes on cases mostly.

Jake paused on a file buried deep in the stack, the name printed across the tab calling to him.

Brandon Tippins

He knew that name.

Why did he know that name?

And the neat handwriting, he knew it too. Jake stilled, his blood freezing over.

No.

The picture in Greg's office.

The one with the date scribbled in the corner.

The slant, that weird, squished loop between the o and n.

It was the same.

If Ethan had been involved in whatever happened to the girl in the picture, Hanna was in serious danger.

▲▲▲

The world began to fade. Darkness crept into the corners of my sight as my consciousness slipped.

Through the swirling shadows in my oxygen-deprived mind, I glared back at Ethan.

If this was how I was going out, I wouldn't beg, not to Ethan.

I was going to memorize every aspect of his face, from the sharp brows and piercing blue eyes to the smarmy snake grin warping his lips, so I could come back and haunt his ass for the rest of his miserable existence.

Precious seconds ticked away. Ethan's smile only grew as the light seeped from my eyes.

Energy drained from my pores like water from a spout as the last of the oxygen fled my lungs.

A slow blink. Another.

Each time harder than the last to open my eyes.

I wouldn't go easy.

I fixed my gaze on Ethan's, forced him to watch.

A cheery ding jumped from Ethan's slacks pockets.

Ethan's jaw ticked with irritation.

For a moment, he glared back at me like he wanted nothing more than to squeeze the last of the life from my body. Then his grip loosened on my throat.

"Hold her."

Ethan shoved me toward his lackey, who was still recovering from my earlier attack.

Slim, deceptively strong arms closed around my torso. Fingers brushed the side of my breast.

Air surged into my lungs, searing across my bruised throat muscles on its way down.

I didn't care.

I could breathe.

It didn't matter that the air was damp and smelled faintly of mildew and the rotten scent of a body left too long unwashed.

It was air, and it meant life, at least for a few moments longer.

Ethan stared down at his phone.

"Fuck me."

I almost smiled as Ethan swiped intently at the screen of his phone.

"What's up, boss?"

I smirked.

"Someone spoil your plans?" I asked, sickly sweet.

▲▲▲

Jake stared up at the bookcase behind the desk as he tucked the file under his arm.

There was nothing special about it. Just a few law books and photos on a whole bunch of open shelves.

Setting his hand on the lower shelf, Jake leaned in for a closer look at a phone in a dark wooden frame.

A younger Ethan stared back at him from among a group of smiling teens. A girl with flowing blonde hair grinned from the center of the group.

"What the—"

Jake knew the man behind Ethan, had seen him recently. His hair was shorter, his cheeks a little less gaunt, but Jake knew he'd seen him.

The van.

The man following Hanna.

Fumbling for his phone, Jake stepped back from the shelf.

The bookcase clicked as his hand lifted from the shelf.

Beneath where Jake's hand had been, a small drawer popped open.

Of course, the bad guy with the torture chamber basement has a secret compartment in the bookshelf.

Needing to find something to win Blair and Carter a warrant, Jake edged closer, leaning in.

Peeking into the drawer, Jake's eyes widened. His jaw hit the floor.

Fuck.

Driver's licenses.

The drawer was half full of them.

All of them women's.

Jake could see several were expired, but there were just as many still active.

As far as Jake was concerned, there was only one reason for someone to have that many women's driver's licenses.

Trophies.

Jake snapped a picture.

It was time to go.

▲▲▲

Jake was in the hall when his phone trilled.

The maid's heels clicked overhead as she returned to work.

"What?" Jake hissed softly into the device.

Blair answered casually, sipping from what had to be a coffee. "Find anything?"

The man was obsessed with those designer drinks.

"He's got a torture chamber in his basement. Cells and a drawer full of girls' IDs." Jake crossed the large room to the open window, more than ready to make his escape.

"I'll send photos when I get back to the truck."

"Woah! Wait a...Hold on, back to? Jake, where are you?"

"Getting you that evidence for a warrant."

Blair groaned through the phone. Jake could almost see the stocky man tugging on his russet beard.

"Please tell me you're not in the house."

"Okay." Jake hauled himself up onto the sill.

Another groan from Blair.

"You know I can't use anything you found while trespassing. It won't hold up."

Jake frowned as he climbed out of the egress ditch.

Right.

The whole law thing.

Fuck.

A crease formed in Jake's brow.

"If I can get a clear shot of the IDs from the outside, will that be enough?" Jake mentally worked his way back through the house to the office.

What side of the house was that window on?

"I don't know. Maybe. Jake, I meant for you to watch the place, to see who comes and goes, not break in and go all commando. If I'd known..."

"He's got people here. Girls." Jake didn't really know that, but if it got Blair moving...

"Alright. Get the photo from the outside, and we'll see what we can do."

Chapter 37

Molley sipped at her tea, a deep crease in her forehead as she watched Jake over the rim of her cup. Her lips twisted in a disgusted grimace.

Herbal tea is the worst.

But after what she'd confirmed that morning, Molley didn't want to risk her usual caffeinated beverage of choice.

Molley watched Jake flip and scan a page. A permanent frown seemed to have affixed itself to his face. It was there when he got home, not that Molley blamed him. Nothing on earth could make her envy the situation he'd found himself in.

Jake hadn't looked up from those files since he stepped through the door.

A nervous energy poured off him, ramping up with every passing hour.

Dark, disheveled hair stood on end on top of his head from all the times he'd raked his scalp in frustration.

The garage door slammed somewhere near the front of the house.

Scrambling claws scrit-scratted across the hardwood floors as a smiling gray-muzzled pitbull barreled into the kitchen to greet her housemates.

The aging pitbull slid into Molley's legs with the gusto of a dog half her age. Molley scratched the top of Estel's bulbous head as she searched for the proper course of action to help Jake.

Shawn Blair called around three that afternoon to ask about some evidence Jake found, but when Molley inquired about said evidence to the brooding man filling her living room with anxious, negative energy, she got only a shrug.

"Don't know what he's talking about."

Molley promised Blair she'd keep pushing and hung up.

Watching Jake pour over those documents, Molley took another sip of her tea and pushed the mug away.

She had to do something.

It wasn't healthy for Jake to get so wrapped up in searching for Hanna. He was verging on obsessed.

Yes, they all wanted Hanna found and brought home safe, but what was Jake going to do that the police couldn't?

Will stepped up beside Molley at the island, his forearms leaning on the counter. The counter creaked in protest as Will glanced at the teabag dangling over the edge of Molley's cup.

"No coffee?"

Molley pasted on an innocent smile as she turned to face him. Her husband had a better nose for a lie than any bloodhound Molley'd ever heard of.

"Thought I'd try caffeine-free for a while," she said before choosing to tack on, "to help me sleep."

Brackets formed around the corners of Will's mouth, but he didn't push any further on the issue. Instead, he pushed off the counter and moved to the pantry in search of a snack.

Molley let out a silent breath and asked about his day. Best to steer conversation away from her shifting habits.

A missed period wasn't anything new for Molley—she'd grown accustomed to the absence of her monthly visitor over the last few years as she struggled with her weight—but the past few days, she woke up with a sour taste in her mouth, feeling like she'd just gone ten rounds in the ring with Mohamad Ali.

When Molley had to pull over the other day on her way home to let an uncharacteristic wave of motion sickness pass, she grew suspicious.

Will didn't know yet. Frankly, she wasn't sure how to tell him.

They'd just adopted Gracie and only had her in their lives a little over three months. Barely enough time to get to know each other.

Will had always been very clear when it came to their future together. Considering his past health issues—years of radiation and chemo treatments—neither one of them thought it was even possible for them to have biological children together.

The two pink lines buried deep in the bathroom trash proved they'd both been wrong.

Will came out of the pantry with a pair of bananas. He set one on the counter in front of Molley before peeling the other.

"How's he doing?" Will nodded toward the living room. He took a bite of banana.

Molley let out a bone-deep sigh.

"Not great."

"You talk to him?"

Molley twisted the string connected to her teabag around her finger as she stared into the yellow steaming liquid.

She'd only manage a couple sips of the bitter brew.

She tried another tiny sip and wrinkled her nose in a way that made the corners of Will's mouth twitch upward.

"Not since he got back."

Will's brows rose over his chocolaty gaze in a look that could only suggest one thing.

Molley let out a low growl and pulled herself off her stool, abandoning her tea on the counter.

She hated when Will was right.

▲▲▲

The concrete was cold beneath my cheek. Beyond the door of my dark prison, footsteps receded down the hall and up the stairs.

Blinking back tears, I bit my lips to keep from making a sound.

My throat ached with every breath. Bruises spread across my neck and peppered my ribs.

Arms closed around my middle.

Please be okay!

I hadn't hit the floor that hard when Ethan and his goon tossed me back into the cellar room, but it was still so early.

Hands pressed to my abdomen, feeling for some sign of the life growing inside me, anything to tell me he or she was okay, safe.

A tear slid past my lashes, over my nose, to puddle on the concrete.

I had no idea how much time passed in the dark silence. Seconds seemed to both crawl and flash by at the speed of light at random. With no other options, I stared up at the square of light peeking in around the boards covering the little window near the ceiling.

I couldn't move.

Could do little more than breathe.

Cold seeped into my bones.

Even as the icy chill on my skin grew unbearable, I stayed still.

Horrors swirled in my mind, every outcome and scenario.

If I shifted, even to pull my knees up to my chest, the fragile bond I'd just begun to form with the life inside me would fracture and fall away, leaving me empty, hollow, without my last tie to Greg.

I still didn't know why those pictures were in his office.

The myriad of nefarious reasons for its existence assaulted my mind, bleeding doubt into the many happy memories I'd built with the man I thought I'd spend my forever with.

In the back of my mind, a tiny voice whispered.

Don't give up hope.

Fight to live.

I pushed up to sitting, backed against the wall.

The little voice in my head was right.

For the life inside me, for the memory of Greg, I couldn't give up.

I blinked at the white light slipping in around the edges of the tiny window. It was my only option. The thick door to the little room was locked; there was no way I'd be able to get through that without getting caught.

Rubbing my hands up and down my arms to bring back a modicum of feeling, I listened to the sounds overhead and around me.

Wood creaked as the building overhead settled on its bones. Birds chirped outside.

No footsteps rocked the floorboards above.

No heavy metal pounded, vibrating in the walls and into the floor.

The building seemed free of life sounds, but was it really empty?

Had Ethan and his lackey really left? Or were they just waiting for my next move?

I blinked away another minute or hour—who could really tell—in the darkness before rolling onto my knees.

When I was relatively certain I was alone, I scrambled across the concrete, moving like someone lit a fire beneath my feet, until my fingers bumped up against the rough, splintering edges of the wood pile beneath the window.

Yes!

Now, to get out.

I stared up at the halo of light sneaking in around the edge of the window.

It was a long way up.

Was it boarded from the inside or the outside?

Who boards a window from the inside? That doesn't make any sense.

I shook my head to clear my drifting thoughts.

I had to get up to that window. It was my only way out.

Frowning, I wiggled my toes, still trapped inside my infernal knee-high boots. Those would have to go. The only way up to the window was over the woodpile. My ankle would snap like a twig if I tried to climb that rickety stack in five-inch heels. The boots worked great for the bar, allowing me to see over the heads of almost anyone in the place, but they were not the best for mobility.

I dropped back on my butt and yanked the boots free, chucking them over my shoulder across the room.

Hopefully, Ethan would trip over them when he came back, break a tooth, or something. An arm?

What was going on with my mind?

Shaking away the out-there thoughts, I stumbled back to my feet.

Why was balance so hard to hold onto?

Vision blurred at the edges.

The dry wood bit and pulled at the bottoms of my feet as I started up the stack of logs toward the window. Skin on the soles of my feet tore as I hobbled over the logs.

A breath fled my lungs in silent thanks to whoever watched over me as my fingers butted up against the edge of the shallow sill.

The splinters embedded in my feet would have to wait.

I hauled myself up to the window and pressed my hand to the blackened space where I should have been able to see outside. The pads of my fingers came up against cool glass.

Boarded from the outside then.

I smiled to myself at the little victories.

Now, to do away with the glass.

The woodpile wobbled as I knelt on top, feeling for a heavy chunk of wood to bash my way out. Finding a piece that might work, I weighed it in my hands, prodded at the jagged, brittle end with my fingers.

It would have to do.

One hand on the wall, I pressed back up to the window.

Here goes nothing.

Gripping the log in both hands, I reeled back and swung the chunk of wood at the window with all my strength.

A sharp crack as glass splintered. Sharp bits rained down on my head. Reverberations from the strike shot up through my arms, numbing my fingers, but I was so close.

Tightening my hold, I swung again, harder this time.

The blow landed in nearly the same place on the window.

I swung again.

Shards of glass flew as the log glanced off the sill, its weight tugging me off balance.

No, no, no!

I fought to stay upright as the logs under my feet began to tumble.

Surprise pulled from my lips as I fell.

Landing in a heap of wood and glass, I sucked in a breath, trying not to cry at the stinging in my knee or the slow throb in my ankle from where it turned on the falling logs.

The echo of the falling woodpile bounced off the walls around me, mocking, taunting.

No way out now.

Tears in my eyes, I glanced up at the window and blinked in surprise.

I'd done more than merely shatter the glass.

Whoever boarded up the window must have done a pretty poor job picking supplies. A small hole busted through the plywood on the other side of the now shattered glass, letting in a beam of waning evening sun.

I followed the beam to where it landed on the floor in a pool against the far wall, my hopes sinking.

It would take forever to stack up the pile of logs again in the dark, and who knew if it would be stable enough to hold my weight.

Then there was the glass.

The evening light on the floor laughed in the face of my misery. A sob worked its way up my throat.

Something shifted overhead.

I froze, eyes widening.

My lips clamped down on the sob.

What was that?

I'd been so sure the house was empty.

That definitely sounded like the legs of a chair scraping on wood floor.

On bated breath, I waited for what came next.

I didn't have to wait long.

Distinct heavy boot tread stopped overhead, sending my heart pounding at marathon speeds as it lodged in my throat.

No, no, no!

Not now!

I forced myself to my feet, scrambling for a plan. But every thought trudged through sludge in my mind in their attempts to come together. Solid, coherent thoughts waited just out of reach. If only I could lasso them and tie just a few together to...

He was on the stairs.

No time for intricate escape plans.

Kneeling, I snatched up the largest log I could find.

Jumping over the mess, I fit myself into the small space behind the door and waited, sure that any second, the light would come on.

My breath refused to slow. It came in long, jagged gulps of air that left me feeling lightheaded and dizzy.

I clung to the log like it was the only life preserver in the ocean of fear flooding my mind.

Seconds ticked by.

The room stayed in darkness.

I listened as the footsteps drew nearer, marching down the short hall to the door.

The lock scraped on the other side of the door, but the room remained black.

Through the thick wood, mumbled curses, soft and higher pitched than Ethan's voice, almost effeminate.

Good.

I waited as Ethan's minion fought with the locks. The muscles in my arms strained from holding the log overhead. But I had to be ready.

It only took seconds for the door to open after the last lock snapped into place.

"What's going on down here?"

The beam of a flashlight sliced across the room, pausing on the tumbled pile of wood in the middle of the room.

Ethan's minion took two steps beyond the entrance, his silhouette just coming visible around the edge of the door.

I held my breath.

With the lights off, he had no way of knowing where I was unless he found me in the shallow beam of his flashlight.

Come on. Just a few more steps.

"Frickin' bitch..." he mumbled as he took one more step into the room and knelt to pick up a chunk of wood.

My brain screamed inside my head.

Now!

As Ethan's goon knelt, I swung the log downward with all my strength, connecting with the man's head with a satisfying thunk.

The man fell forward with a cry, but I didn't stick around to see if he was alive or unconscious.

Stealing my chance, I shot around him and out the door, pulling it closed behind me.

Determined to lock him in, give the guy a taste of his own medicine, I stared at the outside of the door, taking in all the intricate locks.

Once again, my brain was moving through quicksand, unable to piece together through the fog of fear and whatever else was pumping through my system how to work even one of the locks.

No. Too much time.

I had to get away.

But even in my slightly addled state, I knew I was no match to outrun a grown man, even if he did have a concussion.

Unwilling to waste any more time, unsure when Ethan would be back, I threw my hands at the locks, turning and sliding anything that would move in hopes that one of the locks would hold. I turned and darted down the hall and up the stairs.

Chapter 38

Jake glared at the files in front of him.

Papers and notes blanketed Molley's living room coffee table, spilling over onto the floor.

After hours, words bled together on the page. Nothing made sense.

Jake flipped back to the front of the stack of papers before him.

There had to be something in there that would lead to Hanna. Why else would Ethan want to keep the files from the police?

A loud pop sounded as Jake sat up to stretch his neck. His eyes fell on the file from Ethan's office, the name printed on the label tab.

Brandon Tippins.

The name sounded so familiar.

Why?

Jake flipped open the front cover of the file on the coffee table and leafed through the typed pages inside.

Case notes from the looks of it. Lots of them.

A growl built in the back of Jake's throat as he flipped through the beginning pages of the file.

This wasn't working.

There had to be some other way to find Hanna.

"Any luck?"

Jake looked up from the jumble of words on the page as Molley dropped onto the other couch. Over her shoulder, Jake noted Will watching them from the kitchen. Will swiped a coffee cup off the island and set it in the sink.

A bone-deep sigh tore past Jake's lips. Cobalt eyes leveled on Molley.

"Nothing." He dropped the file back onto the coffee table.

"Not. A. Single. Thing."

"I talked to Shawn Blair," Molley said like she was approaching a child with bad news. Jake's attention peeked.

"Did he get a hit on the van?"

Molley's lips thinned, and Jake knew the answer before she opened her mouth.

"No."

Molley's response stung, punching Jake in the gut in a way he hadn't expected.

He'd failed. Again.

He'd failed Hanna.

The voices in Jake's head resurfaced with a vengeance, loud and taunting. Poking and prodding Jake with memories and mistakes he could never outrun.

I should have met her inside.

I should have known something would happen.

I should have stopped them.

A warm, delicate hand settled on Jake's knee, squeezing until he reluctantly met Molley's eye.

"Maybe it's time to step away. Just for a bit."

Though Molley spoke in the gentlest way, it felt like a slap.

How could she suggest such a thing?

Hanna was in danger.

He couldn't stop—not till Hanna was safe, back in his arms.

Jake paled.

The baby.

If anything happened to Hanna's baby, Jake would never forgive himself. He'd tear whoever hurt them limb from limb.

"Maybe something to eat?"

Jake shook his head.

When he met Molley's gaze, there was so much pain in his eyes she had to bite back the urge to pull him into a tight hug.

"You really care about her."

Jake's head bobbed. Exhaustion from the day tugged at him.

"It's happening again, Moll," Jake's voice came out like broken glass. "I can't..."

The muscles along Jake's jaw ticked as he bit back a surge of emotion.

"I have to find her. I can't let what happened to Jess happen to Hanna."

Molley's lips pressed thin. None of this was Jake's fault, but reminding him of that would do little to ease the pain and worry that consumed him.

"We'll find her." It wasn't the soft soprano that answered.

Jake looked up as Will's hand landed on Molley's slim shoulder. Brown eyes met Jake's with a deep understanding Jake never expected to find in the big man.

To say Jake and Will's relationship had been tense would be an understatement.

When Will and Molley started dating, Jake had been in a dark place. Angry and bitter, unwilling to accept that someone else could move forward with their life while he was stuck in the past.

Though Jake and Will learned to live with each other over the years, and much of Jake's bitterness subsided, their interactions tended toward snark and back-handed comments. Jake never expected the level of sincerity he saw in Will's eyes.

Tears pricked at the corners of Jake's eyes. Nodding, he sucked them back. Regardless of the new tenuous territory they found themselves in, Jake wasn't about to cry in front of Will.

"Jake." Molley stared down at the open file Jake left on the coffee table.

"Where did you get this?"

Cobalt flashed to the file and back to Molley.

"I...probably shouldn't say... Why?"

Molley flipped the file closed and pointed to the name on the

"You know who this is."

It wasn't a question.

"I don't..."

Jake's throat went dry.

"Jessie," Molley prompted.

Jake's brow creased.

No.

That couldn't be right.

"But that was Mr. ..."

"He was just the..." Molley coughed to clear the building emotion thickening in her throat. Her next words came out half-strangled. "Buyer."

Jake stared at Molley, the cogs turning behind his dark eyes.

"But then..." Cobalt eyes flashed to the files on the coffee table.

Without warning, Jake shoved off the couch and strode toward the front of the house.

"Jake, what—"

"Get those files to your cop friend," Jake called over his shoulder to Molley as she and Will followed close on his heels.

Jake fished his keys from his pocket.

Outside, the sky was just beginning to darken, the edges turning a deep, purply hue across the horizon.

"Jake, wait. What's going on?"

He couldn't relax. It was like Jake's nerves were on fire. Jitters scurried over the skin on his arms and chest like a thousand little bugs.

Keys jangled in his hand as Jake wheeled to face his friend.

"He has her, Moll. The freak that took Jessie," Jake's voice came out like stone, hard and cold, rigid.

Molley met Jake's gaze, seeing the unyielding resolve there in the dark depths that she'd never seen before. A resolve that not even the football team making it to the state championships put in Jake's eyes.

Every second that passed was like a physical blow to Jake's heart. Both sharp and bludgeoning. Bruising the outside as it sliced deep to his core. If anything happened to Hanna...

Jake couldn't wait around for the police to get their ducks in a row. Hanna didn't have that kind of time. Not if she was with that psycho.

He couldn't breathe around the pit forming in his throat. Try as he might, Jake couldn't swallow back the fear pressing at the back of his throat.

Jake spun back toward the silver truck parked at the curb.

He had to get to Hanna.

Chapter 39

Okay, Hanna.

You're free.

Now what?

Head on a swivel, I took in my surroundings, the decrepit house beside me, the clearing and dirt drive cutting into the forest.

Pine trees loomed in the darkening twilight on the fringes of the long, wild grass, raking the sky like claws.

Have to get away.

Hide.

Vision blurring, I stumbled for the trees, tall grass lashing at calves.

If I could just reach the trees, I'd be home-free.

There'd be plenty of space to run under their sheltering cover. But which way to go?

The gravel road cut a path from a faded red pickup next to the house into the forest.

There. That was my way out.

Through the gloom behind the open doorway, I could see the hall leading down to my prison stood empty.

Good.

I had time.

Beyond the tree line, I was forced to slow to a disjointed jog. It had been a long time since anyone cleared that section of woods.

Trees grew close together. Discarded needles covered the ground, obscuring sticks and rocks that bit into the soles of my bare feet like vicious harpies.

Clambering over a fallen tree, I glanced back over my shoulder.

The locks on the door must have held.

I squinted past the fuzz clinging to my sight, scouring the trees to my left for the gravel path.

It would be quicker to just run up the middle of the drive. Also, incredibly stupid.

Ethan could be back any minute.

From the looks of things, that gravel path was the only way in or out of that clearing by car.

Ethan sure as hell wouldn't be walking in.

Not in his fancy-ass suits.

Grimacing as the arch of my foot came down on a snapped twig, I spotted the path.

The sky darkened.

Soon, I'd be unable to see where I was going, let alone the path that would lead me back to civilization and help.

My corset top pinched at my sides, squeezing my breasts as I fought for air.

When I got back, the first thing I was going to do was buy more comfortable work attire.

This is ridiculous.

For a moment, I considered stripping away the corset, discarding it on the forest floor, and running the rest of the way naked from the waist up, boobs waving in the wind.

But how would that look to someone who was helping me?

Would someone help me?

Some crazy half-naked chick running in the woods?

Probably not.

So, I kept going.

Short bursts of breaths pulled into my lungs around sharp bursts of pain as the ribs of my corset dug into my sides.

I moved as fast as I was able, falling over tree trunks and stumbling over stumps and rocks.

Branches lashed at my bare arms.

Wind pulled at my hair, ripping strands from the long braid down my back.

I couldn't stop.

Not here.

Not safe.

Not with...

I pressed a hand to my stomach.

Was the little life inside me still there?

My baby?

Sixteen weeks was still too early to feel any kind of movement; at least, that's what the internet and the apps all said. Too soon for the little life inside me to give me any indication that she was still there.

I don't know why I called the baby a she.

I had no way of knowing one way or the other. And it just felt wrong calling the little life inside me an it, even if it was more correct. My baby wasn't an it. My baby was a human life, a little girl or boy, though the ultrasound technician in Billings said it was still too early to tell which on the grainy screen.

I picked up the pace.

It was getting dark.

I had to get my baby to safety.

Unbidden, cobalt eyes flashed in my mind.

Smiling and warm.

Jake.

Where was he?

He had to be beside himself with worry. Fear.

That night at his friend's, I hadn't expected his confession in the dark, tiny morning hours as he bared his soul, his deepest torments.

My heart squeezed and twisted.

He'd think this was his fault.

With everything that happened to Jessie still weighing on his conscience, how would he handle my disappearance?

I shook the thoughts away.

It didn't matter. Not now that I was free.

Soon, all his worry would be over.

As the icy wind tore at my hair and clothes, I felt the warmth of Jake's phantom embrace around me.

When I got back, I'd bury myself in his arms and never let go.

I stumbled and almost collapsed to the forest floor.

The thought scared me coming so soon after losing Greg.

Were my feelings for Jake just another mistake?

Another shining example of my poor coping skills?

I shook the thoughts away. I could worry about that later.

Now, I had to get out of those woods before it got too dark, and I lost my way.

Through the trees, I found the road once more.

Despite my aching legs, I picked up the pace.

The highway had to be close.

Nobody made driveways that long anymore. Who would scrape them in the winter?

Shadows descended amongst the trees, casting long lines along the forest floor. Needles crunched beneath my feet, their tips digging into my sensitive soles every other step, leaving the skin prickly and sore, but I couldn't stop.

Not now.

Not with freedom so close.

▲▲▲

Jake gripped the steering wheel, foot heavy on the gas, as his mind raced back through the years.

That night. The night Jessie went missing. Jake was supposed to be there to pick Jessie up after practice.

If he'd just been there, none of this would have happened.

Jessie wouldn't have to fight with her memories every day.

Hanna wouldn't be missing.

If Jake had just been there.

But no.

Instead, where was he?

Out with his friends and some girls he wasn't even interested in.

Jake's truck slid on gravel as he spun the wheel and pulled onto the highway without letting up on the gas.

Now, the same creeps who kidnapped Jessie in high school had Hanna, and again, it was all his fault.

Hands strangled the dark leather steering wheel. Hard eyes glared out the windshield.

If anything happens to Hanna or her baby...

The cool nylon polymer of Jake's personal firearm pressed into the small of his back.

Usually, the Glock stayed locked in a safe under his bed, but since everything started popping off, Jake kept it on him.

If something happened to Hanna...

He'd never shot anyone, but if one hair on Hanna's head was out of place when he found her, Jake had no doubt he'd be pulling the trigger on whoever hurt her.

Shadows collected along the roadside, stretching from the trees lining either side of the road in close-knit rows of evergreen.

Inside, the cab of the truck was silent, but as Jake blinked, he could have sworn he heard the phantom beats of a pop rock band he used to listen to religiously, always on full volume, filling the cab–A ghost of the last time he sped down that road.

Jessie'd been so small, frail from malnutrition and months of being locked away in the cellar beneath Brandon Tippins' house. Her skin was so pale, nearly translucent in the moonlight, stretched thin over the bones and muscles beneath her face like the taught surface of a drum.

And like an idiot, Jake nearly ran her down.

Hanna's words wove through his mind.

It's over now.

It wasn't your fault.

No one blames you.

Jake shook his head clear.

None of that mattered.

The past didn't matter.

He had to get to Hanna.

Without thinking, Jake pressed the gas pedal to the floor.

The quicker he got to that despicable cabin...

Movement in the trees up ahead caught Jake's attention out of the corner of his eye.

Probably a deer.

Even still, Jake let up on the gas.

Jake had a sizable savings, but he didn't need to be draining it on repairs to his truck after trying to drive through a three-point buck.

Jake eyed the thick wall of foliage.

A crease formed in Jake's forehead as he frowned.

Cobalt eyes focused on the point in the trees where he'd seen the movement.

Maybe it turned and went the other way?

Tension slid from Jake's shoulders when nothing jumped out of the trees.

He turned back toward the road.

That particular section of highway was dark. No streetlights lined the shoulder. Just forests and fields as far as the eye could see.

Jake's teeth ground together as he recognized where he was.

The turn for Tippins' cabin was coming up.

Where Jake and Cole found Jessie so many years ago.

"What the—"

A flash of red shot onto the shoulder, heading straight for the road ahead of Jake's truck.

Rising moonlight caught in a long wave of honey and caramel, making it flash gold behind the swath of red.

Cobalt eyes shot wide with recognition seconds before he came aware of his speed.

No!

Too fast!

Jake jerked the steering wheel and slammed on the brakes, but it was too late.

Chapter 40

Were the trees thinning?

Fewer fallen limbs and bramble cluttered the ground between the mammoth pines.

Through a break in the trees, a street sign flashed white, glowing in the moonlight.

My heart leaped.

Yes!

The road!

Just a little bit further.

Then I'd flag down the first car to pass and be free.

A second of apprehension itched at the edges of my mind, triggered by something Ethan's minion said earlier. Was Ethan on his way back to the little house in the meadow?

But it was too late.

Ethan wasn't the type to get his hands dirty, traipsing through the woods, let alone in the middle of the night after an escaped captive. He'd let his underlings scramble around in the dark.

Besides, I highly doubted Ethan was the type to go out of his way to handle business so late. He had a reputation to uphold, events to attend, people to see.

No. There was no reason to worry about coming across Ethan.

But as I stepped through the last layer of trees onto the shoulder of a two-lane highway, the worry refused to ease.

Beyond the tree line, the ground was cold and rocky, littered with bits of glass and trash rather than the soft cushion of pine needles and leaves.

I glanced up and down the road, heart pounding.

Headlights!

My heart pogoed into my throat. Fear-induced nausea swept over me. A thin sheen of sweat formed over my arms despite the chill night temperatures.

Headlights.

What if...

No.

Ethan wouldn't come out here in the middle of the night.

The lights drew closer, and my doubts doubled.

What if it's Ethan?

What if his stooge had a cell phone and called for help?

No.

I couldn't risk it.

Heart hammering in my chest, I stepped back into the trees, knowing I might be passing on my only chance at help.

I didn't go far, just the other side of the first curtain of branches.

An idea spurred in my mind.

Keeping one eye on the approaching headlights, I moved parallel to the highway toward the gravel drive that led back to the house in the meadow.

I just had to get to the other side of the driveway.

If the headlights slowed to make the turn, I'd know it was Ethan.

If not, I'd still have time to flag down the car.

Arms pumping at my sides, I ran toward the gravel road. I was cutting it close. I only had a few seconds before the car would blow past and be lost in the night.

Falling over the far side of the gravel drive, threw myself into the trees at the edge of the highway to catch a glimpse of the approaching headlights.

How fast are they going?

The headlights were way closer than they should have been at the marked speed limit.

Ethan racing to free his accomplice?

The car was going too fast.

Too fast to safely make the turn onto the gravel side road.

My feet acted before I truly had the time to process the information, carrying me out of the trees, across the shoulder to the edge of the road.

It was dark.

I waved my arms.

Any second, I'd be caught in the beams of the headlights.

The driver would see I needed help and pull over.

We'd call the cops.

The headlights were coming fast.

With swift, jerking motions, I jumped and waved frantically in an attempt to catch the driver's attention.

Why aren't they slowing down?

Light speared my eyes as the beams from the approaching car slid over me.

The car was huge, not a car at all but an SUV or truck.

I squinted through the light to make out any details.

Only thirty yards away, I could see the outline of the vehicle looming against the darkened sky.

They're not going to stop!

Why aren't they stopping?

Fifteen yards away.

I'm going to be stuck out here!

Desperate, I called out to the driver, knowing the futility of my actions.

Who would stop for some stranger on a dark highway in the middle of the night?

Could I really blame the driver?

Ten yards away.

My eyes widened as, the next second, the headlights vanished from the road to cut across the trees on the far side of the highway.

Arms fell to my sides. I watched on in horror as the truck lost control, spinning out and running headlong into the thick trunks on the other side of the road.

Screeching tires. Scraping metal bending around the trees faded from the air.

Frozen in shock, mouth agape, I stared at the steaming vehicle where it came to rest, the front end crumpled against the trees.

I willed the driver's side door to open.

For the driver to step out unharmed.

A minute passed.

Two.

My eyes traced over the truck bed to the cab. Moonlight glinted off the silver paint coating the exterior.

Nobody stepped from the truck.

Move!

My mind screamed for me to cross the street.

Help!

I was over the yellow lines before I knew I was running.

A dark cross in the center of the tailgate caught my eye a second before I reached the truck.

Sweat beaded on my forehead, rolled into my eyes to blur my vision.

No.

I stumbled the last few steps into the culvert to the driver's side door.

The dash lights lit up the interior of the cab.

Through the window, I found a dark head hanging over the steering column.

No!

I tore open the door.

Please. Please, no!

"Jake? Jake!" I jostled his shoulder.

Nothing.

Why?

Why'd you have to drive off the road, you big, dumb idiot?

My fingers shook as I fought to unclasp the seatbelt.

I couldn't grasp the latch, couldn't find the button. I pulled on Jake's arm until the mechanism gave, and Jake tumbled out of the vehicle, knocking me back into the dirt.

Jake landed on top of me, forcing the air from my lungs.

A soft groan of pain.

Not mine.

Dirt and gravel dug into the back of my arms and shoulders, but the discomfort they caused was the furthest thing from my mind.

"Jake. Jake, speak to me!" I brushed dark hair back from his face. Fingers came away wet and stained dark.

Blood smeared Jake's forehead from a gash at his hairline, running down over his eye.

His eyes.

Those beautiful, dark blue eyes were barely open, lashes

fluttering over them, only revealing the underlying color in bits and spurts.

A pained moan passed Jake's lips; in it, a single word.

"Hanna."

A warm hand closed around mine.

"Jake—It's going to be okay. Everything's going to be fine."

I squeezed his hand.

The police. An ambulance.

I had to get help.

Like a robot short-circuiting, I searched Jake's pockets in a frenzy before coming away empty-handed.

Frustration and panic tore from my throat.

Where is it?

Where's his phone?

Then it came to me.

Easing Jake onto the ground next to me, I slid from beneath him and dove into the cab of the truck. In the dim blue light off the dash, I groped, nearly blind, between the seats before my fingers closed around the cool rectangular casing of Jake's phone.

I swiped a finger across the screen and dialed.

I climbed back out of the truck as the phone rang and crouched beside Jake. His eyes were closed, but his chest moved steadily with breath.

"Nine-one-one, what's your emergency?"

"Yes, there's been an accident—we need an ambulance!"

"What's your location?"

Why's she so calm!

"It's..."

Where were we?

I glanced up and down the highway for some kind of marker.

What road were we on?

"I don't...I don't know."

"You don't know... Alright, can you give me some landmarks? How many vehicles were in the accident?"

"Just one."

I squeezed Jake's hand, dragging it to my lips.

"How many people involved?"

"One."

Were Jake's fingers cold?

I pressed a hand to his chest and cried out when it took a moment to find his heartbeat.

"Ma'am, please look around. Can you find anything identifiable to help us narrow your location?"

How could she sound so cold?

"I don't... I don't..."

A sigh.

"Are you in town? Can you tell me some of the businesses around you?"

The sound of rapid typing came across the line.

"Trees."

"Trees? Good, that's good. Ma'am, call GPS triangulation says you're somewhere on Highway 395 north of town. Does that sound correct?"

How was I supposed to know?

"Ma'am, can you find a mile marker sign?"

What was with all these questions?

"We need an ambulance."

"Ma'am, I've dispatched first responders, but I need you to help me narrow your location. Do you see anything, a landmark to tell responders where to find you?"

Blinking back tears, I searched my surroundings, noting an empty blue beer box in the ditch. Probably not what she was looking for.

Headlights gleamed in the distance.

Help!

My heart soared with relief.

"I see the ambulance!" My hand found Jake's once more. "Help's coming!"

"Ma'am..."

I hung up and dropped Jake's phone in the dirt.

I pulled Jake's head into my lap, brushing blood from his face with my hands.

Help was coming.

I watched the headlights draw near, turning from tiny white

specks to blinding suns as the car slowed and pulled to a stop next to the pull-off that would lead to the house in the meadow.

A car door opened and slammed.

My brow creased.

Something niggled at my brain.

Something...

Lights.

Where are the lights?

The car parked on the other side of the road was too small to be an ambulance. I guess it could be a police officer, but even then, they would have had their sirens going, blue lights flashing.

"Hello?" I called out. Whoever it was, hopefully they could help.

Jake shifted and groaned but didn't rise.

Silence.

Boots crunched on gravel, drawing closer.

"Please, we need help."

Still no answer.

My lips pressed to a thin line. I moved in front of Jake and stood.

"So, I see you outsmarted Tippins. Can't say I'm surprised."

Chapter 41

Ethan stepped around the end of the truck, a gun leading the way.

I stared up at the towering figure. I didn't need light to recognize that arrogant stride.

Ethan stopped in the road.

"It's not too late to come crawling back, gorgeous. We'll even find you a nice room at the big house."

An icy fear raced down my spine before I could steel myself against Ethan's threats. Something deep down told me I never wanted to go to the big house, as he called it.

"Might even let your boyfriend, there, live if he promises to stay out of our business."

Not likely.

I scrambled to my feet, positioning myself in front of Jake. He was hurt enough, and I didn't know how much more of his blood I could stand to see.

If help didn't get there in time to stop Ethan, at least the ambulance would be there in time to help Jake.

I glanced down at Jake's still form on the ground, only for a second. I didn't dare take my eyes off Ethan for long.

He was a snake. Sneaky, deceptively quick, and could move at a moment's notice. I didn't want to give him an opening.

"And if I refuse?"

Ethan laughed, the sound dark and menacing.

"Darling, there is no refusing. You'll come with me, and your knight in shining armor there will bleed out in the street. Come now, like a good girl."

My hackles rose. I clenched my jaw to bite back a snide remark.

He would shoot Jake. After everything I'd seen back at the cabin, I had no doubt.

But what was going on? Why was he so keen on keeping me?

It had to go beyond a few hurt feelings at his rejected advances.

This wasn't normal. People didn't threaten others at gunpoint for no reason.

Going with Ethan was a death sentence, but did I have any other choice?

I got away once. I'd just have to escape again.

All the bumps and bruises on my body from my trek through the forest ached at the thought, but if there was a chance Jake could get out of this alive, I had to take it.

Teeth closed around my lip.

Was there any other way?

"If I go with you, you'll leave Jake unharmed?"

Ethan's brow rose as he glanced down at Jake behind me in a way that showed he sincerely doubted Jake was unharmed. He nodded.

"Come with me, and I'll leave your Romeo as he is."

The ambulance would be there soon. They'd take care of Jake. He'd be okay. He had to be.

"Okay—" Strong fingers closed around my ankle. A moment later, the unmistakable metallic click of a bullet being chambered.

Ethan's slimy grin slipped for a millisecond. Panic flashed in his eyes as he searched for the source.

"So, you have come to play," Ethan simpered, Lips curling as his eyes dropped to Jake. His words came like a rattler's warning. "Not so big and dangerous down there, are you, mate?"

"Last I checked, a bullet 'll do just as much damage from down here," Jake rasped, each syllable sounding like a battle as they fought to get past his lips.

Ethan's smile broadened.

"Touching, but you know this can't end well for you."

"Says who?" Jake coughed. "Police are on their way. They know all about what you're keeping in the basement of that shiny house of yours."

What?

Ethan's smile melted into a feral sneer, a cornered dog. Real fear sparked in the cold depths of his eyes.

And like that, we were dealing with an entirely different animal.

In a single swift moment, Ethan's face hardened. Pale blue eyes turned to steel. He wouldn't back down. Not now. Probably thought he could lawyer his way out of any real danger if he could just get away. Avoid being caught red-handed.

My world narrowed.

It was just me and Ethan and that gun.

I watched the shaking gun in his hand go still seconds before the blast that stopped time.

My eyes squeezed shut against any impending pain, for the bullet to pierce my skin, rip through muscle and bone until it reached my most vital of parts. I dropped.

Seconds ticked away.

Nothing.

Slow, my eyes blinked open.

Is this shock?

I took inventory of my person. Finding no blooming carnation of blood spreading over my clothing, I turned instantly to Jake, but aside from the blood on his shirt dripping from the gash on his forehead, he seemed fine, too.

Something heavy fell on the gravel.

Ethan lay in a heap on the asphalt, hand clamped over his shoulder. Blood blossomed from beneath his fingers, staining the expensive fabric of his dress shirt. His pistol lay forgotten where it fell in the road.

Surprise and shock mixed on Ethan's face as he paled. Lips moved, but no words came as he stared wide-eyed into open space.

In the distance, sirens blared.

With a grunt of pain, Jake pushed to his feet and limped toward

Ethan. Boot scraping over the asphalt, Jake kicked the discarded pistol out of reach.

Ethan effectively disarmed and immobilized, Jake turned back to me.

Dark cobalt eyes searched my face, cataloging every scrape and blemish. He met my gaze with the same probing intensity and frowned.

A soft click had me flinching as Jake removed the magazine from his gun. The muscles in his jaw tightened and bunched.

There was little Jake missed.

Sirens blared.

Lights on top of a fire engine bathed Jake's face in red and white as the emergency vehicle slid to a stop behind Jake's truck.

A police cruiser skidded to a stop beside it in the road a second later.

Blue mixed with red light.

Jake lifted his hands in the air as two officers stormed from the cruiser, pistol in one hand, magazine in the other.

The world blurred and spun.

I blinked, and the officers were on Jake, pulling his arms behind his back.

"Wait!" I called, but no one heard.

An EMT was at my side, hands closing around my arm, steering me away toward the ambulance, parked a safe distance behind the line of police cars forming.

"No."

"Wait."

"He's not—"

But no one listened.

As the officers dragged him toward the police cruisers, Jake found me. Lips moved, but what Jake said escaped in the wind and sirens.

Tears streamed down my cheeks. I fought the medic to get to Jake, but it was no use. Too late.

The EMT's hold on my arm held firm.

Another set of officers and a medic circled Ethan, assessing his injury, field-dressing the wound before the officers helped Ethan to his feet.

My shoulders sagged with relief. It was over. It was all over.

Sitting on the back of the ambulance, a familiar face approached, the silver star of the county sheriff's office pinned to his uniform.

I watched the other cops walk Ethan, not to the back door of a police cruiser but to the second ambulance.

What?

No.

That can't be right.

"Ms. Montgomery," the officer addressed me from beneath his rusty mustache. Shamrock eyes implored me. "If I could have a minute."

"She needs to get to the hospital," the EMT objected.

"I'm fine," I countered. "Where are they taking Jake?"

"Don't worry about that. I just have a few questions before—"

"No. Jake's innocent. It was self-defense. If he hadn't—"

Officer Blair leveled me with a hard stare.

"Ms. Montgomery, he shot a man."

"To protect me!"

"Nonetheless—"

"No." I tried to push past Blair to get to Jake. "I'm not answering any questions until you let Jake go. Can't you see, he needs to go to the hospital."

The burly officer let me by, though I heard him let out a weighted sigh as he followed me over to where the other officers loaded Jake into the police car.

"Stevens!" Jake turned from the car. I stared into dazed cobalt as the adrenaline faded from Jake's system.

At a signal from Blair, the other officers stepped back.

I flung my arms around Jake's waist and felt him lean into me. His head dropped on top of mine.

I didn't say anything. Neither did he.

Words couldn't encompass the breath of emotion passing between us. In those brief moments spent in each other's arms, a bond forged that can only be crafted through shared experience.

One of the officers cleared his throat loudly.

Jake pulled back, but I kept my arms locked around him.

It wasn't right.

He'd been protecting me.

He was the one who should be loaded into the ambulance, not Ethan.

Where were Ethan's handcuffs?

I intended to find out.

"Hey."

Blinking back tears, I glanced up to find Jake offering up that cocky smile of his and felt the corners of my own mouth rising despite the fog of fatigue I could see clearly at the edges of his eyes.

As Blair led me away toward another cruiser, that dazed gaze stayed with me.

Jake insisted he was fine, that everything would be okay. It was just standard procedure. He wasn't being arrested, just detained for questioning.

It's just how things are done.

Heart squeezing painfully in my chest, I watched the officers load Jake into the cruiser before letting the burly officer lead me to his car.

Chapter 42

I paced the police station lobby. Nervous energy pulsed off me.

What was taking so long?

The incident on the highway seemed miles away.

Once the scene was secured, Officer Blair loaded me into his cruiser. As Ethan was carted off to the hospital, we followed Detective Carter's car, Jake inside, back to the station.

A large clock on the lobby wall ticked away the minutes. When did we get there? Hours ago.

I passed a pair of double doors that led back to the interrogation rooms and officer's offices. Jake was back there with Carter and Blair, rehashing the events leading up to Ethan being shot.

I'd been back there too for a while, only long enough to explain my abduction and escape before getting booted back into the lobby. Eyes narrowed as I passed the doors a second time. Hopefully, Carter and Blair could feel it from beyond the interrogation room wall.

Really, how long did it take to hand over what little Jake could know about the case?

Another lap of the lobby.

The room was unnerving, nothing like I expected from a police station waiting room. All hyper-modernized furniture, no cold metal benches or sketchy individuals waiting to be processed. I expected mismatched, second-hand chairs and wanted posters pinned up to the walls, not sleek black and stainless chairs and landscapes showing images of the Palouse and the surrounding mountains. The way Jessie described the police station back in high school made it sound like some ragtag, Podunk office with few decorative garnishes.

The lobby I paced was sleek and professional, albeit empty at the late hour. The young officer behind the reception desk eyed me wearily like he expected me to make another go for the double doors.

If the detective didn't finish up with Jake soon, I planned to.

Over the receptionist's desk, bright, white fluorescents flickered in the ceiling.

Another lap.

What could possibly—

The seal on the reinforced glass front doors squelched as they slid open with a whir, hauling my attention from the little interrogation room in the back.

In a stylish black suit and sparkling gold heels, Molley strode into the station with the energy and draw of a wild tornado. She flashed the officer behind the desk an award-winning smile as she pulled a dark folder from under her arm.

"Garrett, how are you doing? Could you bring this back to Shawn Blair and the detectives handling the St. James investigation? I think they'll be wanting what's inside." Molley slid the file across the desk.

Molley spun away from the desk before the officer could respond. Bright eyes fixed on me with a laser stare.

"What are you still doing here? Shawn should have... Never mind, how are you holding up?" Molley crossed to where I'd stopped in my pacing. One arm going around my shoulders, she steered me to a bench along the far wall. "Are you okay?"

"They're holding Jake." My voice came out dull and hollow, sounding lightyears away.

"Not for much longer. As soon as they see that file, they'll let him go," Molley assured.

"But—"

"Trust me on this," Molley said with a wink that should have been reserved for stadium crowds. "Just a few more minutes."

It was more than a few more minutes.

An hour passed before the doors behind the reception desk swung open.

Looking worse-for-wear, Jake strode through the double doors like he'd just won State.

I was on my feet in a blink.

"Jake!"

Bits of blood still clung to his forehead where the wound opened again after someone cleaned it, and the cobalt of his eyes was dulled by fatigue and probably a bit of a concussion, but when they landed on me, a familiar crooked grin stretched his lips. The tiniest bit of a spark brightened Jake's eyes.

Jake was across the room in seconds, long arms circling my

waist, pulling me tight to his chest.

I clung to his shirt front, pressed my face into his chest as I breathed in the spicy, distinctly masculine scent I'd come to associate with Jake.

God, how I'd missed him. Something altogether thrilling and terrifying at the same time.

Greg had only been gone a handful of months. What would people think about me moving on so quickly? What would Greg's parents think? Misha?

But in Jake's arms, my heart thrilled and danced like it had when I used to lay in Greg's embrace. Not quite the same. The melody had changed, the turns and leaps different, but the thrill for life was there; the desire to leap into open air without knowing where or how I would land as long as he was there with me carried me away.

Staring up into Jake's eyes, I thought, maybe that was enough. Maybe I could hold onto that feeling with Jake without forgetting or betraying Greg's memory and the time we had together. I knew I could never let go of the love I shared with Greg, of the life we built together, but maybe it didn't matter what others thought if my heart kept dancing.

▲▲▲

"Ahem." Detective Carter cleared his throat.

I stepped away from Jake—not far. Jake's arms stayed tight around my waist as we turned to find Blair and the blond detective beside Molley.

The detective held the dark folder in his hands as he stepped forward.

"Ms. Montgomery, I'd like to offer my condolences on the loss of your husband. He was a good man. Top in his field," the detective said, meeting my gaze directly. "Your husband's help was paramount to solving a very important case."

"Wh-What? You must be mistaken. Greg was a doctor. He healed sick children in remote villages, not..."

The detective nodded.

"Yes. On one of Dr. Montgomery's recent trips, he worked with a group of young women who'd escaped from skin traders in Guatemala. It was his work there that made me reach out to him to consult on my case. With the incites your husband gave us and the new evidence you all brought forth, I think we're finally going to be able to close a case I've been holding on to for a long time."

I blinked.

Greg? A police consultant?

"So...the pictures?" Again, the detective nodded.

"Were from our files."

I frowned. Something wasn't adding up.

"But then...why were they hidden?"

The corners of the detective's mouth fell, deepening the creases in his cheeks.

"I don't... Security, possibly," the detective shrugged, his hands tightening around the file. "It's hard to say. From the looks of some of the notes found in the file from your husband's desk, it looks like he may have been conducting his own investigation. Someone may have caught on to his snooping around."

Jake's fingers closed around mine, offering a gentle squeeze that

I returned.

"I'm sure more will become clear as we tie up the last of the loose ends on this case. For now, you should all return home for some rest. You'll be hearing from me in the coming days." At that, the detective met all our gazes, holding a second longer on Jake before nodding and disappearing back into the caverns of the police station.

Hand in hand, Jake and I stepped out into the night, ready to put the last few weeks and all the crazy behind us, eager to step into whatever life had in store for us in the future.

Epilogue

A cannon blast rang out across the field, signaling another home team touchdown.

All around me, the stands erupted with cheers and shouted excitement. I shuffled into the third row of bleachers in Union Stadium and took a seat beside Molley. On her other side, her husband, Will, cradled their infant daughter to his chest. The baby's little face scrunched up against the noise, but her mouth was open in a wide grin as she reveled in the exciting new sounds.

Further down, Jessie and Cole huddled close together, Jessie snug under Cole's arm as much for protection from the cold as the crowds.

Though Jessie improved leaps and bounds over the last few years, recovering from the trauma she experienced in high school was slow going. Being in crowds was hard for her.

I was surprised to see Jessie at the game at all, but we all wanted to be there for Jake.

"How's it going?" I turned toward the field. My eyes caught on the group of girls in blue and gold cheer uniforms on the sidelines before finding the scoreboard at the far end.

Up by three with six minutes in the final quarter.

Not exactly the score I'd like to see for Jake's first game as assistant coach, but there was still time for them to strike a considerable lead.

"Not bad, but G Prep's tough."

"They always are."

I searched the sidelines for a familiar figure I could pick out of any crowd and found Jake near the twenty-yard line gazing intently out at his players as they set up to kick the extra point. Even from my place in the stands, I could see his knuckles were white from his grip on the clipboard in his hand.

Compared to the head coach beside him, Jake looked like a ticking time bomb ready to blow at any second with all the nervous energy moving about him. Not good.

Jake changed his mind several times about the coaching position over the last month. Some mornings, he'd wake up, never wanting to set foot on another football field ever again; other days, I'd find him still awake at two am going over potential play options.

That morning had been a bad one.

Jake came into the kitchen a knotted, anxiety-riddled mess, convinced he'd call the wrong play and lose the team the game. All I could do was listen and offer soft assurances.

"You know what you're doing."

"You won't call the wrong play."

"You've got this."

It didn't help that they were playing one of the best teams in town. Gonzaga Prep didn't always make it to state, but they'd made it more times than Mead or any other high school football team in town. Most of the players on the private school's team were almost double the size of Mead's players.

Luckily, it looked like Jake's team was holding their own.

I meant to make it to the game sooner, but Ms. Cora called needing a sub for the late class.

Though I finally opened my studio a couple weeks ago, the class sizes weren't quite what I wanted them to be. I'd agreed to continue covering Ms. Cora's classes as needed as long as they didn't interfere with my own. We could really use the extra cash with the coming baby expenses.

On the field, the players in blue and gold looked haggard and exhausted, but among them, there was still a spark, a hunger for victory. As long as that kept burning, they had a chance.

"How are you feeling?" Molley asked, glancing down at my barely rounded belly with a hint of a smile. I hadn't even realized I'd settled my hand there over the growing life inside.

"I'm good. What about you?" My morning sickness, which had nothing to do with the morning time as it turned out and everything to do with stress and long car rides, had subsided the week before, along with the exhaustion. The last few days, I'd been able to make it through my classes without having to sneak away at lunch for a catnap on the couch.

"I'm doing okay," Molley said casually, though her sky-blue eyes widened in warning before flicking toward Will.

Molley hadn't told Will yet about their new addition, though she'd have to soon. In a few more weeks, she'd no longer be able to hide her growing belly behind flowy peasant tops.

Molley was afraid of how Will would react when he found out, but watching him with Gracie, she had nothing to worry about. Will would accept the new addition in stride. Anyone could see how good he was with their daughter. Will's love for both girls in his life shined in his every move. One more addition would bring nothing but joy.

I turned back to the field just as G Prep threw an interception. The stands around us went wild.

▲▲▲

After the game, when the stands cleared and the players all left on the buses, I found Jake still in the stadium, sitting on the sideline bench, staring out at the field with a contemplative look. The clipboard was gone. Now, Jake clutched the winning football in his hands.

Gingerly, I lowered myself down beside him and bumped his arm with my shoulder.

"You were great out there."

The corner of Jake's mouth rose, but his eyes didn't leave the field. Was he replaying the night's game? Or some other game? One where he played a very different role.

"It was all the team," Jake tried to shrug off my compliment.

"Bull."

"W-what?" Jake choked on a laugh. He turned to face me, one hand finding mine.

"They were able to play like they did tonight because of you," I said, "Number 5 wouldn't have been able to spot those pass routes like he did without your coaching. From what Cole was saying, the quarterback had way more time in the pocket to get the pass off than any of the other games this season. That's because of you."

"I don't know," Jake turned back to the field.

My brows drew together as I frowned.

"No. I'm telling you. Because, for some reason, you can't see it," I nudged his shoulder again to get Jake to look at me. I stared up into those dark blue eyes. "What happened in high school, those last few games, was beyond your control. You did the best you could with what you had at the time. So what if you never got to play in college or go pro. Here, now, you've got the chance to make a real difference in these kids' lives. With your help, you're teaching, some of them might get to go where you couldn't.

"I saw how they looked at you in the huddle. They hang on your every word."

"But–"

"No."

"No?" The corner of Jake's mouth quirked.

"Nope. No doubt. They don't care that you only played in high school. They believe in you."

"I don't want to let them down."

I squeezed Jake's hand.

"The only way you could do that is to keep doubting yourself. Believe because they believe," I smiled up at him. "Because I believe."

Jake smiled a smile that wasn't quite sure and took my hand.

He turned back to the field with a sigh.

"I heard from the lawyers today."

Uh oh.

Despite the aching blooming across my lower back, I straightened beside Jake, readying for the coming blow.

The day after Ethan's arrest, the neighbor across the alley came over with footage from his motion camera. The grainy recording showed a busty, dark-haired woman sneaking through my gate just before midnight the night my studio was broken into.

Jake wasted little time contacting his lawyer to draft a formal threat of suit against his ex-wife. We awaited Gina's response.

"And?" I prompted when the silence stretched too long. My fingers tightened around Jake's.

"The footage is too grainy to make out any distinguishing features proving it's her."

Damn.

Foolishly, I'd been hoping to be rid of Jake's ex. It was awkward enough being best friends with his old girlfriends. A psycho-vengeful ex-wife was more than I could handle at the moment.

Jake pulled his hand free from mine. Seconds later, I felt it slide around my waist, pulling my snug to his side.

I relished in the warmth of his body against mine, let my head fall against his shoulder.

"I asked my lawyer to show the footage to Gina anyway and to pass along a message. From the sound of it, she was pretty spooked. We won't be hearing from Gina again."

I straightened, tilted my head to look up into his face.

"Jake, you didn't have to—"

Jake flattened his hand across my rounding belly.

"Yeah, I did."

As if in answer, a series of butterfly light flutters rippled across my abdomen. Jake's lips stretched, feeling the movement, too.

Eyes lined with silver, I pressed a kiss to his shoulder.

"Thank you."

Jake's lips pressed to my hair.

"For you, anything."

NOTE TO THE READER

Oh my gosh, we did it! Never Let Go and the Open Hearts Open Hands series are complete. Honestly, that's something that at times over the last few years, I wasn't sure I'd ever get to say. It will probably get me many glares, but I have had some form of Never Let Go finished for almost three years, but the story and the characters didn't quite fit with the rest of the series. Hanna wasn't in the original version. Instead, I'd created a badass dancing mother on the run from a very bad husband (three guesses which character that was). In the original version, Jake was cop, partnered with Officer Blair. Sometime in the editing process of the original version I realized, not only did it not make sense to add in a completely new main character so late in the series, but there was no *way* Jake was disciplined (or law abiding) enough to be a police officer. So, in comes Hanna. Unfortunately, she'd already been coupled off in a stable happy relationship, so that had to go, and so commenced the complete rewrite of my third novel. I wanted Never Let Go to be a sort of redemption story for Jake, to show how he'd grown over the course of the series.

I have enjoyed every moment I've gotten to spend with these characters, and I hope you have as well. And here's the part where I ask you to please take the time to review Never Let Go. As an indie author any bit of feedback to feed the Amazon machine is always appreciated.

I have several projects in the works at the moment, and while I wish I could tell you now what is coming next, life has decided to limit my writing time with marvelous things like children (whom I love) and my day job (jury's still out on this one), but if you join my email list on my website www.ecollinsbooks.com you will be the first to know which of these projects will be finished first ;-).

Thank you so much for sticking with me on this journey. I would love to hear your thoughts on the book and the series as a whole. You can find me on Instagram and Threads at @author.e.collins. Follow me on social media for updates that won't fill up your inbox or check out my website at www.ecollinsbooks.com for any news or to find out my thoughts on whatever randomness I'm reading.

I hope to hear from you all soon!

ACKNOWLEDGMENTS

I know I've already said this (I just can't get over it!), but wow! I can't believe Never Let Go is finally published. The road to this point has been a challenging one and so I have many people to thank who have all helped me along the way. First, I'd like to thank my husband. Aaron, without your support, and your insistence that I make the time to get through the dreaded editing process, I would still be sitting with a half-finished book. You encouraged me to keep going from the moment you found out I was a writer, so many years ago. I will always be grateful for the time you make for me to focus on my dreams.

Thank you to my parents who taught me the importance of hard work and perseverance but also proved it is possible to live your dreams. You have both been an inspiration in more ways than I can count. I appreciate all the help and encouragement you've given over the years.

Next, I'd like to thank my siblings, Scott, Evan, and Jackie as well as my friends Emily, Chelle, and Carson for enduring my random musings and obscure character development questions. Without you all I wouldn't have been able to create the world and characters of this series. And I'm sorry, but we're about to start all over again ☺.

E. COLLINS

Born a product of the Disney/Crime TV generation, E. Collins grew up in a world of love, happily-ever-after, and murder that put a permanent brand on her story telling before she was even aware. Yes, she loved Disney princesses and happy endings, but in her stories the prince isn't always saving the day, the princess isn't the damsel in distress, and sometime (Rarely) the villain is not bad.

Hailing from Spokane, Washington, E. lives surrounded by family with her loving husband, kids, and their dog, Maggie.